# African Encounter

## by

## Hugh Chare

# Publication data

**African Encounter** © Hugh B. Chare 2006 & 2019

First Published as *Chaya Four One!* in 2006 by Trafford Publishing
Kilihune Books Edition of *Chaya Four One!* Released in October 2009
Title reissued as *African Encounter* in 2012, as an eBook and 2016 in print

**Book and Cover design by Hugh B. Chare.**
ISBN: 978-1-940012-49-0

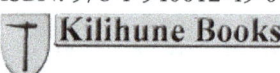 **Kilihune Books**

The James Martin series
*African Encounter*
*Across the Zambezi*
*Just off the Great North Road*
*Well, there you go!*
*Back to Africa*
*The Sagitta Mishap*
*Flight 5 to Johannesburg*

Marieke Englebrecht mysteries
*Death in the Mopane*
*Revenge after twenty years*

Other books
*The journal of Jan Englebrecht*
*British Spy in the Bushveld*
*Federica*

Dedicated to
**Karen**
without whom
this would not be written

# Preface

This novel is set in the late 1960s and early 1970s, in the period shortly following the independence of most of the previous colonial territories in Africa. Attitudes of some of the people of that era were often extreme and would today be regarded as distasteful, abhorrent, and bigoted. Racial slurs and ethnic terms of that era have been retained for the sake of authenticity, but should in no way be regarded as reflecting the opinions and views of the author.

As Zimbabwe had not yet achieved full self-determination, the names of towns and cities used under the Rhodesian regime have been retained. Similarly, place names in South Africa have been kept as they were during that period.

This novel is a work of fiction. Names, characters, businesses, and incidents are fictional with the exception of obvious references to historical figures or events. Any resemblance in the featured characters to actual persons, living or dead, is purely coincidental.

My thanks to Jimmy and Moki for reading the early versions and encouraging me to continue, also to Andrew Coates for correcting my Afrikaans and, most particularly, to Sara Chare for editing the whole work.

My thanks also to those many people who helped me with my questions, including Keith Franson, Cruise Planners, Mrs. F. Steblecki, Automobile Association of Zimbabwe and Vicky Green of the Southampton Reference Library.

# Contents

# En route to Zambia

"May I help you, Sir?" the salesman asked.

James thought that this was very polite considering that he probably looked as if he had barely enough money to buy lunch, let alone anything from Henleys, the Rover Company distributor in Piccadilly.

"Yes, thank you, I would like to buy a Land Rover," he answered.

"Really, Sir, what did you have in mind?"

James loved the way that really came out, so much disbelief and scepticism in the one word, really.

However, he explained that he was leaving for Zambia in a couple of months and wanted to buy a Land Rover to take with him. The salesman perked up a little but clearly needed some form of assurance that the vehicle would be paid for. James was not sure how to convince the man, but he had a promise of the money from his grandmother. He gave the salesman his full name, James Martin and his current address and was finally able to convince the salesman that Henleys and The Rover Car Company would, in fact, get paid.

James was soon to graduate from university with a degree in mining engineering and had accepted a position with one of the mining companies on the famed Zambian Copperbelt. He had debated between flying out on a BOAC VC-10 or taking the boat and then driving up from Cape Town. The boat adventure had won the toss, so now he had to acquire the transport to make it the rest of the way.

James discussed his needs with the salesman and settled on a long-wheelbase Land Rover with heavy-duty suspension and springs and a drum winch. It was a nice light colour, called limestone by the car company, which would be good in the tropics. The salesman suggested a locking post for the spare wheel, a locking cap for the petrol tank, and a locking hasp for the bonnet, all of which James thought sounded like good suggestions and added to the list.

The salesman explained the taxation differences between buying a vehicle equipped to seat ten and one equipped to seat twelve. Although there was essentially no difference in the vehicle itself, apart from a few

1

seat changes, one carried tax and the other did not. As the vehicle was to be exported, the difference was largely moot, but the twelve-seat version avoided the possibility of additional tax payments in case things did not work out as planned and the vehicle had to be re-imported.

The whole transaction had an air of unreality about it, as they were discussing aspects of a vehicle that would be best suited for off-road bush work, whilst outside the window, fashionable London enjoyed a balmy May afternoon. James dragged his attention back to the task at hand and away from the short hemlines as the salesman added up the price and then took down the particulars of the delivery location. Rover actually delivered their Land Rovers to the client, so James was to accept his at his parents' home. The delivery date would be in mid to late July, about a month before his sailing date.

After leaving the Rover showroom, James communicated the details of vehicle type, weight, et cetera, to the mining company, which would now book space on the boat. All that remained was to graduate and prove to the Zambian government that he actually had a degree, and then he would get his work permit. James did not foresee any problems with his graduation, so was happily planning the rest of his trip.

In mid-July, James received a call from a Rover driver to say that he was on his way with the Land Rover. James had already received notice that he had graduated and had communicated this fact to the Zambian Embassy and the mining company. He now had his work permit, smallpox and yellow fever jabs, and was ready to begin the next phase of this adventure. It was exciting to be getting his first vehicle, and a new one at that. He had considered a used Land Rover, but his grandmother talked him out of that idea and told him to buy a new one and had slipped him a thousand Pounds to help with the purchase.

A brand new Land Rover pulled to a stop outside the house, and James could see the neighbours' curtains twitching as they all looked out to see what was happening. James did not live in the kind of neighbourhood where brand new Land Rovers were that common. One was more likely to see Morris Minors and, at best, Ford Cortinas, typically with names like James and Sheila emblazoned on the window. The Rover driver showed James around the vehicle and answered all his questions, and then asked if he could be dropped off near the main road to hitchhike back to the Solihull factory. James did wonder how the black vinyl upholstery would be in the tropical sun, but there were no options for another covering.

After dropping the driver at a convenient spot, James took his new toy off to try it out and see how it ran. He drove around the neighbourhood and then off onto a muddy back lane to find out about the four-wheel drive and transfer case options. By now, the villagers had formed their own opinions about what he was doing, and some remembered that he was supposed to be going to Africa. Many of the people in the village had said that they thought it a little strange to be going so far afield, but it also seemed that nearly all had some relative or acquaintance living in Nairobi, Addis Ababa, Dar es Salaam, or Johannesburg, and they had each provided James with a long list of contacts.

Unfortunately, few seemed to know where Zambia really was, or for that matter, Nairobi, Addis, or Dar. They seemed to think they were just down the road and could be visited easily. One would have thought that in 1969, with television in most homes, there would be better knowledge of geography. After all, the Americans had just put men on the moon, so at least someone must know their way around.

James spent the next week or so alternately cleaning and polishing his new car and then driving off to the muddiest hole he could find. He added a light high on the back of the vehicle to act as a reversing light, and shopped for a few extras like padlocks for the bonnet, a spare wheel and petrol tank, and a high lift jack, rope and shackles. His father's contribution was a Shrader pump for tyre inflation. It worked by replacing one of the spark plugs with the pump and then running the engine to inflate the tyres. There were gaskets and membranes to ensure that the air was drawn from the outside and the petrol vapour was ejected and not put into the tyre. At least, as his father said, he would never need to be stuck with flat tyres.

3

His father also instructed him in the proper use of the starting handle so that he would not break his thumbs. James was amazed that Land Rover still had such things as starting handles, but upon consideration, it was logical as they were intended for out-of-the-way use where battery maintenance and replacement might not be that easy.

In the first week of August, James received a notice from the steamship company that he was to deliver the Land Rover a day before the sailing date of August 22nd. He supposed this was to make it possible to load it with the other cargo. The following week, James made a quick trip to visit with his grandmother to thank her for the generous gift that had allowed him to buy his Land Rover and to wish her farewell. He was surprised at how well she had taken his leaving until she told him about her lost opportunity to go to Canada in 1919 after the end of the Great War. She had regretted it often and did not want her grandson to miss any opportunity.

On the 21st, he drove to Southampton and checked in with the loading agent for the RMS Pendennis Castle. He also took a trunk of personal belongings that would go as hold baggage and was not needed on the voyage. He had been provided labels by the shipping company, UNION-CASTLE LINE & SAFMARINE, that had a large M on them and the space in which to write name, cabin number, vessel, sailing date, and ports of embarkation and disembarkation. His personal effects that he would need on the voyage, he would take with him the following day when they actually embarked. James hung around hoping to see them actually sling his Land Rover aboard, but decided that it might be a long wait, so left and hitch-hiked back to his parents' house.

The sailing day was a day of drama as his idea of a goodbye was to say, I'll see you, but others in the family had different ideas. However, he finally managed to convince them not to make a big deal out of things and to have just his parents drive him to the Southampton harbour. This meant that they both took a day off work, as the sailing time was one in the afternoon and it was a Friday. He checked in at the harbour and boarded the vessel. He found his cabin on the B deck, and his parents were able to confirm that it was not quite the smallest cabin on the boat. At least the cabin had a porthole, which meant it was above the waterline.

Looking out, they could see that the cabin was actually some height above the water. It was on the port side, so at least if posh really did come from port out, starboard home, he was halfway to comfort. The cabin was supposed to be shared with someone else, but a steward told James that the intended passenger had been taken ill and would be delaying his voyage, so he had the cabin to himself.

When at last the call came for all those who were not sailing to go ashore, James said his goodbyes and escorted his parents to the gangplank. They were being very British and keeping a stiff upper lip, though James was sure that his mother would collapse into tears the moment she was out of sight. She seemed to have this notion that he was on his way to do Colonial service and was in some way going to further the aims of, if not the Empire, then at least the Commonwealth. Somehow, the idea that he was actually going to be working underground for a living did not enter her mind.

The passengers lined the rails and threw streamers to those on the dock. At one o'clock on the dot, the boat pulled away, and the streamers tightened and then finally broke. James waved goodbye to his family and wondered how much they would change by the time he was likely to see them again, three years hence. There were plenty of tears to go around with the other passengers and those on the dock. He looked down at the streamers as they hit the water, and another thought struck him. The oily water of the harbour, roiled up by the tugs and the boat, seemed to James to be an unhealthy brownish colour, and even the foam was brown. It was also going to get grubbier as all the streamers hit the water and then slowly disintegrated. He hoped that they would see water elsewhere that looked a little cleaner.

The trip to Cape Town finally began, and for the next eleven days or so, they would be at sea, except for a brief stop at Las Palmas for fuel.

James wandered around the boat and explored. His excursion was barred at one point by a notice that told him that the area he was headed to was for first-class passengers only. So he turned about and walked towards the stern and away from the elite. He looked over the other passengers and tried to guess what they might be doing on the boat. All told, he estimated that there must be about six hundred in the first and tourist classes. They were a real mix of ages, from probable retirees to young families with children. Already, some of the children had taken over the swimming pool and were having a good time.

The weather was fine and, unless they encountered poor weather through the Bay of Biscay, was likely to get better as they headed towards the equator. The boat headed down the sound and into the channel between the Isle of Wight and Portsmouth. James watched the other boats and traffic around, from the ferries to the Isle of Wight to Navy vessels headed into Portsmouth and then a freighter obviously destined for Southampton. As the boat moved out into the Channel, it picked up speed, and the motion increased, and James noticed some of the passengers looking green. He considered himself lucky that seasickness was something he had never been bothered by. He had made a number of ferry crossings of the Channel in all kinds of weather and had never had a problem. Out in the Channel, the wind freshened, and it got quite cool, so he moved inside and went below to his cabin to unpack.

Upon boarding, James had been given information about meal times and seatings, so at the appropriate time, he made his way to the dining room. He discovered he was seated with a young couple and an elderly lady. The elderly lady looked as if she had been out in the sun a long time, but for all she was really well-preserved. The bloke was about twenty-one or so, just under six-foot, and fair. His wife, however, was another matter. She was stunning. James looked her over and noted that she was beautiful to look at, she had auburn hair and green eyes, and as far as he could tell, she had a great figure. James had to pull himself back to the present and remember where he was and that the others were looking at him expectantly.

"Hello," James said, introducing himself. "James Martin."

"Pleased to meet you, Tom Morrison, and this is my wife, Rita," replied the man.

"Alice Blake," said the older lady. "So, what brings you young people to South Africa?"

"Well," said James. "I'm not going specifically to South Africa; I'm actually going to one of the copper mines in Zambia."

"So are we," said Tom. "Which one?"

James and Tom compared notes and discovered that they were indeed going to the same place. James thought that Rita looked relieved.

"I'm glad," she said. "At least now we won't be driving all the way up on our own. That is, if you would consider driving with us?"

"Of course," replied James. "I must admit that the thought of going it completely alone had alternately seemed exciting and then terrifying."

"You will be fine," said Alice Blake. "Young people like you should take on challenges and seek out new and exciting things to do."

"What about you?" asked James.

"I'm going home," she replied. "I will be staying on the boat all the way to Durban so you will leave me in Cape Town."

"How long have you lived in Durban?" Tom asked.

"About twenty years now," Alice replied. "My husband and I moved there from Bechuanaland, he had been assigned there with the Colonial Office."

"Why didn't you retire to England?" asked Rita.

"Because, my dear," said Alice. "England is damp and cold, and I cannot abide the society there any longer. I came to love Africa while we were in Bechuanaland, Botswana, to you, and could not bear to leave altogether."

"How does South Africa compare to Botswana?" asked James.

"Well, I have to admit that the situation in South Africa upsets me more and more these days, and I keep thinking of either moving back to Gabs or doing something completely different, like taking a villa in Tuscany," Alice replied. "At least then I would be closer to my grandchildren who live in Oxford."

"If you were driving to Zambia, which way would you go?" James asked Alice, his mind more on the immediate.

"I would take the coastal route to George, then cut inland across the Karoo towards Bloemfontein. That way, you will limit the amount of time you have to spend in the Karoo. If you go straight to Worcester and then on to Beaufort West, you will see more of the Karoo than perhaps you really want. From Bloemfontein, you could go to Jo'burg and on up to Beitbridge. After Beitbridge, you have a choice of Salisbury and Chirundu, or Bulawayo and Vic Falls, then on to Lusaka and Kitwe," she replied.

"Have you ever driven it?" asked Tom.

"In various stages," Alice replied. "At one time or another, we drove throughout most of South Africa, the Rhodesias, and South West, but the roads were not always that good and sometimes what takes a day now could take a week or more. When my husband was alive, he enjoyed travelling throughout the territories."

After dinner, they sat for a while asking the elderly Mrs. Blake about her early experiences in Botswana. Her husband had been posted to the then Bechuanaland just prior to the Great War, World War I, and she had gone along as a new bride. They had seen all manner of things in their life up to their retirement, and she was happy to tell them about her early life of making a home where there were precious few amenities. Finally, she excused herself and retired for the night.

"Fancy a beer or a nightcap?" James asked the others.

"You two go ahead," said Rita. "I think I would prefer a rum and Coke."

James ordered the drinks and then asked. "So, what do you think about going to Zambia?"

"I think it will be great fun," said Rita. "I'm sure Tom will enjoy his job, and I plan to see if there is anything I can do in the line of a job. What about you, aren't you married?"

"No," said James. "My girlfriend told me that she didn't quite fancy the idea of Central Africa. But the opportunity seemed too good to pass up, so here I am."

"Where did you go to university?" asked Tom.

"I went to RSM," replied James. "What about you?"

"Nottingham," said Tom. "In fact, we both went there; I was a mining engineer and Rita read English."

"Did you grow up in Nottingham?" asked James.

"No, we both come from London, Notting Hill actually," Tom replied.

"That's ironic, someone from Notting Hill going to Nottingham," said James, dragging out the end of Nottingham, making it almost two words instead of one to emphasise the point. He went on to comment that he had stayed in Notting Hill for one term until he could get something in South Kensington.

"When did you two get married?" asked James.

"Last weekend," replied Rita. "So this is something of a honeymoon."

"Well, have fun," said James. He then thought it would be polite to let them be on their own and excused himself and went off to his own cabin. He really envied Tom. At least Tom had a girl to go off with, and what a girl! James wondered what kind of social life he would be able to make for himself in Zambia and how many single girls he would meet, if any.

For the next three days, there was a routine of breakfast, lunch, and dinner, interspersed with lifeboat drills, some deck activities, and evening parties. There were bridge tournaments, deck cricket games, quoits, and the rest. For James, there was the daily gamble of what the log said they had travelled the day before. James also spent a fair amount of time with the Morrisons. He liked Tom and was drawn to Rita. She had a beauty that attracted almost anyone, and James felt lucky just to be able to spend time in her company. He was envious of Tom and wondered often where things might go, or if he might find someone who would replace Rita in his thoughts.

All that aside, they had hit it off well and were planning their drive north. James and Tom both had maps of South Africa and Rhodesia and were looking at the route suggested by Mrs Blake. One night at dinner, they quizzed her about hotels, and she told them that it would really not be difficult to find accommodation along the way. The long school holidays in South Africa were over the Christmas period in the middle of summer, not in late August and early September, so the demand for accommodation would not be so great.

9

James also kept an eye on the water, and it cleared up and became bluer as they headed south. Occasionally, they would see great long swathes of debris that seemed to collect on the ocean surface. They also saw oil slicks, which James could only presume came from the ocean traffic.

The boat was scheduled to make a stop in the Canary Islands on Monday afternoon. It seemed an odd place to stop, but James had heard that the reason they stopped was that fuel was cheaper there and that all the ships stopped there to bunker. They would actually be putting into Las Palmas, the major port of the Canaries. There were a group of passengers at the rail taking bets on who would first spot land. James was sure that would lead to much debate. How were they going to distinguish a smudge on the horizon as clouds or land? When Las Palmas hove into view, they were keen to see what it would look like. What they first saw were the hills of the islands against the horizon, and then more detail became apparent as they neared. The Pendennis slowed and took on board a pilot to take them into the harbour.

They had come some seventeen hundred miles already from Southampton, and they had another four thousand four hundred miles to go to Cape Town. James was amazed at the amount of shipping that there was in the port. There was a Japanese fishing fleet, a Russian fishing vessel, and a number of freighters. The pilot took them in close to the wharf, and then the tugs took over and manoeuvred the vessel into position. James looked at the water over the side and decided that this water was slightly less murky than the water in Southampton. However, it was definitely dirtier than the open ocean.

There was a line of taxis and horse-drawn traps waiting to take passengers for excursions. For the limited time they were in port to fuel up, the passengers were permitted to go ashore and explore. James and the Morrisons debated car or horse and decided on a car. They took a quick trip into town and spent a little time sightseeing. None of them spoke Spanish, and the townspeople spoke only some English, enough to deal with the tourists. The town did have some really beautiful public gardens with palm trees, orchids, and cacti. Things were beginning to look really tropical. They discovered one other fact: booze was cheap, really cheap, probably because it was not taxed.

They enjoyed the trip but were glad to get back to the boat, and looked forward to making the long run down to the equator and on to Cape Town. With all the passengers rounded up and accounted for, they put back out to sea and started the run south. At dinner, they asked Mrs. Blake if she had been ashore. She told them she had seen Las Palmas often enough that she really did not need to make another visit.

The routine continued for the next few days as the boat headed south around West Africa and then across the open ocean straight towards Cape Town. They were steaming fairly fast, and the daily logs showed them hitting close to twenty-two knots at times. The water had cleared up as soon as they had left the immediate environs of Las Palmas. As they headed south, the air heated up, and some of the passengers actually took to sleeping on the deck. Cardboard scoops appeared out of portholes in an attempt to introduce a better airflow into the cabins. James wondered if the first-class cabins had air conditioning; it certainly would make life more comfortable.

Many of the passengers camped out by the pool and stripped down to the minimum. James got his first appreciation of just how much of a stunner Rita was when she appeared one day in a bikini. He found himself staring and wondering. Fortunately, just about every other man around the pool was as transfixed and many were now catching it from their spouses. The resulting cries of pain distracted Tom, and he did not notice the way James was looking at his wife. James recovered himself and found something else to look at for a while, or at least until Rita got out of the pool and covered up.

On Friday morning, the crew cleared the pool and set up for the Crossing the Line ceremonies. They had picked out a Lord Neptune and his consort and set up court by the pool. For any on the boat who had not previously crossed the equator, there was a chance that they could be dragged into the events. James decided that the crew picked out either passengers who had in some way annoyed them as victims for

11

Neptune or those who they decided were quite amenable to some fun. He also decided that they tried to find the prettiest girls they could and get them as wet as possible. He wondered why they had not picked Rita as, in his opinion, she was quite the best-looking on the boat. At least it broke the routine completely and provided some relief from the regimen of the voyage.

James continued his review of the colour of the ocean water, but he got a reminder of why the ocean was getting polluted when he saw the crew dump boxes of empty beer tins and bottles over the stern. He then began to wonder how the boat treated, or did not, wastewater from the baths, showers, and toilets. He asked a couple of the other passengers about the dumping. He did not learn much except that the joke was the captain navigated with a magnet following the trail of empty beer tins lying on the ocean floor. Later that night, James sat out on the deck looking at the stars. Tom Morrison came and joined him, and they started debating which stars formed the Southern Cross. Finally, they asked one of the deck officers, and he pointed out the constellation and a few of the other major constellations, including Corvus and Libra.

The moon was almost full, and the deck officer told them it had been totally full a couple of days before. It was amazing to James and Tom how light it was from just the moon. James thought that without the moon, the star viewing out here must be amazing. He had not truly appreciated how much light pollution there had been where he had grown up. Of course, in London, there was so much extraneous light that on some nights it was hard to see more than the very brightest stars.

The following night, over dinner, Rita asked Mrs. Blake if she had ever met any famous people while she lived in Botswana.
"Well, it depends on who you class as famous," Mrs. Blake replied. "I knew Seretse Khama well before he was exiled in 1950, and before him, Tshekedi Khama, who most upset Mr. Rey. I also met Mr. Smuts. All of them, I thought, were men who were clever and thoughtful. Not everyone thought so, particularly of the Khamas."

"Who was Tshekedi Khama?" asked James. He had heard of Seretse Khama and Jan Smuts, but the other two names were new to him.

"He was the regent in charge of the Batswana people before Seretse was old enough to take over," Mrs Blake replied. "He was in the centre of a storm over a white settler, and Mr. Rey brought up Marines from Simonstown to supposedly keep order. Personally, I don't think there was ever any need, but who was I to express an opinion."

"What about all the other leaders today like Kaunda, Banda and Smith?" asked Tom.

"Ah, yes, the leaders of what was the Federation. Well, we retired too soon to get to know them," was the answer. "They became really active in the 50s, and we were out of things by then, but I do think that Smith fellow is living in a dream world and not facing the facts. But what about you, Mr. Martin, are you related to the James Martin who was a District Commissioner in the East Africa Protectorate?" Mrs. Blake continued.

"I very much doubt it," replied James. "As far as I know, none of my family had been farther than France or Southern Europe. When would that have been?"

"Early this century, following the First World War, up to the 20s," she replied.

"Definitely not," said James. "My father, grandfather, and great-grandfather were born and raised in England, so although it has the air of a romantic tale, not for me, I'm afraid."

What struck James was how little he knew of the real history of Southern Africa. At school, he had learnt about the Boer War and that most of the countries that had been colonies were now independent. But the who, how, what, and why surrounding the events up to those independencies, he had no idea about. He had followed, to some extent, the talks between Harold Wilson and Ian Smith on HMS Tiger, then HMS Fearless. Both of those attempted negotiations had ended in failure, so there were continued problems between the Rhodesians and their neighbours and with the British Government. He also had little knowledge of East Africa, beyond hearing about the famed Lunatic Express, as the railway from Mombasa to Uganda had been dubbed.

The boat continued south with the same routine: breakfast, lunch, and dinner, with activities in between and the opportunity to spend money on drinks at the bar at any time. On Tuesday night, there was a farewell party as they were due to dock in Cape Town on Wednesday morning. The crew went all out, putting on a good show, particularly for the benefit of the first-class passengers. It suddenly struck James that this was all about getting tips for service. He had not thought about it until then and wondered what, if anything, he would do. He certainly had not budgeted for tipping crew members when he had started out, and could not afford much at all, as he needed his cash to pay for the trip north.

James resigned himself to the fact that his cabin steward would think of him as mean and unappreciative, but that was life. He thought a little more and then came to the conclusion, perhaps in a self-serving way, that the steward had probably already pegged him as short of the ready and was not expecting anything. That fitted with the level of service he had received on the voyage, proper and adequate, but not anything special.

On Wednesday morning, he was up very early, almost before it was light. They had already slowed somewhat, and James could see Table Mountain in the distance and on the port beam the coastline of South Africa. He stood looking out at Table Mountain and was joined at the rail by Tom and Rita.
"Are you all packed?" asked Rita.
"Yes, I did that last night," replied James. "All I need to do now is throw in the last few things and I'm ready to go."
"How long do you think it will take to unload everything?" asked Tom.
"No idea," said James. "But I would not plan on leaving today. We should probably get a hotel tonight somewhere in Cape Town."
"It's cold here, don't you think?" said Rita.
"Well, yes, honey, it is still the end of winter after all," said Tom.
"Did you keep out some warm clothes?" asked Rita.
"Yes, they are at the end of the bunk, under my jacket," replied Tom.

The boat slowed down to take on the pilot, and they headed in towards the harbour. They were close enough in now to see all of Table Mountain and could just make out the cable car station on the top. Between the docks and the mountain was the city of Cape Town, wrapped around the base. Mrs Blake came up and joined them at the rail and started pointing out landmarks and areas of the city. To the west was Sea Point, and to the east, more suburbs growing away from the city into the plain beyond. She suggested that they might find a hotel that was reasonable in Sea Point and then recommended a drive around the Cape itself before they left the area. They said their goodbyes, and Mrs. Blake wished them luck in Zambia and hoped they enjoyed their trip.

When the boat docked, the immigration and customs officers came on board and started processing people. The first to go were those whose final destination was Cape Town or those who were going to catch trains. Others, like James and Tom, who had vehicles on board, were in no particular hurry, as they had to wait anyway until unloading was complete. Eventually, James made his way to the immigration line and had his passport stamped. He examined the stamp and noticed that it was in both English and Afrikaans. So Binnekoms meant entry, and Cape Town was Kaapstad. He talked to the customs people and got some paperwork to retrieve his vehicle when it was unloaded. As an in-transit person, they did not seem overly concerned about anything. James also went to the bank that had been set up on board and changed Pounds into Rand. The Rands he noticed were smaller in size than the Pounds, but colourful. He also got some coins as part of his exchange, and the coins were definitely smaller than the shillings and pence he was used to.

James reached the dock in time to see his Land Rover being slung over the side, and then he saw it being manhandled out of the way by about ten Africans. Then it hit him. All the officials had been white, and all the obvious manual labour was black. An obvious state of affairs for South Africa if he had thought about it, but he had not been thinking, so did not notice until he saw the moving crew. Tom and Rita joined him and saw their Land Rover being similarly unloaded. It looked like the twin of the one that James had.

Now they had to find the hold luggage that had been brought up and placed according to last name on the dock. So James and Tom both looked at the M area and found their respective trunks and cases. They also found a porter and had him take their belongings to the cars. Tom and Rita had more than James, and they had obviously worked out how it would all fit. Rita had some large, heavy calico sheets to spread over the cases and boxes they had. She told James that they really did not fancy unloading everything each night, so were making it less obvious and attractive. Not that the sheets did not suggest something was underneath, but at least to the casual observer, there was nothing of immediate interest.

They connected the batteries back up again and checked petrol. They had about enough to drive off the docks and get to the closest petrol station. It was now well past lunchtime and into the early afternoon. Taking Mrs. Blake's suggestion, they drove to Sea Point and found one of the hotels she had recommended. Having deposited some of their bags, they then decided to take a drive around the Cape.

The road wound around the coast, then cut inland over the western end of Table Mountain to Hout Bay. From Hout Bay, they drove around Chapman's Peak and then on to the Cape itself. James stood and looked out at the ocean where the Atlantic and Indian oceans meet, but before long, he felt himself being watched and then noticed a troop of baboons beginning to collect nearby. He decided that it was probably better in the car than out, as the teeth on some of the larger males were huge. James had not realised just how big baboons get and was pleased to drive away. Tom and Rita had also seen them and had started away.

They drove back through Simonstown and headed towards Fish Hoek and Muizenberg. James pulled off the road to look at the bay. He thought he had seen something in the water. Sure enough, in Simonstown Bay was a whale. Tom and Rita pulled in behind him and got out to see what he was looking at.

"Hey, do you see that whale?" James asked.

"No, where?" replied Tom.

"Out there! Watch, it will come up again soon," said James.

"Wow, you're right, there he is," said Tom. "That's a first for me."

"Do you know where this is?" asked James.

"No, where?" replied Rita.

"That is the Simonstown naval base," said James. "That is where the British had a base for a long time and where Mrs Blake said they got marines from to send to Bechuanaland."

The road back into Cape Town followed the base of the mountain past the Groote Schuur estate, which had been Rhodes's estate in the Cape. The de Waal drive presented a great view of Cape Town as they came around the end of the mountain. They had driven through mostly suburbs, and the majority of people they saw were white. James wondered where all the black people lived. He knew that in South Africa that they were separated, sometimes by great distances, and he wondered what their houses looked like. They found their way back to the hotel and decided that they would leave early the next morning to drive to George. The hotel served a good dinner, and they turned in early so as to be up by dawn.

From Cape Town to George was about two hundred and eighty miles. The first part of the journey was out through the suburbs of Cape Town. Now, James knew where all the black people lived; they saw large townships of both regularly constructed houses and shanties. James had noticed that the buses and trains headed towards the city had all been crowded with people going in, presumably to work.

The road stayed fairly flat and straight across the plain towards a range of mountains, which they eventually came to. Past the town of Somerset West, the road climbed quickly into the mountains up a pass named after a Sir Lowry. James wondered who this worthy had been and added it to his list of things to check on one day. At the top of the pass, they stopped to take a look back. The view was spectacular. Sweeping around on their left was the huge expanse of False Bay, and way off in the distance was Table Mountain. The lower slopes of the pass they had just driven up were planted with all kinds of fruit trees, and the mountains behind them had their own rugged grandeur.

They continued their drive through the mountains, finally stopping for lunch in Swellendam. James had only committed one faux pas that morning. They had stopped at a very small town for a drink, and James had gone into a store. Once inside, he had been asked to leave and come back in through the correct door. He had not noticed the *Nieblankes* above the door he came in by, and even if he had, he was not in the frame of mind to translate non-whites. What he could not understand was that once back inside, he was at the same counter, talking to the same people who had asked him to leave and come back properly. Ah well, that was part of the ludicrous nature of the South African political system.

The other thing that James had noticed when they stopped was the noise. As soon as he pulled up, he could hear a high-pitched buzzing sound. At first, he thought there was something wrong with his Land Rover, but it persisted even after he shut the engine off. Outside the vehicle, it was even noisier. He asked Tom and Rita what they thought, and Rita had the answer: insects! It seemed that among the insects they could hear were some called cicadas, not endemic to England, that created an almost constant buzzing sound. James had no idea that just insects could make so much noise. Rita assured him that they certainly could and that some species, though not those they could hear, only came out every seventeen years or so. James asked Rita how she knew about such things, and she told him that she had actually done some research on the trip and had looked up insects as well as mammals and birds. James was suitably chagrined and impressed.

Between Swellendam and Mossel Bay, they ran close to, and then crossed, a railway line, and James spotted a train travelling in the same direction they were going. The locomotive was steam, and the train was all goods traffic of some kind. From Mossel Bay to George was only a short distance, and they were in George in plenty of time to find a hotel and still take a walk through the town. James had seen some suede boots that he fancied and finally found them in an Edworks store. He splashed out and bought himself two pairs; one that came to just above his ankles and the second much higher, fastening with buckles around the mid-calf. He and Tom also found themselves some safari jackets and matching shorts. The salesman tried to get them to buy long socks as well, pointing out all the business people in the street who were like attired. They debated and caved in and purchased some long and some short socks, so that they now had the option.

Rita had noticed that the women, white women that is, were generally fairly formally dressed. There were not many in jeans or trousers, and skirts or dresses seemed to be the thing. She told Tom and James that she was not about the travel that kind of distance, trying to look beautiful and that until it warmed up, she was wearing jeans. She did concede that when, and if, it got warm enough, she would consider shorts or a skirt. James thought that would be a day worth waiting for, as her legs were quite delectable. He looked forward to it.

The next day's drive was to be slightly longer, at about three hundred and forty miles to Colesburg. Tom pointed out to James that that was about the same distance as London to the Scottish border, and that did not get them even halfway up South Africa, let alone to Kitwe. They fuelled up and then set out up the Montagu Pass on the road to Oudtshoorn. There was a sea mist condensing out in the pass as they climbed, and for the first time in South Africa, James needed his windscreen wipers. They passed a train also headed up the pass, and James could see that they were having problems with the damp on the rails and were busy sanding for all they were worth to gain traction between the wheels and the wet rails. At the top of the pass, the road divided, and they turned right to head away from Oudtshoorn and towards Graaf Reinet. James was sure that he was murdering the pronunciation of these place names. How in the world did one pronounce Oudtshoorn?

The next hundred miles were fairly interesting. They climbed ranges of hills, dropped into valleys to cross rivers, and passed a few small towns. On the mountains to the south, they could see odd patches of white from some snow that still lingered after the winter. Then the terrain changed, and the road straightened out. As far as they could see, the road stretched out ahead and behind them, seemingly endless with few distinctive landmarks. Obviously, this was the Karoo. They did not see much in the way of trees for a good while, and they only saw sheep scattered across the land. Occasionally, they saw some cattle, but they did not look very happy.

James realised they had driven for over two hours and he had not seen another vehicle except for Tom and Rita's. All in all, not a very inviting place. One thing James did notice was that the sky had cleared and that there was not a cloud to be seen anywhere. The sky was uniformly blue and stayed that way the whole of the rest of the day. It was just as well that he had brought sunglasses to counter the glare.

They stopped briefly in Graaf Reinet for lunch and then continued on over the Lootsberg Pass to Middleburg and finally Colesburg. By the time they reached the town, they were all ready for a break. At Colesburg, they joined the road that came up from Cape Town via Beaufort West and Worcester. James supposed at least now they would see a little more traffic. They picked out a hotel in Colesburg and put up for the night. They had dinner and then pulled out maps to discuss the next day's trip.

"Where do we head for tomorrow?" asked James.
"Not sure, do we really want to head into the Jo'burg area, or should we stop short?" answered Tom.
"My vote is that we stop short and then bypass Jo'burg and Pretoria the next day," said James.
"I'm all for that," said Rita. "So, what do you think of the trip so far?"
"Interesting," said James. "I don't know quite what I expected, maybe more people, certainly not snow on the mountain tops. I also imagined more Tarzan-type jungles and wild animals at every turn."
"Maybe there were more animals here once upon a time, but I imagine the people pressure has long since driven them away. As for the jungle, clearly not enough rain," said Rita.
"It is a long way, isn't it?" said Tom.

"It is indeed," replied James. "It makes England look pretty small, doesn't it, considering we are not even halfway there yet?"

"Okay then, what about Kroonstad for a stop tomorrow night?" suggested Tom. "We go through Bloemfontein and Winburg and stop there. Then, because it's Sunday the next day, we bypass Jo'burg and make our way north."

"I like that," said Rita. "Didn't Mrs. Blake suggest a hotel just outside Louis Trichardt, what was it, The Mountain Inn?"

"Sounds good to me," said James. "Are we agreed?"

They did in fact stop the next night in Kroonstad and then on Sunday proceeded on through Johannesburg and Pretoria, eventually to Louis Trichardt. James had not realised that Johannesburg was such a large city. As they drove through, he saw the small mountains of yellow dirt left over from the gold workings; the skyscrapers, the huge main roads, and the myriads of parking metres on the streets. Johannesburg was altogether like any other big city. James was pleased that they had not come through on a regular workday, as he could imagine the traffic jams and the delays. There were some people around, but obviously not as many as would have been on a weekday.

North of Pretoria, they pushed on, eager to get to Louis Trichardt. The terrain was changing, getting hillier and with more brush growth. They passed through Warmbaths, then wove their way through a line of hills to get to Nylstrom; then the road generally straightened out a little on the way to Potgietersrus and Pietersburg. James once again thought that some of the names were almost impossible to pronounce and wondered if he would ever manage it. There were large expanses of dry-looking grasslands, interspersed with hills and rocky outcrops that sometimes looked as if someone had just piled together a load of rocks. Just north of the side road that led to a place that rejoiced in the name of Soekmekaar, James pulled over and stopped. Tom followed suit and came over to ask what the problem was.

"We are on the tropic," said James. "Look at the sign."

"What? Oh, of course, Capricorn," said Tom.

"Of course, dodo," said James. "Did you think we had driven all the way to the tropic of Cancer?"

"We need a picture," said Rita. "Get over there, you two and pose."

The Mountain Inn was beyond Louis Trichardt in the Soutpansberg Mountains. The view of the city below was impressive, and the setting was really attractive. The main building of the inn was thatched and had whitewashed walls. The interior had high ceilings with beams and had a sort of safari lodge feel. The rooms were in separate two-storey buildings with outside walkways. They settled in and met for dinner and discussed the day. They all had much the same observations. Everywhere they went, the managers and officials were white and the manual workers were black. Even in the petrol stations, black attendants served them, but there was usually a white person sitting in the building taking the money.

They considered progress to date and looked at what was to come. They had travelled a fair distance that day, over four hundred miles. That plus the previous travel meant that they had now gone over halfway, and there was a little over nine hundred and fifty miles to go. Because of the altitude, the evening at the inn was cool, but they had already noticed that it was generally much warmer, and James decided it was time to break out his shorts and pack the long trousers.

Monday morning early, they left the Mountain Inn and drove north towards Beitbridge and the border. As they drove north of the Verwoerd tunnel, James noticed Tom pointing at something on the roadside and waving them down. James pulled in behind Tom and went over to find out what was up.
"We are in baobab country," said Tom. "Look over there."
James looked, and sure enough, there was a baobab tree. He thought that it was a peculiar-looking tree, almost as if it were upside down.
"You realise that means we are well and truly in the tropics now?" said Tom.

"I wonder what the first real wild animal we see will be?" asked James.
"I think it will be an elephant," said Rita.
"Why?" asked James.
"I just have this feeling," said Rita.

"Hasn't it struck you that we have been driving for miles in this country and we really haven't seen any wild animals?" asked James.

"As I said before, if you two actually remember anything I say, maybe it's because of the people pressures and they have all moved away from the area where the main roads are," answered Rita.

"Maybe they saw your driving and ran away," said Tom.

"Hah, I noticed you sleeping a good deal of the way when I drove," said Rita. "So it can't be all that bad."

"Have you noticed how here the bush has changed and how much more dense it is here?" asked James, changing the subject.

"Yes, before we came up the mountains, there were grasslands and plains; now we have lots of hills and heavy bush," answered Tom.

They filled up with petrol at Messina, drove a little farther north and then checked in with the South African immigration post at the border. James noticed that whereas the entry stamp was circular, the exit stamp was rectangular, and the Afrikaans for left, as in departed, was Vertrek. They crossed the banks of *the great grey-green, greasy Limpopo River, all set about with fever trees,* into Beitbridge. James looked around for fever trees but could not decide which ones they were.

# North of the Limpopo

The Rhodesian immigration officers were courteous but made asides to one another about people who would go and work north of the Zambezi. They were given entry visas for seven days and were allowed on their way. Just north of the border post, they came to a junction in the road that gave them the option of Fort Victoria and Salisbury, or Bulawayo and Victoria Falls. They had talked it over the night before and had elected to go through Salisbury. The road was good enough, but there was not exactly an abundance of other cars on the road.

At the Bubye River crossing, they saw a motel and decided to stop. The Lion and Elephant Motel not only had a bar and restaurant facilities, it also had a pool. The temperatures were now going up, and it had been a hot drive from Beitbridge, so a dip in the pool sounded like a great idea. It did, of course also provide another opportunity to review the scenery again when Rita donned her bikini and took her swim. James covered his confusion by jumping into the pool and creating a large splash. Later, talking to the motel staff, they learned that one of the problems they had was elephants coming into the motel area to drink the water from the pool.
"See, I told you that the first animals we saw would be elephants," said Rita.
"We haven't seen one yet," said Tom.
"Maybe, but we will, you'll see," said Rita.

After lunch, they continued on towards Fort Victoria. It was now getting quite hot, so James opened the vents above the dashboard that allowed air to flow in. He also opened up the roof vents to get a flow through. It certainly helped, but the air outside was now just plain hot. Just past another river crossing, the road changed. Now, instead of a full width of tar, they were confronted by two strips of tar set about the track of most vehicles. They were now on one of the famous, or infamous, strip roads. The going was fine, but James wondered how well he would do if he met someone coming the other way. Still, he would cross that bridge when and if it arose. They had been going for about thirty minutes when James saw piles of elephant droppings in the

24

road. He thought that was the closest they were likely to come to actual elephants. However, he was wrong, and he rounded a slight curve to find himself looking at a herd of about twenty animals. Not quite sure what to do, he pulled up and waited.

The elephants looked at the car but otherwise seemed to ignore him. He tried hooting at them, but that made no apparent difference. Not quite sure what to do next, he considered getting out of the car, but decided that was really not a good idea. After about fifteen minutes, the elephants moved off. Tom and Rita, who had been stopped behind him, pulled up level, and Rita leaned out of the window, grinning and waving her camera around.
"See! See! I told you we would see elephants, but, oh no, you wouldn't believe me," she said.
"Hey Tom," said James. "I'm glad it's you in that car, not me, to have to listen to that for the rest of the day."
"Hah, you're just jealous because I was right," crowed Rita.

Just before they came into the town of Rutenga, they crossed a railway line. James wondered where it ran from and to, and when they stopped in Rutenga for a cold drink, he asked. He learned that the line ran from Lourenço Marques to meet up with the line from Bulawayo to Gwelo. Despite there being a railway line, there was not much in the way of habitation around it. James wondered how many trains ran on the line and what they carried. They continued on towards Fort Victoria past a small settlement called James's Store, and then they saw a sign to a leprosarium, then a mission, and then a sign to The Great Zimbabwe Ruins. James mentally added that to the list of places he would like to see someday, but for now, he was committed to getting to Zambia. The strip road continued until another river crossing, and then they were back on full-width tar. All in all, they had gone about forty miles on the strip road, but had only met two cars on the way, and both had pulled over and passed with one wheel on a strip and the other in the dirt.

They put up for the night at Fort Victoria. The whole area surrounding the town seemed to be dotted with granite outcrops that rose hump-like from the ground. There was a main intersection of roads at Fort

Victoria, west to Bulawayo, east to Burchenough Bridge and thence Mozambique, and north to Salisbury. They also found the railway terminus. The South African Railways system had stopped north of Messina at Limpoporivier, so this system must be connected through Gwelo to Bulawayo. The following day, they continued their drive north towards Salisbury. In Salisbury, they stopped for lunch and a walk around. First, though, they had to find a bank and get some more coins, as nearly all the streets seemed to have parking metres. There was a flower market set up by a park opposite the bank, and Rita looked at flowers while Tom and James looked over a Land Rover with a Kazungula Safaris sign on the side. What attracted their attention was the roof rack and some of the other fittings that had been added.

"Well, what do you think?" asked Rita.

"What about?" replied Tom.

"The flower market, idiot," she said.

"Oh, wonderful," said Tom. "I wonder where all the flowers are grown; do you think they come from around here somewhere?"

"Probably," said Rita. "I don't see any refrigeration vans anywhere unless they came in by railway. What are you two looking at anyway?"

"Oh, we were just wondering how this roof rack was made," replied James. "I rather fancy one like this for myself."

"Why, are you planning to go into the safari business?" asked Rita.

"Well, you never know," said James.

After lunch, they drove north again through Banket and Sinoia and some really interesting sounding places; Alaska, Eldorado and Lions Den, then on towards Karoi. The whole area, after they left the suburbs of Salisbury, was very sparsely populated, but there were a few more people than in the area between Beitbridge and Fort Victoria. They had seen the end of the railway at Lions Den. It seemed from their drive up from Fort Victoria to Umvuma that there were many more, smaller towns, and then from Umvuma into Salisbury, there were almost none, but there was also no railway line between Umvuma and Salisbury. Now they also noticed that after the railway ended, the development also diminished rapidly. James wondered which came first, the railway or the towns.

From now on until they were well inside Zambia, it was back to road traffic only. The road was interesting to drive on; it seemed to swoop down into valleys, then rush up the other side over a hill and then down into another valley. The bush on either side of the road was much thicker, and James was convinced he had seen antelope of one type or another disappearing as they drove by. There was a fair amount of military traffic on the road, and they were actually stopped at one roadblock. But it seemed that the Rhodesian military was not really interested in them, and they were waved on with only a glance.

At Makuti, they stopped for the night. Between Makuti and the Zambia border, there was nothing else, so this was the last chance, unless they went via Kariba and crossed over the dam. The motel at Makuti was fairly nice and again had a pool. However, it seemed that it was also playing host to half the Rhodesian armed forces. As it turned out, it was just a couple of platoons of Rhodesian Light Infantry enjoying a break. Rita was well checked out when she took her swim, not only by the RLI but also by James. It seemed from what they learned from the soldiers that the whole area near the border was heavily patrolled, which explained the roadblock they had gone through. That signalled the beginning of the control zone.

Over dinner, James noticed a middle-aged couple sitting near them. He pointed them out to Tom and said that he had seen them before on the boat, again on the street in Kroonstad, and then again in Louis Trichardt.
"Do you think they are also going to Zambia?" Tom asked.
"Seems likely, don't you think?" said Tom. "Why else would they come all the way up here from Cape Town, unless they are going to the hydroelectric station at Kariba?"
"Why don't you go and ask?" said Rita. "It can't hurt to ask instead of debating and speculating."
"Okay, okay, I'll go," said Tom.
He got up and walked over to the couple and chatted with them. When he came back, he informed the others that, yes, those two were going to Zambia. Their names were Jack and Maureen Bell, and they were going

as far as Ndola, where they apparently taught at a technical school. They had invited the three of them to have a drink after dinner.

Over drinks, James introduced himself, as did Tom and Rita. The Bells had been on leave in Europe and were now headed home with the new car they had purchased in England. James and the others were keen to find out more about Zambia from someone who lived there. The mining company had given a briefing, but that was only an hour or so, and there was so much they really wanted to know. It turned out that the Bells had been teaching there for over fifteen years and had stayed on after Independence in 1964. Jack taught mathematics, and Maureen taught chemistry. The Bells liked Zambia and the people. They talked about the desire of the people to learn and the lengths to which they would go to get an education.

Clearly, the Bells were Zambia supporters and were concerned that opportunities be available to all. They mentioned briefly the different societal groups that formed. There were the expatriate mining company people, the local white miners, the farmers and the business people. There were further groups among the indigenous Zambian population. James was not sure that he really grasped why the expatriates and the local white population did not mix well, but thought he could understand why, with the historical baggage people carry around, the races might not mix.

The Bells also explained the significant presence of the Rhodesian army. It turned out that three years earlier, there had been a shootout between the army and some insurgents at Sinoia, a town they had driven through earlier that day, and then again in 1967-8, there had been various actions either along the river or in the western part of the country near Wankie. So this made the area somewhat of a combat zone. Wonderful, was the thought that all three had upon hearing this. The Bells asked them when they were supposed to arrive in Kitwe, and James explained that they were just to check in when they actually arrived. Jack Bell suggested that they stay with them overnight and drive to Kitwe the following morning, so that they would be sure that the mine personnel offices would be open.

Wednesday, the final real day of the trip! They left the Makuti motel fairly early and headed to the border. Just north of Makuti, the road started to descend the Zambezi Escarpment. They rounded a corner and pulled over, and stopped. The view was amazing. They could see the Zambezi Valley ahead of them and to the right as it continued down the valley towards Mozambique. Tom and Rita came back to talk to James.

"Well, James," said Tom. "Wasn't it Hemingway who said *miles and miles of bloody Africa*?"

"I don't know for sure," replied James. "But if he did, it was probably in *Green Trees of Africa*. It is amazing though, isn't it?"

"You're right," said Tom. "Well, I suppose we'd better push on."

They continued on, and the road wound down the escarpment road and as they descended, the bush got denser and more lush. They came to a gate and a shed in the road. James wondered what it was, but then saw the signs that told them it was the tsetse control gate. James drove his vehicle into the shed, and a couple of control officers came around with spray guns and fly nets. After they had given the wheels a few squirts, they let James drive on. He waited for the others and then drove on to the border at Chirundu. The Rhodesians were fairly casual about the process and said that they were sure they would be seeing them again.

Another Beit bridge to cross, this one was the Otto Beit Bridge. James was not sure if this Beit was the same as the one for which Beitbridge in South Africa was named, another thing to add to the now long list of things to look up one day. This Beit bridge took them across the Zambezi. The Zambian immigration and customs took a little longer. The travellers filled out forms and provided information until they felt that there was nothing left to tell. Part of the work permit process included a travel authorisation stamped into the passport in the form of a visa good for a single entry, valid for three months from the date of issue.

The immigration officer must have received a new stamp, as he took great delight in using it to stamp *Utilised* across the visas. The customs officers would have liked to have all the cases, trunks and boxes out of the vehicles into their office for inspection. However, Jack Bell had given them a tip; provide the customs officers with serial numbers of cameras or something similar that they could enter on their forms, and honour would be satisfied.

James wondered how the all-black Zambian officers got on with the all-white Rhodesian officers across the bridge. Jack told him not to be totally deceived by politics. There was an uneasy kind of truce between the two sides. The officers obviously knew one another and, absent politicians, would probably actually get on fairly well. However, cross-border incursions in the past had soured relations and would likely not improve things as time went on. The presence of Zimbabwe freedom fighters in Zambia was going to make things worse in the future, but for now, at least, things were fairly quiet.

From Chirundu, the road continued in the valley for a while past an area of petrified forest and then through another tsetse gate. Elephants held them up again, this time for about ten minutes. Finally, they started the climb up the Zambian side of the escarpment. In a couple of places, they saw remains of trucks that had gone over the edge. James surmised that it was probably because of brake failure. There were remnants of an old road here and there that they could see. There was very little traffic on the road except for a couple of cars with boats going the other way on their way down to Lake Kariba. There was little in the way of habitation in this area, certainly no towns and only a few villages.

They came to the junction with the road to Livingstone and took the northerly fork towards Lusaka. Not long after the junction, they crossed the Kafue River. James noticed that the bridge had members of the Zambian army standing guard. James did wonder what they were guarding against. Then he considered that perhaps the Rhodesians might even strike north and take out the bridge, which would be devastating to the economy, as all road traffic north crossed the one bridge.

From the Kafue bridge into Lusaka is only thirty miles or so. Between the river and Lusaka, they picked up the railway lines again, as the road ran near the line from Livingstone to the Copperbelt. The bush had changed back to a general low tree cover, uniformly brown as they were well into the dry season. It was quite different to the lush growth in the Zambezi Valley. The road into Lusaka from Kafue came to a large roundabout where the Great East Road and Great North Roads met. Straight over took them on to the Great North Road that continued on to Kabwe, Broken Hill, to old timers and the Copperbelt.

James, Tom, and Rita had discussed the idea of stopping to take a look around Lusaka, but by now they just wanted to get to Kitwe and the mine. James promised himself that he would try and get back to Lusaka sometime just to look around. Just out of Lusaka, the road and railway split again. The road took a most westerly track and swung away from the railway. Between Lusaka and Kabwe, there was surprisingly little development, except for one road junction, named for some reason, Landless Corner.

Kabwe turned out to be quite small, really, centred on the lead and zinc mine of Broken Hill. The road and railway joined again at Kabwe, and just through the town, they crossed. They decided not to stop for lunch in Kabwe but went on to Kapiri Mposhi. Kapiri's claim to fame was that it was the junction with the road to Tanzania; otherwise, it was one of those places that, if you blinked when you were driving, you missed it. There was a café in Kapiri where they found a good lunch. Jack told them that Kapiri was an important road junction because the Zambians were trying to route increasing amounts of traffic through Dar es Salaam and cut back on reliance on the southerly routes through Rhodesia, either to South Africa or Mozambique.

Parked all over the place were green Fiat trucks and trailers. These were the workhorses of the run-up to Dar es Salaam. Jack had also told them that there were negotiations going on among the Zambians, the Tanzanians and the Chinese regarding a railway to be built from Dar es Salaam to Kapiri. When and perhaps if this railway was built, it should relieve the burden on the road and provide an alternate railway link to the sea that did not go through Rhodesia, South Africa, or Mozambique.

Beyond the town of Kapiri Mposhi, they passed the only road junction to the northeast that eventually would lead to Dar es Salaam. James was surprised that there was nothing more than a couple of stop signs and a road sign that said Ndola and Kitwe that way, and Serenje and Mpika the other way. There were a few huts and houses scattered around, but otherwise not much in the way of development. Short of Ndola, they followed Jack onto the right fork in the main road and onto the road that took them into Ndola.

For some reason, there was a cut-off road that missed Ndola and headed straight off towards Kitwe. Once in Ndola, they followed the Bells through the town to the Hillcrest area where they lived. They had a bungalow with a well-developed garden surrounded by tall, thick hedges and large spiky cacti. James was a little taken aback at the security precautions with screens on the windows and extra locks on all the doors. Jack told him that the drift into the urban areas and lack of employment made this inevitable. Jack also told him that the cacti were a very good deterrent as they were almost impossible to climb through or over without being pricked by the vicious spikes on the ends of the leaves.

It was good to spend the night and be well-fed. Apparently, the Bells had telegraphed ahead, and their cook had come in earlier and prepared dinner for all five. The house servant had also been in and made up beds in the guest rooms. James asked Jack if he had any other people working for him, and was told that there was a gardener and another who came on an irregular basis to help the gardener with heavier work. The whole concept of house servants was new to James, and he was not sure what to make of it. Jack pointed out that it provided some further distribution of wealth through the salaries that were paid. Later that night, Tom and James discussed with Jack when they should leave the next day. He suggested that they time their arrival in Kitwe to be in the early afternoon. This meant that they could sleep late and depart about lunchtime.

The road from Ndola to Kitwe went first west towards Luanshya until it met the cut-off road that bypassed Ndola. At that road junction, they turned right and headed towards Kitwe. The road to Kitwe undulated through the bush in a cut in the tree canopy. Occasionally, the undulations turned into hills as they descended into valleys and crossed over streams and rivers that cut across the road. The surface was mostly good, but heavy truck traffic had broken it up in places, and the corrugations were so great that there were diversions through the bush. Quite what this would be like in the rainy season, James couldn't imagine.

Each detour was through deep, fine red dirt that billowed up in huge dust clouds as they passed. James tried to hang back far enough so as not to get completely covered in dust. Once back on the main road, James noticed that the sides of the road fell off steeply into huge ditches, obviously graded for significant rain runoff. The crown on the road was much greater than any roads that he had driven on in England, and he wondered what would happen if he were driving and fell asleep and ran off the road.

Approaching Kitwe, the bush started to thin, and the houses multiplied; there were more side roads and lots more traffic. James had his first real sight of a squatter township built on the edge of the mine housing. There were people, chickens, and dogs everywhere. The squatter shacks were built of sticks, bricks, tarpaulins and corrugated sheeting, any building materials that they could get their hands on. James now saw what Jack Bell had meant when he had told them the night before that population drift from the rural areas to the townships created problems in that insufficient employment was available for the number of people. They then built housing wherever they could and eked out an existence through odd jobs, subsistence farming, begging, and theft.

Adjacent to the squatter township was the mine housing. This was originally built for the African workers and consisted of neat rows of brick-built one or two-room houses with corrugated iron roofs. Some of them were showplaces of care, including brightly painted walls and cultivated patches for vegetables. Others looked as if they were barely occupied.

As they came into town, James turned onto Central Street and found his way to the mine offices. Tom and Rita pulled in behind him. Jack Bell had been right; they were assured that the offices were open and there was someone there to attend to them. The personnel department introduced them to Piet van Rensburg, who would be taking care of them for a while. There were a couple of others in the office who were obviously also just checking in. They were introduced by van Rensburg as Lionel Fairfax and George Walker. They had apparently flown in that day. James learned that he would be staying in the single quarters, as would Fairfax and Walker, and the Morrisons were to be taken to the house assigned to them. Piet van Rensburg sent the Morrisons off with one of the other managers, and he then took James and the other two bachelors to the single quarters.

They were each given a set of keys and shown to individual flats.
"Rest up this afternoon and tonight," van Rensburg said. "I suggest you eat at the mine mess and then I will pick you up at 7.30 in the morning to get you all signed on at Personnel. Here's a fifty kwacha advance each that should do you for a beer and dinner tonight and breakfast in the morning, and some more besides. Later tomorrow, you should be able to get to a bank and organise your own finances."

The flats were minimally furnished and had the basic essentials in the kitchen. The walls were painted off-white, and the floors were red: it looked to James as if the floors were concrete with some kind of paint or polish finish. There were at least curtains and lampshades. Stacked on the end of the bed were towels and linens, so obviously they were actually expected and someone had been to drop off basic supplies. There was nothing in the fridge, except a plastic bottle of water and nothing in the pantry, except the cockroaches. James dumped his stuff and wandered down the corridor, and knocked on the door to George's flat. He figured it was time for a beer and to get to know the two others. "You fancy a beer?"

34

"Absolutely," answered George. "Let's get Lionel and head on over to the mine club."

"These single quarters are not very inspiring," James remarked.

"Don't worry," replied George. "We'll find ourselves a leave house and get moved into somewhere decent."

"Leave house, what's that?"

"When you have been here for three years or so, you can take a long leave of three months, and then it makes sense to have someone stay in your house, so we do the staying and get to live somewhere decent for a while, and they feel happier about leaving their house. Once you become known as a reasonable house sitter, there will be plenty of possibilities," explained George.

They gathered up Lionel and walked down the road to the mine club. The sun was just setting, early for the Brits, who had come from the mid-summer higher northern latitudes, but there was still enough light to clearly see around them. To the right of the road, on the other side of some railway lines, was a playing field with a rugby team practising. On the left of the road were houses that looked unoccupied. Although there was not much traffic on the road, George assured them that at shift change time, there would be plenty.

The mine club was past the rugby field, farther down the road on the opposite side and had obviously been there a year or two. The bar had a few patrons already, all of them sitting up at the bar. They found themselves a table and sat down. A waiter detached himself from his perch along the wall and came over to see what they wanted. George ordered three Castles, a locally brewed beer, he told them. The beers were brought and were cold, and went down well after the long day.

"Okay," said George. "What do you chaps plan to do tomorrow?"

"Maybe open a bank account so that we can get some money," James tried as an opener.

"Transport, a decent place to live," suggested Lionel.

"Right, and while you are at it, you might think about a social life. You, Lionel, have the best start on a social life, working at the hospital," added George.

"Why?" asked Lionel.

"Because the sunshine girl nurses work there and that may be your best chance of finding a girlfriend here, unless you fancy the local girls?" continued George. "Look, you have to understand the situation here. There are all kinds of blokes like us who are here and single. Most of the women worth looking at here are married and bored, but not interested in us; we have no money, no status and, with all due respect to you two, none of us is an Adonis. The other options are the local white girls, who are daughters of farmers, business people, and old-time miners, many of whom are Afrikaners, or, God forbid, the blacks."

"Why would the women here be bored?" James asked. So far, everything he had seen was fascinating.

"Because they don't really want to be here. They get a servant to do all the housework and look after the children if they have any. They have nothing to do in the day, so hang out in coffee cliques and then get drunk in the afternoon, or fool around with the rich higher-ups or local business people. Some work, but they are in the minority. The ones employed by the mine either work in the hospital on contract like us, or they have been here forever and are old and past it. There are very few professional women on the mine; those that are here are mostly geologists, mineral technologists, or metallurgists. Remember that in Zambia it is against the law for women to work underground, and you won't get promoted up the management chain on the mining side unless you have worked underground," answered George.

"How come you know so much?" asked James.

"I was here last year as a student," said George.

"You mentioned the Afrikaners," said Lionel. "What's wrong with them?"

"Rude, arrogant, and ugly, speaking a bastard language, and they all have names that are impossible to pronounce," answered George.

"Was van Rensburg an Afrikaner?" asked Lionel.

"Couldn't you tell?" said George. "Thick as two short planks, hates the blacks and couldn't get a job anywhere else if he tried."

"Well, so apart from knowing where the women are, how do we get to meet them?" asked Lionel.

"Look to joining one of the social clubs," answered George. "Do you play rugby, tennis, golf or go fishing?" he asked. "Those are probably the most active clubs on the mine. Mind you, they are now accepting blacks as members."

"Maybe you're right," said Lionel. He seemed keen to head off this line of conversation. He probably felt as uncomfortable as James did with George talking about blacks when many of the club patrons and all the waiters were black and moving around them all the time. "Don't you think it's time we ate?" he added.

"Why don't we try the mine mess, across the street?" suggested George.

They paid the bill and walked the short distance to the mess. The night was clear and the stars brilliant. It was amazing to James that there was no twilight; it had gone from daylight to pitch black in about half an hour. Even with the light pollution from the streetlights and the mine, he thought that there were more stars visible than he had ever seen. He wondered what it would be like if you went into the bush away from the town.

"Which is the Southern Cross?" Lionel asked the others.

"No idea," said George. "I never took an interest in the stars, and besides, they all look the same to me," he added, laughing at his own joke. However, James remembered what he had learned on the boat and pointed the Southern Cross out to Lionel.

The mine mess was basically a large square room with access to a kitchen at the back. Tables for four were set up all around the room, and about half of them were filled. There were no other white faces in the mess, except for someone who looked like a manager, but they were not treated as anything particularly unusual. Attached to the wall high in one corner was a television set that was playing an episode of *Star Trek*. Some of the customers were obviously watching the show, and James was intrigued by their level of involvement. They would comment on the action or dialogue and would talk and give instructions and suggestions to the actors as though they could be heard.

A waiter brought menus and asked if they wanted anything to drink. Three more Castle Lagers were ordered, and the menus were then studied.

"What the hell is Monkey-gland steak?" James asked George.

"Surely not actual monkey steaks?" asked Lionel.

"No," replied George. "I think it is just your basic steak, but with a fancy sauce." Dinner was ordered and brought, and they ate in silence. With only airline food for the past night and day, George and Lionel were ready for something to eat. They ordered coffee, and James asked George if he knew any of the people he would be working with.

"Yes," replied George. "I met most of them last year while I was here. Most of them are okay, with one or two exceptions."

"Do you know anyone at the hospital?" asked Lionel.

"No, afraid not," was the answer. "I don't know any of the doctors, nurses or techs, nor do I know any of the mining types. You are on your own tomorrow."

They called the waiter over and paid the bill, and then walked back to the single quarters. The street was lit, and around each of the lights were clouds of insects. The night was noisy with the chirping of some kind of bug, the identity of which none of them knew, even the supposedly knowledgeable George. They could smell the sulphur dioxide coming from the smelter, and James wondered which way the prevailing wind was from and how bad the smell might get. The single quarters had lights on, so obviously, some of the other residents were now home. They split up and turned in for the night. Before he actually retired, James had to sort out his clothes and put them away somewhere. He decided to make up the bed, emptied his bags into drawers in the wardrobe, took a shower, and turned in.

Van Rensburg arrived at seven-thirty the following morning. None of them had been up early enough to walk to the mine mess and get breakfast. They were driven to the mine offices and introduced to the Personnel Manager, Henry Mwanza. They also met Tom and Rita there. There were employment agreements to sign, photographs for identity cards taken, and basic employment policies discussed. They were all assigned a number for identification and told that their mine number was the key to just about everything associated with the mine and its operation. To ease the settling-in process, there was an allowance paid, less the fifty kwacha advance. Travelling expenses were also recompensed, other than the prepaid boat or airfare. Then Henry Mwanza asked which bank they wanted their pay cheques to be deposited. The choices were National and Grindleys, an affiliate of Lloyds, Barclays or Standard Bank. They each picked one, either randomly or because they had past associations with either Barclays or Lloyds. Van Rensburg then drove them into town to visit the banks, set up accounts, and get some cash for daily living. Inside the banks, most of the tellers were black, with a few whites in the back offices or in management positions. James was intrigued to see that in the bank of his choosing, the telephone receptionist was blind, but obviously very good at his job.

Van Rensburg suggested that they find their way about town and get some supplies for themselves. He took them to the local stores, OK Bazaars and ZCBC, then the produce markets, where they bought fruit and vegetables and finally to a butcher. The problem was that James didn't think any of them knew what to buy, as they had given no thought to meals. Breakfast cereals and milk seemed a good start, then potatoes and steaks. James was amazed at the low price of the steaks. Growing up, steaks had been something that were almost never seen at home. Lionel asked van Rensburg where they might start looking for transport.
"You want new or second-hand?" asked van Rensburg.
"What are the prices of new or used?" asked Lionel.
"Anything from four hundred to four thousand five hundred kwacha," van Rensburg said. That was not very useful. Each of them had a base salary of nine hundred kwacha a month, out of which came taxes, room rental, and other deductions. Spending a lot on a car would be hard to do.

"We need to think some more about this," said George. He obviously had a scheme, but was not saying yet what his idea might be.
"Why don't I run you back to the single quarters?" said van Rensburg.
"This afternoon, you each need to report to your own departments."

"Before we go back, can we just stop at the Post Office so that I can send a telegram letting my family know that I'm still alive and here?" asked James.

"Sure, sure," replied van Rensburg. "What about you other *ouks*?"

They assumed that by *ouks* that he meant blokes, so he got one other taker and a Post Office visit was added to the journey. James thought that he should have mentioned it sooner, as the Post Office was almost opposite the last bank they had been in, and they would have been able to avoid another drive around looking for parking. They drove back to the personnel offices to drop Tom and Rita, then van Rensburg said that he would drop each of them at their appropriate offices that afternoon, and then he was done with being a taxi service. He gave Tom directions on how to get to the shaft complex where the training school was located and said to meet them there. He then got the others back to the single quarters for the lunch break.

# The mine

James fixed himself a light lunch, a cheese and pickle sandwich and was ready when van Rensburg came for them at one. Van Rensburg dropped George off first at the main offices for the smelter, then Lionel at the hospital, and James followed him to one of the shaft complexes. This was the location of the underground training school. Van Rensburg introduced him to Koot Strydom, the Mine Captain, who ran the school.

"Here's another *Rooinek* for you, Koot," said van Rensburg.

"I suppose this one is brilliant, like all the rest?" muttered Strydom. "Okay, *boetie*, tell me about yourself."

"My name is James Martin, I graduated from the Royal School of Mines, and I'm single."

"Okay, that's enough. Well, tomorrow you will join the other trainees and start the training program. There will be about a month in the school and then another two to three months as a learner official in the mine," Koot Strydom said. "You will need to learn the language we use and also see if you can do better than the other new *Rooineks* at some of the basic tasks our people do every day. In the meantime, is there anything you want to know?"

"How does the management structure work?" James asked him.

"I suppose you want to be an underground manager next week," said Strydom, then he continued. "The lowest level of official is the Section Boss, then Shift Boss, Mine Captain, Assistant Underground Manager, Underground Manager, Manager Mining, and General Manager. You will start as a learner official, and when you get your blasting licence, you can start as a Section Boss."

"How many others will be in the classes?" James asked.

"Well, there are three other *Rooineks* like you and five local boys," answered Strydom.

They were interrupted by a knock at the door. "Coffee *Bwana*?" asked a Zambian.

"*Ja*, for three, Gibson," answered Strydom. Gibson was back almost immediately with a tray on which were a large coffee pot, three cups, milk, and sugar. He set the tray on the desk and withdrew. James

41

wondered why van Rensburg had stayed on and had not spent any time with either George or Lionel. It turned out in subsequent conversation that van Rensburg had worked underground for most of his career and had only recently joined Personnel. He had left the underground because of health problems. Sustained exposure to silica dust over the years had left him with respiratory problems that precluded his continued working in a mining supervisory position, and he did not have the academic qualifications to go further in mine management. He felt most comfortable with his friend in the mining school and did not associate very much with the other professions on the mine. Strydom called for Gibson and told him to take James to the mine stores and get him equipped with overalls, boots, hat, belt, safety glasses, and gloves and then bring him back to the office.

"Don't bloody lose him!" was his parting shot to Gibson.

The mine stores were only a short distance from the school office. In the other direction, James could see the shaft complex that provided access to the mine itself. The rest of the buildings near the shaft were changing rooms, offices and workshops. At the mine stores, the only thing the storekeeper wanted to know was his mine number, the universal mode of identification. Equipped with the clothing and safety gear, James was taken back to the office. Then Strydom took him to a classroom and introduced him to the rest of the class.

"This is Felix Mwewa, Rice Chikonde, Greg Young, Hippo Zimba, Joy Mwamba, Bill Harrison, Tom Morrison, and Samson Kachepa. Meet James Martin. Oh, of course, Morrison and Martin already know each other. You will all start here at six thirty tomorrow morning," they were told. "Bring your own lunch and something to drink. As I'm sure you will be only too happy to know, Saturday is a short workday, so you will be finished early. Okay, *voetsak,* and be ready to go to work in the morning."

James went out with the others and discovered that Bill Harrison had no transportation.

"Can I give you a ride back to the single quarters?" he asked.

"Thanks a lot," said Bill

They drove past the mine complex to the single quarters. Tom pulled up behind them and got out to see what single quarters looked like.

"Where do you live?" Bill asked Tom.

"We were assigned a house on Geddes Street, the other side of Central Street," replied Tom.

"Where are you from, Bill?" James asked.

"I come from Newcastle and went to university there as well," added Bill. "How about you two?"

"I grew up in the Thames Valley close to Marlow and went to RSM," James replied.

"I grew up in London and went to Nottingham," said Tom.

"What's a *Rooinek*?" James asked.

"It is an Afrikaans word for an Englishman," answered Bill. "It is supposed to come from the sunburn on the backs of the necks of the English. The Afrikaners also use the words *Engelsman* or *soutie* for us," he added.

"How long have van Rensburg and Strydom been here?" asked Tom.

"Much of their lives, I understand," said Bill. "They both moved here from South Africa in the late 1940s, when this was still Northern Rhodesia and stayed after Independence in 1964."

"Well, I had better be going," said Tom. "Rita will be expecting me to be home soon to tell her about the day."

After he had gone, Bill asked James if Rita was worth going home to. "Definitely!" was the answer.

"Do you want taking in the morning?" asked James.

"Yes, please, thanks," Bill replied.

They swapped room numbers. James was a little confused. He had heard that the South Africans, particularly the Afrikaners, did not believe that the Africans could run their own affairs, let alone a country, yet here were two of them who had willingly stayed on in Zambia under a black government. James had no idea how van Rensburg and Strydom actually felt about the Zambians and doubted that he would learn any time soon. He did wonder if the two older men were, in a way, trapped by basic economics and tied to the mine and the jobs that they had. As for the Zambians, so far his own contacts with the

Zambians had been reasonably positive, and his impressions were favourable.

There was a knock at his door, and George and Lionel came in.
"Dinner?" asked George.
"Why not?" James replied. "Do you mind if we ask someone else to join us?"
"No, who?" asked Lionel.
"Another bloke I met at the training school today, he's called Bill," he replied.
They found Bill's flat and banged on the door.
"You fancy joining us for dinner?" James asked. "This is George Walker and Lionel Fairfax, meet Bill Morrison."
"Where to?" Lionel asked.
"I suppose the mine mess again," said George. "We really do need to get some transportation so that we are not constrained in our choices."
"Well, I could drive you; do you have anything in mind?" James asked.
"No, the mess will be fine," replied George.

Early the following morning, James awoke at five thirty and got some breakfast and was ready for Bill at six. It was chilly out as the sun was not yet up. The drive to the training school did not take thirty minutes, so they were early at the shaft complex. Koot Strydom was there and showed them the change house for the school.
"Be ready to go down as soon as the others are here," he said.

At about 6:40, they all were changed and ready and were shown to the lamp room to collect their lights. Issuing the lights gave a count of how many people were underground at any time and served to indicate who had not yet returned to the surface. James threaded his belt through the lamp hooks and then noticed that Bill had a different belt, which provided a much easier way to clip on the lamp. He determined to ask where he could get one of those belts. James slung the light and its cable around his neck, rather than attaching the lamp immediately to his helmet, so that he would not look too much like a newcomer, not that it was not immediately obvious with his new overalls and bright shiny helmet.

44

They then went to the shaft and got into a cage. The cage was essentially a lift with a larger-than-usual car for passengers. The cage was strictly utilitarian, plain steel walls, floor, and ceiling. The capacity was sixty people per deck, and there were two decks. The cage was full by the time they were aboard, and most of the other people in the cage seemed to know who Koot Strydom was. He passed comments with some of them and got some laughs with whatever it was he said. Mwewa and Chikonde looked as if they had had a good night and were suffering for it. Zimba said, beer, too much, and laughed.

The descent to the training school was quick, as it was relatively close to the surface. James had been in mines before and felt at home going underground again. The cage rattled and clanged as it dropped into the mine, then stopped, and they got out into a 'station' which was a level underground, off which led a tunnel, with railway lines laid down in it. The station walls were whitewashed, and electric lights were slung from the roof. The floor was concreted right at the shaft and then turned to compacted dust and dirt. Running alongside the railway lines was a drain with a slight trickle of water running through it. The air was cooled by the draft that came down the shaft and went into the haulroad. They walked down the haulroad until they came to a junction with a crosscut. The school had a classroom off the crosscut, cut out of the rock. Once inside, they met the rest of the staff.

"This is Ron James," said Strydom. "He will be your instructor while you are here. Simon, Adam, and Seventeen will assist him. In the future, come down here directly and be here by six-thirty, and I will stop by some times in the week to see how you are progressing. Ron is in charge here, and you take your instructions from him"

The first class was language. The workers on the mine came from many different language groups within Zambia and also from Tanzania, Malawi, and a few from Mozambique. Because they were from so many groups and spoke different languages, the mines had long ago adopted the practice of the South African and Rhodesian mines and used a *lingua franca* or pidgin language. In South Africa, it was known as

45

Fanagalo, in Rhodesia, ChiLapalapa and in Zambia, ChiKabanga. Fanagalo was derived by the South Africans for use in the mines and was basically Zulu and Xhosa with English, Afrikaans, and the odd Portuguese word thrown in. ChiLapalapa and ChiKabanga both had changes to the language that were driven by local usage and pronunciation. As the workforce had become more educated and time had progressed, English became more widely used and in time, would probably displace ChiKabanga as the language of the mines. It would probably also please the Zambians to be rid of a language that was so closely associated with Colonialism. But, for now, ChiKabanga was the only reliable way to communicate.

"Okay, listen to me, people," said Ron. "Your instructor this morning will be Adam, who will start you out on ChiKabanga. This afternoon, you will split into three teams, and Adam, Simon, and Seventeen will start you out next week on some timberwork. Okay? Right, Adam, they are all yours."

"*Inzwa na mina*," said Adam "*namusha, tina kuluma lo kabanga*. Listen to me: today we will speak ChiKabanga. *Ena lo isando, lo sumali, lo ithumbu*. This is a hammer, a nail, a hose," continued Adam.
The class went on through the morning until they all felt that they were getting some of the words and expressions. There were times when James felt that he would never get the hang of this language, but by the end of the lesson, he had at least learned to say why and when. The Zambians did a little better at this than the expatriates, as some of the words had common roots with their own languages. They finally broke for lunch, and the first question was for loos.
"It's called the *chimbusu* down here," said Ron "It's down the haulroad towards the shaft. You will see it, there is a sign."

After the lunch break, they were essentially done for the day. The instructors were keen to be gone, so they all went back to the surface to shower and change. James took Bill back to the single quarters and then wondered what he would do for the rest of the day. He decided to take a drive back into town and take a look around. There was a cinema, the Astra, a couple of banks, and several large-looking stores. James drove through the centre of town and out onto the road to Chingola. The road dipped to cross a stream and then climbed up again past a large hospital, which he later learned was the Kitwe Central Hospital, previously the Llewellin Hospital. Past the hospital, he found a place to turn around and then drove back into town and to his accommodations.

In the parking area, he found Lionel and asked him if he fancied a beer. Lionel was only too keen and suggested that they try the Edinburgh Hotel. Lionel knew roughly where it was, so James drove back through town and up the hill again, then turned right and found the hotel. It was definitely a cut above the mine mess. The food was good, and the bill clearly reflected it. Still, it was a welcome break, and they enjoyed the evening out.

Sunday, James decided that he would spend the time filling out some of the postcards he had purchased earlier and taking an easy day. He saw Bill being collected by someone and then saw a couple of the other residents come and go. It was a good time to take a break and recover a little from the trip out and the drive up. There had been a lot packed into the last couple of weeks. He found a quiet spot under a large tree and wrote his postcards. There was a rugby game going on just down the street, so that provided some entertainment until the light went out, and it was really too dark to see much.

Monday came early enough. James found Bill and drove to the mine to start work. The day was set up to be language lessons in the morning and practicals in the afternoon. After the lunch break, James was assigned with Rice Chikonde and Tom Morrison. They went off with Seventeen to a different part of the school and were shown timber supports that held up the roof. The idea was that they should learn how to make these supports and actually put some up themselves. What looked simple turned out to be more difficult than they had imagined.

The timber was a local wood called mukwa, and it was hard: it was heavy and therefore hard to handle, it was tough, so it was hard to saw, hard to drill, and hard to put nails in. When they tried to saw through

47

it, the saw would stray off the line wanted. Hammering in nails was almost a waste of time, as they seemed to always bend. Part of the problem was that the only light available came from the lamps on their helmets, so they could only see what they were directly looking at. With no whitewash on these walls, the only reflection was from the water in the drains, and without the meagre light of the lamps, it was utter darkness.

Seventeen shook his head a lot and said *Aikôna* often. James had learned enough to know that this meant no. It became frustrating. He felt that it was unnecessary to go through this exercise. He was a graduate of a renowned mining school and was back to doing manual labour and not using any of the skills he had spent years learning. Tom, however, was fairly adept at the skills required to work the wood, but Rice was about as hopeless as James. Occasionally, Seventeen would wave them aside and, without apparent effort, would cut, shape, drill and nail pieces together. Clearly, there was skill required to do this work well, either in the understanding of the wood and its behaviour or in the use of the tools, or both.

The level of conversation rose and fell with the level of intensity of work. James discovered that Rice had been to university in Russia. He had attended a language school in Moscow first and then had gone to a mining school in Kiev. Rice said that there was some attempt to politicise the students, but most of their time had actually been spent on mining engineering. His education was part of the aid package that the USSR provided to Zambia. Rice said that his biggest complaint was the cold in the winter months. He had never experienced anything like it and hoped never to again. They kidded Rice about looking green in the morning, and he laughed and owned up to being out with some of his friends the night before. They had been to a club and had drunk more than a few beers. They quizzed Seventeen and learned that he had been with the mine for over twenty-five years and had moved into the training school two years before. He had most recently been a Section Boss in stoping operations, which was the main production function.

At the end of the shift, they stowed the tools and equipment and walked out to the shaft. There was a small crowd waiting for the cage. James joined the group and settled down to wait. Several times, the cage rattled by their station on the way up with loads of men. The crews waiting called to those in the cage and got calls of derision in answer. Several times, newcomers came up and rang on the bell system used to communicate with the hoist operator. Each level had its own identification call, and they were letting the driver know that there were men waiting to go to the surface.

Finally, the cage stopped and everyone at the station crushed on board. Each deck was supposed to take sixty men, but James estimated that there had to be at least eighty per deck. Once on board, the cry was taken up, *Chaya* four one. The signal of four rings followed by one ring was the instruction to the hoist operator to proceed to the surface without further stops, in other words, Take us to the top! As the training school was at the level closest to the surface, this was the only logical signal for the onsetter to give the engine driver.

Once on the surface, James headed over to the change house to take a shower and get back into his street clothes.
"Wait a bit," called Tom. "Aren't you going to turn your lamp back in? If you don't, they will think you are still down there."
"Oh, shit," James replied. "Forgot."
He checked his lamp in and then went off to the showers. Back in his clothes, he looked around for Bill. James wanted to be sure that he would be available to give Bill a ride back to his flat. The others in the group had all headed off towards the parking area.
"You chaps want to come to the house and meet my wife?" asked Tom.
"Thanks," said Bill. "You want us to get you some beers on the way there?"
"Sure," said Tom. "We can swing past a bottle store in town and then go home."
They drove into town and found a bottle store, and picked up a crate of beer.
"You prefer Lion or Castle?" asked Bill.
"I can't really tell the difference," said Tom. "Get Castle."

"What will Rita drink?" James asked.

"She will take a beer or a Coke," Tom answered.

"Better get some Cokes as well, then," said Bill.

From town to Tom's house was only a five-minute drive, mostly through lower-density mine housing. A few of the houses looked pretty unkempt and run down, but most had the manicured look that James had now come to expect of the low-density housing. Some of them had huge growths of trailing vines that covered fences, hedges and structures. Others had large trees in the yards with fruits hanging on them.

"What do you think those are?" asked James, pointing to some trees in a yard they were passing.

"I think the taller tree is avocado, the shorter ones are mango, and it looks like some orange or lemon and a couple I don't know, the stuff with the purplish-looking flowers is bougainvillaea," answered Bill.

They turned off Kantanta Street onto Fourteenth Avenue and then onto Geddes Street and drove down it for a little way and then turned into one of the houses. The yard had a large pile of rubbish in the centre and was overgrown. They pulled in behind Tom and got out. "I have some work to do," said Tom. "Give me something to do at the weekend."

"When do you have to get local license plates?" asked Bill.

"I don't know," said Tom. "Probably should find that out from Ron or Koot."

"Yeah, before you get arrested," laughed Bill.

"I never thought of that," James said. "What about driving licenses?"

"I'm sure we will need Zambian licenses," said Bill. "But don't ask me yet how we go about getting them."

Tom led them to the back door of the house and unlocked it, showing them the kitchen. "Come on in," he said. "Sweetie, I'm home!" he yelled. From the front of the house came a call, be right there.

"Brought some of my partners in crime," called Tom. "Better make sure you are decent."

Rita came in from the back of the house.

"Oh, hi, James," she said. "How are you today?"

"Rita," said Tom. "Sweetie, meet Bill."

"Nice to meet you," she said. "Won't you come on in?"

They moved from the kitchen into the living cum dining room.

"Grab a seat," said Tom. "And I will get us some beers."

"So, how are you settling in?" asked Bill.

"Fine, but there are some things I would like that we don't have, like a washing machine and a floor polisher," answered Rita. "These floors are just plain concrete with some kind of paint on them, and it looks like they get polished," she continued. Tom came back with the beers and asked if Rita had met any of the neighbours yet.

"I met Elaine McPherson from next door this morning," she said. "They have been here six years. They come from Glasgow. He works in some kind of engineering workshop. They have two children, both away at boarding school, and she sits at home all day. She told me that I need to get a Bembamatic to do the floors. What's that?"

"I think she was having you on," said Bill. "The dominant local people in this area are the Bemba, and most expatriates have house servants, hence Bembamatic."

"How come you seem to know so much?" James asked.

"My brother lives in Luanshya," said Bill. "He has been coaching me a little."

"So, are you married?" asked Rita.

"Not yet," replied Bill. "Though my brother keeps telling me that he is trying to fix me up with some nurse that he knows in Luanshya."

"Tom and I have been married only a couple of weeks," said Rita. "Our honeymoon was basically the boat trip to Cape Town."

"What do you do?" Bill asked.

"I was a reservation agent for BOAC while I was at university," replied Rita. "I used to book people to places like Zambia, but never guessed that I would actually go there."

"Have you thought about working here?" Bill asked.

"Actually, I have already met someone from UTA, and they have a job. I can speak French, which helps with UTA, if not the local population, and they want me to come in and see them soon." Rita said.

"Another beer?" asked Tom.

"Thanks," said Bill. "We should think about dinner soon, and don't want to impose." Bill and James then drove back to the single quarters.

Back at the single quarters, they decided to see if George and Lionel were in and maybe get some dinner. George was in, and he told them that Lionel had been called out to the hospital.

"How about dinner then?" James asked.

"Sure, Ernie's again?" answered George. They walked to the mess and asked George about his first real day.

"I started to learn the sign language that they use in the smelter," said George. "It's too noisy to talk much of the time, so they have devised a bunch of hand signals." He went on to say that he had met some of the people that he knew and had a line on a car for himself, a leave house that he was looking at and had been invited to a *braai* at the weekend.

Bill explained to James that a *braai* was a barbecue, done South African style, lots of meat, few, if any, vegetables and plenty of beer. George's *braai* was going to be at the house of one of the supervisors at the smelter, whose contract was almost up and was not renewing. He was due to leave soon, and it was his car that George figured he would buy. James could not help but be a little envious. He had no line on leave houses, and no one had invited him out yet. He presumed that what George was telling them was true and that he was not bullshitting, as he had begun to wonder how much of what George did and said was true.

James drove himself and Bill to the shaft complex the next morning. They met Tom, who was already there, as Rita was taking his truck in order to be able to go to an interview that day. They got changed and then waited for a cage down to the school. As they got into the cage, Simon, Adam, Seventeen, and the rest of the training class joined them.

"So, *kanjani, zonke ena mushle namusha?*" asked Adam with the standard, how are you, is everything good today?

"*Mushle,*" replied Felix, who apparently was well.

"*Lo skopu ka mina yena cheesa,*" said Chikonde.

"Why does your head hurt?" asked Adam, switching back to English.

"Too much beer," said Chikonde. "My brother got married and we had a party."

Following the language class that morning, James asked Greg Young about himself. "I grew up in Dundee, went to a school of mines in Cornwall with Mwewa and Mwamba. I married a girl from Redruth last month and came out here by boat, then drove up country, stopping in Jo'burg for a week to visit my cousin at Springs. How about you?"

"Well, I went to RSM, got dumped by my girlfriend when I said I was coming here, came in from the south a day or so ago," James replied.

"Which boat did you come out on?"

"The Vaal, which boat did you come on?" asked Greg.

"The Pendennis Castle," replied James.

"Why don't you join us for dinner tomorrow night?" asked Greg "Come to think of it, we should get Tom and Bill to join us as well."

"Sure, where do you live?" James asked.

"On Phillips Street," said Greg. "It's the one over from Central Street, and you get to it by turning left just past the infants' school and then right."

James wondered about the others in the class and asked Greg about Mwewa and Mwamba.

"I tried a few times to socialise with them in Cornwall," said Greg. "But somehow we seemed to have so little in common that it never quite worked out, and even though they are supposedly educated with degrees and all, they are still *munts*."

James was a little taken aback by this statement and could think of nothing to say for a minute, and then they were joined by the rest, and the conversation switched to cars.

The afternoon was more timberwork with no apparent improvement in the skills of James and Rice. Seventeen was critical and polite in the way that sergeants can be polite towards new young officers. Ron James came along and added to Seventeen's comments, remarking that he had rarely seen such poor work. James wondered if this was all part of the education process to ensure an appropriate level of humility in the new graduates.

At the end of the shift, Bill asked Ron James if he knew anyone with a car for sale. Ron said that he thought that Simon might know, as he was the local car fanatic.

"Simon, who has a car for sale?" he asked.

"Try the Bufalari Garage," said Simon. "I think they have some for sale."

"You could always check the classifieds in the paper," suggested Ron. James told Bill he knew where the garage was; he had seen it when driving through town the previous day with Tom. Bill also said he had checked the classifieds every day in the *Times of Zambia* and the *Zambia Daily Mail* and had yet to see anything that he really fancied.

Friday was much the same as Wednesday and Thursday, with language classes and then more manual labour. James finally managed to drive some nails into the timbers without them bending, and Seventeen even smiled slightly and said, *Ena so*. James was looking forward to something different for dinner. The mine mess got old, and his own cooking skills were very limited.

James and Bill met at six and drove down Central Street to Greg's house. They arrived at almost the same time as Tom and Rita. Greg's house looked the same as Tom's house, but with a yard that was a little more developed. Someone had taken pains over this yard, and it still looked reasonably good. Bougainvillaea grew up over a back porch, and the driveway was lined with bushes, which were covered in white flowers that gave off a really strong scent. Greg saw them arrive and invited them in. Inside the layout of the house matched that of Tom's. Greg ushered them into the living room and introduced them to his wife, Shirley. He offered beers all round, and they all introduced themselves.

"How do you like Zambia?" asked Rita.

"I hate the place," said Shirley. "It's hot and dusty, the blacks are unpleasant, and I feel afraid to walk the streets to do my shopping. I don't know why we had to come here; we could have stayed in Redruth, and Greg could have gone to work at South Crofty."

Just then, Greg came back with the beers, and Shirley did not say any more.

"How was your interview with UTA?" James asked Rita.

"Super," replied Rita. "I start next week. Do you think that you might work here, Shirley?"

"No, I don't think so," said Shirley. "I'm not sure what I would do."

"Have you thought about getting a house boy?" asked Bill.

"God, no. I couldn't stand the idea of one of them creeping around the house and going through my things," said Shirley. "What about you, Rita?"

"I may," said Rita. "With the job at UTA, I may need to in order to stay ahead of the housework."

"You mentioned that you had tried to socialise with Mwewa and Mwamba while they were in Cornwall," James said. "What was the problem?"

"I just hate *kaffirs*," said Greg. "The bloody *munts* are thick and stupid, and how they figure they can run a mine, let alone a country, is beyond me. My cousin told me about his experiences in South Africa, and there, let me tell you, they know how to manage their *munts*."

"How can you say that?" asked Bill. "Do you think the Brit colonial powers did anything to prepare the people for self-rule?"

"What are you, a *kaffir boetie*?" asked Greg.

"Not particularly," said Bill. "I don't see myself as a particular friend of the blacks, but don't you think they should be allowed to run their own country, make their own mistakes, and grow?"

"That's a problem because they don't have the basic intelligence to learn what they need to know," said Greg. "Studies show that they don't have the same amount of brain and therefore they don't have the ability to think. They are only good for manual labour."

"Where do you get this stuff?" asked Bill. "If you really don't like it here and don't like the people, why come, is it just the money?"

At this point, Shirley felt it was time to intervene and defuse what could grow into an argument. She announced that dinner was ready and that we should all take a seat.

Whatever else Shirley was, she was a good cook. They had avocado shrimp cocktails, followed by chicken à la king, then a rhum baba with coffee, and brandy to finish. Dinner conversation focused generally on life in England and the various cities that they came from. Shirley had been raised in a mining family. Her father worked at one of the tin mines in Cornwall, as did her brother and several of her uncles. Greg had been her first love, and she wanted him to return to England as soon as possible, where she had a life mapped out for them. It looked like they were going to be there for the first three-year contract and no longer. After dinner, they talked some more about the houses and what could be done to make them more attractive and where furniture could be acquired that was more presentable than the basics that the mine provided. Finally, Tom got the message from Rita's kicks and suggested that they should go home. James and Bill left at about the same time. On the way home, James remarked to Bill that Greg would make a great companion for George.

Saturday was another fairly short working day. It started out at six thirty but again finished earlier, just after one in the afternoon. It was good to be able to spend some time in the sun. The long days underground tended to keep one out of the sun, except late in the afternoon. After work, Bill asked James to take him into town, he had decided to get his own car. James took him into town, and they went to a garage that Simon had mentioned. The garage owners had an old Land Rover for sale. It was a long-wheelbase station wagon, a sort of greyish-green colour that had been fitted with extra fuel tanks and a winch. It had a diesel engine, but Bill didn't mind; it ran, and the price was within the amount he had budgeted. He spent some time dickering with the Italian garage owners over the price, and eventually, they agreed, and he took ownership of his new vehicle.

Now Bill was independent, and he no longer had to rely on others to get around. He had, of course, to get it licensed and to get insurance, but the Bufalari brothers told him how to do that. They asked if there were any others like him who needed vehicles, as they had a few other vehicles for sale. James thought of Lionel and said he would pass the message along. The transaction complete, James and Bill drove back to their quarters. Bill wanted James to follow him, as he wanted assurance that he would at least make it back without a breakdown. His misgivings were unwarranted as the vehicle proved to be in good condition and ran well. They parked outside the single quarters among the growing collection of Land Rovers and the few other cars that were already there.

Lionel saw them drive up and came down to see the new acquisition. While they were admiring Bill's new Land Rover, George drove up in his newly acquired Ford. He had, after all, been telling the truth. The supervisor leaving had sold him his car and George was now also independent. Lionel now felt that he should get with it and organise himself. James told him of the Bufalaris and their garage with the cars for sale. Lionel admitted that what he really wanted was a motorbike, and he would keep looking until he found one. Lionel really needed transportation to get to the hospital, but did have the advantage that if he were called out, the mine police would collect him if necessary and take him to work. George said he was leaving to go to the *braai* he had been invited to.

After he was gone, James asked the others if they fancied a drive. They said yes, and together they set off to explore. They drove through parts of Kitwe and then took the road to Kalulushi. Partway down was a side road with a signpost to the boat and fishing clubs. These clubs were located on a slimes dam, which contained the outflow from the concentrator. At one end of the small lake was the dam wall. At the other end were the clubhouses of the fishing and boat clubs. At the entrance to the boat club was a guard who stopped them and asked if they were members or guests. Fortunately, they were spotted by Ron James, who came over and told the guard that they were his guests.

"*Howzit*, you *ouks* fancy a beer?" asked Ron.
"Only if we are not imposing on you," James said
"No, man, that's fine. Come on in and have a beer." Ron took them in and introduced them to his wife, Elizabeth, and friends, John and Carol Watson and Koos and Sussana Englebrecht and got them all beers. James introduced himself, then Bill and Lionel. There were a number of people at the club, but James noticed that the only black faces were those of the waiters.
"Are there no Zambian members?" James asked.

"Yes, me!" replied Ron. "I am a Zambian, became a citizen on Independence. Seriously, boating is not a sport that many of the Zambians have yet the means to take up. The fishing club next door has quite a few Zambian members, including Mwewa from your class."

James looked around at the others in the bar and failed to recognise anyone else.

"So, how has your first week been?" asked Elizabeth.

"Oh, fine," said James. "A little overwhelming sometimes."

"I have seen things that I had read and studied about, but never expected to actually see," said Lionel. "One thing, though, there are a couple of really nice-looking girls at the lab that I don't think are married."

"One of them is my daughter," said Ron. "So watch what you say."

"Which one?" asked Lionel. "Catherine or Sheila?"

"Catherine," said Elizabeth. "She'll probably be here later with a couple of her friends."

"Maybe we should think about leaving soon," said Bill "We need to get ourselves organised for dinner."

"Eat here," suggested Ron "We do a *braai* later that you can pay for and get yourselves dinner."

"Okay with you chaps?" asked Bill.

"Great," said Lionel and James together. They relaxed a little now that there was no need to hurry or leave. James looked out onto the lake and noticed what appeared to be small islands that all had the same basic conical shape.

"What are those islands?" he asked.

"Oh, those, they are anthills, or more correctly, termite mounds," answered Ron.

"They are tough, tough, let me tell you," said John. "I bush clear and I hate those things." "John runs a contracting firm that does open-pit mining," explained Ron. "Koos runs a transportation firm; I think he moves most of John's equipment around for him," he continued.

"So, where do you *souties* stay?" asked Koos.

"We are all in single quarters for now," James answered.

Koos called over a waiter and ordered another round of beers.

"We should get these," said Bill.

"No man," said Koos. "It's okay."

Ron stood as some girls came into the club. James looked them over, and although they were nice enough, they were still not in the same league as Rita. Ron called them over and introduced them to the newcomers. "This is Catherine, Jane and Theresa," he said. "Girls, meet Lionel, Bill, and James."
"Lionel, I know from the lab," said Catherine. "What do you two do?"
"We work in the mine, currently in the training school," said Bill.
"So, what are you doing tonight?" Elizabeth asked Catherine.
"We are going to the bioscope and then maybe to a session," she replied. "*Oom* Koos, what is Katrina doing tonight?" she asked.
"She is dancing at the Little Theatre," answered Koos. "I think the show goes until eleven."
"There is a theatre in town?" James asked.
"*Ja*, it is an amateur thing," said Sussana. "Our daughter, Katrina, is dancing with four others there in a show. We saw her on opening night and will go to the last night and the cast party. They are good, I'm telling you."

"When did you come to Zambia?" James asked Koos.
"In 1948, we came up to work on the mines and then branched out into other things. We get back to South Africa once in a while to see the rest of the family."
"How does the Zambian Government treat you?" asked Bill.
"Oh, fine," said Sussana. "There is usually some drama at the border, but they are mostly doing that for show. The Government would prefer that all companies were fully Zambianized and Zambian owned, but they realise that this does take time, and it has only been five years since Independence, and the major mining companies have the priority."
There was a break in conversation as two men who had been at the bar joined them. They obviously knew Ron and his party.
"Attie, Darryl, meet Lionel, James and Bill," Ron said.
"You *ouks* just get off the VC-10?" asked Darryl.
"*Sies* man," said Catherine. "You are only rude."
"It's okay," answered Bill. "We all did get in a few days ago, James by boat and Lionel and myself by air. Do you chaps work at the mine?"

"You chaps! *Ag*, no man," said Attie. "I work for John, and Darryl works for the local Cat dealer."

"Are you staying here or coming to the bioscope?" asked Catherine.

"What's the flic?" asked Attie.

"Romeo and Juliet at the Rhokana or The Dirty Dozen at the Astra," answered Catherine.

"No man," said Darryl. "Maybe we will see you later at the session."

The girls left, telling Ron that they were off to see Romeo and Juliet and that they would be home late. The others sat back down and started to talk about fishing. Ron said that he and Koos were going fishing the following weekend, downriver on the Kafue. This led to a long discussion between Ron and Darryl about rods, lines, and bait types. This looked as if it would go on for a while. John asked the rest of them if they were ready to eat and then led the way to the *braai*. There were *braai* packs available for purchase that each contained steak, *boerwors* and pork chops and baked potatoes. Vegetarians would not do well here. Dinner was good, and James was reluctant to leave, but the others said they were beat and wanted to turn in. They drove home, and James thought about the evening and Ron and Koos's hospitality and wondered where George got his ideas about the Afrikaners.

Sunday was a day to lie in and be idle. James was sitting on the wing of his Land Rover studying the engine when George came down. "So how was your *braai*?" he asked.

"Oh, okay," replied George. "It was at some superintendent's house in Parklands. The men all got to talking about going home to England soon, and the women sat in a group talking about pregnancy. What did you do?"

"Oh, we took a drive," said James. "And found the boating club."

"So how was that?" asked George.

"Oh, fine," replied James. "We met one of our instructors from the mine school and some local business people."

"Huh, local yokels," said George. "They only seem to be interested in shooting and fishing and seem to have more money than is good for them. My boss told me that it's the same in Jo'burg. The Afrikaners and some of the English-speaking whites seem to live for nothing else." On that note, George took off, saying he was going to visit an acquaintance in Chingola.

A Land Rover pulled up at the single quarters, and a mine policeman got out. He asked James where *Bwana* Lionel stayed. It turned out that, because Lionel had no phone and it was his call-out turn, they had come to inform him of the call-out and take him to the hospital. Bill came down and asked what was up.

"Oh, Lionel has a call out," James said. "He told us not to bother waiting for him if we planned to do something. So what do you fancy doing today?"

"I don't know," said Bill. "Anything you fancy?"

"Well, George has gone to Chingola, so maybe we should go somewhere else," James said. "How about the Mufulira Rapids? Then maybe we could check out this theatre this evening."

"What are the Mufulira Rapids?" asked Bill.

"Ron was telling me the other day that in the Kafue there is a set of rapids close to the road to Mufulira," James said.

"Sounds like a plan," said Bill. "Why don't we grab some lunch in town and then drive over there?"

They drove into town and had lunch at the Edinburgh Hotel. As James had discovered before, this was a little pricier but a much better lunch than the mine mess. While they were eating, Bill was gazing distractedly out of the window.

"What are you looking at so intently?" asked James.

"Those birds," replied Bill. "They look like crows, but they are black and white, more like a magpie."

"Huh, you're right," commented James. "Maybe that's a local Zambian type of crow. Funny looking though, being black and white."

"Well, if you think about it," said James. "There will be many birds here that we have never seen."

"True," commented Bill. "I wonder if any of the summer migrants to England come here to winter?"

"Could be," said James. "Better eat your lunch and worry about birds later. Maybe we'll see some real birds around here sometime!"

"What about those three we met last night?" asked Bill.

"Pretty good, but not quite the right one yet," replied James.

After lunch, they drove out on the Chingola road to the Mufulira turn-off, then to the Mufulira rapids. Looking at the river, they thought that it might be fun in the future to get some kayaks and run the rapids. Then colder logic set in, and they remembered that the pools below the rapids could be full of crocodiles. Although they could see no crocodiles, they actually did see hippos in the pools. So whatever they were to do, they should try not to fall out of any boat. Then surprise, there were a couple of people going over the rapids in large inner tubes. They looked as if they were having fun. They also saw a couple of powerboats trying to make their way upstream.

"How can they do that?" Bill asked a man who was fishing from the bank.

"They are jet boats," he was told. "The New Zealander, Hamilton, came up with the idea, and it has grown. They draw very little water, and with a big enough engine and pump, you can climb amazing rapids."

"Thanks," said Bill. "You catching anything?"

"A few bream and a pike."

"You know?" said James, turning to Bill. "A month ago, if anyone had told me that I would be spending a Sunday afternoon looking at a river, I would have thought they were crazy. There must be more to life than this."

"You're right," said Bill. "We need to work on a social life a little harder. Why don't we take a look at that theatre that Englebrecht mentioned last night?"

They made their way back to Kitwe and found the Little Theatre on Kantanta Street. Tickets were available at the box office. They went back to the mine mess for a quick dinner before the show and got back in time to get reasonable seats. The show was good, and as *Mevrou* Englebrecht had said, the dancers were good.

"Which one do you think is Katrina?" James asked.

"I don't know," said Bill. "But who cares, they all look pretty good to me, they all have legs that go on forever."

Bill was right. The dance numbers were costumed for tight outfits, and the dancers all had great figures. It was a little difficult to see what they looked like because the costumes and makeup hid most of their features. After the show, they tried to see where the cast might go, but missed them, so went back to their quarters disappointed.

"So, see you in the morning?" James asked.

"Yes, we had better be there in good time," said Bill. "We still have to prove to Ron that we have some idea what we are doing so that he will let us out into the rest of the mine."

# "I spy"

The following morning, James fixed breakfast, organised some lunch and then gathered up Bill for the drive to the mine. On the way, they saw Kachepa walking along the road. They stopped and picked him up and then asked what had happened to his car.

"Stolen," said Kachepa. "I was at the Astra last night and the *skelms* stole my car."

"Did you report it to the police, and do you think they might recover it?" asked Bill.

"Those people, they said that it is already in Zaire," answered Kachepa.

"Is it much use there, surely the steering wheel is on the wrong side?" asked Bill.

"They will use it for parts."

They arrived at the mine and changed into their work clothes. The others arrived, and they got the cage down to the school.

"*So, kanjani namusha?*" asked Ron.

"*Mube, bwana,*" said Kachepa. "*Lo skelms yena bambili lo car ka mina.*"

"Sure?" said Ron, not surprised that Kachepa was having a bad day.

They went on to discuss the theft of Kachepa's car and its likely fate. Then Ron called a halt and said it was time to go back to work. The discussion about Kachepa's car had all been in ChiKabanga, which was actually quite challenging as the language had been devised as a command language. It was never conceived or developed as a language for philosophical discussion.

They continued language drills until lunch and then divided back into their teams for more practical instruction with timberwork. James's crew went with Seventeen to a disused haulage way and were shown the task of the day. They were to build a chute used to load ore into the rail cars. The timbers and steel were all there, and it was now a question of working out how to actually put it up. They were struggling with a hoist, raising some heavy steel sections up when Ron came by.

"So, when will this be done?" asked Ron.

"*Manje, manje so,*" answered Seventeen.

"Sure?" asked Ron, not really believing it would be done soon, no matter what Seventeen said.

"*Sure, Bwana, aziko indaba*," Seventeen assured him that this would not be a problem.

Ron was sceptical and said he would be back later to see. When he had gone, Seventeen showed them the easy way, and then the hopper went together with a lot less effort. Ron did come back and saw that the chute was in place and looked in good shape. He gave Seventeen a look and walked off to see the rest of the crews. James guessed that part of the assessment of Seventeen was how well his students actually did, and Seventeen was not about to let the other instructors outshine him.

At the end of the shift, they went back to the surface and met up with the rest of the class. James asked Kachepa if he needed a ride, but was told that Mwamba had already fixed that. Tom asked if they fancied a beer and was told. "Yes, what did he think!" They drove to Tom's house and discovered that there was an ulterior motive to the beer offer. Tom had been cleaning up his yard and needed to pull some posts out of the ground.

The previous resident had put little fences all over the yard. They were made of steel posts set in concrete and had cross pieces welded to them. Tom's idea was to use the Land Rovers and some heavy cable and tow them out. This worked and did not take long, and they were soon finished. Tom handed out the beers, and they asked him what he planned to do now that the little fences were all gone.

"I think I will just let it grass over," said Tom. "Perhaps I will also put in some vegetable beds. It should be possible to grow just about anything here."

"What will you do about water in the dry season?" James asked.

"There are two water supplies to the house," answered Tom. "One potable and one for the garden, that's what those taps are for in the corners of the yard."

"Where does the garden water come from?" James asked.

"It comes direct from the Kafue; I was reading something in the paper about the supply the other day," said Bill

"Shit," interrupted Tom. "I had better go and get Rita before she thinks I have forgotten, I was supposed to pick her up at five."

"Okay, Tom," James said. "We'll push off and see you tomorrow."

Bill and James drove back to the single quarters and found George and Lionel there. "Fancy some dinner?" asked George.

"Sure," said Bill. "Where shall we go?"

"There is an Indian place in town," said George. "Why don't we try that?"

They piled into James's Land Rover and drove into town and found the restaurant.

"So, how is it going, Lionel?" James asked.

"Oh, fine," said Lionel. "You wouldn't believe some of the things we see every day. I have seen ringworm, terrible burns from charcoal fires, malaria, and the worst of all, kids vomiting up round worms. It is a real difference from the suburban medicine I saw in England."

"I don't know why you bother," said George. "These *kaffirs* are not worth bothering about. They have too many kids and, from what they tell me on the furnace line, place more faith in the witch doctors than they do in real medicine."

"Sometimes I wonder how much good we actually do," continued Lionel. "We manage to bring down the infant mortality, but then the death rate goes up for two-year-olds. We offer cures for disease but don't alter the basic living conditions or habits of the people."

"Hey, this is getting a little too philosophical for me," James said. "I need to eat."

All of them considered themselves to be reasonably expert in Indian food, as England had any number of good Indian restaurants, run by immigrants and the children of immigrants. The food, when it came, was actually pretty good, and they were in good spirits when they returned home.

The following day, immediately after work, James went into town to the government offices and licensed his Land Rover. He also got himself a Zambian driving license. This turned out to be a relatively simple procedure of producing his British license, filling in the appropriate papers, and providing a photograph. His new license looked almost as if he had made it himself. It had a green soft card cover and inside was a photograph, officially stamped over, his address, signature and the endorsements for vehicle types. James was convinced after this that government employees are the same everywhere, slow, generally disinterested and somewhat incompetent. Certainly, his experience here in Zambia matched his experience in England. Insurance was next, and that was soon taken care of. He was now compliant with the local laws, or at least hoped he was. He also went to the Post Office and rented a mailbox so that he could receive mail. With a Post Office box number in hand, he went to the bank quickly to make sure they had his new address.

James then decided to take a look at the railway station to see if there were any trains in. He was fascinated with the trains. The gauge of the track was less than in England, 3' 6" instead of the usual 4' 8-1/2". Even so, the equipment was still about the same size as he was used to. He pulled up, and there was indeed a train in the station. It was a mixed goods and passenger train with a large steam locomotive at the head. The passenger cars were painted in chocolate and cream colours, and each had a large round crest on the side that said Rhodesia Railways. The locomotive was different from any that James had seen before. It was like having two sets of driving wheels connected by a frame, on which sat the boiler and the driver's cab. This was the first of the famous Beyer-Garrett locomotives that he had ever seen. James was fascinated and got his camera out and started taking pictures.

"What are you doing? You must stop. You cannot take pictures here!" a man told him. Others joined the speaker, and they took him by the arms and hustled him off the platform into an office. James was confused and a little frightened. He had no idea what was wrong, but clearly, the people who had brought him in there did not want him to take any photographs. They had taken his camera and seemed to be waiting for someone. A few moments later, a man came in, followed by several others, all of whom were loudly telling him about this incident. The newcomer introduced himself as Angus Turnbull and said that he was the stationmaster. He showed James to another office and thanked the others for their help.

"So, I hear you have been spying for the racist Rhodesians," Turnbull said.

"What?" James asked.

"Spying for the Rhodesians," said Turnbull. "I presume that you weren't really spying, but you need to give me some particulars and let me explain the situation. Give me some details about yourself and what you were doing."

"Well, my name is James Martin; I have just started at the mine in town as a trainee and will work underground. I came from England a little over a week ago and have always had a fascination for steam locomotives. I didn't think there was any problem with taking some photographs," answered James.

"Fine, you understand that we will probably check with the mine to see if, in fact, you are employed there. In the meantime, this is the situation. About a year after Independence, the Rhodesians declared UDI in late 1965. Earlier this year, President Kaunda issued a manifesto on Southern Africa stating that Zambia would rather negotiate than destroy, but that Zambia would support the local people against the oppressors. This means that we expect the Rhodesians to make some moves against Zambia, politically and economically. The railways are part of the lifeline of this country and are considered of strategic importance. Anyone seen taking pictures of the trains, bridges or other items that could be considered strategic is assumed to be potentially a spy," said Turnbull.

"But, would the railways not have been a shared asset under Federation, so the Rhodesians would already have all the information they need on the rolling stock and the bridges?" said James.

"That may be true," replied Turnbull. "But you need to learn to be sensitive to the feelings of the local people."

"I see. I'm sorry if I caused problems. I did not intend any harm." James said. "Is there any way I can keep the film I have exposed and the pictures?"

"Of course," said Turnbull. "We are not totally without discretion. Providing you do actually check out to be who you say you are, I can get you a permit to visit the locomotive sheds we have here in Kitwe, and you can get back the film that is in your camera. Come back next week, and I will have the permit ready for you and the films for you to collect."

"Thank you, sir," James said.

"Mr. Mwewa," called Turnbull.

A man came into the office. It was one of the people who had apprehended him earlier.

"Show Mr. Martin to his car, and we will see him next week when he comes to collect his permit, so that he behaves properly," said Turnbull.

"Yes, Mr. Turnbull," Mwewa said. "Mr. Martin, please come with me."

James was shown out and escorted to his car. After he had driven away, he got the shakes, brought them under control and then breathed a long sigh of relief.

By Saturday, James was looking forward to some entertainment, and George suggested that they all go to a rugby match in Kalulushi. Apparently, the mine in Kitwe had a team that was playing against the team from the Chibuluma mine in Kalulushi. After work on Saturday, Bill, Lionel, and James took off with George in his car for Kalulushi, about ten miles west of Kitwe. The rugby match was fun, if not particularly professional. After the match, they found their way to the bar at the Chibuluma Rugby Club. At the club, they met Greg and Shirley, and Tom and Rita from Kitwe. James introduced George to Greg and suggested that they might have much in common. Greg and George went off to share views and experiences and had clearly found common viewpoints and interests.

James asked Rita how the job at UTA was going.

"Fine," she replied. "There is a lot less activity than we had at my last job. A lot of the travel is for people taking leave to Europe or local leaves somewhere in Africa, or the neighbouring islands like the Seychelles."

"Do you think it will be worth staying at?" James asked.

"Oh yes," said Rita. "There may even be some travel benefits for me. So what did you do this week?"

"Oh, probably much the same things as Tom did. I did get a Zambian driving license, licensed my car, and nearly got arrested," James answered.

"What do you mean, nearly got arrested?" asked Tom.

"Well, I tried to take some pictures of trains at the station and landed up in front of the station master. He turned out to be okay and is fixing me up with a permit to visit the loco sheds in Kitwe," James answered.

"What's wrong with taking pictures of trains?" asked Tom.

"Well, as I understand it," James said. "Anyone taking pictures of trains, bridges, or other significant installations is potentially a spy for the Rhodesians. So, unless you want to land in hot water, or maybe even get deported, watch what you take pictures of."

"Weren't you scared?" asked Rita.

"Scared almost shitless," James said. "I could see myself in gaol or being deported any minute. But I think that the station master understands that Brits are weird about steam locomotives and figured that I was either just dumb or a really ballsy spy for the Rhodesians."

George came over to them and asked if they fancied staying much longer, as he was thinking of leaving. Tom told George not to worry, as he would run them back to Kitwe. George took off, and James saw him leaving with Greg and Shirley.

"Next time we go anywhere, I will drive myself. I'm really beginning to not like that idiot," James said. "Do you and Rita plan to stay for the *braai*?"

"Yes," replied Tom. "We have made no plans to do anything else this evening."

"Well, what do you think of this crowd?" asked Bill.

"A little different from the boat club," said Lionel. "These blokes are mainly expatriates, and if you took away the mining types, there wouldn't be many left."

"That's true," James said. "There are quite a few I know here from my year and previous years at RSM."

"No single women, though," said Lionel. "You know, we had better luck at the boat club. At least I got some dates out of our meeting with Catherine and Jane. I have been out with Jane a couple of times."

"So what is this Jane like?" asked Rita.

"Real smasher," said Lionel. "Looks great, nice person to be with, and we have another date tomorrow evening to go to a dance."

"What does she do?" continued Rita.

"She works for her dad, who runs a big equipment dealership in Kitwe," answered Lionel.

"What about you, James?" asked Rita.

"Oh, he is still trying to meet the mysterious Katrina," said Bill.

"Who's Katrina?"

"Well, she's the daughter of this chap we met last week. The only thing we really know about her is that she is a dancer, and if she was one of the ones we saw last Sunday has legs that don't stop," said Bill.

"Okay, okay, why don't we just eat?" James said. He didn't really want this to continue, as he was embarrassed, partly by his curiosity to meet this unknown and partly because he was hoping that someone would come along to take his mind off Rita.

"Well, what about you, Bill?" asked Rita.

"My brother in Luanshya is still trying to fix me up; he has something set up for tomorrow. He is coming over to Kitwe to pick me up tomorrow morning and then go to someplace called the Seventeen Mile Dam, wherever and whatever that is," replied Bill.

They were joined by a couple of others whom James knew from his college days.

"So, what brings you to Kalulushi James?" asked one of the newcomers.

"We came with a chap we started with to watch the rugby," James replied. "This is Rita, Tom, Bill and Lionel, meet Chris and Mick."

"So, you all work in Kitwe?" Chris asked.

"Yes," James answered. "Tom, Bill, and I work underground, Lionel works in the hospital lab, and Rita works for UTA. You are with the Chibuluma mine, right?"

"*Ja*, Mick and I are both shift bosses in production at Chib," replied Chris. "You chaps staying for the *braai*?"

"Well, we need to eat," said Rita. "And I want some food in these idiots before they think about driving home."

"Not to worry," said Mick. "The only breathalysers in the country are used by the mines and the railways. So, providing you don't hit someone or run off the road, you should be fine."

"Maybe," said Rita. "But considering how many beers these three have already had, I want them to eat."

Rita got her way, and they ate.

The routine continued with language classes and more basic schooling until, after the first month, they graduated from the underground school. They were assigned to working sections of the mine as learner officials who would shadow an experienced supervisor. James was assigned to a development section in the southern part of the mine, mining new drifts to make ready for future production. Bill was assigned to a production section in the same part of the mine, and the others were all placed into different parts of the mine, actually located about three miles away in the main section.

James had stopped at the railway station again and picked up his permit and his film. He had then had an escorted tour around the locomotive sheds of Zambia Railways. He had taken his fill of photos and thanked his guide profusely. In the latter part of the month, Lionel had found his motorbike and George had moved out into a leave house, but had been unable to take anyone with him, so Bill, Lionel, and James were still looking. Lionel had taken Catherine's friend Jane on several more dates. Katrina was still a mystery. Mwewa had got married, and Mwamba was seriously involved with one of Mwewa's sisters. Unfortunately, Mwamba was having difficulty coming up with the *lobola*, the bride price. He had agreed on five cows, or the cash equivalent, with the prospective bride's father, and until he could come up with the *lobola*, he was stymied. Mwamba had tried to borrow enough to pay the *lobola*, but his history of managing his money made people reluctant to lend.

On the first day of his new assignment, James first reported at six to the shift boss, in whose area he would be working. This was Abel Mwewa, elder brother to Felix Mwewa. Abel took him to the section boss, Isaac Kayumba, with whom he would actually be working. Kayumba gathered up his things and asked if James was ready. They collected their lamps and went to the cage and joined the rest of Kayumba's crew. In the cage, Kayumba gave instructions to some of his people. He assigned them work in teams of two, each to a different level.

They got out of the cage at the 2570 level. This put them at 2,570 feet below the surface, and Kayumba's section ran from that level to the haulage level below at 2,830 feet. It was hotter at this level than at the training school. There were large refrigeration units in a chamber off the main haulage, and chilled water was piped throughout the mine to heat exchangers set in the intake airways. Kayumba led the way along the haulroad to the working section and stopped off at a small crosscut where there were some red steel boxes. Kayumba unlocked one of the boxes and stowed his bag.

"*Wena funa faka lo chola ka wena lapa?*" he asked James.

James thought quickly and interpreted this as "Do you want to put your bag here?"

"Okay," he replied.

Kayumba went on to say that they would check out each of the working areas. It was a responsibility of the section bosses to check the working areas for safety. James went with Kayumba, and they climbed down to the first level below the main haulroad. Then they went to the end of a six-foot by eight-foot tunnel. Kayumba grabbed a steel bar and tapped the roof to see if it was sound or loose. They were listening for the ringing sound that a sound roof makes, or the dull thuds that loose rock makes. The strikes that Kayumba made against the roof rang nicely. Kayumba said to James. "*Okay, ena mushle, manje, bamba lo tumbu, vula manzi!*"

James was delighted to hear that the roof was fine. There is nothing like a solid roof over one's head to keep the day going nicely. He grabbed the hose and turned on the water, as had been requested. They washed down the end and checked for misfires from the previous blast. The blast had gone well, and there were no remnants of explosives left. They marked up the next drilling pattern with sticks of a waxy yellow crayon and had a few words with the crew that was going to drill this end.

Kayumba and James then made their way to the next level, climbing down the steel ladders that were placed in the raise. They went to the end of this level, and the operator here had already made a start.

"Kossam, *kanjani?*" asked Kayumba.

"*Ena mushle*," replied Kossam. "*Mina azi chaya lo manje manje so, ena kona lo munya?*"

James gathered from this exchange that Kossam was confident that he would have this end drilled quickly and was asking if there was another to be drilled.

"*Ena so, skati wena azi chayili lo, hamba panzi lapa* 2720," he said. So when this was finished, he was to go down to the 2720 level. James also realised that Kossam must have a blasting licence to be able to proceed independently.

They left Kossam and climbed down two more levels to the 2770 level and found the next crew. This crew was unloading gear from a small hoist that ran down in one of the raises that ran up the vertical length of the section.

"*So, Banda, inindaba wena aikôna chaya?*" asked Kayumba.

Poor Banda appeared to have no real answer as to why he was not yet drilling.

"*Lo jombolo yena aikôna mushle,*" replied Banda.

Kayumba took a look at the drill steel and told Banda that it looked fine to him and to stop stalling and get on with the job. He and James then barred down the working end. Even after knocking down loose rocks, the roof still did not sound good. Kayumba told Banda to get a timber crew and get some supports installed before they drilled the next round. In the meantime, he was to go to another level and drill a pattern that had been marked up the previous day. They then washed down the end and checked for misfires and marked up the next drilling pattern. Kayumba then decided he should check the progress of the advance of the tunnel. He got James to hold the end of a tape against a peg hammered into the roof, and he went forward to the face and measured the distance.

"Fifteen point five metres," he said. "*Bala lo.*"

James made a note of the fact that from the survey peg in the ceiling, the face was now 15.5 metres farther into the rock. They would note this on the drawing later and compare this against the plans.

"Okay, *tina hamba pezulu,*" said Kayumba. They left this working area and made their way back up to the top of their section. Kayumba found a crew there that was installing pipes. He told them to go down to the level where Banda had been working and install some timber supports in an area that was unsound. Next, Kayumba and James moved explosives from the magazine to the raise and lowered some cases to the different levels for use later. They went back down the ladder way and found that Kossam had finished his first round and had moved down to the next level. Kayumba got a hose and copper tube and, with James's help, proceeded to clean out all the holes to ready them for charging. Into each hole they pushed sticks of explosives and rammed them home with a charging stick, a rubbery, flexible stick about six feet long that had brass threads on the ends to add other sections or a rubber head.

Finally, Kayumba took a stick of explosive and stuck a hole in it with a six-inch nail and threaded a fuse and detonator through it and placed that into the hole. Strictly speaking, this was a no-no, as they were supposed to use copper tools to do this. But copper tools get lost, stolen or forgotten, and six-inch nails are common. When all the holes were charged, Kayumba then took some igniter cord, a plastic-looking, thick thread and connected up all the fuses, working the igniter cord to the middle to time the blast. This finished, they then placed a charging stick across the tunnel to indicate that the end was charged and went to the next end for charging.

At about one in the afternoon, they took a break and waited for all the crews to leave. They climbed back down the ladders and checked that all the ends were properly charged. Kayumba had only to charge three of the ends as Kossam, having a blasting licence, had charged one of the ends he had drilled that day. Nevertheless, Kayumba checked Kossam's work to see if it was satisfactory. Finally, they went back up the ladders to wait for the word to blast. Because of the ventilation system and the airflow, there was a strict schedule for blasting, and they needed to wait for the section above them to let them know it was safe.

James felt terrible. His head had started to ache, not just ache but pound. He sat down with his head in his hands and moaned, he felt it would be better to just die; it would be less painful. Kayumba looked at him and grinned.

"*Lo skopu ka wena, yena cheesa?*"
James wondered how Kayumba knew his head ached. "*Ja, yena cheesa sterek*", he replied.
"*Ena lo powder*", said Kayumba. "*So sorry, mina aikôna lo muti*", he explained that the explosives were causing the headache, and he had no medicine. He also promised that in time, James would get used to it and it would no longer bother him. James was not sure he actually believed him, but figured that Kayumba probably did know what he was talking about.

Finally, the crew from the upper section appeared and told them it was safe to blast. Kayumba went to the raise and yelled down it, '*Cheesa!*' This was the signal to the section below that he was going to blast. They climbed down the ladder way and walked quickly to the first end. Kayumba took some matches out of a tin that he had in his pocket and lit the igniter cord.
"Okay, *hamba checha*," he said.
They quickly left that end and ran down the ladders to the next level and repeated the process at each level until they arrived at the lower haulage level. As they neared the lower level, they could hear the blasts going off in the ends above them. Kayumba was counting to see if the right number actually fired. Once down, they passed the word on to the next section and then walked out to the shaft.

At the shaft station, they met up with others who had also finished their day and were returning to the surface. James saw Bill coming down the haul road and asked him how his day had gone.
"Great," said Bill. "We drilled loads of holes and charged up a pretty big blast for today, how about you?"
"I don't think I have ever climbed up and down so many ladders in my life," James said. "I think Kayumba was taking delight in seeing if I could make the grade. I also have a headache that could kill."
"Oh, you have a powder headache. It is the nitroglycerine in the explosives that is absorbed into the body. It dilates the blood vessels, including those in your head. That is what causes the headache. I have one, but I brought some painkillers, not that they do much good. Here have some. Tell you what, though," said Bill. "I need to bring more

water to drink tomorrow. It was hot in that section. You know what else is weird? We have plans marked in metres, we use three-foot drill extensions, measure hole depth in metres with six-foot rods and pay footage bonuses!"

While they were waiting for the cage, Kayumba did his paperwork. There was the work plan that they were following and the gang card, which was basically the timesheet for the crew. James noticed that against Banda's name, there were a number of Xs.

"What does this indicate?" James asked.

"He is an alien," answered Kayumba. "He is from Malawi."

"So what does that mean?" asked James.

"He cannot get promotion," replied Kayumba. "Those jobs are for Zambians only."

The station filled up with men, and many of them rang for the cage. Finally, a cage stopped, and they crowded into the two decks. Many shouted '*Chaya* four one!' but the cage was not yet full, and they went up to the 2570 level to pick up more people. After the stop at 2570, they were full, and the onsetter did strike four-one, and they went to the surface.

Once up James went with Kayumba to report to the shift boss, Abel Mwewa.

"So, how was your first day?" asked Abel.

"Good," James replied. "I think Isaac is trying to see if I'm capable of climbing ladders. I also have my first powder headache."

"Two occupational hazards," said Abel. "You need to go to first aid classes starting tomorrow," he continued. "You will need a first aid ticket and a blasting licence to get your section boss's assignment."

"Okay, where do I need to go?" James asked.

"There is a classroom at the first aid station by the smelter," answered Abel. "Be there at two-thirty tomorrow afternoon for the first class, and they will give you more details. Also, Ron James at the training school wanted to see you."

"Thanks," James said. He loved the way the Zambians spoke English. They had a singsong way of speaking with a completely different intonation from the Brits. For some people, it was hard to understand, but James seemed to have no problem.

James went to the training school and found out from Ron that one of the mine captains was leaving for a three-month break shortly and was looking for someone to stay in his house. Ron suggested that they drive to the main shaft area and meet with him. James got directions and met Ron there. The mine captain was a Piet van de Merwe, and he was leaving for an extended visit to South Africa, driving down through Rhodesia and then on to the Cape. Ron made the introductions, and Piet suggested that James come to the house and meet his wife. Piet gave him directions and suggested he be there at six. As they left, James thanked Ron for the help and also asked what he would have to do to join the boat club.

"Why don't you come out on Saturday and meet the membership chair, and we'll get you a membership," said Ron.

"Is the process complex?" asked James.

"*Ja*, you pay, we make you a member," said Ron.

Later that evening, James stopped by Piet van de Merwe's house. It was fairly large, larger than those occupied by his friends, and set back from the road. It had a huge hibiscus hedge along the front and thick bougainvillaea hedges down the sides. Bougainvillaea grew up and over a porch that led into the back of the house. Piet saw James arrive and opened the gate and let him drive in. As he got out of his Land Rover, he was checked out by the two dogs, and Piet told him that they lived in the house. Piet led James into the house and introduced him to his wife. They discussed the house and the need for a house sitter. Piet and James agreed upon a moving date, and Piet went over the feeding for the dogs and the garden chores he needed to have done. They arranged for James to come on the weekend and meet the houseboy and garden boy. James thanked them for the opportunity and took his leave. He drove back to the single quarters to tell Bill and Lionel what had happened.

"So, you are leaving us?" asked Bill.

"'Fraid so," James said. "This leave house is nice and conveniently close to the mine."

"We'd better get our act together and see what we can come up with," said Lionel.

"Are there any doctors planning on leave soon?" James asked.

"Don't really know," answered Lionel. "I should ask the pathologist. He knows all the hospital staff and what they are doing."

"Maybe we should also talk to Ron James," said Bill. "If he could come up with something for you, maybe there could be something for us."

The next day, they were back at work, and James met up with Kayumba at the office to get instructions before going underground. They also checked the section boss's logbook to see what the previous shift had done.

"These people," said Kayumba. "They say they did not lash out all the ends."

"So, what do we do?" James asked.

"We must lash the ends ourselves," said Kayumba, clearly unimpressed by the prospect of the manual labour that would be involved, lashing being the local term for shovelling the broken rock out by hand.

They made their way underground and walked into the section. They then climbed down through the section to see what actually had been done the night before. They found the end that had not been lashed out. Kayumba grunted and swore, and they left to start the drilling crews on the main work of the day. After the crews were well at work, Kayumba and James returned to the uncleared end. Apparently, the lashing crew had not cleaned the end because they claimed it was not well-ventilated. They looked at the flexible ducting that brought air to the end, and Kayumba decided that they should extend it so that the discharge was closer to the face. They found a section of duct and added it to the existing ductwork. They also added pipe sections to the air and water lines that were hung along one wall of the tunnel. When this was done, they checked the roof, washed down the rock pile, and then set to cleaning it away.

"*Bamba lo fosholo*," said Kayumba to James, making it clear that they were really going to do the work themselves. They both got shovels and started to clear away the blasted rock. It was a case of filling the wheelbarrows and then dumping them into a raise that was used for the waste material. James had not worked so hard in years and had a greater respect for the lashing crews when they were done. He figured that they had moved over 15 tons of rock. With all the blasted rock gone, they then checked the roof again and washed down the exposed face and checked for misfires. All was well, and they marked up the end for the next round.

They went up to the haulage level and organised the explosives for the day's blasts. James was amazed at the cockroaches that came pouring out of the powder boxes. They moved the explosives to the various levels where it was needed and started on the task of charging up the drilled ends. James had to admit Kayumba was right. After a while, the body got used to the nitroglycerine, and the headaches went away. While they were doing this, the shift boss, Mwewa, came by. He said that he liked to check each section once a day if he could, but that he spent most of his time in those sections that had problems. Kayumba ran a fairly good section, so was left alone a lot.

They waited until all the crews came out of the section; their day finished. Now it was time to wait for the section above to give them the all-clear to blast. Eventually, that came and they started down to light up the first end. Kayumba got out his matches from his tin and struck them, nothing! He tried more, nothing!

"*Malabishi Mulilo Fire*," said Kayumba. "*Yena aikôna mushle, ena kona manzi. Hamba lapa station bamba lo munya.*"
Kayumba was clearly unimpressed with the Mulilo Fire brand of matches, figuring that they had become damp and would not strike. He wanted James to go back up and then out to the station and get some more that were not wet. James ran up the ladderway to the haulage level and set off for the station. He needed to get a move on as the sections below them were waiting for their clearance to blast. James reached the station and started asking if anyone had matches. Fortunately, the copper mines were not like coal or gold mines and smoking and naked lights were not banned. Finally, he found someone who gave him a nearly full box of matches. James tried a couple before he started back, and these worked.

James ran down the haulage way back towards the working section, careful to keep the matches away from the water that streamed down in places from the roof. He reached the section and almost slid down the ladder. Kayumba was waiting.

"*Wena kona?*" he asked.

"*Sure, mina kona, futi lo ena mushle,*" answered James. These matches were okay.

They called down the raise to warn the people below and then lit the end. Quickly, they worked their way down the section, lighting all the charged ends. At the lower haulage level, they gave the word to the next section and then walked out to the station to get the cage to surface.

Once up, James had to move quickly to get to the first aid training course. The wet matches had caused them to be later than usual. On reaching the first aid station, he found the rest of his training school class, including George and some others from the smelter, about twenty people in all. The instructor started them off with an outline of the course and then started on basic anatomy and injuries. Apart from crush injuries, the most common underground injuries were cuts, burns, and blast accidents. The smelter was a little different, but only in the sense that there were no explosive-related incidents, but more serious burns.

After class, James went to dinner with Bill, Felix Mwewa, and Joy Mwamba. They were going to try a new restaurant, or at least a restaurant that was new to them. Over dinner, James asked Joy how his quest for bride price or *lobola* money was going.

"Not good," said Joy. "I have not yet enough money for the cows."

"Does her father really want cows?" asked Bill.

"Sure," said Joy. "The *madala* is trying to become the biggest cattle owner on the Copperbelt."

"No, no," said Felix. "My father is just trying to be sure that he will have enough for his old age."

"So, how is married life?" James asked Felix.

"Good," he replied. "We should have a child soon."

"But, didn't you just get married?" asked Bill.

"Oh yes," said Felix. "But you would not marry a woman who could not give you children. So you must be sure first."

"So, how was Cornwall?" asked Bill.
"It was always cold and damp," said Joy. "And many of those people are racists."
"What, even Greg?" asked Bill.
"That man," said Felix. "He is like a baboon. You watch a baboon in a *mealie* patch; the baboon thinks it is very clever. It takes one *mealie* and puts it under its arm. Then it gets another and puts it under the same arm, thinking it now has many. But it has lost the first one and will go through the whole patch picking all the *mealies*, but finishing with only one. Greg takes from whatever is there at the time, but in the end will have little."
"We were fine with some of the people there, but Greg and those other people are afraid," said Joy.
"Afraid of what?" asked James.
"Afraid of what they do not know," said Joy.
"I wonder why he came here then?" asked James.
"I think because he thought this would be an easy job and he wants the money you people get as a bonus for being here for three years," said Felix.
"Do you think he will last the three years?" asked Bill.
"Well, if he doesn't, he has to pay back some of the travel and other allowances and will not get the bonus that Felix mentioned," replied James.
"That man will have problems," said Joy.
"Why?" asked Bill.
"Because he talks of the people as macaques, and it is dark in the mine," replied Joy.

"Do you think you will stay in the mines for a long time?" James asked Felix.
"Sure," said Felix. "I will become the first Zambian general manager. But not like these people who are the leaders of ZIMCO and are friends of Kaunda."

"Yes, those people are all politicians, but none of them understand how the business is done," said Joy.

"Isn't it a little dangerous to be talking like this?" asked Bill.

"I am not UNIP," said Joy. "One day, these people will realise their mistake. You will see, we will have a one-party state soon, and that will lead to disaster, then common sense will finally come back."

"My friend, you will be in Kamfinsa soon if you continue to talk like that," cautioned Felix.

"What is Kamfinsa?" asked Bill.

"It is the prison that is between here and Ndola," said Felix. "But maybe it will not be Kamfinsa but Lake Benguela!"

"Is that worse?" asked James.

"Oh yes, it is detention at the President's pleasure," answered Felix. "Once you go there, we will not hear about you again."

"Maybe we had better change the subject then," said Bill. "I for one don't want to see Joy hauled off just yet."


"When did your brother become a shift boss, Felix?" asked James.

"He started as a lasher, then worked his way up in the mine to section boss. He got his appointment as shift boss two years ago," answered Felix.

"Is he much older than you?" asked Bill.

"Yes, he is the son of the senior wife of my father," said Felix.

"Do you have other brothers and sisters?" asked James.

"Yes," said Felix. "Four of each. How about you?"

"There are three of us, my older sister is a lawyer, and my younger brother is still at college," said James.

"Well, it is time for me to be home," said Felix. "I will see you chaps tomorrow perhaps."

"Hah, the new wife is already keeping you from your friends," said Joy.

"She thinks that perhaps I have a girlfriend in the compound," said Felix. "How could I afford one of those girls?"

"Well, you had better not keep her in suspense," said James. "See you tomorrow."

"Well, we had also better be off," said Joy. "Bill and I are going to my club."

Saturday, after his shift, James went to Piet van de Merwe's house. Piet introduced him to Silent, the house servant and to Evansi, the gardener. Piet had made arrangements for them to be paid while he was away and made it clear to James that he was to make full use of their services. James was sure that Piet was having them keep an eye on him as well. Silent and Evansi had both been with Piet for twenty years. It seemed incongruous to call Silent and Evansi "boys" as they were both quite middle-aged, even elderly men. James decided that the term 'boy' was a hangover from Colonial days and wondered how long it would continue to be used before it created considerable ill will. Still, he realised that he was unlikely to change the habits of a lifetime. He was given a set of keys and was shown around the house. The van de Merwes were leaving the next day, so he would move in after lunch on Sunday.

After finalising his arrangements with Piet, James drove back to the single quarters to see if Bill or Lionel wanted to go to the boat club with him. Lionel was off on a date, and Bill said he was also otherwise engaged. He drove to the club and found that Ron must have made some kind of arrangements with the gate guard, as he was expected and waved in. He parked and walked into the clubhouse.

"So, you made it," said Ron. "Are you still up for joining the club?"

"Of course," said James.

"Okay, let's go see the club president and treasurer and get you signed up," said Ron.

This process did not take long, and James then stood the first round as a minor celebration.

"I hear that you decided to stay in Piet van de Merwe's house while he is away," said Ron. "If you need anything while you are there, be sure to let me know."

"Thanks," said James. "I met Silent and Evansi, and I get the feeling that they will be keeping an eye on me."

"*Ja*, they have both been with Piet for years," said Ron. "What about Bill, anything turned up for him yet?"

"I don't think so," said James. "But he was off somewhere today."

"Well, we must *maak 'n plan* and help him find something," said Ron.

At about that time, Ron's friends Koos and John arrived. They asked if anyone wanted to take a boat out onto the dam. James said yes and went off with Koos to launch his boat. It was a jet boat with a large Volvo Penta engine mounted amidships. Koos backed his truck down the launch ramp, and they got the boat floated off and then made fast to the dock. They boarded the boat and took off. The jets gave the driver great control over the boat, and once up on the plane, it really moved. James noticed that when they were on the plane, there was actually less obvious wash than when they were travelling slowly. Koos handed the wheel over to James and told him to take them to the far side of the dam, close to the dam wall. Koos spent the next few minutes looking over the stern at the trim tabs that were mounted there. He was trying to set the boat up for a race that would be held the next day.

"What do you do for a race course?" asked James.

"We pick out ant hills or place buoys in the dam and then agree a course around them," replied Koos. "We will then race a number of laps around the course."

"How many boats?" asked James.

"*Ag* man, maybe ten," replied Koos. "It should be no problem to leave them all behind."

"Do any crocodiles live in this dam?" asked James.

"Once in a while, one comes in, but they do not like this water," said Koos. "But there is plenty for them to eat with all the fish."

"Are they big enough to take people?" asked James.

"*Ag* man, sometimes, I have seen them in the Kafue at 16 feet or more and have seen people swimming in the same part of the river," answered Koos.

"Jesus," said James. "Does anyone ever get taken?"

"*Ja*, lots of Zams and some idiot VC-tenners," replied Koos. "You can tell if a river has a bad reputation for crocs, watch the Zams, if they scoop water out with their hands and always seem to be watching the water, you can bet that crocs are there."

Koos then asked James to steer them back to the dock, and they took the boat in. It took only a few minutes to get the boat back on the trailer and out of the water, and then they retired to the bar.

"So, did you enjoy your spin around the dam?" asked Ron.

"Yes," said James. "I had no idea it was quite so big."

"Well, all the concentrator tailings have to go somewhere," said Ron. "And we can't just dump it in the river or back underground."

"Where did you learn to handle a boat?" asked Koos.

"When I was at college, I used to drive the coaching launch for the rowing club," answered James. "But we only had outboards, and they were never as fast as your boat."

At about that time, Attie and Darryl came in. They had been trying out Attie's new car on the way-leave for the power lines, getting ready for the local version of the East African Safari. Attie wasn't sure what his chances might be for finishing, let alone placing, but he wanted to enter. Darryl had been roped in as navigator and was looking fairly green. The way leaves were just rough dirt roads, bulldozed down the strips cut through the bush for the power lines, and no attempt had ever been made to reduce the curves or gradients. With his head down calling out gearshifts, Darryl had no visual reference outside the car and was feeling a little car sick.

"So, *howzit*?" asked John.

"That is only a potent car," said Darryl. "It needs a fine little tuning, but suspension is fine, gearbox ratios are good."

"So how much is this going to cost us?" asked John.

"*Bichana*, not much," said Attie. "There really isn't that much more to do."

"Do you sponsor them?" asked James.

"*Ja*," said John. "Koos and I both give these *ouks maningi mali* to waste racing around the *bundu*; I only hope that the money is well spent."

"We saw your *boetie* Bill last night with some Zam," said Attie.

"Sure? I think he may have been out with Joy Mwamba from our class at the training school," replied James. "They seem to have become fairly friendly."

"Joy is probably trying to sell off one of his sisters so that he can pay his *lobola*," said Ron.

"So, are you coming to the race tomorrow?" Attie asked James.

"Maybe," said James. "I would like to see who else races boats around here, but I'm moving tomorrow, so might not make it. Are you chaps coming?"

"*Ja*, us chaps are coming," said Attie.

"What time will you start?" asked James.

"Early, early man," replied Koos. "Before it gets hot and the wind gets up, maybe around eight."

"Are your family coming this evening?" asked Attie.

"*Ja*, they should be here now now," replied Koos.

"*Bwana* James is dying of curiosity to meet Katrina," said Darryl.

"*Voetsak*," said James.

"Ha, wherever did you learn such language?" asked Attie.

"Oh, some *ouks* like you that I met underground have started to teach me all kinds of new words," said James.

Koos was right, and his wife and daughter came into the club and joined them. James had learned enough of local customs to stand as *Mevrou* Englebrecht joined them and offer her a seat.

"*Dankie*, James. Have you met Katrina yet?" *Mevrou* Englebrecht asked.

"No, nice to meet you, Katrina," said James.

Katrina was tall, over 5' 8"; she was not so much beautiful, in the way that Rita was beautiful, but striking, the kind of girl you looked at and then again to be sure that you had seen her correctly. She had long, dark brown hair and beautiful brown eyes. Her complexion was dark, very reminiscent of Southern European or Middle Eastern. She had a spectacular body with the legs and the build of a dancer. Until now, James had thought that Rita was the most beautiful girl he had met, but, in his view, Katrina eclipsed Rita. She had to be the most alluring and exotic girl he had ever come across, let alone have the chance to actually meet. It was not as if she were more beautiful than Rita; in many ways, she was not. But the overall effect had such an impact on James that he thanked his lucky stars that he had been stuck on Rita long enough to avoid other girls up till now. He was struck dumb and realised that if it was possible to fall head over heels in love on a first meeting, he had done so. He was confused enough that he was glad when she turned to Attie and asked them how the car was doing.

"*Ag*, Darryl almost threw up when I ran him down the way-leave track," said Attie.

"Man, if you could hear better and follow directions, you would have made the trip faster, and I wouldn't have felt so bad," said Darryl.

"*Sies*, you two sound like an old married couple," said Katrina. "So, James, what do you do?" she asked, looking him over.

James, by now, had recovered enough of his composure to feel that he would not make a complete idiot of himself.

"I have recently come from England and work underground in the mine," he James.

"*Ja*, he is one of the new class of trainees we are trying to teach something," said Ron.

"What about you, Katrina?" asked James.

"Oh, she runs my business," said Koos.

"Not quite," said Katrina. "But I do help out and manage the scheduling of the transporters." She had this contralto voice with an accent that James decided he could never hear enough of.

"Look, we are all going to the bioscope after the race tomorrow, why don't you join us, James," said Darryl. "Katrina will be coming, Attie and Catherine and maybe a couple of others."

"Sure, what's showing?" asked James.

"The Thomas Crown Affair at the Astra at seven," replied Katrina.

"Okay, I will see you all at the Astra tomorrow then," said James.

Sunday, James got up late and packed his stuff, ready to move into the van de Merwes' house. He made his way to their house in time to see them off. Piet van de Merwe was pacing around his car, muttering about women and how long they could take to get organised. Eventually, Mrs. van de Merwe appeared, and they took off. Silent, the houseboy then took James's stuff and moved it into the house for him. As James was sorting his belongings, Silent came and asked if he wanted coffee. He also asked if James would be in for dinner. James said yes to the first and no to the second; he would likely be out and returning late after the movies.

Early evening, James drove into town to the Astra cinema. The others were already there and had got the tickets. James felt awkward. This was like going on a blind date, but he wasn't even sure if Katrina considered this a date. He paid Attie for his ticket, and they went in and found seats. Attie and Darryl were deep in conversation about cars and changes they wanted to make to the rally car. Catherine and another friend of hers, Shirley, were talking about Shirley's upcoming wedding, so James and Katrina were left to talk to each other.

"You were second from the right, weren't you?" asked James.
"What do you mean?" asked Katrina in reply.
"At the theatre show, you danced second from the right in the line-up, didn't you?" repeated James.
"Yes, how did you know?" asked Katrina.
"I don't know. Maybe it's the way you move, walk or something, but I remember clearly," replied James.
"I think I will take that as a compliment," said Katrina. "Although I wonder if I should."
"Please don't be offended," said James, anxious now to redeem himself and not antagonise her. They sat in silence for a few moments, and then Katrina asked;
"So, why aren't you married?"
"I was dumped when I announced that I was going to Zambia," replied James.
"Shame, why, what's wrong with Zambia?" asked Katrina.
"I don't know. I think a lot of people think it's in deepest darkest Africa, with no amenities, no entertainment, and no life," said James.
"So, you came on your own?"
"Yes, I rather fancied the idea. The mine had a job, it pays okay, and I have a chance to see some of Africa. So far, I have not been disappointed. The job is okay, the place is fascinating, and most of the people I have met have been really nice. If you don't mind me asking, are you dating anyone particular at the moment?" said James.
"No, I just haven't met the right person yet," replied Katrina.
"Ssh! You two, the movie has started," whispered Attie. "You can hold hands and whisper to each other later."

After the movie, James asked if Katrina was driving herself home or if she needed a ride. Katrina said that her dad had dropped her in town earlier. James offered to take her home if she would tell him how to get there.

"Go to the next robot and turn left, then right onto Independence Avenue," Katrina told him. "That will get you on to the Chingola Road and out of town."

"What the hell is a robot?" asked James.

"A traffic signal, what else would you call it?" Katrina replied.

"Traffic lights," said James.

They drove out on the Chingola road until they passed the Mindola compound and crossed the railway. Then Katrina told James to watch for a road to the right about two and a half miles past the crossing. They turned right, crossed back over the railway again, went through the Garneton Township, and down a dirt road towards the River Kafue. They finally came to a large farm, with a main house and a number of outbuildings. As they drove up, the car was surrounded by a number of Great Danes. It looked to James as if there were a hundred of them, but Katrina assured him that there were no more than sixteen. Katrina explained that her mother bred Great Danes and that they had the run of the farm.

"Do you want to come in?" asked Katrina.

"Will I make it to the house alive?" asked James.

"It's fine. You're with me, so the dogs won't bother you," said Katrina.

"If you're sure I will live, I would love to come in," said James.

"Did you ever have dogs when you were growing up?" asked Katrina.

"No, we had no pets of any kind," replied James.

They got out of the car and made their way into the house. Apart from being thoroughly sniffed by the dogs, James made it without a scratch.

"Coffee?" asked Katrina.

"Thanks," said James.

James stayed for a while but then had to excuse himself, as he had to be at work early in the morning. He did ask Katrina if he could take her to dinner later in the week. They set a date for Friday, and he asked if she had a phone number where he could reach her. She knew he was staying at the van de Merwes' and knew the number there. James drove back to town singing to himself. He could hardly believe that someone

90

as gorgeous as Katrina would actually agree to see him. He did wonder how in the world she had not been spirited off by someone long before. When he arrived at the house, Silent was there to meet him.

"*Bwana, kanjani? Zonke ena mushle?*" Silent asked, grinning like a Cheshire cat.

"*Sure, Silent, zonke ena mushle,*" James replied.

Yes, James thought, everything was good. The job, although frustrating at times, was interesting. He had just spent an evening with a beautiful girl, and he had a date for later in the week. What could be wrong? He did wonder, though, just how Silent seemed to know where he had been and who with.

# Mishaps

On Tuesday, James and Isaac were checking out one of the ends. The roof, when tapped, still sounded dull, and there was no ringing sound. They used the bars to pull down what seemed to be most of the loose rocks and then started tapping again. The tapping loosened more rocks, and the whole roof looked as if it were coming down. Isaac was struck aside by a piece of timber, but James was hit by a large slab of rock. When the dust settled, Isaac was bruised but fine. James, however, was winded and was lying under a pile of rock and dust trying to get his breath. Isaac started pulling rocks from James and eventually had all cleared. James was gasping for breath; it seemed to him that he could not get any air into his lungs. Finally, he was able to catch a breath and fill his lungs. His chest felt bruised, but nothing seemed to be broken.

"*So, Bwana, kanjani?*" asked Isaac.
"I'm fine, sorry, *zonke ena mushle,*" replied James.
"*Mushle, kabanga tina aikôna chela lo Mwewa,*" said Isaac.
James agreed that they would just clear things up and not tell the shift boss, Mwewa, what had happened. He felt that he would be embarrassed to admit that they had been caught in a roof fall, and Isaac probably didn't want to admit that he had endangered the life of a *muzungu*. They cleared up the work area and tested the roof again. The fall apparently had cleared all the loose material, and the roof now rang properly. However, as a precaution, they called in a timber crew and had some supports installed. After this was done, both of them felt better about setting the drilling crew to work.
"Well," thought James. "So much for everything being great; the job seems to have more risks to it than I thought."

Later that day, James called Katrina and confirmed their date for Friday. He then told her about his experience that day, happy to be able to unload onto someone. Katrina asked if he was hurt, and James assured her that he was fine, just a little shaken up and bruised. Only after talking to her did James think that maybe he should have kept quiet. The community was fairly small, and Katrina knew most of the old-time white residents, which included Ron James. If she told him that

James had been caught in a roof fall, then Ron would probably tell Abel Mwewa. Well, that was a risk that he would have to live with. It was good to talk to Katrina. He couldn't understand now what he saw in his last girlfriend in England. Katrina, by any standard, was exotically beautiful and shaped to kill. She was intelligent and was fun to be with, and, most importantly, she was there in Zambia.

On Thursday, they were at the lower end of their section when they heard an explosion below them. In some ways, this was not unusual, as the tramming crew that worked on the haulage below them would place bombs on the grizzlies when rocks were hung up. However, this time, something was wrong.

"*Wena inzwili lo whistle?*" asked Isaac.

"*Aikôna, aziko whistle, aziko cheesa,*" said James.

"*Fuck,*" said Isaac. "*Fanika lo muntu ena fili.*"

There had been an explosion below them, but there had been no alarm whistle and no warning shout. Now, Isaac thought that someone might have been injured or dead. They climbed down the ladder way to the grizzly level and ran along the drive. The drive was full of smoke and dust. As they came to the working grizzly, the scene was horrible. There was a man lying slumped on a pile of rocks. Isaac climbed over and pulled at the man's shoulder. The man rolled over, and they could see that his chest had been badly damaged and that his hands and much of his arms were gone. James couldn't believe that there was not more blood. Then he realised that the blood was mixed with dust and water and was there, but just not obvious. He wanted to heave and had trouble holding down his breakfast.

"*Lo muntu yena fili?*" asked James.

"*Sure, yena ifwa,*" said Isaac.

"*Ubani yena?*" asked James.

"*Lo yena Mhango, lo pikinin ka lo Mhango, lo yena sebenza na lo Chikonde,*" replied Isaac.

So, he was dead, and Isaac had identified him as the son of a man who worked for Chikonde, one of the shift bosses. As they were talking, the rest of the tramming crew came up from the haulage level.

"*Kanjani lo Mhango?*" one of them asked.

"*Yena ifwa,*" said Isaac. He then turned to James.
"*Hamba lapa shaft, telephone lo Bwana, kuluma na yena, chela yena lo muntu yena fili.*"

James was glad to get out of there; he was to go to the shaft and telephone the surface with the news. He stopped partway down the drive and retched. The man's injuries had been horrific, no hands or arms and almost no chest. This was the first major accident that James had ever seen. He barely recovered himself, climbed down to the haulage level and ran off down the haulroad to the shaft. As he was headed towards the shaft, he met the tramming shift boss and a mine captain in the haulway. He explained what had happened and was told to return to the grizzly area. The mine captain came with James, and the shift boss went back to the shaft to report the incident.

With the arrival of the mine captain, Isaac and James were told that they could return to their work section. They had recounted all they knew and could add nothing further to the investigation. Both were told to be prepared to answer more questions later from the safety department and perhaps from the Mines Department. As they climbed back up, James asked Isaac what he thought had happened. Isaac said that he thought it was likely that Mhango had been placing a bomb on the grizzly to unclog a hang-up that had occurred, and for some reason, something had fallen onto the bomb and set it off. The cold sweats hit James around then, and he started to shake. For a couple of minutes, he had to hang on to the ladder to avoid falling. He kept seeing the mess on the grizzly, with the bits of flesh everywhere mixed in with the dust and dirt. Finally, he recovered his composure and carried on up the ladder.

When they came to do their own blasting, James was a little apprehensive. He had seen the effects of an explosion on a person, and the results were not pretty. Isaac seemed to sense the problem and told him that he would learn to live with it. James wasn't sure quite how to take this. He couldn't believe that Isaac was really as insensitive as he appeared. Later, he was proved correct as he saw Isaac in a dark corner, mourning the loss of one of his friends and workmates. It looked as if the daylight had left Isaac at least for the moment, and it was some time before he rejoined the rest of the crew and appeared to be at least handling the situation.

Later that day, as they were leaving, James ran into Bill, and he seemed to know all about the incident. James asked him how he knew, and Bill told him that the Africans seemed to know almost as soon as it had happened.

"You know, Bill, Sunday I thought everything was going great, now two things have happened this week to make me wonder," James said.

"Yes, I heard about your fight with the roof and now this," said Bill. "You fancy a beer?"

"Absolutely," said James. "Maybe three or four with some Scotches thrown in."

"So, how was your weekend?" asked Bill.

"Oh, fine," replied James.

"I heard you had a date," said Bill.

"Oh, really, who from?" asked James.

"Simon Kachepa told me," answered Bill.

"How the hell did he know?" asked James.

"These blokes seem to know everything that's going on, some kind of bush telegraph, I suppose," replied Bill.

They went to the mine club, and James got his beers. He had one Scotch but passed on the rest. They had been there only a short time when Tom came in. He had heard that James had blundered into an accident and wanted to see how he was doing, and guessed that they would be at the club.

"*Howzit?*" Tom asked.

"Oh, fine," said James. "I have just had a shitty week so far."

"Well, maybe your date tomorrow will cheer you up," said Tom.

"How the hell did you know I had a date tomorrow?" asked James.

"Our houseboy told me," said Tom.

"So how did he know?" asked James.

"I understand that he heard from the houseboy next door, who is a friend of the houseboy where you are staying," answered Tom.

"Well, how did he know?" asked James.

"Who are you going out with?" asked Tom.

"Katrina Englebrecht," said James.

"Do the Englebrechts know the people in whose house you are staying?" asked Tom.

"Oh yes, they know the van de Merwes very well," said James.

"Well, there's your answer, James," said Tom. "The Englebrechts' houseboy is in touch with the van de Merwes' houseboy."

"You know, you couldn't get away with anything in this bloody town; everyone seems to know what you are doing," said James.

"So when are you going to introduce us to this Katrina?" asked Tom.

"Maybe next week, if this date tomorrow goes okay," said James.

"How is Rita doing in her job?" asked Bill.

"Super," said Tom. "She really enjoys it, but never seems to be overworked."

"How about your search for somewhere else to live?" asked James.

"I'm fixed up," said Bill. "I have a leave house that belongs to a manager from the smelter."

"Do you know if Lionel is fixed up yet?" asked Tom.

"Yes, lucky bugger," said Bill. "He moved in with Jane, you remember her, the one with great legs."

"That was fast! Have you had any luck with the ladies yet?" asked Tom.

"I told you that my brother from Luanshya was trying to fix me up. Well, it turned out that, for once, he was actually doing the right thing, and he fixed me up with a nurse. She is really nice and I have been spending a fair amount of time in Luanshya," replied Bill.

"Sorry to leave you chaps, but I need to get home," said James.

"Ha! You just want to get back and talk to this Katrina bird," said Bill.

"Piss off," said James. "I'll see you both."

James drove home and was greeted by Silent.

"*Kanjani Bwana?*" Silent asked.

"*Aikôna mushle, Silent,*" James answered. "*Namusha, lo muntu yena fili.*"

"*Ja, mina azi,*" said Silent.

Silent obviously knew all about the accident and the death. James was struck again by how fast information seemed to travel. He got Silent to bring him some coffee and then called Katrina. When she answered the phone he told her about his day and asked what kind of day she had had. Katrina told him that business was doing quite well, but that spare parts were getting difficult to obtain as the border to Rhodesia was getting difficult and alternate routes were long and unreliable. Although the railway border to Rhodesia across the Victoria Falls Bridge was officially closed in 1965, wagons were exchanged across the border and traffic continued, but it was slow.

The railway line through Zaire and Angola to Lobito Bay ran occasionally, but only occasionally and was not at all reliable. The other route was the Hell Run, or the road from Kapiri Mposhi that eventually reached Dar es Salaam. Italy had provided a huge fleet of Fiat trucks that were equipped to carry fuel in and copper out. James had seen some of these trucks on the drive-up. The road, however, had never been built to take this level of heavy traffic and was torn up, especially in the rainy season. So loads were delayed or even went missing. There were also tales of local "entrepreneurs" who were supposed to have stolen truckloads of goods.

James confirmed their date for the next evening and then had dinner. Silent was actually a pretty good cook.
"*Skuzi, Bwana?*" asked Silent. "*Kusasa wena aikôna tenga lo skofu lapa?*" James answered Silent by telling him that, indeed, tomorrow he would be eating out. That night, James slept very badly. He kept seeing the scene of carnage in his mind and wondered if he would ever get over it. Finally, after a couple of whiskeys, he dropped off and almost overslept.

The next day, the mine safety department interviewed James and Isaac. They were unable to shed much light on the incident. They told what they had heard and not heard, seen and not seen, but would not speculate on causes. Later, an official of the Mines Department also interviewed them. Again, their testimony was factual but confined only to events that had clearly followed the incident. The tramming crew were the ones that would have to spend the most time explaining what they had been doing. James asked Isaac if Mhango had any family of his own. Isaac told him that Mhango had no wife, but that he had been saving to get the *lobola* and had planned to marry.

After work, James went straight home to spruce himself up. Silent was lurking around, grinning his head off. He had pressed the clothes that James had put out that morning.

"*Upi wena hamba Bwana?*" asked Silent.

"*Lo Blue Room lapa Luanshya,*" answered James. "*Wena azi lo?*"

"*Aikôna Bwana,*" said Silent.

James thought that perhaps it was unreasonable to expect that Silent would know of the Blue Room restaurant. It was, after all, in another town and not likely to be on Silent's list of eating places. He drove out to the Englebrecht farm and, as he approached, was announced by the pack of hounds. Koos Englebrecht came out onto the *stoep* of the house and shooed the dogs away.

"James, *howzit?*" he asked.

"Fine, thanks, Mr Englebrecht," James replied.

"Come in," said Koos. "You will have to wait, Katrina isn't ready yet."

"*Dankie, Meneer,*" said James.

James followed Koos into the house and waited. Eventually, Katrina came into the room and asked James what her father had been saying. James was surprised and said that Koos had actually left him alone and gone off somewhere. Katrina seemed relieved and told him that her father was not above embarrassing her by doing or saying something odd.

They drove back through Kitwe and then on to Luanshya and found the Blue Room. The restaurant was nowhere near as exotic as it sounded, but it was better than anywhere James had eaten lately. Dinner was good, and Katrina was fun to be with. As they were waiting for coffee, a group approached their table, and James saw that it was Bill and Joy Mwamba with two girls.

"James, we didn't know this was where you would be tonight," said Bill. "I would like you to meet Mary Chisenga, you already know Joy, and this is Susie Mwewa, Felix's sister."

"Hi," said James. "This is Katrina."

"We don't want to disturb you two," said Bill.

"I started at the training school with these two," James told Katrina. "Bill still works fairly close to where I work, and Joy has been moved to a section that is in the newer part of the mine."

"We were just leaving," said Bill. "See you at work tomorrow?"

"Should do," replied James. "That is, if I can find my way back to Kitwe in the dark."

"Don't worry," said Katrina. "I think I know the way, even some back roads if you prefer."

"Ha! Watch out, James, she will lead you astray on some dark road and abandon you," said Joy. "Then we will never see you again."

"I haven't annoyed her that much yet, but don't give her any ideas," said James.

"Okay, okay, we will leave you to your romancing," said Bill. "*Bonne nuit mes enfants!*"

They finished their coffee and left to drive back to Kitwe. Once out of Luanshya and on the road to Kitwe, the night was pitch black. There were no lights on the road, and there was no moon, but there were stars by the thousand. As they drove, James asked Katrina if they would see any game on the road.

"Maybe," replied Katrina. "But nowhere near as much as when I was little. The growth of the towns and the traffic has forced the game away from here."

"What might we see?" asked James.

"Kudu, impala, leopard," replied Katrina.

"No monkeys?" asked James.

"No, they roost up in the trees overnight away from predators," answered Katrina.

"How much game did you used to see?" James asked.

"Well, the best time was at dusk, and we would see monkeys, baboons, buck, even an elephant or two. When I was really a lightie, it would take the best part of a day to go from Kitwe to Ndola and back. Of course, then there was no bridge across the Kafue coming out of Kitwe, we used a pontoon over the river," said Katrina.

"It must have been very exotic growing up here," said James.

"Exotic, no, I don't think so," said Katrina. "It was all I knew. I always used to think that people who grew up in London had an exotic upbringing."

"Where did you go to school?" asked James.

"I went to a boarding school in Bulawayo," answered Katrina. "We would go on the school train."

"What's that?" asked James.

"At the beginning of the school year, there was a special train run up from Bulawayo to pick up all of us going to school. There were teachers on the train to chaperon. It took two days and a night to get there and two nights and a day to come back. The train ride was fun, especially crossing the Vic Falls Bridge."

"Somehow my school days suddenly sound mundane," said James.

"What are you doing tomorrow?" asked James.

"Nothing particular," said Katrina. "Why do you have something in mind?"

"Well, not really, maybe we could get a beer and dinner somewhere," replied James.

"Tell you what, why don't you come by the house after work, and I will find something for us to do," said Katrina.

"You're not dancing at the moment?" asked James.

"No, we have a break between productions; we should start rehearsing for the next production in a few weeks," replied Katrina.

The following day, James was back at work with Isaac. They did not see Bill in the cage on the way down, so James had to assume that he had either got an earlier cage down or was running late. They had a good day and were able to finish up in good time. For once, everything ran smoothly, the matches were dry, and they had no problems setting their blasts. James did wonder why they used safety fuse and not an electrical method of blasting. It was a question to which he never got a really good answer.

After work, James cleaned himself up and was about to leave when he saw Bill. Bill looked as if he had been through a wringer.

"What happened to you?" asked James.

"Oh, we went to a *shabeen* after the movie," said Bill. "I was introduced to Chibuku."

"Chibuku, isn't that the maize beer that they drink here?" said James.

"Yes, I think I prefer Castle," said Bill. "It is tough driving when you have had too much of that stuff. I nearly drove off the road a couple of times between the Luanshya turn-off and here this morning."

"So who is Mary?" asked James.

"She is the nurse I told you about from Luanshya," said Bill.

"Well, how is she?" asked James.

"Active," said Bill. "She wore me out last night and this morning, I finally had to leave and speed over here to get to work. I got here late enough to be in the same cage as all the shift bosses. I didn't fancy answering any questions, so I rode in the upper deck with everyone else."

"You didn't tell me that she was a black Zambian," said James.

"Did you tell me that Katrina was white?" asked Bill. "What difference does it make?"

"No, you're right," said James. "I apologise, I just wasn't thinking. Was this the girl your brother was fixing you up with? Does your brother work with her in Luanshya?"

"Yes, works for the Government Hospital as a pharmacist" answered Bill.

James left Bill and drove out to the Englebrecht farm. Katrina met him outside and escorted him through the guard of the dogs to the house. Koos Englebrecht was there with his wife, Sussana.

"James, *howzit*?" asked Koos.

"Fine, thanks, Mr. Englebrecht," replied James.

"I hear you had an exciting week," said Koos.

"It was excitement I could have done without," said James. "It was my first sight of an underground accident and hopefully my last."

"What are you two doing tonight?" asked Sussana.

"*Los dit*," said Koos. "*Jy vra te veel vrae.*"

"We are leaving to go to the boat club, will we see you there?" asked Sussana.

"Perhaps," said Katrina.

When they had gone, James asked Katrina what her father had said to her mother.

"Oh, he told her to leave it and that she was asking too many questions," said Katrina.

"So have you any brilliant ideas of what we might do?" asked James.

"Well, as most of the day has already gone we can't go too far afield. Maybe we should just drive out to the dam and get dinner there," said Katrina. "Next weekend we must *maak 'n plan* and go somewhere on Saturday, stay the night, and come home Sunday. That way, we can go a little further."

They drove out to the dam, got themselves a beer, and sat out under one of the *chitenges*, small thatched umbrella-type shelters, watching the sun go down. Their peace was interrupted by Greg Young and his wife, Shirley.

"James, how are you?" asked Greg.

"Fine, thanks, Greg. Katrina, this is Greg and Shirley Young," said James.

"*Meneer, Mevrou*," said Katrina.

"James, I hear your mate Bill is a regular *kaffir boetie*," said Greg. "I hear he is actually going out with a *munt*."

"Where did you hear that?" asked James.

"Oh, word gets around," said Greg. "A friend of mine saw him at the movies in Luanshya yesterday with three *kaffirs*, one man and two women."

"Well, that's his *indaba*, what Bill does is his business," said James. "If you will excuse us, we need to rejoin the rest of our group."

"Oh, sure," said Greg. "We just stopped in for a quick beer before dinner with the engineering manager; he is a cousin of my mother's."

James and Katrina fled into the clubhouse and looked around for Koos and Sussana. They went over and joined them.

"So soon?" asked Koos.

"Sorry to disturb you," said James. "But we were trying to get away from a bloke I know."

"Why, what's he done?" asked Koos.

"*Hy is baie verkrampt*," said Katrina. "I'll explain later."

"We were talking about where might be nice to go next weekend," said James,

"Why not take the boat and go out to Muchiyas ferry?" asked Koos.

"Where's that?" asked James.

"It's close to the confluence of the Luswishi and Kafue, out past Mpongwe and Munkumpu," said Katrina. "I know where it is and how to get there, but I think the river will be too low at this time of the year, which will make the rapids higher."

"Maybe you had better go to the Mita Hills dam instead," said Koos. "You can take the truck and the boat on Saturday, I will be sure that there is petrol."

"*Dankie Meneer*," said James.

"So, you have often been fishing?" asked Koos.

"No, never," said James.

"Well, time to try. Katrina will teach you. Take some rods and a gun with you, Katrina," said Koos.

"What's the gun for? I thought we were going fishing?" asked James.

"In case you have problems with lions," said Koos.

"Can you use a gun?" James asked Katrina.

"Of course. I suppose that's another part of your education that's lacking?" she said.

"Never handled a gun before," said James.

"*Moenie* worry *nie*," said Koos. "Katrina is a good shot."

"We will have to camp out. I assume you have camped before?" asked Katrina.

"Oh, yes," said James. "But not in a place where the local wildlife could actually eat you."

"*Moenie* worry *nie*, most things in the bush are more afraid of you and will leave you alone," said Katrina.

On Sunday, Katrina called James, but only to ask how he was and tell him that she had a previous commitment and would not be available that day. As James had not suggested anything, he was thrilled that she had actually called him. Being at a loose end, he drove out to the boat club after lunch for a beer. He met some of the other members and watched people in rowing boats. As hot as it was getting, he could not imagine why they were putting in so much exertion.

His reverie was broken by Greg and Shirley, who seemed determined to talk to him.

"James, we may not have got off on the right foot," said Greg. "But we need to talk to you."

"What about?" asked James.

"Well, we noticed yesterday that you were here with that girl," replied Greg.

"Yes?" asked James.

"Well, we don't think it's right that a real Brit like yourself should be going out with a Rock Spider. You really should stick to your own kind. You know these local yokels are only interested in hunting and fishing and have no culture. We are only thinking of your own good," replied Greg.

"Well, thanks for your concern," said James. "Quite what does this have to do with you?"

"Well, we've been talking to the others in our group, and we can introduce you to a real English-speaking girl that you would be much better off with. If you persist in seeing this Katrina, you could land up like the local yokels, and it could affect your career," said Greg.

James could hardly believe what he was hearing. He strongly suspected that, although Greg might have something to do with this, it was more likely Shirley and the other women who were the instigators. He could see them being green with envy over Katrina.

"You know that this Katrina has the reputation of being something of a scrubber, don't you?" asked Shirley.

"What?" said James.

"Oh yes, I was talking to some of the other women on the mine, and they know all about her and the number of boyfriends she has had," continued Shirley.

"Jesus, are you serious?" asked James.

"Oh yes," said Shirley. "We just don't want you to go off the rails. For all we differ on some things, you are at least not going out with one of the jungle bunnies, and we would rather see you with people you can relate to."

"Well, thanks for the advice," said James. "I will bear it in mind, if you will excuse me, I have an appointment in town I need to keep."

With that, James left. He was really pissed off. Who did these people think they were? He could not believe their nerve, telling him how he should run his life and then telling him that the girl he had lost his heart to was a *scrubber*. Just fucking charming. How the hell was he ever going to lay that one to rest? He thought that it was just as well it was a public place, or he may have thumped Greg. Of course, he had no appointment; he just needed to be out of there. He went back to the house and sat and brooded for the rest of the evening.

Monday morning, James met up with Isaac, and they got their instructions from Abel Mwewa. He saw Bill, and they rode down in the cage together. James debated whether to tell Bill about Greg Young but decided not to. He reasoned that it really was Bill's *indaba* and none of the business of Greg or anyone else, and he had no desire to mention to Bill what Greg had said to him or the comments Shirley had made about Katrina.

James and Isaac walked into their working area and organised the work for the crews. They were one machine short as they had had several breakdowns and not all the units were repaired yet.
"*Tina funa lo munya jackhammer,*" said Isaac. "*Tina hamba panzi, bamba lo ka lo Kabeyo.*"
Isaac was suggesting that they go to the section below, which belonged to Kabeyo and "acquire" another jackhammer. James was new to this and agreed to go along to carry the stuff. They set off down the ladder ways with some rope and entered Kabeyo's section. No one was drilling yet; they all seemed to be still at the section boss's box getting their instructions. Isaac led the way, and they soon found a couple of jackhammers stashed behind some timbers.
"*Mina azi, yena kona lo munya,*" said Isaac. He seemed to know that Kabeyo had some spares, and more importantly, where he kept them. They took one and hauled it back up into their own section. James had no doubt that Kabeyo would start looking for his machine at some time, particularly if he had problems. He asked Isaac if that would be a problem
"*Aziko indaba bwana,*" Isaac replied. "*Munya skati, lo Kabeyo yena bambili ena no lo munya section.*"

105

So it seemed that wholesale movement of machines was fairly common, as this machine had been previously lifted from yet another section.

The additional equipment enabled them to put all the crews to work. Isaac and James checked out each end and measured progress. Where necessary, they extended ventilation lines and water and air lines. One of the tasks given to the drillers was to put holes in the sides of the tunnels at suitable intervals so that they could hammer in steel stakes on which to hang the pipes as the lines were extended. Isaac asked James how his first aid classes were going. James replied that he was learning and would have no problems with the test when it came.

Later in the day, Abel Mwewa, the shift boss, came by to see how they were doing. As the developments were proceeding to schedule and were going in the right direction, there was not too much to discuss. Abel asked James how he was after the accident and if he still felt capable of doing the job. He also asked how he was doing with his study of the Explosives Regulations, which would be the basis of the blasting licence test. James said that he still had nightmares but that he was learning to accept things. He was also very comfortable now with the blasting regulations, having had a great incentive to actually review them and try and understand them. He answered Abel's questions quickly and easily. Abel also told James that in about another week, he would be moved to another section for further training. It would either be production or big-end development, big-end development being the mining of large tunnels, which were typically used for trains or vehicular transport.

# Mita Hills Dam

By Saturday, they had decided where James was to go next. He was to report on Monday to Jim Brown, a mine captain, who ran a production section in the deeper part of the mine. Jim would tell him which section boss he was to be placed with. James had no doubt that trainees were a mixed blessing. Whereas they were needed to provide future supervisors, they also took time to educate and train. James asked around to find out who were the shift bosses and section bosses who worked for Jim. He had met some of them and generally would be happy to work with any of them. There was one change, though; he would need to go to one of the other shaft complexes to go to work. It meant going to the north end of the mine, rather than the current south end. As James was leaving the mine, he saw Bill and told him where he was next assigned. Bill told him that he had been reassigned as well and was going to stay in the same area but switch to big-end development.

James left the mine and went home to change ready for his trip to the river. He drove out to the Englebrecht farm, and Koos was out hooking up a boat trailer to a Land Cruiser.

"James, *howzit?*" said Koos.

"Fine, Mr. Englebrecht, how is it with you?" said James.

"*Ag* man, these dogs will clean me out before long. Two of them were taken by crocs last night, and we have just been at the vet getting another two sewn up." Koos replied. "Everything is ready for you. The *bakkie* has a full tank of petrol, and the cans in the back will fill the boat. The rods and other *katundu* are also in the back; the gun is behind the seat. Katrina is supposed to be ready, but you know, women, they would be late for their own funerals."

"I'm sure she won't be long," said James. "What is *katundu?*"

"Your stuff, man, you know, all the things that you are taking, your luggage," said Koos. "James, remember that the lake is behind a dam and is full of dead tree stumps. You should be fine. Katrina knows the lake well. Now all you need is that *meisie* of mine to decide that it is today that she wants to leave."

"Pappa, how can you say that?" interrupted Katrina. "I'm not mommy who is always late. Are you ready, James?"

"Ready when you are," said James. "Shall we go?" He noted that Katrina had on shorts that showed off her legs to great advantage. She really was good-looking and was built fabulously. This was going to be a fun weekend.

They drove off, with Katrina at the wheel and headed through Kitwe south on the main road until a little before Kapiri Mposhi. They were basically retracing the route that James had followed on his way north, except for the Ndola cut-off. They turned off the main road, just after the glass works, onto the road to Serenje for about twenty miles. Here, they turned off the main road onto a side dirt road going south. Once on the dirt, they threw up a large dust cloud behind them. James hoped that they wouldn't come up behind anyone, as then they would be riding in a similar dust cloud. The road was corrugated, and the choice was to drive slowly or very fast to minimise the effects of the ridges.

Katrina chose to drive fast, and James had to hang on a couple of times as they rounded corners. She spent most of the time on the wrong side of the road as the corrugations had less of an impact that way. When one of the few cars they saw came the other way, she moved over to the right side of the road, but only briefly. James also found himself looking back occasionally to see if the boat was still there. The Land Cruiser must have had plenty of power because they were doing 70 down this dirt road without apparent effort.

Katrina slowed down briefly as they passed by villages, but she sped up again as soon as they were clear of the children and dogs. They finally reached the dam, and there was a rough boat ramp that the local farmers and miners had pushed into the lake. Katrina turned the truck and trailer around and backed it down the ramp into the lake. James had loosened the tie downs and held the bow line while Katrina drove the truck. As the trailer got into deeper water, the boat floated off, and James pulled it into the bank.

With the boat in the water, they loaded in their supplies and *katundu*. Katrina parked the truck and trailer and locked it up. They climbed into the boat, fuelled it, and took off downstream. As they picked up speed, the boat climbed up onto the plane. Katrina steered skilfully around the tree stumps that cropped up occasionally. It was obvious that she was at home in the boat and had been on this part of the lake before. Katrina explained to James that the lake was low as they were well towards the end of the dry season. James wanted to know which river had been dammed to form this lake. She told him that it was the Lunsemfwa and that below the dam it went over some waterfalls and then through a beautiful gorge, known locally as Wonder Gorge, before joining the Luangwa. From the boat, the view was strange. All around, dead tree stumps stuck up out of the water like broken teeth, and James wondered how many were just below the surface, not visible, but just there waiting for an unwary boater.

From the boat, they saw some buck, and James asked Katrina what they were.
"Man, don't you know anything? The larger woolly-looking ones are waterbuck," she replied. "And the smaller ones are puku, same family as the Uganda kob."
There was much more game than they ever saw around Kitwe. Katrina told James that, as the dry season was well advanced, most of the water-dependent game had moved closer to the river. She pointed out crocs on the bank and hippos in the water in the deeper pools. There were thousands of birds, some in huge flocks that swirled around like clouds.
"What are those?" asked James.
"Quelias," replied Katrina. "Some of the Africans call them 'feathered locusts'. They can make a mess of a maize crop."
"Herons I recognise," said James. "What about the eagle over there in that tree?"
"That's a fish eagle," said Katrina. "Speaking of which, we should probably find somewhere to tie up soon and get some fish ourselves for dinner."

Katrina then slowed down and headed the boat towards an inlet; she found the backflow in the stream and idled the engine. They got out the rods, and Katrina showed James how to attach a spinner and cast it into the water.

"What are we fishing for?" asked James.

"Bream, pike, it depends," said Katrina. "Either is okay to eat, but pike have a lot of bones."

They played the spinners for a while, casting into the deeper waters.

"I've got one! I've got one! What do I do now?" shouted James.

"*Magtig,* but you are only a real townie. Strike the rod to set the barb and then play the fish to land it," said Katrina calmly.

James tried to follow the advice that Katrina was giving him and, perhaps more by good luck than skill, he pulled in a large bream.

"Boy, that's shit hot," said James. "That's the first real fish I've ever caught."

"Well, keep it up, hotshot. We need a couple more for dinner," said Katrina.

As they fished, they heard hippos honking on other parts of the lake. James wondered if they would be bothered by the hippo and how you could tell if one was close or not. He also watched Katrina, mulling over the accusations that Shirley had made and wondering, again, how to lay that demon to rest.

A short time later, they saw another boat coming down the lake. James recognised the driver; it was Angus Turnbull, the stationmaster from Kitwe.

"Afternoon," said James.

"Ah, it's the spy," said Turnbull. "What's the fishing like here?"

"Pretty good," said James.

"Where are you camping tonight?" asked Turnbull.

"About a mile from here, on the western shore, by the grove of sausage trees," said Katrina.

"I know it, that's where we are camping too," said Turnbull. "See you there later."

After Turnbull had pulled away, Katrina asked James what the spy business was all about. He told her his story about taking pictures of trains and his subsequent interview with Angus Turnbull.

"Well, Jamesey Banda, *nikisi nikisi seven,* we should get ourselves to the campsite before the sun goes down," said Katrina.

Katrina spun the boat around and opened up the throttle. She weaved down the lake until they came to a bay in the lakeshore. Katrina turned into the inlet.

There were two other boats there. One James recognised as belonging to Angus Turnbull, whom they had seen earlier. The other, he did not know.

"Do you know whose boat that is?" he asked Katrina.

"No, I don't recognise it," she replied. "It looks new, maybe first time out."

"Is it safe to get out of the boat here?" asked James.

"Yes, I see no hippo here, and if you climb out onto the higher part of the bank, crocs should be no problem," replied Katrina.

James jumped out onto the bank and took the bow line to tie the boat up. With it secured, he helped Katrina unload their stuff. Katrina was right about the grove of sausage trees. The trees were huge and got their name from the fruits, shaped like giant sausages hanging from the branches.

They met up with Angus Turnbull and were introduced to the rest of his family. Katrina then saw the other people who were there. Setting up mosquito nets was Koot Strydom.

"*Oom* Koot, when did you get the new boat?" asked Katrina.

"Yesterday, Katrina. Do you like it?" he replied.

"It looks nice, how does it handle?" she asked.

"Fine. I came down here earlier today and have been trying it out. I didn't know you'd be here with young Martin. *Is hy jou nuwe skat?*" asked Koot.

"*Miskien,*" she answered.

"What are you two talking about?" asked James.

"Oh, nothing," said Katrina. "When you are older, I will tell you. In the meantime, why don't you get a fire going so that we can cook these fish?"

"No, man, it's okay," said Koot. "I came here with my cook, Styrah and my tracker, Rice. Styrah can fix the fire. Why don't you give him your fish, and he will cook them?"

"Are you sure he won't mind?" asked James.

"*Ag* no," said Koot. "Styrah is the best bush cook in Zambia; he enjoys proving to people that anything is possible. Styrah, *bamba isabi.*"

James pulled Katrina aside and asked her if this was okay. He felt as though they were taking advantage of Styrah. Katrina assured him that it was okay. She told James that Styrah was probably being paid for the weekend by Koot to do the camp chores while he and Rice did the hunting.

The idea of taking personal servants along on a camping trip was new to James. It was a different and strange experience; he almost wondered if they would see a line of porters walking through the bush with loads on their heads. It was difficult for James to adjust to the idea of always having personal retainers around. He wondered if they ever got any time off. Katrina told him that the better employers made sure that their retainers got time off, which usually meant an extended trip back to the area they came from. She also told him that other employers could not care less about the welfare of their people, and typically, they had a quick turnover of people. She went on to explain that their own house servant, Gibson, had been with the family for over twenty-five years, so she had grown up with him in the house all the time. She laughed when she told James how Gibson used to protect her from her mother and clear up after her before her mother could see the mess she left behind.

James helped Katrina clear away branches and rubbish and then laid out their sleeping blankets. Katrina hung a couple of mosquito nets. Whatever ideas James might have had about a romantic weekend in the bush were now shot. There were just too many people for James to be comfortable. As far as the food was concerned, Koot was right. Styrah performed miracles with their fish, and a magnificent dinner appeared out of nowhere. How he did it with an open fire and just a couple of cooking pots, James could not quite understand.

After dinner, they sat and talked for a while. It was hot, and the others told James that this was normal for mid to late October. He learned that October was known locally as suicide month. The heat and humidity built up during the month until the rains broke in early November. The conversation then switched to the people present, and James learned that the Turnbulls were working out a contract with Zambia Railways. They had another two years to go and would probably not renew. Koot Strydom told them of this early life in Zambia, or Northern Rhodesia as it was then. He had come north with only an offer of a job and had made a life for himself and his family. He recognised that he had advanced as far as he could go, but was happy with his current position. He would probably stay until he retired, and then he was talking about going to the Cape, possibly somewhere around Fish Hoek.

He also told stories about the Englebrechts and of Katrina growing up, some much to Katrina's embarrassment. James listened carefully to see if there were any clues as to whether or not Greg and Shirley were just being spiteful. There were no clues. Eventually, they turned in and went to sleep listening to hippo in the river and a leopard coughing.

The next day, James and Katrina got up with the dawn. Katrina picked up her gun, and they took a short walk along the water's edge.
"What sort of gun is that?" asked James.
"A 9.3," answered Katrina.
James looked at her enquiringly.
"The calibre is 9.3 millimetres," said Katrina. "Does that mean anything to you?"
"Jesus! That's a lot bigger than a 303," said James.
"Well, yes," said Katrina. "But you need enough gun if you need it."
James was not quite sure what to make of this logic and let it go.
They walked on along the bank; it was already fairly warm and promised to get hot when the sun rose higher in the sky. They could see the tracks where the hippo had come out of the lake to graze overnight. By now, they should all be back in the water, and they would not find themselves between a hippo and its intended refuge for the day. They could hear guinea fowl and francolins and saw a fish eagle take a large

fish from the lake. James asked Katrina what type of birds they could hear. Katrina identified them by sound and then tried to find them. Finally, she spotted them and pointed them out. The guinea fowl were coming down from their overnight roosts, and the francolins were just letting other francolins know that this was their territory.

The guinea fowl calls changed from the monotonous "come back, come back" call that they used when undisturbed to their alarm call. Katrina looked around and tried to work out what had disturbed them. She hoped it was nothing that would bother them. James asked Katrina if there was much game in the area. She told him that they were near a maize and tobacco farming area and that there was plenty of game in the area, including lions, hyaena, and leopard, but most of it would flee long before they could get close. Katrina pointed into the bush.
"What are we looking at?" asked James.
"Jackal," said Katrina. "See under that baobab."
"Where? I still don't see anything," said James.
"*Kyk* man, it is to the left side of that baobab moving from left to right," she replied.
"Ah, okay, I see it now," said James. "What is it looking for?"
"Breakfast, what do you think?" Katrina said. "They are mostly nocturnal so you are lucky to see it."
The jackal looked at them briefly, then turned and took off into the bush. They could follow its progress by the alarm calls of the birds.

They walked back and began to pack up their stuff and load the boat. Angus and Koot were up and about, and Styrah had some coffee ready. James and Katrina got some coffee and then breakfast.
"Are you going to do some more fishing?" asked Koot.
"*Ja*," said Katrina. "James thinks he is hot stuff with a fishing rod."

When they were on the lake, Katrina announced that she was going to have a talk with her father. James asked why.
"Because he only lent us the *bakkie* and the boat because he knew that Koot would be here," she said.
"Do you really think so?" asked James.

"Of course," she answered. "They are old friends, and Koot probably mentioned where he was going, so Poppa suggested we take a trip to Mita Hills."

"Do you think he knew the Turnbulls would be there as well?" James asked.

"Probably," she said. "He is such a *slim kêrel*, or at least he thinks he is."

"What's a *slim kêrel*?" asked James.

"Oh, sorry, it means a cunning person; we use the expression normally to talk about someone clever. In this case, he is just a cunning old *aasvoël*," answered Katrina.

"You did it to me again, what's an *aasvoël*?" said James.

"I think you had better begin to learn my language if we are to spend more time together," said Katrina. "Oh, and an *aasvoël* is a vulture."

"Have you been on weekends like this before?" asked James.

"Man, *maningi* times with my dad, but this was to be my first trip on my own," replied Katrina.

James brightened up a lot. It hardly sounded as if Katrina was the loose woman Shirley had accused her of being, and it looked as if Katrina was telling him that they had a future.

They travelled slowly upstream, stopping occasionally to fish, until they came to the boat ramp. Katrina put the boat onto the shore, and James got out and tied it up. After unloading their stuff, Katrina fetched the truck and backed the boat trailer into the water. James then manoeuvred the boat onto the trailer and cut the engine. They tied off the line to the bow and winched the boat firmly up onto the trailer, then Katrina pulled it out of the river with the truck. After tying the boat down onto the trailer and putting the cover on, they were ready to go.

They drove back towards Kapiri Mposhi and then onto the main north road. They were about halfway between the Ndola turn-off and Kitwe when they saw a Land Rover by the roadside. Standing by it was Tom Morrison. James asked Katrina to pull over, then he ran back to see if everything was all right.

"Tom, anything wrong?" asked James.

115

"Bloody thing!" said Tom. "As best as I can tell, I just broke a half shaft on the back axle."

"Hang on a minute while I check something," said James.

"Katrina, can this *bakkie* tow the Land Rover and the boat?" he asked.

"No man, it will be fine, just hitch the boat to the Land Rover and then look in the *bakkie* for the rigid tow bar that should be there," said Katrina.

"I thought she just said no?" said Tom.

"Yes, she did, but that's not what she means," said James. "Just do what she says."

"Katrina, this is my friend Tom, and that's his wife Rita sitting in the front," said James. "Why don't you entertain Rita while Tom and I re-arrange the tow?"

They found the tow bar in the back and enough bolts, nuts, and other components to rig up a tow hitch on the front of the Land Rover. With that in place, they hitched the boat to the Land Rover and then hitched the Land Cruiser to the front of the Land Rover.

"So this is the mysterious Katrina," said Tom. "She is exotic. Where have you been this weekend?"

"We went to the Mita Hills dam and camped out," answered James.

"So, did you get any?" asked Tom.

"You have a dirty mind," said James. "But, to answer your question, no. There were other people camping at the same place we were, and they all seemed to know either Katrina or her father and to quote people here. "He is only a potent *ou*."

"Let's see what these girls are talking about," said Tom. "How are you two doing?"

"Fine, can we go home now?" asked Rita.

"Absolutely," said Tom. "James, do you and Katrina fancy joining us for dinner?"

"If it's all right with Rita," answered Katrina.

"Please do," said Rita. "I could use some conversation other than mining for a while."

"We were visiting some people we know in Luanshya," explained Tom. "The conversation was probably a little limited."

They drove back to Kitwe with Katrina driving the Land Cruiser with Rita and the two others sitting in the Land Rover. James took the opportunity to swear Tom to secrecy, even from Rita and then told him all about the conversation with Greg and Shirley. Tom said that he would find out what Greg was talking about. James was ambivalent; on the one hand, he wanted to be sure, and yet part of him didn't want to know or care. After arriving at the house of Tom and Rita and disconnecting the various hitches, Rita set about cooking dinner, and she and Katrina spent time in the kitchen talking about something. Tom and James got themselves a beer each and kept out of the way. Later, James took Katrina home and collected his own truck and drove back to the van de Merwes' house. The drive had been fairly quiet as James's mind was in turmoil. He could not believe what he had been told by Greg and felt really bad about even considering the possibility.

Early Monday morning, James reported to Jim Brown and was assigned to a shift boss who passed him on to a section boss, Samson Chazeema. James and Samson took the cage down to the 2570 level, and then they walked along the main haul road, passed the refrigeration chambers, to the sub-vertical shaft, which was another shaft system that went farther down into the mine. They descended another 600 feet to their level, got out, and walked to the production section. James was familiar with the basic layout of the section because he had just been working in a section preparing the tunnels for use by production teams. Samson showed James where to stow his *chola,* and then they started down to visit the work crews.

The operations here were a little different to the development areas. Large drilling machines were set up on bars and fans of holes, anywhere from 10 to 40 metres long were drilled. The fans were repeated every few metres along the tunnel, and then explosives were charged into the holes and set off to break the ore up to pull it out of the bottom of the chamber, called a stope, that was created. The drilling could take several days to complete each fan of holes. Bill had already told James that they used three-foot extensions for the drill string, and he saw stacks of rods by each of the machines.

They visited each of the levels and talked to the workers who were busy drilling. Samson checked progress and, on one level, marked up the next round to be drilled. James asked how long it took to move the drill rig from position to position, and then from level to level. Samson told him that sometimes they could lose three days of drilling with a big move.

It was much warmer in this section than where he had previously worked. He now understood the need for the large refrigeration units he had passed on the way down. They fed chilled water to large heat exchangers placed in the intake airways and cooled the air. Without the cooling, it would be really hot. The temperature of the rock, before being exposed by blasting, went up by one degree Fahrenheit for every 100 feet they went down. Exposing the rock to the airflows dropped the temperature somewhat, but all that heat had to go somewhere. So, it was hot and humid in the working levels.

They took a break for lunch, then went down to the level where they expected to blast. Samson had a crew specially designated for loading explosives, and they were hard at it when Samson and James arrived. James watched the process. They took a large stick of explosive, punched a hole through it and threaded some Cordtex, a detonating cord, through the hole. They then pushed the stick into the hole, paying out the cord as the explosive went into the hole. They then pushed more sticks into the hole until the correct length of hole had been charged. Finally, they took the last stick and pushed a detonator into the stick and pushed it into the hole, paying out the electric wires as it went. Samson checked each of the holes that had been charged and made sure that the wires were properly twisted together, or shunted, for safety.

When the charging was finished and the crew had left, Samson and James started to connect up the detonators from each of the holes. They then connected the wires up to a cable that they ran out to the raise that went down to the haulage way below. They climbed down the ladderway to the haulage level and picked up the cable again.

"*Mangaki lo madoppie ena kona?*" asked Samson.

"Four rows of ten," answered James, thinking back to the number of detonators they had installed.

"*Okay, mangaki metres na lo drift, futi, mangaki metres na lo raise?*" asked Samson again.

James thought and then replied. "*300 metres lapa drift futi 50 metres lapa raise, futi munya 50 metres kalapa.*"

They were working out how many metres of cable they had paid out along the drift or used down the raises. They would then use this information, together with the detonators they had installed, to calculate the resistance of the circuit. James had a set of numbers in his notebook for the resistance of the type of detonators and the different kinds of cable that they were using.

"Say 4 lines of ten in parallel at 2.07 ohms per detonator plus 300 metres at 0.0338 ohms per metre plus 100 at 0.0085 ohms per metre, or a total of 16.165 ohms," said James, after he had scratched a bit on some paper.

"*Okay,*" said Samson. "*Faka tester.*"

James put the tester into the circuit and read the number out to Samson, who nodded in approval. Apparently, the circuit was good because they got an appropriate reading, and the result was close enough to their calculations to be acceptable. They then sat down to wait for the okay to blast from the crew before them.

"*Wena sebenzili kudala?*" James asked Samson.

"*Aikôna, two years kupela,*" replied Samson.

Having established that Samson had not worked at the mine a long time, only two years, James thought that he must be pretty bright to have got so far in such a short time. James was not sure what else to talk about. They had only met that day and had yet to get to know each other.

"*Kanjani lo England, ena mushle lapa?*" Samson asked James.

"*Munya skati ena mushle, ena kona maningi bantu lapa, futi munya skati ena makhaza,*" said James as he told Samson that England was good sometimes, but there were a lot of people there and it was cold. James wanted to say more, but his command of ChiKabanga was limited and his Bemba was non-existent.

"So in England, it is cold too much?" asked Samson.

"Too much!" said James.

They settled in to wait. They could feel and hear other blasts from higher up and farther out in the mine. Finally, the crew ahead of them came along the haulroad and James was surprised to see Greg Young. He hadn't known that Greg was assigned to this area of the mine. The section boss, with Greg, launched into a long discussion with Samson in Bemba. James was curious about their conversation, as he was sure that it was about Greg, judging by their body language.

James decided that he had better be polite and not let Greg know how much he had been unsettled by their previous meeting.

"So, Greg, how was the day?"

"Huh, these idiots can't even run a simple calculation for working out the resistance of the blasting circuit," replied Greg. "I had to show them what they were doing wrong."

"What's your section boss like?" asked James.

Greg pulled James aside and then whispered. "Between us, I can't see how he got the job. It just proves my point that these people are not ready to run the mines, let alone the country."

Samson interrupted them to tell James that they were clear to blast. Greg and the other crew took off down the haulroad, and James and Samson went to the blasting point. Samson used the tester one more time to check the circuit, then he connected the cables to the blasting box and told James to wind it up and shoot it. James turned the handle quickly until the charged light came on, then he pressed the blast button. They felt the blast and then heard it. As far as they could judge, it had gone well. They would see the next day and would also get a sense of the success by the tramming results for the night.

As they were walking out to the shaft, James asked Samson what he and the other section boss had been talking about. Samson dismissed it as nothing important. However, James was still convinced that they had been talking about Greg, particularly after he had heard Greg's comments about the section boss. He told Samson that he thought Greg was not a good man and left it at that. They came to the station, and the others had already gone. They resigned themselves to another wait and sat down. Samson got out his paperwork for the section and started to record the drilling advances for the day. They looked over the progress and estimated that they would be ready for a major blast soon. In the meantime, there were some other blasts to be done, preparing a new stope for production.

Once on the surface, James quickly showered, changed, and went off to his first aid class. The classes had become much more real since he had seen the accident. He knew that there was nothing they could have done for Mhango, but it was possible that in the future, he might come across something that he could help with. He took it seriously and didn't expect any problems when it came to the certification test.

After the class, Tom suggested they get a beer. Bill joined them, and they went to the mine club. Tom and Bill both wanted more details on James's trip with Katrina.
"Where did you go?" asked Bill.
"To Mita Hills," said James.
"Ah, but James's style was cramped by all the other campers," added Tom. "He told me all about it last night."
"There was nothing to tell," said James.
"Oh, sure," said Bill. "A weekend in the bush with the bird I saw you with, and there is nothing to tell!"
"Look, you pricks, as I told Tom yesterday, there were *maningi* others there, and besides, it's none of your business," said James.
"Why, don't you know what to do?" asked Bill. "Maybe we should get some of Mary's friends to give him a few lessons."
"Thanks, but no thanks," said James. "From what I have seen of you on Monday mornings, I couldn't stand the pace."
"Jealous," said Bill.
"Now, now *mapicinin*, don't argue," said Tom. "Why don't you two come with me, we'll collect Rita and go get a curry?"

The following day, James met up with Samson at the section boss's office, and they checked the logbooks for the night shifts. Everything appeared to be in order. They got the cage down and walked to their section, where they checked on each of the work crews. All were busy drilling. Samson then said that they should go and start charging up what he called a slot. In starting a new stope, they needed an open space into which the broken rock could go. They had a double row of holes to charge up, varying from a few metres in length to about fifteen metres.

They started with sticks of explosives, but because there was open space underneath, they had to use some tricks to stop the explosives falling through. Samson punched holes through the stick and threaded the Cordtex. He then took his knife and cut the paper wrapper down the length of the stick. Next, he lowered the stick into the hole, paying out the Cordtex carefully, measuring the amount paid out as he went. At the right depth, he stopped and started to tap lightly on the stick of explosive with the charging stick, while holding back on the Cordtex.

Samson's technique worked, and they moved on to the next hole and repeated the process. With the bottoms of the holes anchored, James was able to quickly add the rest of the explosives in each hole and top them off with the detonators. They shunted each of the detonators for safety and then took a break for lunch.

"*So, bwana, wena hambili lapa shateen?*" asked Samson.
"*Ja, mina hambili lapa Mita Hills,*" replied James.
"*Wena kona lo umfazi?*" asked Samson.
"*Aikôna,*" said James.
"*Mina inzwili wena hambili lapa shateen na lo umfazi, yena aikôna lo umfazi ka wena?*" asked Samson.
James wondered how Samson knew he had been out in the bush and with whom. Now he was asking if he had a woman or a wife.
"*Ja, mina hambili na lo umfazi. Mina aikôna azi.* Hell, I can't think how to say this in ChiKabanga. I don't know yet if she will be my woman," answered James.
"Ah, I see," said Samson. "I am so confused. Why go with a woman who you do not know is yours? *Wena enzili lo jig-a-jig na lo umfazi?*"
"*Ini lo jig-a-jig?*" asked James.
Samson then made it quite clear what he was talking about. James wasn't sure whether to tell Samson the truth or not. On the one hand, Samson would probably think less of him if he said nothing had

happened, but if he said yes, and word got back to Katrina, who knew how she would react. So, he took the safe approach and just laughed.

Fortunately for James, the drilling crews started arriving to report their progress before knocking off for the day. As each of them told his story, Samson marked down the progress on his worksheet. With all of them reporting in, they then went back down to the slot level and started connecting up the wires for the blast. With the detonators all connected up, they wired in the main lines and went down to the haulage level.

"*Okay, bala mangaki,*" said Samson.

So James sat and did the calculations for circuit resistance. Samson then put the tester into the circuit and got nothing like the thirteen ohms he had expected. James looked at it and concluded that they had an open circuit, so there must be a break on one of the lines. They started back up the raise and at each junction tested the circuit. They were lucky and isolated the fault fairly quickly in the crosscut to the slot.

"*Tina kona lo new waiya?*" asked James.

"*Sure, lapa pezulu,*" replied Samson.

James understood that, as the new boy in the section, it was his job to run up the ladder ways to the top of the section and bring down the new cable. This took him only a few minutes, and they laid a new cable in the crosscut and then tested the system on their way back down to the haulage level. Greg and his section boss were waiting for them as they came down.

"What's the problem with you people?" asked Greg.

"Oh, we had a problem with a faulty cable," said James.

"See, I told you," said Greg. "*Non capabilus.*"

"*Ini lo, non capabilus?*" asked Samson.

"*Aziko indaba,*" said James. "*Lo Greg yena kuluma fanika lo picinin.*"

"Piss off, James," said Greg.

James was really beginning to dislike Greg, and he had the feeling it might be mutual.

After the others had gone, Samson passed the word to the next crew, and they set up the blasting box. Today, they were back into Samson's routine, and he handled the blast. Yesterday, he had allowed James to fire the circuit, but not today. The shot sounded good. They would inspect the slot the next day to see if it had opened up properly. They walked out to the shaft and got the cage up to the 2570 level. They quickly walked out to the main shaft and then had a good fifteen minutes to wait before they could get to the surface. Apparently, the shaft had been in use earlier by crews lowering equipment into the mine, and they had done some minor damage. So, the shaft had been shut down for about an hour while things were repaired.

Once on the surface, James showered and then drove to the first aid station. Today they were to take the test for the first aid certificate. The test was a series of questions to check their basic knowledge of first aid, and then practical tests to see if they knew how to assist respiration, bandage wounds, and set bones. It was quite different from coming across a man who had been half blown up by an accidental explosion. No amount of artificial blood could set the adrenaline pumping and send cold shivers up the spine like a real situation. Having seen the horror of it, James took it seriously and fervently hoped that he would never have to see it again.

They all passed the test, which was probably a greater credit to the instructors than the diligence of the trainees. Afterwards, Bill suggested that they all get a beer at the mine club to celebrate. Ron, James, and Koot Strydom from the training school joined them and stood the first round.
"So, young James, tell me about your visit to Mita Hills?" said Ron.
"I went fishing," said James.
"Ah, yes, but who with?" asked Ron.
"*Oom* Koot," replied James.
"Koot, I get the distinct impression that he is being evasive," said Ron.
"*Ag* man, you know how it is when you have something to hide," said Koot, winking at James.
"I give up," said James. "Why don't I buy you *ouks* a beer? You can't drink and talk at the same time?"
"You know, I'm not sure it is a good idea for you to be dating someone outside your social group," said Ron.
"What do you mean?" asked James.

"Well, what do you have in common with someone from here?" asked Ron.

"Isn't that something for us to worry about?" replied James.

"Okay, but don't say I didn't warn you when problems arise with your parents wanting to know who it is you may bring home one day. Have you ever thought that she might not want to leave here?" asked Ron.

James stayed long enough to be sociable and then left for home. Now Ron was telling him to back off. What the hell was going on? Silent had coffee ready and had prepared dinner. After dinner, James called Katrina and she told him that she would be starting a new theatre production soon and would have to learn a whole new set of dance routines, so would be unavailable for a while. They did, however, arrange a date for the following evening.

Wednesday, after work, James drove into the industrial part of Kitwe and found the company that Koos Englebrecht ran. It was located close to the dealers for large equipment. To get to it, he passed the Coke bottling plant and the slaughterhouse. He had been told that there were huge pythons that lived in the ditches close to the abattoir. They were reputed to live on the offal and off-cuts that were disposed of during the butchering process. The Englebrecht's yard was really just a parking area for the transporters and a workshop for repairs. There were a couple of ramps built for loading. Towards the back of the plot, there were older, apparently broken-down tractors and piles of old tyres. To the side of the workshop was an office, and there, James found Koos.

"James, *howzit*?" said Koos.

"*Goed, Meneer,*" replied James. "*Is Katrina hier?*"

"*Nee,*" replied Koos. "*Sy is nie hier nie.*"

"Sorry, *Meneer,*" said James. "My Afrikaans isn't that good yet."

"*Ag,* man, she is out for a while delivering a load for me," said Koos. "She will be back just now."

"She drives these lorries?" asked James.

"Well, she can when we really need another driver," answered Koos. "But, I prefer that she doesn't. Can I get you a coffee?"

"Thanks," said James. "That would be great."

"Bwalya, coffee *na lo bwana, futi ka mina,*" said Koos.

James was still struck by the fact that an offer to get something usually translated into an instruction for someone else. Bwalya brought a tray with the coffee and some coarse-looking biscuits.

"What are these?" James asked Koos.

"Boer *beskuit*," replied Koos.

There were two varieties, one sweeter than the other. They were like hard rusks and were good for dipping into the coffee.

"Excuse me for asking, sir, but do you have a problem with me seeing Katrina?" James asked.

"No man," replied Koos. "I saw too much hate in Katrina's *ouma* against the English after my older brother married an English-speaking girl from Bechuanaland. She refused to go to the wedding and didn't talk to them for years. They now live in South West, near Mariental. I decided that whatever Katrina did, if she was happy, I was happy. If she chooses an *Engelsman*, then she will have to stick with her choice, no matter where that choice may take her. She was engaged to be married once, and then she found out that the *ouk* was a *los gat* so she got out of that fast. She has had many *ouks* chase her since, but she gives them no time, I can tell you, and she can *get the moer in* fast with them if they persist. You must be different because she has seen you more than once."

This was an amazingly long speech for Koos, whom James had never heard say more than the bare minimum. They sat in silence for a while until a large low-loader pulled into the yard, and Katrina got down from the cab. She came into the office and looked at the two men.

"So while I'm out working, you two sit around drinking coffee?" she said. "I thought it was only the Bemba who put their wives to work while they sat under the trees, drank Chibuku, and debated the greater meaning of life?"

"Well, now that you have delivered that one load, when can we expect our dinner?" asked Koos. Katrina's answer was to throw the logbook at him. She stormed out of the office and came back a few minutes later with her own coffee to find Koos still laughing.

"You are not setting a good example for James," she said. "He will begin to think you are serious. So, where are you taking me, James?"

126

"I thought maybe we could check out a restaurant in Ndola," replied James.

"Okay," said Katrina. "Can I go home and get changed first?"

"Well, you can go dressed like that if you want," replied James. "But, I think you may want to change."

"Why, don't you think my dungarees are suitable for a flashy restaurant in Ndola?" asked Katrina.

"Sure, we can go to Chikonde's bar and grill if you want," answered James.

"I'm half convinced that you would actually drag me there," said Katrina. "But, I think I would rather do a little better than Chikonde's."

They left the yard and drove out to the Englebrecht farm. James was interested in the large truck that Katrina had been driving. It was a make that he was not familiar with.

"Where does the Oshkosh tractor that you were driving come from?" James asked.

"Oh, some small town in the States, I think in Wisconsin," replied Katrina.

"Huh, I thought it might be Japanese, the name sounds Japanese to me," said James.

"No, strictly Yankee stuff," said Katrina. "It's better than anything the Brits have, and I like it better than the Kenworths we have in our fleet."

"Don't you ever think it is a little unfeminine to drive large equipment?" asked James.

"*Jy kan maar kak praat!* Why are you so *verkrampt* that you worry about the types of jobs men and women should have?" asked Katrina.

"Well, until now I really hadn't thought about it," replied James. "But it just didn't strike me as the kind of job a girl would have."

"What kind of jobs should a girl have then?" asked Katrina, with a big emphasis on girl.

"Something tells me that is a question to which there is no safe answer, rather like when did you stop beating your wife," parried James.

"Well, why don't you think about it while I change, or maybe you are just like all the rest and cannot face a woman who can do things you cannot?" said Katrina.

James was rescued at that point by Mrs. Englebrecht, who came in and sent Katrina off.

"Please excuse Katrina," said Mrs. Englebrecht. "She is the only child we have, and *Meneer* Englebrecht would have liked a son, so now Katrina thinks she must do everything that a son would have done."

"Oh, that's all right, *Mevrou*," replied James. "She has made me think a little."

James sat and talked to Mrs. Englebrecht while he waited for Katrina to shower and change. She told him a little of their struggles to make the business work, and then she asked him how his job was going. James was sure she had seen any number of other young men start at the mine and had followed their progress, so she probably had a better idea of where he was than he did. Katrina came back from her shower and asked James if he thought he could organise himself enough to take them out.

The drive to Ndola was a little quiet, and James kept wondering if he had asked the wrong question. Over dinner at the Savoy hotel, it became apparent that Katrina had forgiven him for his foolishness. He was also reassured by her father's comments and wondered how he could have even begun to doubt Katrina. On the way back, they stopped along the road at the crest of a hill where there was a fairly wide gap in the trees, and the view of the sky was not obstructed and got out to look at the stars. With no light pollution from the towns, the view was spectacular.

They also saw that the clouds were beginning to build up and the stars were being obscured. Then the lightning started. It was strange for James to watch the amazing lightning display, hear the thunder, and yet for there to be no rain. He asked Katrina if this was usual and was assured that, yes, it was usual and that the lightning could continue throughout the night. They stood holding hands by the road until Katrina remembered that they both had to go to work the next day.

"Time to go, I think," said Katrina.

They got back into the truck and drove back through Kitwe to the farm. The evening finished on a high note; James got an extended good-night kiss when he dropped her off.

The next day, James was back down the mine with Samson. They were going to try and get two blasts off, as the following day was Independence Day and a holiday. James and Samson lugged boxes of explosives to the raise and lowered them down to the right level. At 25 kg per box, they were careful to count down each load, so as not to tax the hoist. They had decided to do little drilling that day and set most of the crew to transporting explosives and equipment in preparation for the blasting.

The first blast they set up was on one of the main production levels and seemed to James to be a very large number of holes, which meant a lot of explosives. At the rate they were loading the holes, they were going to use 12 cases per fan of holes, and there were 6 fans of holes to load up. At 25 kg per case, they were going to set off 1,800 kg of explosives, which should make a fairly large bang. They wired up the detonators, safed and isolated the circuit, and went down to the slot level to set up the second blast.

"So *Bwana* James, *ini wena azi enza kusasa?*" asked one of the crew who was helping them charge up. James thought for a minute and then realised that he really had no plans for the next day. He had agreed to call Katrina, and they were going to meet up at the boat club; from there, who knew?
"*Mina aikôna azi*, Ben," James replied. "*Kabanga mina azi hamba lapa shateen.*"
Ben considered carefully the news that *Bwana* James might be going into the bush and then asked if he planned to go fishing. James wondered where this conversation was going, and it finally worked its way around to fishing with explosives. Ben apparently saw himself as a kind of commercial fisherman who supplied his customers through the use of explosives in the rivers.

It also transpired that the steel cables they used to lock up the boxes in which they stored their personal things made good snares for poaching. James began to wonder what kind of crew he had fallen into. They had markets for everything, including the heavy copper wire that was used for the overhead power supply for the trains underground. James wondered how much risk there was in getting the copper wire down with the power on and decided he didn't want to try and find out.

With the slot charged up and wired, they went back to the upper level and connected up the first blast. They then ran back down the ladders, connected up the slot blast to the cable network and then went down to the blasting station on the haulroad to await the signal. They did not have to wait long, as everyone was eager to get away for a long weekend. It was an impressive bang. They could feel it go, and James wondered what it felt like on the surface. With all the blasts going on at the end of the shift, there must be a whole series of apparent seismic events every day. James wondered how you ever sorted out real seismic events if ever there were any.

The cages going up were packed. They had to wait about forty minutes before one stopped at their level. James estimated that there must be close to 80 or 90 people per deck instead of the supposed 60. James had never been jammed into anything like such close quarters with anyone before. It was almost claustrophobic. The cage stopped at the next level up and, unbelievably, they managed to jam in more people. The conversation was all about the day off coming up and the individual plans that each had. Some were taking the Saturday off as well and going off into other parts of Zambia to visit relatives. Some were going to be marching, but the greater majority planned to just stay close to home and enjoy the day off.

James had arranged to meet Tom at the Mine Club after work. Tom had told him that he had some information for him. James got a beer and waited for Tom to join him.

"James, *howzit?*" said Tom, coming up to him in the bar.

"Fine, thanks, Tom. Had a good day?" asked James.

"So, here's the deal," said Tom. "I talked to the shift boss who is over the section I'm in. In a roundabout way, I got talking about some of the local girls. Your Katrina has quite a reputation, but not in the way that Greg and his wife suggested. Lots of blokes would love to take her out, but I gather that she will have none of them. I also understand that anyone out there who brags about sleeping with her is full of shit."

"So, the idea that Katrina is some kind of *scrubber* is, shall I say, not quite an accurate representation?"

"I think that is putting it mildly," said Tom. "I think you can go back and thump young Greg in the mouth."

"No, I won't do that," said James. "I will just ignore the sick bastard and his stupid wife and try and get past the guilt I have now for ever thinking anything untoward about Katrina. You didn't tell Rita, did you?"

"Hell no, man," replied Tom. "This was between us, but I have to tell you, Katrina was quizzing Rita about why you were kind of distant when you went away."

"Shit, I wondered whether I had managed to cover, but apparently not well enough," said James. "Well, I'll let you know how things go tomorrow. Thanks for your help, Tom."

"Hey, it's okay. It's not every day that you get to meet a bird like Katrina. If I didn't have such a catch in Rita, I would be out there making your life a misery," said Tom.

"So what are you planning to do tomorrow?" asked James.

"Rita and I had nothing special planned; we were thinking of taking a drive out to the Luisiwishi River for a picnic. Want to join us?" replied Tom.

"I'll ask Katrina," said James. "If she says yes, when and where do we meet?"

"Why don't we meet at the Mine Club at around nine in the morning?" suggested Tom. "As we have no phone, we will wait until nine-fifteen, and if you are not there by then, we will go on alone"

"What about food and drink?" asked James.

"Don't worry, Rita has already put enough together to feed an army, so the four of us should manage nicely, you won't even have to bring the beer!" replied Tom.

"Great," said James. "Hopefully, I will see you tomorrow."

James drove home and checked to see that his truck had a full tank of fuel and that he had water and oil in case, and a rope. Who knew when that might come in useful? He called Katrina and checked to see if she fancied a picnic in the bush, and that it was ok to be going with the other couple. James was delighted that she agreed and relieved that she had no objection to tagging along with others. The only thing she suggested was that they take James's truck so that they would not be tied to anyone else and so that if either truck had problems, they could get home.

# A day out

Independence Day was hot and humid. As the dry season came to an end and the rains were anticipated, the level of discomfort increased. The humidity climbed to levels that almost reached those of the deeper underground levels. The rate of suicide went up in the country with the choice of technique being the power lines. There were parades and rallies planned to celebrate the fifth anniversary of Independence and there were undoubtedly going to be meetings and demonstrations throughout the town.

James was in no hurry to get up; it was nice to lie in for a while, or at least until seven instead of the usual five-thirty. He got up and threw together some breakfast. He had told Silent and Evansi to take the day off, so he was alone in the house, as they had left the night before. He fed the dogs and then locked up and drove out to the Englebrecht farm. Koos was in the yard and provided him with safe passage through the dog horde that descended when he drove up to the house.

"So, James, *howzit?*" asked Koos. This seemed to be the standard greeting for Koos, and James was beginning to expect it.
"*Goed dankie Meneer,*" replied James. "Is Katrina ready?"
"*Miskien,* but you know women *ou maat,* she should be out now now or just now," said Koos. Turning to the house, he yelled. "*Meisie, jou skat is hier.*"
James had learned enough Afrikaans to blush at the *skat* and wondered if that was how Katrina felt about him. Evidently, today was a now now day because she came out of the house. A just now day would have put their departure time into the realm of the unknown. She was dressed in a T-shirt and shorts with a pair of *takkies* on her feet. She launched into a tirade of Afrikaans at her father. James lost the drift of it after the first two words. Whatever she was saying did not bother Koos in the least as he just stood there grinning at her. It seemed that a certain amount of embarrassing was Koos's way of having fun with his daughter.

Katrina put a large sack of oranges in the back of the Land Rover and another bag full of something else, then she got in and told James to go.

She did smile and wave to her father as they pulled away, so whatever had been said was either not unusual or was not half as bad as it sounded. Only when they were well up the road and almost to the main road did she lean over and kiss James good morning. "You had better not do too much of that while I'm driving," said James. "I might lose my concentration completely and drive us off the road."

They drove into Kitwe and passed a number of groups of people all headed towards the centre of town for rallies and parades. There was even a small band forming on one side street. Katrina told James that there had once been a police band and that as a young girl, she had followed them down the street as they marched. She had been really impressed as a child by the drum major with his leopard skin and staff.

They met up with Tom and Rita at the mine club, and after a brief conversation to sort out what they planned to do and where they were going, set out in convoy. The road led them out across the railway line that serviced the mine and then headed towards Kalulushi. Before reaching Kalulushi, they turned off onto a side road and proceeded in the general direction of Kabompo. Very quickly, the road turned to dirt and was heavily corrugated with patches of thick dust. James dropped back a fair distance to be out of the dust cloud that Tom and Rita's Land Rover was throwing up. Even so, it came into the car, and they could taste the red laterite soil. There were groups of people on this road as well, headed towards town to take part in one rally or another. James waved to them as they went by and got smiles back. He felt a certain amount of guilt about these people. He was creating this huge dust cloud, which billowed all around the people walking along the road, and had to get into everything they had.

Katrina reached forward and opened the vents above the dashboard and below the windscreen. Then she opened the sliding windows behind them and created a through draught that cooled things nicely. It did tend to bring in a little more dust, but the overall effect was better rather than worse. Katrina then kicked off her *takkies* and put her feet up onto the dashboard. "You know, if you were really brave, you could set the hand throttle on this *bakkie* and do the same thing," she commented to James.

"Thanks, but I don't think so," he replied. "I rather fancy being in control in case we came across the unexpected."

"Why is it that the floors of these *verdomde* Land Rovers are always so hot?" Katrina asked.

"The exhaust pipe," replied James. "It is where they run the exhaust pipe, and there is no insulation between us and the exhaust except the thin piece of aluminium that is the floor.

James found it extremely difficult to drive and keep his eyes on the road when he had Katrina's legs propped up next to him. As Bill had commented when they first saw the dancers at the Little Theatre, they went on forever, and James was entranced by the shape and colour. "So does the rest of you look the same?" he asked.

"What do you mean?" asked Katrina.

"I mean the colour. You're such a nice colour, I wondered if it is the same all over?" replied James.

"*Oppas boetie, jy soek my?*" said Katrina. "What does it matter to you what colour I am?"

"Well, it's such a pretty colour, I wondered if all the rest was the same as your legs?" said James.

"Are you the same colour all over?" asked Katrina.

"No," said James. "I have a tan line around my arms and legs but the rest of me requires very careful exposure to the sun, or I look like a lobster."

"Well, perhaps one day you will show me," said Katrina.

James almost drove off the road. He decided that if they planned to get to the Luisiwishi in one piece, without Tom and Rita coming to look for them, he had better change the subject, or he would drive off the road.

After about half an hour, they slowed down and passed through a small village. Katrina told James to slow down and then stop by a group of children. The children immediately crowded around them. James had never taken the time before to look at the native Zambian children. They were all shapes and sizes, with all styles of dress from the minimum to what almost looked like a school uniform.

"Shame, aren't they cute," said Katrina. She got out of the car and opened up her bag of oranges and the other bag, which turned out to be full of bread rolls.

"Here *maPikanin bamba lo*," she said to the children and started to hand out oranges and rolls to every child that came up.

After they had all received some, there were only a few left in the bags, which she gave to a *madala* who had come up to the car with the children. James had watched her during this and had seen the way her eyes lit up when she was dealing with the children.

"Why do you do that?" asked James.

"It's a small enough thing, don't you think, James, to give a little of what you have?" replied Katrina. "I try to do this each time I go into the bush, sometimes at the same village where they know me."

They drove on and caught up with Tom, who had slowed down when he had finally missed them in his dust cloud. For the next hour, they drove, generally on the wrong side of the road, where the ride was better, exchanging small talk and barbs. James was becoming more and more entranced with Katrina. Everything about her was exciting and fascinating. He loved the way she looked, the way she talked, and the way she thought. He realised that he had really fallen deeply in love and hoped desperately that he would not be rejected and heartbroken.

Finally, they saw that Tom had really slowed down and was turning off the road to a side track. He had been given some directions by one of the section bosses on the mine to a side road that paralleled the river. Off this track, they could see a number of possible spots for a picnic, and Tom finally decided on one and pulled over between the track and the river. James followed, and they parked under some sausage trees overlooking the river. After the drive and the noise of the engine, it was relatively quiet in the bush; they could hear just the sounds of the insects and the birds. Rita started to set up their picnic between the two cars. Tom was right; she had brought enough food to feed an army. Tom offered drinks all round and James and Katrina each took a Castle.

They sat on the riverbank, listening to the bush sounds, drinking their beers, and watching the river run by. Rita came over and joined them and asked Katrina to name the various birds they could hear and the trees they could see. They saw a family going by in a dugout canoe. The man was poling the canoe, and the balance of the family sat in the front along with packages of belongings. Katrina called to them in what James assumed was Bemba and had a brief conversation. She told the rest that the family were going fishing farther down the river and that they would be out until the next day, when they went back to their village. They saw some buck on the other side of the river.

"Those are lechwe," said Katrina. "They are more common in the south in the Kafue Flats. They have adapted to life near swamps and can be found near permanent water."

"What about those animals that you can just see in the bush behind them?" asked Tom.

"*Mboo*, about the meanest things in the bush," said Katrina.

"Who or what are *mboo*?" asked James.

"Oh, sorry, buffalo," said Katrina. "They're good to eat, very similar to beef. But, if you shoot one, make sure you do a good job or he will come for you now now. He will be the hell in and you will be *ifwa*."

Rita took some photographs and then got them together in groups for people shots. Then she and Tom took a walk along the riverbank.

"Don't go too far," said Katrina. "I have nothing with me to rescue you if you meet something unpleasant. Just make some noise and scare off the beasties in front of you."

When they had gone out of view and out of earshot, Katrina sat close to James and took his hand. "Do you know what they say about you?" she asked.

"No, what?" replied James.

"Oh, some of my friends told me that you had had a couple of affairs since you came to Zambia," said Katrina.

"What?" said James. "With whom and when, for God's sake? I hardly know anyone, let alone have had affairs with anyone."

"I know," said Katrina. "But one of my friends, or perhaps ex-friend now, thought it her duty to warn me about you."

"That's funny," said James. "Because Greg and Shirley thought it their duty to warn me about you. They tried to tell me some story about you.

Why do you think these people are so bound and determined to make our lives their business? Did you mention it to anyone?"

"Yes, I asked Rita what she thought, and she told me that you had been so busy that she didn't see how anything like that could be true," replied Katrina. "How about you?"

"I talked to Tom and he told me I shouldn't listen to such crap," said James. "In fact, he told me that I should go and punch Greg in the mouth."

"Oh, well, so now Tom and Rita know all our secrets and our shady pasts," said Katrina.

"Katrina, I love you," James blurted out.

"I know *Liefling*. I love you, you know, even though you are a *groot kak*," said Katrina as she leaned over and kissed him.

"Are we interrupting anything?" said a voice.

James and Katrina both started and looked up to see Tom and Rita staring at them. "Is everything all right?"

"Perfect," replied James and Katrina in one breath.

"So, should we be celebrating?" asked Rita.

"*Ja*," said Katrina. "James and I want to thank you for your help to each of us and hope that you will stay our friends."

"Why, what did we do?" asked Rita.

"Well, you helped me, and I gather that Tom helped James," said Katrina.

"What did Tom do?" asked Rita.

"Oh, he sorted out my mind for me," said James.

"He didn't tell me," said Rita.

"Well, I wasn't supposed to," said Tom.

"Hey, you two, don't fight over us," said James. "We like you both too much to have you fighting. What matters is that I have found the girl of my dreams, and I owe it in part to each of you. Thanks!"

At the end of the day, James's drive home was far too short. It seemed that the miles and the time just shot by. It was dark, really dark, as there was no light anywhere. The road was relatively easy to follow as the side berms where the graders had thrown up the dirt reflected the lights from the trucks. Occasionally, they saw eyes reflecting, which made the trip eerie. As they drew closer to the towns, they could see the lights of Kalulushi and Kitwe in the sky, and their view of the stars became less clear. Katrina warned James to slow down as there was likely to be the odd person on the road who had drunk a little too much. The most dangerous would be the whites driving cars and who thought they were quite capable of handling a vehicle at speed, although they were drunk as lords.

They crossed the railway lines as they headed into Kitwe, and Tom and Rita turned right and headed home. James and Katrina turned left and wended their way through the outskirts of town, back to the Chingola road and then on to the Englebrecht farm.

Saturday was a short workday. Many of the crews were on skeleton staff as a lot of the workers had taken leave days to make up a four-day weekend. James joined Samson, and they took the cage down to their working level.

"So, *Bwana, ini wena enzili?*" asked Samson.

"*Mina hambili lapa shateen,*" answered James, wondering if the quick trip the day before to the Luisiwishi qualified as a trip to the bush.

"Ah, *wena hambili na lo mfazi ka wena,*" said Samson.

"*Kabanga,*" replied James. *Mfazi* was such a convenient term. It could mean wife, girlfriend, or whatever, so covered most situations. James then asked Samson what he had done. "*Wena, ini wena enzili?*"

"*Mina shalili lapa kaia na lo mapicinin,*" said Samson.

Samson had stayed at home with his children. James asked how many children he had and how old they were. Samson told him that he had three: two boys and a girl, aged between eight and twelve.

The cage arrived at their working level, and as they walked into the working area, they continued their conversation. James learned that children were considered wealth, as children could take care of their parents in old age. When Samson's daughter was old enough, either she would find a suitable husband, or Samson would help her arrange a marriage; either way, there would be a *lobola*, or bride price payable. The two boys would find wives, and he might have to help them with their *lobola*.

139

Samson lived in Wusikili, not far from the stadium, in one of the mine houses that James had seen when he had first arrived in Kitwe. James was sure, knowing Samson a little by now, that it had to be one of the one or two-roomed houses that were brightly painted with a well-maintained garden. He was right. Samson was proud of his vegetable patch and even had his older son sell some of the extra produce around the town. James had seen any number of these vegetable sellers. They travelled around town on bicycles and sold vegetables to those who either did not want to go into town and buy them or who had forgotten something. They would ride up to the gates that protected most houses and ring the bicycle bell or call out to attract attention. Samson's son only did this at weekends. During the week, he was too busy with school to have the time. Samson told James that he hoped all his children would finish school and perhaps even go on to ZIT to learn a trade, or even to the University. In this way, he could be assured of a comfortable life when he got too old to work anymore and retired from the mines.

By now, they had arrived at their section and set about the tasks for the day. Samson set the rest of the crew to drilling at existing set-ups. What he and James were going to do that day was move some of the drilling equipment between levels and set it up ready for drilling operations to restart after the weekend. This was harder work than James had imagined. First of all, they had to tear down the setup that existed. That entailed taking the drill off the horizontal bar that it was attached to, then pulling the horizontal bar out of the clamp that held it, then knocking out the chocks that held the vertical bar wedged between the floor and the roof. None of these items was lightweight.

Apart from these larger pieces of equipment, there were the drill strings, tools, spare water tubes, cans of "*black shit*", otherwise known as grease, drill bits, and other junk that the operators seemed to collect. The tools were large spanners that were used to "*bopa sterek*", or tighten up, the nuts on the clamps. It was not unknown for some of the drillers to add pipes to the ends of the spanners and then put in crowbars to provide better leverage. Often this led to the bolt being turned off and broken.

With the set-up torn down, it all had to be transported to the next drilling location, either farther along the same drift or to a different level. Moving to a different level meant moving all the equipment to the raise, lowering or lifting to the appropriate level and then moving it all to the new location. Samson had set up a new drilling location on the level below the one that had been in use, so they had a good few hours' work ahead of them. There was at least a hoist that was used for equipment moves. This was simply an open rectangular bucket on the end of a steel cable. The hoist was run using an air motor situated on one of the upper levels. One of them had to climb up to run the hoist while the other gave directions. It took two to load some of the pieces into the bucket, and this meant that one of them, James, did a lot of climbing up and down the ladderways. The equipment raise was at least a nice four-foot diameter hole drilled through the rock, so the bucket slid easily up and down on the smooth surface.

After moving all the equipment, they then set it up for drilling. They first had to dig into the loose fines and small chips that made up a covering on the floor until they hit solid rock. Then they put in the vertical bar and wedged it tightly between the floor and the roof with timber wedges.

The rest of the setup was a matter of mechanics until they came to lining up the drill to the hole pattern marked up on the wall. First, they made an approximate alignment using the marks on both sidewalls to get the right direction, using the horizontal bar only, before they added the drill. This gave them the right direction for drilling. Then they set up the appropriate hole within the fan of holes. Samson took the water tube out of the drill and shone his light through it while they moved the drill clamp around the horizontal bar to align the beam of light onto the hole. They were now set up for the drillers to start on Monday. Samson made sure that the water and air lines were extended far enough into the drift to service the setup, and they also extended the ventilation ducting to ensure a good supply of air. This all done, they called it a day.

James asked Samson how often holes were drilled in the wrong direction. Samson told him that that was not usual unless there was a 'new one' surveyor who did not know which end was up. It had happened in the past with the operators trying to tell the surveyor that it was wrong and being told off for their pains. The upshot of the episode that Samson was describing was a new assignment for the surveyor, where he could do no harm and a long wrangle about footage bonuses, as the holes drilled were not usable, but the drillers still wanted to be paid the bonus for drilling them.

They left the section and joined the others, who were all eager to leave the mine and enjoy the rest of the weekend. They were not going to do any blasting that day, so did not have to wait for anyone else. They let the section below them know that they were going and took off for the shaft. As there were far fewer people than normal at work, the cages were nowhere near as crowded as they had been the day before the holiday. Still, the cage took some time to come, and James was glad to be done for the day. He saw none of his friends on the surface; they had either already gone or were still down in the mine. Samson wrote up notes in the Section Bosses' logbook and told James that they were now officially finished for the day. James was at a loose end as Katrina was off with her folks visiting some friends near Lusaka for the rest of the weekend.

James drove back to the house and let himself in. He had told Silent and Evansi to take the day off, so he had the dogs to feed. There was a barbecue set up in the backyard, and James decided to cook himself some dinner. The barbecue was essentially a forty-four-gallon drum cut in half longitudinally and set on legs. There was a bag of charcoal nearby and some lighter fluid in the house.

The charcoal lit easily enough, and James waited until the coals had died down before throwing on his steak. He had also found some aluminium foil and had wrapped up a potato and some other vegetables. This package he also put on the coals. Controlling the rate of cooking of the steak turned out to be more of a trick than he had thought, but beer at least served well to cool the meat down so that it did not dry out. It did seem rather a waste of good beer, though!

Eating his dinner, James reflected on all that had happened since he left the UK, from the boat trip to the drive up through South Africa, and the job so far. He was still not sure about the training school and the tasks required, but accepted that the language part of it was essential. The time he had spent with the different section bosses had been really instructive, if only to learn how the theory of the mining method translated into everyday tasks.

# A turn-up for the book

Sunday, James decided, as there was nothing that had to be done and there was no one of his acquaintance around, that he would explore Chingola. Chingola was built around the N'changa mine, particularly the open pit. He drove out of Kitwe onto the Chingola road, eventually passing the Mufulira turn-off and then on until he came to the outskirts of Chingola. For much of the trip, the road paralleled the railway, and he was rewarded with a close-up view of a train headed in his direction. Whether the ultimate destination of the train was Chingola or Bancroft, he could not guess. The train was all goods and seemed to be supplies for the mines, including some earth-moving machines presumably destined for N'changa. The route to the mine was fairly simple; at the first roundabout in town, he took the middle exit and drove through the centre of town until he came to the pit.

There was a viewing area where one could drive up and look over into the mine and watch the operation. There was not a lot happening as the Independence Day weekend had shut down many of the activities, but still, James was amazed at the size of the equipment. There were trucks with tyres that stood taller than his Land Rover. The shovels used to load the trucks had their own electric cables running into them and moved around on oversized crawler tracks. Looking down from the viewpoint, the trucks that were running looked tiny at the bottom of the pit, which gave James a sense of how large the operation really was. He had read somewhere that it was only eclipsed in size by Bingham Canyon in the US and Chuquicamata in Chile. There were a couple of Land Rovers running around that he guessed were being driven by mine supervisors. It looked like a very different kind of operation to manage than the underground sections he had been in to date.

Another car pulled up near him, and James saw out of the corner of his eye a couple get out to look at the view. They did not see James at first because he was hidden behind his Land Rover. James got a real shock when he looked at them. Here was his old girlfriend, Susan, who had dumped him because she did not want to go to Zambia. The bloke she was with was someone James knew from college. He was a minerals technology type, so would probably be working in a concentrator somewhere. James did not know what to do, but was spotted before he could turn away, and it was obvious that he was also unexpected.

"Oh, hello, James," said Susan. "Fancy meeting you here!"

"Susan, Patrick," was all James could manage. He was flabbergasted. All that bull-shit about not wanting to go to Zambia, and yet here she was with Patrick! James now began to wonder when she had taken up with Patrick and how long it had been going on.

"We were married in early September and came out by boat. I must say we did not expect to see you here as we thought you were in another town altogether," explained Patrick.

"Well, I hope you are both happy and congratulations," replied James.

"No hard feelings then?" asked Susan.

"A couple of weeks ago, I would have said yes, but not now," replied James. "Are you working here in Chingola then?"

"No, we are in Bancroft and only came over here to sight-see," answered Patrick.

"Well, good luck, and maybe we will run into each other again," said James. "I must be getting back to Kitwe as I promised to meet someone there."

On that note, James got in his Land Rover and drove off. His mind was in turmoil; how long had Susan been seeing Patrick? At the same time, she was supposed to be dating him. The bitch! And how bloody British! "Oh, hello James, fancy meeting you here." What the fuck was he supposed to say to that? James wondered if he should have stayed and talked longer, but about what? He had nothing to say to them, particularly to the two-faced bitch who had called herself his girlfriend. Or had he been deluding himself and only imagined her feelings for him? Now, thinking about it, he could begin to understand the gaps in their dating and the weekends when she was supposedly visiting her aunts in the country. Likely story that! She had probably been shacked up in some country inn somewhere shagging the arse off bloody Patrick. No wonder Patrick never really talked to him at college, even when they had the same classes. The bastard!

145

This was something he could get really steamed up about, but then he had a momentary vision of Katrina and realised that it was his self-esteem that he was pissed off about. Now he had found his own piece of hot stuff that, in all honesty, made him wonder what he saw in Susan. Maybe that was a little unfair. Susan was good-looking, but he had just never met anyone as good-looking as Katrina. Then he thought some more, and he now began to have more self-doubts as to whether she really was with her folks visiting friends in Lusaka. Was this going to be another letdown?

The visit to Chingola had at least occupied the morning and given him something to think about. And what a thing to think about; Susan married to Patrick. Shit, how the hell was he ever going to live this down with the friends he had made since coming to Zambia and how many of his friends who were in the UK knew about Susan dumping him and probably now knew about her marriage to Patrick. As he thought about it again, he knew that the main issue he had was one of ego, but that was at the intellectual level. At the emotional level that mattered not a whit, it was enough to rile a saint!

James thought later that he remembered little about the drive back to Kitwe. He clearly made it in one piece and managed not to hit anything, which was a miracle as he was hardly focused on his driving. When he got back into town, instead of going straight home, he went to the house of Tom and Rita on the off chance that they were in. Fortune was with him, and they were at home, both working in the garden. James's arriving gave them a good reason to break off and rest. Tom pointed to the grass under a tree and told James to take a seat while he got a couple of beers.

"So, James?" Rita asked. "What's the problem?"

"Why should I have a problem?" replied James.

"Because it's written all over your face," replied Rita.

"What is written on his face?" asked Tom. He had come from the house with a tray full of beer bottles and glasses.

"Problems in his love life, I think," said Rita. "Pour some beer into him, and maybe he will tell all."

"Okay, okay," said James. "I suppose I will have to tell you sooner or later. I just met my old girlfriend, the one who dumped me because I wanted to come to Zambia. It turns out that she married someone else and is in fact in Zambia, living in Bancroft!"

"Wow! What, where, and how?" asked Tom.

"Well, I went to Chingola this morning to look at the Nchanga pit and who should come swanning up but Susan, my ex-girlfriend, with a bloke I knew from college, telling me that they are now married," said James.

"So, how does this change your feelings for Katrina?" asked Rita.

"Not a bit," said James. "But, I have to wonder now if Susan could string me along, is or will Katrina going to do the same?"

"Stupid boy!" said Rita. "How can you be so blind? Katrina is head over heels about you, and I like her, so just be sure you tell her about this in the right way and don't upset her!"

"Why does he have to tell her at all?" asked Tom.

"Because, idiot, as you may have noticed, this is a small community and someone will find out who Susan is and how she is related to James and make it their business to tell Katrina," replied Rita.

"I still don't see why he needs to tell her, just deal with it when and if it comes up," said Tom.

"No, no," said Rita. "If she finds out from someone else and then discovers that James knew all along, she will be upset that he did not tell her himself."

"But, won't she worry that James still has the hots for Susan?" asked Tom.

"Not if he tells her properly and gets rid of that stupid look of bewilderment that he has on his face at the moment," replied Rita.

"When and how do you plan to tell Katrina?" asked Rita.

"I don't know," said James. "I'm only just getting over the surprise myself. Do you have any ideas?"

"You should tell her soon and not over the phone, you need to do this face to face, and you need to be sure that she understands that this does not change your feelings for her at all," said Rita.

"But how do I convince her of that?" said James.

"Be honest," replied Rita. "Tell her what happened and how, and tell her that you love her. I presume you do?"

"Oh yes!" said James. "I have a hard time sometimes understanding what she sees in me, but yes, I love her."

"So, when is she due back?" asked Tom.

"Wednesday," replied James.

"So when she gets back, take her out somewhere quiet and have a chat," said Tom.

"This is not a chat," said Rita. "This is serious stuff; he must be serious, open, and honest."

"God, I hate it when women talk about being open and honest," said Tom. "I always wonder what I should have said or not said and what I may have forgotten that will come to light later."

"Lucky for you, I know all your dark secrets," said Rita.

"Why don't you stay for dinner, James?" said Rita. "Then we can think about how you can tell Katrina."

"That would be great," replied James.

"So, what are we going to have?" asked Tom.

"I don't know," replied Rita. "You are the one cooking tonight."

"In that case, it will be a *braai*," said Tom. "I'll go and get started on the fire."

James stayed for dinner, and they talked about his problems. When he thought about it, there was really not much to tell. A girl he had once been serious about had dumped him, married someone else, and they just happened to be living in Zambia. The real problem was his own self-esteem. He had to get over that and focus on his current situation and new love.

By Wednesday, James had fretted enough and was more at peace and ready, if not quite eager, to give Katrina the news. He planned his big speech that he was going to give over dinner, and the answers to whatever questions he could think of. As it turned out, it was all a bit of an anticlimax. James told Katrina that his ex-girlfriend, Susan, was married and living in Bancroft, and her only comment was that she hoped that Susan really loved the other bloke, as she came to Zambia with him. Katrina was more eager to tell James all the news about her trip. Their friends in Lusaka had just bought a new plane and were planning to fly up to the Copperbelt the following weekend, and would James fancy a quick trip?

James asked where her friends got the money for a plane. Katrina told him that they ran a group of farms in different areas and grew maize, tobacco, tomatoes, and other produce. Apparently, the plane would cut down travel time between the different farms and was a business expense as well as a new toy.

By Saturday, James was excited about the upcoming flight. His only concern was the weather. The clouds were building, and the air seemed to be full of static electricity. The rains looked as if they were about to break, so flying would be tricky. His fears were confirmed when Katrina left a message for him at the mine to let him know that the flight was off as the weather was not cooperating between Lusaka and the Copperbelt. It seemed to be the week for roller coaster anticipations and anticlimaxes. Instead of flying, James picked up Katrina, and they went to the boat club.

As they sat on the *stoep* of the boat club, James heard thunder in the distance. Then he saw lightning. It seemed that the storm was coming towards them. However, for as much as the lightning flashed and the thunder boomed, there was no rain. It was the first time in his life that James had seen an electrical storm without any rain. The lightning flashes came at short intervals until it seemed that the sky was constantly lit up, and it was possible to read things without the lights.
"Is this the way the rains usually come?" James asked Katrina.
"Sure, we only get *meningi* storms like this," she replied. "All light and sound and no rain. Then one day the rain will actually come and it will only but rain, hard, hard until you cannot see in front of your car."
"Really?" said James.
"I'm telling you," replied Katrina. "*Ag* man, the rains are only *lekker*, you can hear it, but most of all you can smell it,"
"What do you mean, smell it?" James asked.

"You will see," said Katrina. "The earth smells so good when the rains hit, like nothing else. You can watch the raindrops bounce up as they hit the ground and the dust rises until it is dampened down by the mist of the disintegrating drops. I think it is the wet dust in the air that you can smell"

"Wow, you make it sound almost mystical!" said James.

"It is, in a way," said Katrina. "You have to remember that we don't see rain for months, and when it comes, it is magical."

# Big ends and Lobola

Monday morning, James reported to the mine offices and was assigned to a new section. He was introduced to his new shift boss, Mike Morris and section boss, Henry Chikonde. After giving some basic introduction to the job, Morris told them to go down and he would see them later. James left with Chikonde, and they proceeded underground. They went down as far as they could on the main shaft, then walked over to the secondary shaft that took them farther down. At the lowest station, they got out and walked to the end of the main haulage road. This is what they would now be working on. Their job was to extend the haulage road so that the sections above would have someplace to dump waste and ore. As the haulage ways were used as main airways, they were also extending a parallel tunnel that would be used as the return airway.

Henry collected his crew together, gave them some instructions and told them who James was. Then Henry took James to the face, and they checked it for misfires and residual explosives. After washing down the workplace, Henry brought up one of his teams, and they drilled some holes into which they placed steel rods. On top of these steel rods, they built a work platform. Henry and James climbed up and marked up the next round to be drilled and blasted. They went to the other tunnel and started the crew clearing the broken rock from the previous day's blast. There was an air-powered machine that James recognised from a previous job as a rocker shovel. The shovel was to be used for the removal of the broken rock. There was also a temporary railway line along which they pushed wagons to be loaded.

After the initial flurry of activity, the crews got down to the serious business of mucking, as the removal was called, and drilling holes and James and Henry took a couple of minutes' break before their next activity. James looked around the work area to see what was involved. They were extending tunnels that were about 4 metres wide by 3 metres high. There were drains running along the sides of the tunnels and occasionally timber supports to hold up uncertain areas of the roof. Along the roof were painted lines that set the direction that they were to advance in, and along the side walls were other lines that set the gradient of the tunnel so that any water drained back to the shaft and the pumps. James noticed a pipe lying on the ground by the drain and wondered if it had just been left and forgotten.

James asked Henry how long he had been working on the mine.
"Too bloody long" was the answer. Henry went on to say that he had been working there for over twenty years and was looking forward to a different life, preferably back in the village where he grew up. It seemed that he had kept a family there and ran a successful market garden. Henry was also a football fanatic and a big supporter of Mufulira Wanderers. He knew all the statistics of the games and was friendly with many of the players. He was an especially big fan of 'Zoom' Ndhlovu. As far as Henry was concerned, 'Zoom' was already a legend and was destined for even bigger awards.

As some of the drilling crews finished their work and started removing their equipment from the face, Henry told James that it was time for them to bring up the explosives and charge up the holes. Henry led the way to the magazine that was located some distance back up the haulage road, and they started carrying sacks of explosives back to the face. This was not the sticks that James had been using up till now; this was ANFO, and it came in bags in the form of prills, or little balls. It smelled of the diesel fuel that it was mixed with, and James noticed that it got used a lot to degrease hands and equipment.

Charging the holes was also a little different. They had a venturi device, simply an air pipe connected to another pipe that sucked the powder from the bag and blew it into the hole. The trick seemed to be starting out with the outlet pipe far enough into the hole to properly load the hole, but at the same time not blow everything out at them. When each hole had enough ANFO in they inserted a regular stick of dynamite with a fuse and detonator attached. The fuse length was 12 feet, so at a burning rate of thirty seconds a foot, they had only a few minutes to light up all the holes and leave, giving themselves enough time to retire to a safe distance.

While Henry was putting the finishing touches to their blast for the day, he told James to go to the other tunnel and make sure that all was properly clean and that the equipment was stored away neatly. James collected his own bag and went into the return airway to see how the crew was progressing. They had finished, and the workplace looked clean and orderly. The crew then went back through the crosscut to the main haul road and then back to the next safe place. James checked the fan that was installed in the crosscut and the ducts that would take the gases from the blast into the return airway. Everything looked fine. He turned the fan on and immediately felt the airflow change. Henry then came running back. "*Hamba checha!*" he said to James. James thought that it was probably a good idea to go quickly. As they went along the haul road towards the next crosscut, James heard one light shot go off. He looked at Henry, who only nodded and said,
"*Zonke ena mushle!*"
They reached the crosscut and then stopped in to join the others and closed the steel door behind them, and waited until they heard the blast.

When the blast went James could see the others trying to count all the holes as they went off. It was difficult as there were multiple explosions that seemed to occur at the same time. After the last one had gone off, they waited a few minutes to be sure, then left the safety of the crosscut and headed off towards the shaft. As James looked back, he could see the gases being drawn by the fan into the return airway and away from them. There was some debris that had been blown back towards where they had been waiting, but not much; most of it had been dropped very close to the blast. Henry seemed pleased. James asked him what the earlier shot was.

"*Ena lo safety,*" said Henry. "*Tina azi bamba lo fuse, futi tina azi juba ena kabanga four feet. So, lo twelve foot ena lo eight foot. Manje tina azi kona two minutes ku hamba.*"

Now James understood. By cutting a fuse down by 4 feet, they knew that they had two minutes to get to a safe place before the first shot was supposed to go off. This was necessary because Henry said the fuse batches all burned at slightly different rates, although the nominal was thirty seconds a foot. As they were lighting each fuse individually, it took some time, and the operators all wanted a way to give themselves warning that the first explosion could take place soon. James wondered where they put this fuse and detonator. Henry told him that they put it in the pipe that was lying by the drain.

At the shaft, they met the rest of the crew who had left earlier and were still waiting for a cage to take them up. James thought about the workday and decided that it was actually fairly short if you deducted the time it took to come down in the morning and go back up again in the afternoon. Total travel time could be as much as an hour each way.

For the next two days, the routine underground continued. On the surface, things were quiet except that on Wednesday, Katrina told James that the more British members of the boat club were going to have a party and bonfire to celebrate Guy Fawkes Day. James asked Tom if he and Rita would like to join them. He also asked Bill, but Bill was otherwise engaged. After work, James picked up Katrina from work and then drove out to the dam. Tom came later after he had picked up Rita. It was a very humid and hot evening, and there was thunder activity in the distance. They sat out on the veranda looking out at the bonfire that had been built.

"James, it is only going to rain, now now," Katrina said.

"How do you know?" asked James.

"I can smell the rain in the air," said Katrina. "I'm telling you, they will light that bonfire, and it will rain."

"How can you be so sure?" asked James. "It has been hot and humid like this all week, and we seem to have less thunder and lightning than we had earlier in the week."

"Wait and see!" Katrina said.

After dark, they congregated around the bonfire and, with much ceremony, one of the Brits put a torch to it. The pile quickly caught, as everything was dry wood, and the flames soon licked around the guy. James wondered where the clothes came from for the guy, as they looked better than some of the clothes that the waiters were wearing.

He felt that it was a shame that they could not have swapped them and given someone a good set of clothes.

In the end, it was James who first noticed the rain. He felt one large drop and then another and another. He pointed it out to Katrina, who suggested that they retire to a safe place before it really came down. They almost made it. James was surprised at how quickly it came. In only a few moments, it was pouring down to the extent that they could no longer see the bonfire from the clubhouse. Katrina was right. What James noticed most of all was the smell. He could also hear it on the corrugated iron roof of the clubhouse. It was amazing how much noise it made. At the rate it was coming down, James could now understand the need for the large ditches that were by the sides of the roads and the significant crown on the roads themselves. The rain just needed somewhere to go.

Well, so much for the bonfire. The rain quickly turned the stack of wood into a smouldering pile. Katrina told James that she wondered why the Brits kept building these bonfires on Guy Fawkes Day, as it seemed to be the signal for rain. She could only remember a few years when the rains had broken after November 5th. Katrina was almost convinced that the Zambians thought that the Guy Fawkes celebration was a British way of making rain.

After about an hour, the rain stopped and the skies cleared, revealing the stars. It seemed to James that there were more stars now than he had seen before. It was probably just the fact that the skies were clearer now with less dust and smoke in the air. The rain had cleaned the air significantly. Katrina asked James if he could take her home as she had an early start in the morning. As they drove out, they had to negotiate a couple of large, deep puddles that were at least 2 feet deep. It was the first time that James had waded his Land Rover through such deep water. Katrina told him to put it in low range and keep the engine rpm up and not to build up too much of a bow wave. They had no problems, apart from getting wet feet from the water that came in under the doors, but it was obvious that some of the others that would follow would have problems until the water ran away. On the drive to the farm, Katrina told James that she would start rehearsals for a Christmas show later that week and that it would take up most of her evenings for the next month or so.

The following week, James was now into the routine of drilling and blasting the big ends. Henry was skilled at his job, and the ventilation and surveying experts who came to check could find no fault. The shift boss, Mike Morris, had been to check on them, but he had other issues to solve elsewhere, and he seemed to have confidence in Henry. James had been permitted to light up the end, which he had done with great apprehension, concerned that he got all the fuses lit before their warning shot went off.

James had missed Katrina over the weekend as she was at the theatre getting the choreography and the costume requirements for the Christmas show. The rain had been coming with regularity. There had been a major storm every day, and inches of rain had fallen each time. The drains and ditches had been washed clean of debris and now flowed properly, so that the incidence of flooding was less.

After his shift on Thursday, James was waiting at the station when Joy Mwamba joined him.
"So, Joy, how goes it?" asked James.
"Oh, fine," said Joy. "I'm beginning to learn what the job is really about and wonder why sometimes I went to university."
"I know what you mean," said James. "I suppose there is logic behind this approach, but I have difficulties seeing it at times."
"What do you think of Zambia now that you have been here a while?" asked Joy.
"Fine," said James. "You know I really am enjoying the job, even though it is frustrating at times, and I even found a girlfriend."
"Yes, I heard about that," replied Joy. "Do you think it will lead to anything permanent?"
"I don't know yet," said James. "But what about you, how is the marriage going?"

"Oh, fine," said Joy. "You know I'm trying to get the *lobola* together so that I can get married. Well, I'm having a problem getting enough to match what the *madala* wants for his daughter."

"How much are we talking about?" asked James.

"I need about five hundred kwacha more," replied Joy.

"Wow," said James. "How are you going to get your hands on that much and live at the same time?"

"Well, the banks won't lend you *lobola*, so I have to find another way," said Joy.

"How?" asked James.

"There are people in the compound who will lend you money," replied Joy.

"At what kind of interest rate and what happens if you don't pay?" asked James.

"It is probably a little extreme," said Joy.

They both sat quiet for a while as others came to the station. James had an idea but was not sure how to broach the subject and was unwilling to with so many people around. Once on the surface and in a quieter place, James raised the subject again. James was not sure what drove him to make the offer he was about to make. He had the money as he had come from England with some that he had saved from a job he had had. He was also not sure how Joy would react, but he could only try.

"You know, Joy, you can't put yourself in the hands of those people," said James.

"Which people?" asked Joy.

"Those money lenders that you think you may have to use to get the *lobola*."

"Yes, but what choice do I have?" asked Joy.

"I would rather lend you the money myself than see you in the hands of those moneylenders," said James.

"Really? Why? You would do that for me?" asked Joy.

"Well, yes!" said James. "I might want to get married myself one day, and who knows what kind of help I will need. I would like to think someone would help me out."

"But I don't know when I will be able to repay you," said Joy.

"I know where you work and can probably find out where you live," said James. "You are not planning on leaving the country, are you?"

"No, of course not," said Joy. "I just never expected that you might offer to help me."

"I have to confess I didn't see myself doing this either, but I just think that this is the right thing to do," said James.

"Yes, but!" said Joy.

"Hey, Joy, no buts, okay?" said James. "Just say yes!"

"But, well, James, okay, I promise that you will be repaid as soon as I can," said Joy. "Do you need a legal agreement?"

"No!" replied James. "Joy, if we get lawyers and their ilk involved, who knows how things will turn out?"

"You are probably right," said Joy. "I give you my word that I will repay and with interest."

"Forget the interest, Joy," said James. "Consider that a wedding present. Now to practical matters, when do you actually need the money?"

"Well, as soon as possible," replied Joy. "I need to get it to the *madala* as soon as I can."

They worked out the details, and James promised to get the money to Joy later that evening.


Joy had left, and James was preparing to leave when Greg appeared. He apparently had been lurking behind some of the lockers and had overheard the conversation.

"James, are you completely out of your mind?" Greg asked.

"What do you mean?" replied James.

"Lending money to one of the *munts*, even if he is a trainee like us, must be about the stupidest thing I ever heard of," said Greg.

"Why is it any concern of yours?" asked James.

"It's not. For all I care, you can let your sister marry one, but you can say goodbye to that money," replied Greg.

"How can you say that?" asked James.

"Look, everyone knows that the *munts* couldn't organise a piss-up in a brewery, so how do you expect to ever get your money back from Mwamba?" said Greg.

"I believe that he is as good as his word," shot back James. "Perhaps if you took the people here more at their word, then you might get on better with them."

"Fat chance," said Greg. "The only good *kaffir* is a dead *kaffir*, as the saying goes and lending money to them or trusting them will get you taken for a ride."

"Why did you come here?" asked James, feeling a little bewildered by Greg's antipathy towards the Zambians and yet his apparent willingness to work there.

"The money. I worked out that I can make enough in the three years I'm here to go to Rhodesia and start a business there," replied Greg.

"Why Rhodesia?" asked James.

"Old Smith has the right idea. Tell the Brits to bugger off and then control the country properly," said Greg. "I have been talking it over with my cousin, and he thinks we have a good shot of making some real money there."

"Doing what?" asked James.

"Tobacco," replied Greg.

"But, if you don't like to work with the *munts,* how are you ever going to run a tobacco farm where you will be totally dependent on them?" asked James.

"My cousin from Springs will join me, and together we can discipline the *munts*," replied Greg.

"You'd better be careful not to talk like that too much around here, or your time here may be short," said James.

"Oh, don't worry. I checked and all the *munts* are gone. It's only you and me, *kaffir boetie*," said Greg.

"Fuck off, Greg!" said James. With that, he got up and walked out into the fresh air. He was glad to get away from Greg and his constant negative attitude. It was hard for James to work out why Greg had gone there, and just how he proposed to operate a tobacco farm surpassed human understanding.

James left the mine and went into town to withdraw the money from his bank account. He was a little nervous having that much cash on his person, but he was soon able to turn it over to Joy whom he met at the bar of the Edinburgh Hotel. Joy was delighted, but still a little confused as to why James was doing this. Truth be told, James was also a little confused, but he was determined. Joy was now in a new dilemma. Should he invite James to his wedding or not? If he did, James would be the only white face at the ceremony, and Joy was not sure how his family, or his wife's family, would accept him. He also wondered if James would even accept an invitation. He decided to try the roundabout approach to test the waters.

"Where is your next assignment going to be, James?" Joy asked.

"I go on to the afternoon shift, tramming next Monday," said James.

"Oh, I see, so you will be busy the Saturday afternoon and night following?" said Joy.

"Afraid so," replied James.

"My wedding date is set for that Saturday. I saw the *madala* today and told him that I now have all the *lobola*, so now he wants to move things along quickly," said Joy.

"Congratulations, Joy," said James. "Glad to be of some help. I hope all goes well."

"So do I," said Joy. "I now have to go to the housing people and see about getting a different house."

Joy felt relieved that he did not really need to address the invitation issue. He did resolve to get a thank you to James as soon as he could from both him and his new wife. James had wondered if Joy was going to invite him to the wedding, and he was, in turn, relieved not to have to put Joy in an awkward position. Work called, and he would be deep underground at the time of the ceremony.

"Out of curiosity, Joy, what is the bride's name?" asked James.

"Suzie," replied Joy. "You know she is the sister of Felix Mwewa?"

"Oh yes, I remember now. What does she do all day long?" continued James.

"She works at a bank as a cashier," replied Joy.

"Can you get preferential terms for loans?" asked James.

"No, unfortunately not," said Joy. "Sometimes I think it is even more difficult to get anything from the bank if you work for them. Perhaps they are being very careful to be sure that there is no problem with embezzlement and similar things."

"Well, anyway, Joy, good luck with the wedding and name the first child after me," said James.

"Maybe," said Joy. "If it is a boy, he should be called after my father, George. But, maybe I will add another name."

"Don't worry, Joy, I was only joking," said James. "I'll see you tomorrow."

The following day, James met up with Henry and learned how to mark up the cross-cuts that connected the parallel drives. They suspended chains from the roof and marked up the main direction of the drive, and then calculated the entry point of the cross-cut and marked up the entrance that was at a perfect right angle to the drive. In a few days, they would find out how many days it would take to connect the two tunnels. Calculating things, James estimated that it should take five days to reach the other tunnel. Following that would be the installation of airtight doors and other equipment, perhaps another two days. But long before that, James was due to be reassigned to another area to learn more, so he was unlikely to see the completion of this stage of development.

After work, James called Katrina and caught up on the progress of the Christmas show. He found himself jealous of the time Katrina was spending on the show and wished it were over. He also felt guilty about this as he realised that Katrina had every right to do what she wanted. Katrina was rehearsing again that night, so was unavailable. James had not realised how much he had come to look forward to seeing Katrina most days and felt a little lost now that he was essentially back on his own again for a while. Oh well, it would all be over after the Christmas show, until the next time. They did arrange a date for Saturday, as Katrina would not be rehearsing that day. Apparently, the dance instructor would be away for the weekend.

Friday of that week, when James returned to the surface, there was a message for him to see George Bullock. He wondered what he had done wrong, as George was an Assistant Underground Manager and thus several rungs above him on the ladder. James could not think of anything that would have caused the assistant underground manager to notice him, and no one else in the chain of command had made any comments. He saw Tom and Bill and asked them if they had any ideas, but all he got was grief from them about being picked out of the masses for greater things. Some help they were. Therefore, he was mainly just curious when he stopped by the office to report to Bullock.

"Ah, Martin, come in," said Bullock.
"Good afternoon, Mr. Bullock, I understand you wanted to see me," said James.
"Yes, have a seat. How are you doing?" replied Bullock.
"Fine, thank you," said James, still at a loss as to where this might be going.
"I wanted to see you because I gather you are house-sitting for Piet van de Merwe?" said Bullock.
"Yes, that's right," replied James. "He is due back on January the 4th, and I will be moving out on the 3rd," he continued.
"Ah, good," said Bullock. "I'm leaving on the 2nd of January for my long leave and am looking for a house sitter. Could you come by tonight and meet my wife, and we could talk about it?"
"Of course," said James.
"Tell you what, why don't you come for dinner?" asked Bullock. "That way we can get to know you a little better."
"Thank you, sir," said James.
"Don't dress up," said Bullock. "Come at about seven tonight, here is the address, and we will be expecting you."
"Thank you again, sir," said James. "I will be there at seven tonight."

With that, James left and went off to find Tom and Bill.
"So, did you get the axe?" asked Bill.
"No, he just wants me to house-sit next year and wants me to go to dinner tonight so that they can check me out," replied James.
"Wow, dinner with the *bwana mkubwa's*," said Tom. "So, do we have to pay to speak to you now?"
"Right, Tom," said James. "It will cost you five ngwee a time because that's probably all my conversation is worth to you."
"So expensive!" said Tom. "I was only thinking of about one ngwee at a time."

"Well, make sure that you are on time, not too early, not too late and wash behind your ears," said Bill.

"Ha ha!" replied James. "Why does it have to be me?"

"Because you have a reputation now," said Bill. "And it probably doesn't hurt that you're seeing the daughter of one of the big businessmen in town."

"Reputation for what?" asked James.

"Well, you haven't burned the house down yet, have you?" asked Bill. "Nor do I recall any wild parties, unless there have been some and we haven't been invited."

"Or they have been intimate parties for two," suggested Tom.

"Of course, why didn't I think of that?" said Bill. "Party for two, James and Katrina, now serving on the veranda!"

"Very funny!" said James. "What about your love life, how is that going?"

"Changing the subject, huh, James?" said Bill. "If you must know, it's going well and I'm even thinking of popping the question."

That stunned both James and Tom, and for a minute, they could think of nothing to say.

"What's the problem?" asked Bill. "Cat got your tongues?"

"Are you really serious?" asked James.

"Actually, yes, I have never been more serious," replied Bill. "What did you guys think, that I would get my bit of black, then get serious and find a nice English girl to settle down with?"

"Actually, I'm not sure what I think," replied James. "I'm a little surprised at how quickly you have got this far, you have only been in the country, what, two months?"

"True, but haven't you ever fallen in love with someone when you first met them?" asked Bill.

"Admit it, James, you have fallen for Katrina, haven't you?" asked Tom.

"Bill's right, I fell for Rita the first time I saw her and knew that she was the one. But it did take me a little longer than two months to get around to proposing."

"Yes, but I haven't thought that far yet," replied James.

"Why not?" asked Bill. "Maybe you should, if, of course, you are really serious."

"Have you thought about what her family and yours might think?" asked Tom.

"Yes, a little," replied Bill. "But, they are not the ones getting married, are they?"

"Will you have to pay *lobola*?" asked James.

"Probably," replied Bill. "The question is how much?"

"Should we go get a drink to celebrate?" asked James.

They left the mine and drove to the mine club, where James stood them a beer and then asked Bill when he planned to ask Mary. That led to a discussion on whether or not Bill should follow the accepted local traditions, should he talk to Mary's father first, then pop the question? Bill was careful to point out that he had not yet even broached the subject with either Mary or her father. He had discussed it with his brother, who had been first amused, then horrified, and finally resigned to the situation. His brother had told him that the responsibility for telling their parents was to be Bill's alone; he was staying well out of it and would find a good reason to be unavailable when the news broke so that he did not have to answer any questions. Bill led them to believe that his brother now regretted introducing him to Mary. He also seemed to think that his brother was interested in a sexual relationship, but nothing more serious.

James then excused himself as he had to clean and change for his dinner engagement with George Bullock. He drove home, showered again, changed, and then drove to Parklands to the Bullock home. He tried hard to be sociable and polite, but was very much preoccupied with the news that Bill had sprung on them earlier. James succeeded in maintaining a veneer of interest, and the Bullocks were entertaining. They reached agreement on the house-sitting, and James promised to stay in touch with George and make more definitive arrangements closer to the date.

# The road past Kamfinsa

Saturday, James spent his last shift with Henry. He was not thrilled about going on nights, but he knew that it was part of the job, and it was only going to be for a short stint. Henry was sorry to see James go, as he had enjoyed having someone with him to talk to and to ask questions of. James was eager to finish for the afternoon as he had his date with Katrina later. Katrina had told him that they were going to a party at Darryl's house, one of the rally car team whom James had met early on when he had first arrived.

After work, James showered and changed and then sat down for a quick chat with Tom and Bill. Tom was also going to spend a couple of weeks with a tramming crew, and Bill was scheduled for a fortnight with an afternoon shift lashing crew. He asked the others what they were doing that weekend and learned that Tom and Rita were taking an expedition into the bush out towards Solwezi, and Bill was going to Luanshya to broach the subject of his impending marriage proposal. He said goodbye to the others and then drove back to the house for a change of clothes more suitable for a party. He drove out to the Englebrecht farm and was saved from the gauntlet of dogs by Koos, who shepherded him into the house.

"So James *hoe gaan dit?*" asked Koos.

"*Goed dankie*," replied James. "Is Katrina ready?"

"Well, you know James," said Koos. "These women can only take time to do things, so who knows? Coffee?"

"Yes, please," said James.

"Where is the session tonight?" asked Koos as he poured out two cups of the strong coffee that he preferred.

"Thank you," said James, taking his coffee. "I don't think it is a session," he added. "I think we are going to a party at Darryl's house. Do you know where that is?"

"*Ja*, he stays in Parklands. Katrina can give you good directions," replied Koos.

"Excuse me for asking, sir, but what do you think of marriages between white and black?" asked James.

"Why do you ask?" replied Koos, looking at James a little sideways over the rim of his coffee cup.

"Well, a bloke that I work with told us today that he plans to marry a Zambian girl from Luanshya," said James.

"*Ag* man, there has been more time wasted and hate generated over those issues. Let me tell you, I had an uncle, Koot, who lived in South West near Gibeon. He lived with a black, and most of the family would not speak to him. My father sent me to stay with them a couple of times, and they were fine. She was kind to me and, as far as a twelve-year-old can tell, *Oom* Koot loved her," replied Koos. "You must tell your friend to do what he will and be dammed to the people who criticise."

"Who must do what?" asked Katrina as she walked into the room.

"Oh, my friend Bill is thinking of getting married. I will tell you about it later. You look wonderful, are you ready?" replied James.

"Of course, are you ready?" said Katrina.

"Off with you two!" said Koos.


James and Katrina made it partly to Kitwe before it started to rain. It was coming down hard enough for James to pull off the road and wait for a while until the rain abated a little. While they were waiting, Katrina asked James about the story with Bill. James told her what was going on and then waited for her reaction.

"Oh, I knew about that," said Katrina. "One of the drivers told me today that your Bill was going with a girl from Luanshya and was going to marry her."

"How did he know, when Bill only told us today?" asked James.

"I think he got it from a girlfriend of his at Luanshya who works in the hospital there," replied Katrina.

"So, she knows that Bill is going to ask her to marry him?" asked James.

"Maybe Bill hasn't told you everything," said Katrina.

"Or maybe, Bill has underestimated his bride-to-be and she has already worked out what he plans," suggested James. "So, what do you think?"

"About what?" asked Katrina.

"About Bill marrying a Zambian," said James.

"Well, I cannot imagine a situation where I would marry a Zambian, but I suppose if he finds this girl attractive enough, he will do what he wants," replied Katrina.

"Don't you think he will have problems either adapting here or helping her to adapt to life in England?" asked James.

"Of course, it won't be easy, and it's possible that it may not last. I imagine I would have problems understanding England. I have never been there and only know what I have read, been taught, or learned from people like you. Are you going to be invited to the wedding?" asked Katrina.

"I don't know; probably yes, as Bill does not know many people in Zambia," replied James.

"Will you go?" asked Katrina.

"If I can, probably," replied James. "Would you come with me?"

"If you go, I will go with you," answered Katrina. "Look, the rain has almost stopped!"

"Great, let's get moving, and perhaps we can get to this party before it's over!" said James.

The party was fun. Darryl and his friends knew how to have a good time. Many of the people there worked for the service companies that supported the mines, a few were in agriculture, and some worked for the government hospital. The only people James knew were Darryl, Attie, and Lionel, who was there with Jane. It looked as if Lionel and Jane were quite an item now. James was asked a few times why he didn't spend more time with the rest of the expats. He was now beginning to understand what the Bells had told him about the different social groups. The people at the party had nothing particular in common with most of the expat mine workers that he knew, and even he had a hard time identifying with many of the things these guys were talking about.

At some level, the sarcastic comments about the local yokels thinking about nothing but hunting, shooting, and fishing were correct. However, the views held by the expats, the VC-tenners, were a little simplistic. Most of the long-time residents really loved the country and were determined to enjoy life as much as they could. They all recognised that Zambianisation would eventually affect them all, and those who still had South African passports would have decisions to make. Many of the South Africans didn't really relish the idea of trying to start new lives in the south. They also knew that they could not go to England, so were left with the choice of staying in Zambia or trying Australia or Canada. Most of them were trying to put off having to make any decisions for as long as possible.

One disadvantage of the party was that James did not get to spend too much time with Katrina on his own; there always seemed to be others around. Katrina evidently felt the same way because a couple of times she looked over at him, raised her eyebrows, smiled, and shrugged her shoulders. Whenever Katrina smiled at him, James felt that he would go weak at the knees, and he was afraid that he was wearing an inane grin that would be obvious to everyone that he was smitten with her. Finally, Katrina and James left the party a little after midnight, and James drove back to the Englebrecht farm.

"I'm sorry I did not get to spend more time with you," said James. "It always seemed as if there was someone in the way when I wanted to talk to you."

"*Moenie*, worry *nie*. What are you doing tomorrow?" Katrina asked James.

"Nothing so far, do you have something in mind?" replied James.

"I thought that if you weren't busy, we could go for a picnic somewhere," suggested Katrina.

"That sounds nice," said James.

"I thought we could take a ride out towards Ndola along the back road past Kamfinsa," suggested Katrina.

"Okay, you'll have to show me the way," said James. "Shall I organise food?"

"No, I'll get my mom to put something together for us," said Katrina. "Why don't you pick me up at ten?"

"Sounds like a plan," said James.

They said goodnight, and as Katrina kissed him goodbye, she whispered in his ear, "Let's see if we can't have a day to remember." On that very suggestive note, James drove home agog with anticipation.

The following day, he picked up Katrina at ten. He saw her parents briefly and was loaded up with what seemed like a mountain of food, drinks, and other stuff. They drove back through Kitwe and out onto the Ndola road. Not far past the mobile police unit station, Katrina pointed out a dirt road to the left, which James took. The road seemed to roughly follow the railway line that ran from Kitwe to Ndola. They had not gone far when they came to the entrance to the Kamfinsa prison that James had heard Felix and Joy talking about. Katrina told James that there was supposedly another prison near Lake Bangweulu for political prisoners, which had the reputation of a place of no return. They drove past the prison entrance, and several miles farther on, they came close to the Kamfinsa stream. Katrina suggested that they turn off the road and follow the stream for a while.

She told James that they were probably only a mile or so from the Congolese border and needed to stay to the west of the road and the railway line so as not to stray over the border. She told him that the Congolese border guards had a reputation for being corrupt and sometimes brutal. However, they did not seem to cross the border into Zambia. Some distance from the road, they found a great place for a picnic that had access to the stream, shade from some trees, and was completely secluded. After leaving the prison locale, they had seen no people or cars, so they were very much alone. There were a couple of coveys of guinea fowl close to them, and they quickly settled down to their regular foraging and made no more alarm calls. James began to suspect that this had been planned out fairly carefully and perhaps even reconnoitred ahead of time, as the guinea fowl would give ample warning of anyone's approach.

Katrina set out blankets, food and drink, and they had a leisurely lunch. James kept looking at Katrina and wondering exactly what she meant by "a day to remember". They made small talk, and Katrina brought James up to date with the progress of the Christmas show. James then told Katrina what he would be doing in the next couple of weeks. After lunch, James helped Katrina as she packed things away. She then produced a towel each and stripped down to a bikini and lay back on her towel. Never having seen her in a bikini, James was entranced and couldn't help staring.

"What?" Katrina asked.

"Oh, nothing," James replied. "I was just wondering again whether you are the same colour all over."

"*Ag*, still curious are we?" said Katrina, smiling at him.

"Of course, wouldn't you be if you were me?" kidded James.

"Why don't you judge for yourself?" suggested Katrina.

With that, she stood up and peeled off her bikini pants, then unhooked her bra and, in short order, was standing in front of James totally naked. James could only gaze at her open-mouthed as she slowly turned around in front of him; her breasts were not overly large, they were firm with quite dark nipples, her stomach was flat from the exercise she did, and her legs and buttocks were muscular and well defined. Her dark hair was long and hung loosely down her back and on her front, partially covering her breasts. He noted that there were faint tide lines at what would be her bikini line, but the difference in skin tone was not significant. She really was a beautiful brown all over. She also had a really dark, luxuriant mass of hair in a definite triangle below her belly, shaped like an arrow pointing to her sex below. James couldn't help his own reaction and felt himself stiffening quickly.

"Well?" asked Katrina.

"You know you really are amazingly beautiful," replied James.

"Don't change the subject! Am I the same colour all over?" queried Katrina. "You seem to have been looking long enough now to form an opinion unless you're colour-blind."

"Not quite," said James. "I don't think I could ever look long enough. You do have some faint lines there and there," he continued, pointing to her breasts and lower belly. "How come you're so brown, even there?"

"It's probably some of the skeletons in the background of one or both of my parents," Katrina answered. "Remember, our family has been in South Africa a long time, and there are skeletons in all our cupboards."

"Really?" said James.

"Okay, you've had your look. Now, what about you?" said Katrina. "*Kom, kom*, get them off, now now!"

"Okay," said James.

He had a little problem with his shorts and underpants as he had an erection that made things most difficult.

"Ah, I see what you mean about tide marks," said Katrina. "You know you are fairly well built under that shirt and shorts you always wear."

"It's all the climbing ladders that I do that keeps me in shape," replied James.

"That's not all that I meant," said Katrina.

"Katrina, I don't have anything with me," said James, beginning to panic now he realised what was likely to happen next. He was silently furiously kicking himself for not reading more into the "day to remember" comment and being better prepared.

"*Moenie* worry *nie*," she replied. "I have been looking forward to this moment, and I went on the pill. Sit down there and let me sit on your lap."

After that, things proceeded quickly to the inevitable conclusion. Afterwards, they clung to each other just enjoying the closeness. The first to break the silence was James, who asked. "You know I love you, don't you?"

"Yes, I do. When did you first realise that?" Katrina replied.

"As soon as I met you," said James. "You were this vision of unobtainability that I never thought I would be with, that just bowled me over. What about you?"

"The first time we met, I decided that you were the one," replied Katrina.

"You know that it is unlikely that I will stay in Zambia in the long term and will probably go somewhere else, don't you?" asked James.

"Yes, I knew that from the beginning. But if you really love someone, what does it matter where you are?" asked Katrina.

"True, but what about your folks?" responded James.

"Oh, daddy knows what it is to move away from your family, he told me one day that when I met the right one, then my place would be with him," said Katrina.

"What about your mother?" asked James.

"She just wants me to be happy, the way she has been with Pops," replied Katrina.

"I'm not sure my folks have the same attitude," said James. "I am sure that they think that this Zambian thing is a phase and I will grow out of it soon enough and return to England."

"Why were you circumcised?" asked Katrina. "Are you Jewish or something?"

James was thrown by the complete change in direction of the conversation and was momentarily confused. "I have no idea," he answered. "I believe it was done a few days after birth, I don't know why, I never asked. And no, I'm not Jewish. If I were, would that matter?"

"Hell no! I don't really know what it is about you, but there is something that just drives me wild. You have no idea how the hell in I was when we went to the Mita Hills dam and all those others were there getting in the way," said Katrina.

"Really, I thought I was the only one who was disappointed," said James.

"So, would you like to show me how much you were disappointed?" said Katrina, lying down on her towel and holding her arms out for him. This time, they both took much longer, enjoying each other before they culminated with another joint climax. James rolled off Katrina and they both lay quietly looking at each other, whispering endearments and caressing.

They were thinking about another round of lovemaking when the rain came. They managed to get everything in the car before it got too wet and then stood in the rain just enjoying the sensation on their skin. The rain poured down in torrents and sluiced off them in rivulets. It poured off Katrina's nipples and from her pubic hair and off the end of James's penis, making it look as if he were constantly peeing. James laughed and hugged Katrina, and that led to another round of lovemaking, this time up against the side of the Land Rover. As the rain started to let up they climbed into the car and looked for the towels to dry themselves. They dried themselves as best they could, but Katrina had to be content with wringing out her hair and letting it air dry.

"Perhaps we should start to make our way home now?" suggested Katrina. "The sun will be going down soon."

"Okay," replied James. "Do you think there will be any problems with the rain?"

"No, we should be fine," said Katrina. "I don't remember any big dips where water would accumulate."

"You planned this, didn't you?" James asked.

"Of course, did you think I would wait forever for you to work up the courage to make some kind of move?" replied Katrina.

"No, I mean the place and everything," he added.

"*Ja*, we *Boergies* don't do anything unless we *maak 'n plan*," replied Katrina, laughing.

The drive back was too fast for James. They seemed to arrive in Kitwe almost immediately and then went on through the town towards the farm. It had truly been a day to remember, and James wondered if his expression would give them away to Katrina's parents. He asked her what she was going to tell them about where they had been and what they had been doing when the rain came. Katrina surprised him by telling him that she would tell them that they had enjoyed their picnic and had sat out the rain, then, later, she would confide in her mother.

"Do you tell your mother everything?" asked James.

"Yes, she is my best friend, always has been. I have always told her everything, it's easier that way. Then she knows everything and there are no surprises," answered Katrina.

"Wow, that's different for me! Will she tell your dad? He strikes me as someone I would not want to be on the wrong side of," said James.

"Sure, sure, she will tell him, if he hasn't guessed already. Don't worry about Daddy, he thinks you are okay," replied Katrina.

"How much will you tell your mom?" asked James. "Everything?"

"Well, not quite everything, just the basics," replied Katrina, laughing. "I wouldn't want her to get jealous of my own potent *ou*!"

They reached the farm, and Katrina asked James to come in. James was nervous. He was sure that his face would give him away. If it did, the Englebrechts were very gracious and chose not to comment. James did see mother and daughter disappear for a short while into the kitchen, and then both came back smiling broadly. He was sure Koos knew as he started to call him "James, my son". James stayed for coffee, then excused himself to go home. Katrina saw him off and whispered in his ear to thank him for the day and suggested that they do it again as soon as was practical.

# Tramming

Monday, James slept in until Katrina called him and told him that it was time he was up and about. Her argument was that if she had to be at work, he could at least be up and doing something. James was thrilled to talk to her and teased her over the phone, knowing that there were probably others in her office. James asked her if she was free for lunch and was delighted when she told him to stop by and meet her. Just before noon, James left the house and drove to the industrial area and made his way to the Englebrecht transportation company yard. It turned out that Katrina's idea of lunch was a little different from what James had first imagined. She had set out a cold lunch in the office for herself, James, and her father. It was difficult to say what he wanted to Katrina with her father present, and James wondered if she was having fun with him. He caught himself a few times looking at her hungrily and blushing, and wondered if Koos had noticed. Katrina did brush up against him a couple of times and felt an electric thrill run through his body.

After lunch, James went back to the house and thought that perhaps he should write to his family. He had not done so since first arriving in the country, except for the brief telegram he had sent upon arrival, and was beginning to feel guilty about keeping them in the dark for so long. He sat down and composed a letter that told his story so far, with only the briefest mention of a girl that he had met towards the end of the letter. He wrote longer letters to his sister and his grandmother and was a little more forthcoming about Katrina in those. Later in the afternoon on his way to work, he swung by the Post Office and mailed the letters and picked up the little mail that he had received.

At the mine, James found and introduced himself to Piet Lamprecht, the shift boss in charge of tramming for that area of the mine. Lamprecht called in a young man and introduced him to James.
"Jimmy, *hier is 'n rooinek vir jou*, what was your name again?" asked Lamprecht.
"Martin, James Martin," replied James.

"Oh, I have heard about you," said Jimmy. "You're the bastard who is taking Katrina Englebrecht out."

"Oh, is he the one?" asked Lamprecht. "Didn't you date her once?"

"No," said Jimmy. "She was too *hovaardig* to go out with me!"

"Oh great," thought James. I am to spend the next two weeks with a bloke who has every reason to hate my guts.

"So, *neefie*, you ready?" asked Jimmy.

"Ready when you are," said James.

They left the office and proceeded underground. In the cage on the way down, they saw Tom Morrison in the company of another section boss, Samson Bwalya. It seemed that they were headed for a section below the one James and Jimmy were going to. Whereas Tom and Samson were chatting comfortably, James and Jimmy had little to say to each other as yet. At the 2830 level, they got out of the cage and walked down the haulage road. James had been here before when he had been with Kayumba.

Jimmy stopped by a crew that was connecting a locomotive to a series of cars. He gave them instructions on which working areas to pull from and then started to make out a tally sheet on which to track tonnage hauled. They were pulling ore from stopes on both the north and south of the shaft. Not far from the station, the haul road split into two, and the tracks went in opposite directions, matching the workings above. James took the chance of this break to look at the locomotives and the cars. The locos were electric-powered and took their power from the overhead lines strung along the haul road. There were a couple of battery-powered locos nearby that were on charge. The cars were arranged so that they would tip out of their sides; there were eight of them to a train.

At last, Jimmy put his papers away and sent the trains off to get their first loads. He then pulled out a chair from behind some support timbers, sat down, put his feet up on a box, turned his light off and went to sleep. James was unsure what to do. Sleeping underground was a serious offence, but who was James to make anything of this behaviour. For all he knew, Jimmy might not be asleep at all, but just resting until the train came back. Not sure what to do and what he was going to learn from this experience, James decided to just wait for a train and see how they emptied the cars into the storage hopper. That hopper then discharged into the skips that hauled the rock to the surface. There were two chutes that the cars could be emptied into, one for waste and the other for ore. Obviously, it was less than desirable to mix the two.

A train returned and discharged its load into the ore chute and left again to collect another load. When this train returned, Jimmy roused himself enough to log in the two loads that the crew told him they had brought. James asked Jimmy if it would be all right if he went with the crew and observed the loading of the trains from the drawpoints. Jimmy told him that as far as he was concerned, James could do what he liked, including jumping down the shaft. James talked to the crew and joined them on the locomotive. They pushed the empty cars down the track and made their way to the drawpoints under the appropriate working section. As each car was manoeuvred under the drawpoint, one of the crew members yanked on a chain and opened the chute to allow the car to fill.

Occasionally, the rock would not flow well, and they would jab at it with crowbars to clear jams. James realised that this was a hazardous thing to do and he asked the crew if there was not another way to clear the jams. They told him that occasionally they used really small explosive charges, but that that was even more risky because the chute could break and all the rock would come out and block the haul road. They also told him that they sometimes had to wait quite a long time for the other train to clear the station area before they could dump their load.

When the train was full, they went back to the shaft and emptied the cars into the storage hopper. This routine continued for several more trainloads before the shift was at an end. The tramming crew were at least chatty and talked about all kinds of things. Sometimes James was completely lost as they went off into Bemba, rather than ChiKabanga. However, it did pass the time.

At the shift end, James waited at the station with Jimmy for the cage.

"Well, *neefe,* enjoy your evening?" asked Jimmy.

"Yes, thank you," replied James. He had decided to play things really low-key and raise no fuss or issues.

"So, you learn anything?" Jimmy continued.

"Sure," replied James.

"Talkative, aren't you?" said Jimmy. "*Ag,* well, I suppose I can put up with you for two weeks."

"Thanks," said James.

Fortunately, the cage arrived right then, and they climbed aboard. James moved to the back of the cage and saw Tom there. Jimmy stayed towards the front and talked on and off to the on-setter. Tom asked James how his evening had gone. James was non-committal and indicated to Tom that they should wait until they were on the surface and away from Jimmy.

On top and after a shower, Tom and James left the mine together and drove to Tom's house. It was late, but Tom assured James that it was okay. Rita was up waiting and happy to see Tom.

"So how was the day?" she asked them both.

"Great," said Tom. "I learned lots and had a good time."

"How about you, James?" Rita asked.

"The section boss they put me with tried to date Katrina once, and she turned him down. So he was a load of fun."

"Sorry to hear that," said Tom. "How was your weekend?"

"Oh, great, thanks," said James.

"All right, what else are you not saying?" asked Rita.

"Nothing!" said James.

"It's written all over your face. Why don't I get you two a beer each, and you can think about your answer," said Rita.

"What does she mean?" asked Tom.

"How would I know?" said James.

Rita came back with the beers and asked James if he had anything else to say.

"Why do you ask?" asked Tom.

"Can't you tell?" Rita answered. "He has something he is not telling us, but I can guess it has to do with Katrina. You didn't ask her to marry you, did you?"

"No, we haven't got that far yet," replied James.

"Then what else?" she pressed. Then light dawned. "Ah, I know, you have gone to the next level!"

"What's that supposed to mean?" asked James.

"I think it means you are beyond holding hands and kissing," said Tom, grinning his stupid head off.

"Can I have another beer?" asked James, blushing furiously.

"I'm right! Look at him, torn between guilt and smugness," said Rita.

"Does this mean we can look forward to wedding bells sometime in the future?" asked Tom.

"Maybe, we'll see," replied James. "Look, I really must go as I'm sure Rita wants to get some sleep before work tomorrow."

"Okay, maybe I'll call on you for lunch tomorrow," said Tom. "Unless, of course, you have other plans with a certain young lady?"

"I don't know," said James. "I'll let you know."

"No, I think I will call Katrina myself and ask her to lunch," said Rita. "It will be interesting to see what she says about James."

The following day, James heard a car outside the house, and it was Tom coming to pick him up to go for lunch. Tom told James that Katrina and Rita had set a lunch date and were going to the Edinburgh.

"So, where shall we go?" asked James. "The Edinburgh to see what those two are up to, or somewhere else?"

"You know, we would probably be better off leaving well enough alone and trying somewhere else," replied Tom.

"Okay, what about the mine club in Kalulushi?" suggested James.

"Good plan," agreed Tom.

They drove off through town and made their way to Kalulushi, found the mine club, and sat down for lunch.

"Well?" asked Tom.

"Well, what?" countered James.

"How was it?" asked Tom again.

"You know, Tom, Katrina is just incredible," said James. "I can't imagine why she decided to go with me, but I thank whatever gods there are that she did."

"So, she was worth it, huh?" asked Tom, leering at him.

"Piss off, Tom," said James. "But, to give you some solace, she, it, was incredible!"

"I'm happy for you," said Tom. "I know you were making eyes at Rita before you met Katrina, so I'm happy for you and me. Now I won't have to beat you up!"

"I'm sorry, Tom," said James, a little crestfallen. "It's just that before I met Katrina, I was jealous of you and Rita."

"Well, let's hope for your sake and mine that you and Katrina make it together," said Tom. "Shall we go?"

When James reported for work that afternoon, Jimmy was a little more communicative and they went underground with Jimmy telling James the hows and whys of the tramming business. James wondered what had caused this change in heart and attitude, but could come up with no real answers. At the 2830 level, they spent some time at the station setting the work schedule for the shift and then Jimmy told James that they needed to go and check on the drawpoints. They were watching a crew pulling ore from one drawpoint when James saw three headlamps coming towards them. He nudged Jimmy and told him that they had company. It seemed that Jimmy had suspected that they might, as he had not pulled his chair out tonight and was taking an active role in the operation. As the lights came nearer, they saw Lamprecht and two others coming to join them.

"Ah, Jimmy, how goes it?" asked Lamprecht.

"Fine, we will make the production targets tonight," replied Jimmy.

"You know Harry Black, my boss. Do you know James Ross?" asked Lamprecht, basically ignoring Jimmy's response. "Mr. Ross is the Assistant Underground Manager in charge of all afternoon shift operations on the mine."

"So you are Jimmy van de Merwe, and you must be James Martin," said Ross.

"Yes, sir," replied Jimmy.

"Well, Jimmy, just make sure that the production targets we have are met!" said Ross.

Then he continued in a rising tone that sounded as if he was venting some severe frustration and anger;

"You people need to get your shit together and stop fucking around and meet the targets that I set. If you and Lamprecht can't handle it, maybe I should get some people down here who don't *waiya waiya* all the time! Black, Lamprecht, come, let's see if the rest of your sections are as big a fuck up as this one."

With that, they left to see another of the crews. James and Jimmy watched them go without saying anything for a while.

"Wow," said James. "What the hell was that all about?"

"*Ag* man, the fucking *does* must be looking for a promotion, so he wants his numbers to look good!" replied Jimmy.

"Yes, but does he think that is the best way to get results?" asked James.

"Think he cares?" asked Jimmy. "It's my job on the line, not his."

"Why don't I take the south stopes and help you out?" suggested James.

"Why would you do that?" asked Jimmy. "Look, I have never been able to make the tonnages they set!"

"His attitude just pissed me off!" said James. "He sounds like a real prick."

"Hey, *oukie,* you might be all right after all. Take the south stopes, you need to pull six trains of eight cars from the 1500 south stopes, can you manage that?" asked Jimmy.

"Okay, I'll give it a try, see you at the station later," replied James.

James left and quickly went back to the station and then off to the south haul road. He found the tramming crew and asked what they had done so far. He went with them to the drawpoints and started to load another train. There were a few problems, but they were handled quickly enough, and the crew took the load back to the shaft. The shift proceeded, and it was soon apparent that they would not make the target; there was just not enough time in the shift. It also seemed that there was a conflict between the north and south trains meeting at the station. At the end of the shift, James met Jimmy at the station and they compared notes. Jimmy had moved some ore from the north stopes, but the combination fell short of the target that Ross had referred to.

"Hell, man, that was only graft, hey?" Jimmy said. "What do I tell Lamprecht?"

"There is a problem, you know," said James.

"What?" answered Jimmy.

"I don't think we could make the targets, even if everything was perfect," said James. "I think the targets are set too high."

"*Sies*, man, you think that *ou* would do that?" asked Jimmy. "How do you know they are too high?"

"Well, I did some quick calculations and the numbers don't add up," replied James.

"Can you prove it and get my *gat* out of trouble?" asked Jimmy.

"I think so," said James. "Do you have any sets of dice that you can bring tomorrow?"

"Dice, what the hell do you want dice for?" asked Jimmy.

"An experiment, you'll see," replied James. "I want to be able to prove that the whole set-up does not work."

"Do you think that Bwalya has the same problems?" asked Jimmy.

"Here comes the cage, why don't we ask them now?" suggested James.

In the cage were Tom and Samson. They both looked as if they had had a bad day.

"What happened to you two?" asked James.

"Did that arse Ross come and shit all over you tonight?" Tom asked.

"*Ja*," said Jimmy. "Hey, Samson, *wena enzili zonke namusha?*"

"*Aikôna*," replied Samson. "*Lo muzungu kuluma fanika lo picinin.*"

"You know, I think that Ross suffers from short man's syndrome," added Tom.

"I think you're right," agreed James. "*Lo* short one *muzungu* Ross!"

"That's fine for you, but what do we tell Lamprecht?" asked Jimmy.

"Have you ever made any of these targets before?" asked James.

"No, why do you think I gave up trying? They have always been beyond me," replied Jimmy.

"Well, just tell him what the numbers are, let him rant and rave if he wants, and tomorrow we'll give him another story," suggested James.

As it turned out, they need not have been concerned because Lamprecht was having his own problems with Black and Ross, and they were only part of the bigger picture. James told Tom what he had in mind, and they agreed to meet in the morning at Tom's house to run through some simulations. The following day, James called Katrina, before she could call and tease him about lying in bed all day long, and told her about the evening. It seemed that Ross had a reputation for pushing all his people. Katrina laughed at Tom's comment about "short man's" syndrome and asked James if he was doing anything for lunch. He told Katrina that he was going to meet Tom, but that he would be sure to join her at one if that was convenient. Of course it was.

James went to Tom's house and they quickly set some rules for loading times, tramming times, unloading times, and the amounts by which each of those could vary. First, they calculated a theoretical maximum, assuming that all went perfectly each time and that there were no conflicts at the shaft. Then they used the dice that Tom had to introduce random variations at different times. That worked well for each train, but they had to make adjustments for the conflicts that two trains arriving at the same time would cause. The upshot of this effort was to prove that the targets were set beyond the theoretical capacity of the system and well above the likely practical experience. They tried adding cars to each train and found that adding one to each train got them closer to the target and that two cars per train put them over with some margin for random variations, assuming, of course, that the locomotives could handle the longer trains. They worked out how they would explain this to Jimmy and Samson, and then James had the brilliant idea of asking Katrina if they had a typewriter so that he could type it up to give to Jimmy.

James drove to the Englebrecht yard and found Koos and Katrina busy trying to sort out how to move several large pieces of mining equipment from the disbanded coal mine at Nkandabwe, near Sinazongwe in the south of the country, to Chingola.

"James, *hoe gaan dit?*" asked Koos.

"*Goed, dankie Meneer,*" replied James.

"I thought you weren't coming until one?" asked Katrina.

"Why do you want me to go away?" replied James. "Aren't you pleased to see me?"

"If you two are going to fight, I'm leaving," said Koos, who then got up and left the office and went off into the workshop. Katrina pulled James towards her and kissed him, and whispered in his ear.

"I knew you couldn't stay away for long. I just willed you to come. Did you feel the power pulling you?"

"Won't your dad come back?" asked James.

"Probably, just at the wrong moment, knowing him," said Katrina with a laugh. "How much longer is this afternoon shift stuff going to last?"

"Only a few more days, what are you doing Saturday lunchtime?" asked James.

"Rehearsals," replied Katrina. "But, what about we *maak 'n plan* for Sunday? Where would you like to go?"

"I don't know, you pick a place. I think I can rely on you, don't you?" suggested James.

"For you, anything, pick me up at ten, and I will have worked something out," replied Katrina.

"Now, for the other reason I came, do you have a typewriter I can use?" asked James.

"So that's the only reason you came to see me, to borrow a stupid typewriter?" teased Katrina.

"Of course! A typewriter doesn't have the distractions that you do," replied James.

"What distractions are those?" asked Katrina.

"Oh, I could think of a few things," replied James.

"Well, do your typing quickly and I'll try not to take your mind off things too much," said Katrina, brushing up against him and kissing him.

It was as well that Koos returned or James may never have finished what he wanted to get done before the shift started. He got paper and carbon paper and typed up his analysis, conclusions and suggestions, then he and Katrina went to one of the Indian stores and picked up an order of samosas that they sat and ate in a park. Katrina then told him about her lunch with Rita. It seemed that they had spent a fair amount of time on girl talk, and James wondered just how much Katrina had actually told her. He told her that he and Tom had been over to Kalulushi and had eaten there, not wanting to spy on the two girls.

After promising to call Katrina in the morning, James went to work and met up with Jimmy, Tom, and Samson. As they waited for the cage, he explained to Jimmy and Samson what he and Tom had done that morning and gave Jimmy two copies of the typed-up numbers they had come up with. Jimmy looked at it carefully and then said that the probable numbers that James and Tom had arrived at through their simulation matched almost exactly with his own experience. He pulled out his charts for the past few months and showed them. Jimmy had actually been doing better than the random numbers indicated was likely. Samson asked if they could do the same for him, and after getting tramming times for his section, Tom said he would have it done by the next day. Jimmy asked about the dice, and James explained how he had used dice to throw in random variation. Jimmy grasped the gambling aspect of it very quickly and then understood how it was done.

At the end of the shift, James suggested to Jimmy that he go off to see Lamprecht on his own and make his proposition for getting more cars allocated to his section. Jimmy agreed and gave Lamprecht the analysis, and was able to answer all his questions. Lamprecht wanted to know how Jimmy came up with this analysis, and Jimmy said that he had had help from James, not that James had done it all. They had discussed this before and agreed that this was the best approach with Lamprecht, as he was more likely to listen to Jimmy than to James. Lamprecht took some convincing but finally saw what the issue was and said that he would go off and see Black immediately. Black, unfortunately, was not around, but Lamprecht could now see a way to get Ross off his back and was not going to let it drop. He would get hold of Black right at the start of the shift the next day and make his request for more cars.

The balance of the week followed a routine pattern: up at about nine, a call to or from Katrina, perhaps lunch, then to work, and then back to bed late. It seemed that the analysis that James and Tom had done had stirred up a hornet's nest as they were visited by 'experts' from the planning department who wanted to do a 'proper' analysis of the tramming function. The experts were complaining bitterly about having to visit the sections in the evenings, as they normally only worked the usual day shift. As it transpired, the experts came up with no significant difference in numbers from the ones given to them. There was no longer discussion about targets, and in fact, they were given new targets, temporarily, until additional equipment could be obtained and assigned to the sections. James felt that he had finally contributed something and that all his learning had not actually been for nought. Jimmy was happier as the pressure was now off, and he also saw the value of discreetly questioning the numbers given and not just accepting them because they came from on high. Whether or not they had now made an enemy in Ross, only time would tell.

Saturday after work, James had a beer to celebrate Joy Mwamba's marriage. He sat outside the house on the *stoep* and watched the rain as it fell and poured off the roof. There was enough light from the street lamps to see how hard it was coming down without having too many of the house lights on. James found it very relaxing to sit and listen to the noise the rain made on the corrugated iron roof and almost tumbled out of his chair as he started to fall asleep.

Sunday, James picked Katrina up at ten, and she told him that she thought they might go to the Milomfwe Falls, a little south and west of Kalulushi. They drove out past Kalulushi, and then Katrina pointed out a dirt road to the south. They drove past the Saint Joseph's school for the deaf and on past Mushimba, then onto a side road until James had to stop and put the Land Rover into four-wheel drive and low range. The track had become really rutted and had large puddles. It was apparent that there had been no vehicles along this portion of the track in a while, as the ruts were old and the puddles were clear water with no mud.

On the edges of the puddles, there were swarms of butterflies that would take off in clouds as they drove near them. Occasionally, they could see animal tracks crossing the road and once they actually saw some buck racing away from them into the bush. It was quite tricky driving through it all, but they progressed and did not get stuck. Eventually, they came to where they could see the falls through the trees. James turned off the track and, with Katrina navigating, bundu bashed his way to the river and found a place to park. With the engine off, the noise from the falls was loud, almost drowning out the bird calls that they could hear. Looking around, James saw that there were large numbers of birds in the trees nearby, and there soon appeared the omnipresent guinea fowl and francolins. Soaring way above them, there were a number of vultures and eagles, and Katrina wondered what might be dead or dying near them. Certainly, the number of vultures seemed to be increasing, with James estimating at least fifty to seventy of them circling the sky above them.

Katrina had brought lunch; however, they both had other things on their minds before thinking about food.
"Do you think the water is safe to swim in?" asked James.
"*Ja*," replied Katrina. "It is not really croc habitat, the pools are too small for hippo, and the water is running too fast for bilharzia snails. We should be fine."
"Race you in!" said James, stripping off.
"You think so," said Katrina. She ran past him, shedding clothes as she went and jumped into the pool and swam towards the falls themselves. James quickly followed, swam up to her and pulled her under. With no swimsuits in the way, the swimming quickly turned to other things, and they made love in the water. James found that he could stand in the pool comfortably with his head above the water, so Katrina wrapped her legs around the small of his back, her arms around his neck and mounted him where he stood.

With the buoyancy provided by the water, James found that he did not have to support her much, so his hands were free to explore her body. And what a body! He had missed her the past week and was delighted to re-explore the body that he had been introduced to only a week ago. It seemed that the feeling was mutual because Katrina was obviously enjoying him as much as he was her. After the first passionate bout of lovemaking, they started again at a much slower pace and took their time to reach their climax. Katrina was whispering in his ear, but she suddenly stopped and looked intently towards the direction of the road. "There's somebody coming," she said.

"How do you know?" asked James.

"The birds are telling me," she replied. "Perhaps we should put some clothes on!"

"Okay, if you insist," said James. "How long before we see them?"

"About ten to fifteen minutes, I should think," said Katrina.

They swam to the edge of the pool, climbed out, and collected up their clothes strewn along the way back towards the Land Rover. They had time to get dressed before they could hear a car engine over the noise of the waterfall.

They watched the birds fly off, and a couple of bushbuck who had been hiding in the grass also ran off. The engine noise got louder, and soon another Land Rover came into view along the road. It ran past where they had turned in, stopped, reversed, and then came in along the tracks they had made getting to the river. Whoever it was then drew closer and finally stopped almost next to them. James was less than thrilled when he saw that it was Greg and Shirley Young.

"Oh great," he said. "It's that stupid bastard Greg, how the hell did he ever find this place?"

"I'm sure someone had to tell him how to get here," suggested Katrina.

"Hey, James," shouted Greg. "Fancy meeting you here. I was told by my section people on the mine that no one ever came here!"

"Well, I had inside information," replied James. "Katrina showed me the way."

"It looks as if Katrina has been showing you the way to a lot more than that," said Shirley, giggling.

"We were leaving, actually," said James. "Enjoy the water!"

"You don't think we are actually going to get into that water, do you?" asked Greg.

"Why not?" responded James.

"There's probably snakes, crocodiles, insects, and God knows what in there; you would have to be crazy to get into that pool!" commented Greg.

"You're probably right," said James. "It pays to be careful because who knows what you might pick up. See you!"

Katrina happened to be closest to the driver's seat, so she got in and started the engine. James climbed into the passenger side, and they took off.

"I hope you don't mind if we go?" said James.

"No, no, it's fine," said Katrina. "He's the *rooinek* who's *regte verkrampt*, isn't he?"

"He is indeed," replied James. "I'm sorry he had to come as it's rather upset things."

"No, no, that's fine," said Katrina. "I don't particularly like the *ou* and would just as soon spend the afternoon at home than with them."

"Are you sure?" James asked Katrina.

"Hell, man, of course I'm sure!" she replied.

They were part of the way back when they came across another vehicle stuck in one of the puddles. A local Zambian farmer had been trying to wade his overloaded vanette through a large puddle and had obviously had problems, stalled, and was now stuck. Katrina pulled up close to the puddle and asked the farmer if he needed a tow.

"Please, yes, madam," was the reply.

"Okay, James, do your stuff," ordered Katrina.

"What?" asked James.

"Take the cable of the winch, pay it out and hitch it to the vanette," she said. "But first, let me reverse a little onto more solid ground."

James waited a minute or so until she had put their Land Rover where she wanted it, and then James unhooked the cable and waded out into the pool to the vanette. He felt around under the front until he found a suitable hitch point, then hooked on the cable and walked back to the Land Rover.

"Okay, *madala, tina azi donsa ena manje manje so*," said Katrina. She revved the engine, and James pulled the lever that started the winch. The vanette came out of the puddle easily enough, and once on dry land, James shut off the winch, disconnected the cable, then wound it back. Katrina shut off the engine, then asked the farmer to open the bonnet. Everything was wet, including all the electrics. Katrina asked James for some cloth, and then she set about drying off all the important components. She had obviously done this sort of thing before, because when she told the farmer to try and start the engine, it fired immediately.

"*Okay, madala, zonke ena mushle manje,*" Katrina wished him well as he prepared to start out on his way again.

"Very much, madam," he kept saying.

"What does he mean?" asked James in a whispered aside.

"He has heard the *muzungu* use the term "thank you very much" and is just using as much of it as he remembers," replied Katrina. "*Ena mushle madala. Munya skati aikôna hamba checha na lo manzi, hamba poli poli! Ena kona munya manzi lapa side,*" she added, pointing down the road. "*Hamba gahle!*"

"You know you really are the most amazing girl I have ever met," said James. "Is there anything you can't do?"

"Of course, idiot!" replied Katrina. "I don't speak French, I don't really know how to cook, I can't do the job you do; shall I go on?"

"Okay, okay, I surrender!" said James. "Now that we've stopped, shall we have some of that lunch?"

After lunch, they drove back to the farm. They made it inside the front door, and then it rained. James was amazed again at how hard it could rain and how much noise it made on the roof. As they were into the rains by a few weeks now, there was not the same smell of damp soil and dust that was obvious at the first rains. They found that the rest of the family was out somewhere, and in the kitchen, Katrina came across a note telling her that they had gone to Ndola for the day and would be back much later.

"Come with me!" said Katrina.

"Where are we going?" asked James.

"To my *boudoir*, silly!" said Katrina.

"I thought you didn't speak French?" said James.

"I know "*voulez vous coucher avec moi ce soir?*"," said Katrina.

"I wasn't actually thinking of doing any sleeping just at the moment!" said James.

"Oh, weren't you? What do you have in mind?" asked Katrina.

James whispered in her ear, and she looked at him and nodded. Then Katrina took James by the hand and led him through the house to her bedroom. It was a beautiful room with large windows that overlooked fields that sloped down to the river. James looked out of the window and could see no other houses or buildings. Katrina told him that the rest of the farm buildings were off on one side and that there was no one on the other side of the river. As there were no obvious curtains, James was pleased that they would not be spied upon. He mentioned it to Katrina, and she told him that there were, in fact, curtains, but that they pulled back into closable alcoves when not in use. Katrina had a large bed and there was also a wardrobe in the room together with a chest of drawers, a small table and chair, and a box that she referred to as a kist. James put his arms around her and kissed her. Katrina responded passionately and started working on undoing his clothes. It was only a short time before they were on the bed, limbs entwined and making love.

Later, when they lay spent from their exertions, James suggested a bath. Katrina said that that sounded like a great idea, so he got up, picked her up, and asked her to direct him to the appropriate room. He managed to avoid hitting her feet and head on the wall and door jambs too many times before getting her into the bathroom. Once there, Katrina ran a bath and they climbed in together. Bathing together was a new experience; it was not like swimming in the pool by the waterfall or standing in the rain. They had hot water and a confined space, which meant that they had to fit their legs around each other, and they had to be close.

"You need a bigger bath!" laughed James.

"Why? This way you can't be too far away and I don't have to reach to get hold of you," said Katrina.

They took turns soaping each other down, and the slipperiness of the soap, particularly when applied between the legs, led to more lovemaking. They managed to avoid splashing too much water on the floor and found all new ways to enjoy each other.

After drying each other and then cleaning up the floor, they dressed, and Katrina asked James if he wanted coffee. They were seated in the kitchen drinking their coffee when they heard a car in the driveway and saw Katrina's parents coming home. James wondered how guilty he looked and then began to think about what Katrina would tell her mother. They greeted her parents as they came into the house and then exchanged details of each other's trips. James excused himself to return to Kitwe. Katrina saw him off and told him that lunch was out the next day as she had business to conduct in Chingola and would be gone the best part of the day. James kissed her goodnight and left for home.

Monday lunchtime, James went to Tom and Rita's house. Tom was working in the garden and was happy to take a break.
"*Howzit,* James?" Tom asked.
"Fine, Tom, what are you doing?" responded James.
"Removing these bushes so that I can plant some different ones," replied Tom. "What have you been up to?"
"I went out to some waterfalls with Katrina yesterday," answered James. "Saw that arsehole Greg and then towed some poor old farmer out of a huge puddle of water!"
"So, how are things with the incomparable Katrina?" asked Tom.
"Great, how about you and Rita?" said James.
"You know that everything is great between us," answered Tom. "Did you have lunch yet?"
"No, that's why I came over. Katrina is gone all day, and I wondered what you were doing?" said James.
"Well, Rita is busy, so why don't we get something from the house and go find a tree somewhere to sit under," suggested Tom.

Later that afternoon, they both reported for work and joined the crowd getting into the cage. Jimmy was happier because he had had a good weekend and because he now had production targets that were at least viable. Samson Bwalya was also there, and he seemed happier with life. They were surprised when Greg got into the cage. James had not been aware that he was working in this particular area of the mine. James, Jimmy, Tom, and Samson spent a few minutes talking about their tramming targets, then the conversation turned to more mundane matters.

"*Ini wena enzili isolo?*" Samson asked James.

"Yesterday, he was out in the bush fucking his fancy woman, Katrina," interposed Greg loudly.

"*Ena so?*" asked Samson, looking at James.

"*Lo aikôna lo indaba ka lo Greg,*" said James, trying to hide his confusion over this public announcement about what Greg assumed he had been doing. He found it difficult to outright deny it but yet he was embarrassed to admit it.

"Who is this *does?*" Jimmy asked James.

"This is Greg Young," replied James.

"Hey Greg, *jy soek moeilikheid?*" demanded Jimmy, putting himself directly in front of Greg, in what could only be described as a threatening manner.

"What?" asked Greg.

"Fucking VC tenner," said Jimmy. "Leave my *boetie* alone, hey!"

"What's this, James, can't fight your own battles?" asked Greg.

"Listen, arsehole," said Jimmy. "I'm just saving him the trouble of having to *donner* you!"

"Forget him, Jimmy," said James. "He is just a sad case and enjoys stirring the shit."

Fortunately for all concerned, they reached the station where Jimmy and James were to get off, so the conversation was suspended, at least for now. Jimmy was muttering about Greg for some time, and James was a little surprised at Jimmy's reaction. He tried to understand why Jimmy had sprung to his defence and learned that although Jimmy had once been turned down by Katrina, he had a fierce loyalty to anyone of Afrikaans extraction and did not really appreciate negative comments from what he saw as an interloper. Added to that was the fact that James had, from Jimmy's point of view, gone out of his way to help him in his job.

They got down to the business of tramming ore and waste from the different drawpoints to the shaft. As they had done the previous week, they divided the work; James took the north side and Jimmy the south. James had seen two train loads to the shaft when one of the crew came to find him. It seemed that several of the cars had jumped the tracks, and they needed to re-rail them all. This was a job James had not seen done before, but the course of action seemed fairly straightforward. They had a couple of jacks on the locomotive, which they used to re-rail each car in turn. Then they took a look at the track itself and could see the problem. Several of the bolts that held a fishplate in place at a rail joint had come out. This opened up a gap in the rail, and the trucks had come off. James told the crew to get some spanners, and they put the bolts back, installed the nuts, and tightened everything up. Then James and one of the others went ahead of the train, tapping at the bolts on each of the joints. There were several others that needed tightening, and they fixed those.

James told the crew to go back to tramming, then he quickly went back to the site of the derailment and walked back to the shaft, checking the rail joints as he went. He came across a few more problems, which he fixed and went on to find Jimmy. He told Jimmy what they had found and what the problem had been. It seemed that there was a continuing issue of who was responsible for the track maintenance. The track-laying crews claimed that they were only required to lay the track, not to maintain it. The tramming crews said that they were there to transport material, not fix the lines. James commented to Jimmy that it would probably serve them well to quickly walk the tracks each day before tramming started in earnest in order to detect problems early. Tightening loose bolts took a lot less time than re-railing cars. Jimmy agreed with James and gave instructions to his crews to check the lines before starting work. Even with the delays caused by the derailments, they managed to meet their new targets and were happy with the night's work.

Tuesday, he called Katrina and discovered that she was leaving for Nkandabwe, which was close to Lake Kariba, a long way to the south, with a group of trucks to move some equipment to the Copperbelt. James recalled that he had heard Katrina and Koos discussing the job earlier. It seemed that Katrina was in charge of the move and was escorting six low-loaders south in order to pick up the loads. The job was going to take until the following Sunday, so Katrina was concerned about missing rehearsals for her Christmas show. It was likely that she would not be back until late Sunday, so they planned no date for the upcoming weekend. James went off to work and was decidedly moody for the whole shift. Jimmy asked him a couple of times what the problem was, but James did not feel like elaborating.

By the end of the week, James had cheered up somewhat and was looking forward to talking to Katrina on Monday. He said goodbye to Jimmy on Saturday night and learned from Lamprecht that he would be switching to a lashing crew for the week. Jimmy also learned that Greg would be joining him for the next two weeks. That didn't sit too well with Jimmy, who was not impressed with Greg. However, there was no choice in the matter, and Jimmy was stuck with him. As he left the mine, James ran into Tom, who had also been reassigned. He asked what he and Rita were doing on Sunday, and Tom told him that they were taking a trip to Broken Hill for the day. Tom knew someone who worked there, and they were going to visit him.

Sunday, James found himself at rather a loose end, so he drove out to the dam and went to the boat club. He got himself a beer, went outside, sat under a chitenge, looked out at the dam, and wondered what the love of his life was doing at that moment. His reverie was interrupted by Koos, who came to see what he was doing.
"James, *hoe gaan dit* man?" asked Koos.
"Hello, sir, fine thanks," replied James.
"You miss her, hey?" continued Koos, looking at James and seeing right through him.
"Desperately," said James. "I never thought that one person could mean so much."
"*Ja*, it is the same with Sussana and me," remarked Koos, commiserating.
"Do you think she will be back today?" asked James.
"*Ja*, she called from Broken Hill and will be in the yard by six tonight," replied Koos.

"Maybe I will come and see you at lunchtime tomorrow?" suggested James.

"*Ja,* that would be good," said Koos. "So, what are you two going to do? Do you have any plans for the future?"

"If I were to ask her to marry me, would you approve?" asked James.

"Would it matter to you if I said yes or no?" asked Koos.

"Yes, sir, it would matter. I would like to think that if I were to marry Katrina, then I would have your blessing," said James.

"And if I were to say no?" asked Koos.

"Then I would have a problem," replied James. "I would be torn between looking for your blessing and planning how to elope with Katrina."

"Well, that would not be good, would it now?" said Koos. "James, you need to ask Katrina before she drives us all out of the house."

"Why, what do you mean?" asked James.

"She, what is the English, mopes around the house when you are not there and yells at us," said Koos.

"Really?" asked James. "She doesn't really yell at you, does she?"

"Not quite, but you'd better ask her soon!" said Koos. "I know what you should do; come to lunch on Christmas Day and make your proposal."

"Why would that be a good day?" asked James.

"I proposed to Katrina's mother on Christmas Day; it is a good day," assured Koos.

"You don't mind the fact that I'm English and will almost certainly leave here one day?" asked James.

"*Ag* man," replied Koos. "I said before that it does not matter. What matters is if Katrina is happy."

"How did you come to be in Zambia?" asked James.

"I was looking for a better job," replied Koos. "I had a job on the mines in the Union, but there were better opportunities in Northern Rhodesia."

"Was it difficult to leave all your family?" continued James.

"No, we were all going to different places back then," answered Koos. "It was probably better for Katrina that we moved here."

"Why?" asked James.

196

"Well, her great-grandmother on my father's father's side was black, and so was her great-grandmother on her mother's father's side, so there was always the chance that she would not pass the pencil test in the Union," elaborated Koos.

"The pencil test, what's that?" asked James.

"It's when the *verdomde* authorities check to see what classification you should be in," replied Koos.

"What do you mean, classification?" asked James.

"Man, whether you are *blankes*, *nie blankes*, or coloured," replied Koos.

"How do they do that?" asked James.

"Among other tests, the story goes that they put a pencil in your hair and see whether it falls out. If your hair is short and tightly curled, it stays, and you are *nie blankes*, non-white," said Koos.

"How does that affect you?" asked James.

"It changes where you can live, work, and even marry!" replied Koos. "Bloody stupid *verdomde* rules that the Nationalists keep pushing."

James thought about this for a while and tried to imagine the upheavals in a family that that would cause. He just could not picture how any government could behave in such a way, but he was beginning to get some insight into the attitudes of people down South.

"Her ancestors, is that why she is so tanned all the time?" asked James.

"*Ja*," replied Koos. "You should see her if she gets in the sun and the ocean for too long. Her hair goes frizzy and she gets dark, dark, really like a Cape Coloured."

"Does she know?" pressed James.

"*Ja*, but she keeps it to herself. Boarding school in the Union would have been impossible for her if the other lighties found out," replied Koos. "Even though most of them probably have similar histories."

James asked Koos more questions about his family and learned much about the peculiarities of the South African system. He also learned more about the brother that Koos had in South West Africa and the sister that Katrina's mother had in the Northern Cape. The family was not very close, and they rarely saw one another. Although Koos did say that when they did get together, it was as though they had never been apart. Their conversation was then interrupted by one of the club

197

waiters, who came to tell Koos that there was a phone call for him at the clubhouse.

Koos came back with Sussana and told James that it was Katrina calling from Kapiri Mposhi to say that one of the low-loaders had blown a couple of tyres and that they were fixing the problem, but that she would be about an hour later than her original estimate. James asked Koos if he thought everything would be alright. He was concerned that she would run into more problems. Koos assured him that it would be fine and that the crews of all the low-loaders looked upon her as a kind of talisman and would ensure nothing happened to her. James asked if she had led such trips before. Koos thought for a while and came up with five other major jobs that she had organised and led. He had every confidence in her, but he did admit privately that he wished she were not so determined to be independent and give him more grey hairs each year. Sussana told James that there were nights when she didn't sleep at all because she was worried about where Katrina might be. She added that she was almost as concerned about James and his friends, who went down the mine every day.

At about a quarter to seven, just as the sun was setting, James left the boat club with Koos and Sussana and drove to the company yard to await Katrina and her convoy. She arrived pretty much as she had predicted and rolled in just after seven. There was just enough room in the yard to accommodate all the low-loaders and the equipment perched on top of them. It struck James that most of the loads overhung the trailers by a fair amount, and he wondered how they had managed on the road. Katrina pulled her Land Cruiser into a space by the office and got out to greet her parents and James. Even in overalls, Katrina looked good to James, and he was happy to see her. She said hello quickly, then turned to the task of checking in each of the loads and sending the drivers off to their homes. The final delivery would take place later in the week. Katrina was delighted to see everyone, including James, but all she really wanted was to go home, shower, and sleep. James promised to call her the next day and left her in the care of her parents.

# Katrina's show & a Blasting Licence

Monday dawned, and James realised that it was already the 1st of December. Time was actually going fairly fast. The new week meant the start of the assignment to the afternoon shift lashing gang that Lamprecht had told him about on Saturday. He called to talk to Katrina, but learned that she had gone to Chingola to arrange the delivery of the transported equipment. So James whiled away the day, then reported for work and met up with George Kachepa, the section boss he had been assigned to. Their first task was to review the shift log books to see what ends had been blasted and therefore needed cleaning. George made a list of the work to be done, and they then headed off to the cage to go underground.

While waiting for the cage, James was surprised to hear that all George wanted to do was ask him about Greg. It seemed that Greg had been particularly critical of the way that George ran his section. James got the impression that George was checking to see if he would also criticise or if he would accept things more as they were. James had learned enough from the other section bosses to realise that they were generally a lot smarter than they were given credit for. He also realised that the section bosses were comparing notes on the trainees and their attitudes towards them were largely based on the reports they were receiving. Apparently, James had not alienated too many as George was prepared to talk to him and even discuss Greg, so he had to be aware that there was no love lost between himself and Greg.

James went with George to the operating section, and George set about detailing his crews off to particular development ends where there was work to be done, as James had cleaned one of these ends with Isaac some time before he knew what the job entailed and had some sympathy for these young men. James went with George to each of the working areas to check on them. They ensured that there were no misfires and washed down each pile of broken rock before the crews started shovelling them out using short-handled steel shovels and wheelbarrows.

James wondered if there wasn't a mechanised system that could be used like the one he had seen in the big end development or like the one he had seen in Ireland the previous year, but then realised that there were just too many of the development ends to equip each one with the mechanical means of cleaning them out. He also realised that the disposal of the waste would be a problem with mechanical scrapers (generally known in the business as slushers). Where would they pull the waste to? The layout of the operation was such that it did not really lend itself to that type of mechanisation. Using rocker shovels, as they had in the big end development, was also not an option, as what would they empty the buckets into? James began to recognise that he perhaps did not know as much as he thought.

James settled into a pattern of work for the week. On Tuesday and Wednesday, he lunched with Katrina and learned more about the trip she had taken to Nkandabwe. Apparently, things had not been as organised as they should have been, and it had taken some ingenuity on her part to load all the equipment and get it tied down for the trip. James asked her how they managed with the overhang that was obvious on most of the equipment, and she coyly asked if he did not remember a welding truck that was part of her convoy. Apparently, she had cut the railings off some of the smaller bridges and then welded them back up after everything was over.

James was curious to learn if any part of the officialdom of Zambia was aware of this and how they reacted. Not to worry, he was told. Of course, they knew; it just took the right kind of facilitation. By that, James inferred bribe. He wondered how much and was relieved to know that it was usually as little as a packet of cigarettes, some vegetables, or some petrol for the police Land Rovers. He had not pictured Katrina as someone who would negotiate with the local police and get things organised, but realised that, of course, she had to be able to do this, as she had been successful in the past in managing similar situations.

Thursday night at work was made more interesting because half the round had not detonated, and they had to pump out all the misfires before the crew could go to work. They connected a water hose to a long copper pipe and started working the pipe into the holes that had not fired. The ANFO came out fairly readily, and eventually, with the water coming out of the hole were lumps of the initiator explosive and the fuse. It took a little time, but they managed to clean all the holes and washed everything down with copious quantities of water. James wondered what the risk was of flushing the remnants of the explosive into the drains and thence to the pumps to be pumped to the surface with all the other water that accumulated in the mine. He consoled himself with the notion that it was sufficiently dilute as to pose no immediate hazard, but did wonder if they were eventually going to poison their own water supplies with all the chemicals they were flushing away.

The work was messy and wet. No matter how they tried to avoid the return water, it was impossible not to get soaked. James learned quickly to stand away from the airways until his clothes dried a little, as he began to get chilled from the evaporation. After the lashing crew cleaned the end, James took a look and tried to work out why the blast had not gone as planned. He decided that, without having seen the tie-up of the fuses to the igniter cord that it was impossible to tell. There was nothing wrong with the spacing and angle of the holes. It was one of those mysteries to which he would not learn the answer for some time to come.

Saturday, James met Katrina in the morning to ask for her help in choosing Christmas cards to send back to England. He drove out to the farm and arrived just as the heavens opened. He saw Katrina on the *stoep* and she waved to him. James looked around for the usual horde of dogs but did not see any. Ignoring the rain, James left the shelter of his vehicle, and just the quick dash from the car to the *stoep* was enough to get him soaked.
"Why didn't you wait a few minutes?" asked Katrina.
"I thought you were waving for me to come in," replied James, gathering her up in an embrace and kissing her.
"*Ag* man, you are only wet," said Katrina, pushing him away. "Now you are getting me wet too!"
"Where is the menagerie?" asked James.

"Oh, they are all in the barn with Pops. He is dosing them all for worms," Katrina answered.

"So, would you come into Kitwe with me and help me buy some Christmas cards?" James asked.

"If you need me to," replied Katrina. "What and how many are you looking for?"

"I worked it out the other day," said James. "I counted up fifteen that I probably need to really send, so I guessed on weight and bought some stamps already. As for what, are there Zambian-looking cards, or are they all more typical of cards we would get in England?"

"Why don't we go and have a look?" Katrina replied. "I'm ready, *kom ons ry!*"

They drove into Kitwe and found cards. It took a little while to select those that James thought might be suitable. He was a little disappointed that there were very few that he would consider of a more Zambian theme. It seemed that Christmas card themes were an export, even though almost no one locally would ever be able to relate to snow, robins, and sleighs. With cards in hand, James then had the task of writing in each of them and addressing the envelopes. He and Katrina found a coffee shop and started on the task. Katrina offered to help by putting stamps on the envelopes and addressing them, which James thought would be a great idea, particularly as it would confuse the recipients, as the handwriting would be unfamiliar. James was a little lost as to what to say and generally limited himself to simple good wishes for the New Year. Katrina just shook her head and asked him if he ever actually talked to any of those he was sending cards to.

They were both busy with their respective tasks when James heard himself addressed by someone who had come up to the table. He looked up and saw that it was Joy Mwamba with, James assumed, his new wife, Suzie.

"Hello, Joy, how goes it?" asked James.

"Good, let me introduce you to my new wife, Suzie. Suzie, meet James Martin," said Joy.

"I'm pleased to meet you," she said. "Good morning, Missy Englebrecht," she added.

"Good morning, Miss Mwewa. Oh, I'm sorry, it's Mrs now. Please introduce me to your husband," replied Katrina.

"This is my husband, Joy Mwamba," she said proudly. She turned to Joy and told him that she knew Missy Englebrecht from the bank. It seemed that the Englebrechts had their business accounts at the bank at which she worked. So Katrina saw her regularly and had heard that she had taken time off to get married. At the time, she had had no idea who Suzie was getting married to; now she knew.

"Would you care to join us for coffee?" asked Katrina.

"No, thank you," replied Joy. "We are just off to ZCBC to look at some things for the house, and we just happened to see you here and thought we should say hello."

"Well, thanks, Joy," said James. "Just make sure that he buys what you want, Suzie, and not something he would be happy with in his single quarters!"

Suzie laughed and dragged Joy off to look at household furnishings. After the two newlyweds had gone, James and Katrina returned to the job at hand. With cards signed and messages complete, James checked to see that the right card was put into the right envelope, and they then left the coffee shop, went to the post office, and mailed them all.

"What now?" asked James.

"Well, how long before you have to go to work?"

"About three hours," replied James.

"Why don't we get some sandwiches and go down to the river and watch crocs for a while?" suggested Katrina.

"Sounds like a plan," agreed James.

Sandwiches in hand, they drove to Central Street and followed it all the way to the end, where it met the Kafue River. There were a few other people there, some of whose children were splashing around in the river. Katrina looked at them and remarked to James that they had no idea of the risk they were taking. James asked why because he saw no crocodiles. Katrina told him that it was a river and that rivers in Zambia had crocodiles, always! Then she looked at the river and pointed out the crocodiles to James. At first, he could hardly see what she was indicating, but finally he caught on and began to see how many there were and where they were skulking in the river. All that was showing were nostrils and eyes.

Katrina told James that the crocs could move much faster than most people thought and that they regularly took dogs and other animals along the riverbank. Finally, she couldn't stand it any longer, and she got out of the car and went over to the people with the children. She asked them if they were aware that there were crocs in the river, and was roundly told to mind her own business. "We have been coming here for months and have never seen a crocodile!" was the comment. Katrina shrugged and told them that they were being short-sighted and foolish, but not to say that they had not been warned. She left them with the comment that she could see eight crocodiles from where she stood at that very moment, not that the newcomers took any notice; they just dismissed her as a scaremonger.

When it was getting time for James to go to work, Katrina suggested that she drop him off. She said that she would then go to her rehearsal and then pick him up afterwards. James was concerned that she would be waiting around for a long time, but was assured that after practice, if there was time, she would go home and then drive back into town to collect him. James pressed to be sure that this was acceptable to her and then agreed. Katrina drove him to his house, and there James packed some dinner for himself and a flask of coffee. She dropped him off at the mine with the promise to pick him up at the end of the shift.

George had seen James being dropped off and was full of questions as to the identity of his chauffeuse. It seemed to James that they spent less time that night supervising the crew and more time discussing the necessity of ensuring that a potential bride was capable of bearing children and the outrageous state of *lobola* amounts that prevailed. George had recently taken a wife and was still smarting over the *lobola* amount that he had had to pay. He was curious to know if the Europeans paid *lobola*, and if not, how the marriages were arranged or contracted. James found that it was actually a little difficult to explain, given the culture of Zambia and the accepted practice of *lobola*.

The shift end came soon enough, and James, freshly showered, waited for Katrina to collect him. He did not have long to wait before Katrina pulled up in his Land Rover. She had obviously been home and changed since James last saw her, as she was wearing a short skirt and a loose top. James asked her how the rehearsal had gone, and she told him that they were as ready as they were going to be; it was now just a question of finishing the costumes. Katrina motioned for him to get in the passenger seat, and then she drove off towards Central Street.

"Where are we off to?" asked James.

"To your house, of course," replied Katrina.

"Don't you want me to drive you home?" continued James.

"I thought I would spend the night with you," said Katrina.

"Really, do you know where the van de Merwe's house is?" asked James.

"Yes, I have lived here most of my life, you know," Katrina replied.

"What about clothes and stuff, what about your folks?" was James's next question.

"Man, you only have *meningi* questions," Katrina commented; then she went on to say. "I have everything I need in a bag behind you, and don't you think I'm old enough to stay out all night if I wish?"

"Oh," was all James could really find to say.

When they arrived at the house, Silent was still up, and he opened the gate for them and closed it after them. When he saw Katrina get out of the car, his face broke into a huge grin. He was still grinning when James opened the door and ushered Katrina into the house. James wished him good night and then had the sinking feeling that news of his overnight guest would be all over the neighbourhood by the following morning.

"Breakfast tomorrow, Bwana?" Silent asked.

"No, it's okay, Silent," replied James.

"Bwana, but the madam, *munya skati yena funa lo skofu kusasa*," insisted Silent.

"Okay, okay, at nine then," said James, wondering if Katrina really would appreciate being referred to as the madam.

"Sure, sure, Bwana, nine," repeated Silent, apparently happy that now he could keep an eye on proceedings.

James said goodnight to Silent then went into the house and locked up for the night. Inside, Katrina was laughing at him and his confusion. She assured him that Silent's behaviour was quite typical of house servants and was only partly driven by curiosity; he also felt deeply responsible for the running of the household and that any guest should be properly taken care of. It would embarrass him deeply if the other houseboys heard that he had not taken care of the house-guest.

"Where do you sleep?" asked Katrina.

"Through here," said James, indicating the way.

"Do you want to bathe before we go to bed?" asked Katrina.

"Good idea," replied James, even though he had showered at the mine less than thirty minutes before. He took Katrina's bag, put it on the bed and then led her to the bathroom. While he ran a bath, Katrina went back to the bedroom and got stuff from her bag. When she came back, she kissed James and then started taking his clothes off. James undid Katrina's skirt and then, with her help, removed her top. Underclothes quickly followed, and he lifted her into the bath, into which he also climbed. It was larger than the bath at the Englebrecht's house, so it provided more room for the two of them. As he soaped Katrina, James asked her about her day. She told him about the rehearsal, the aches and pains that followed and the frustrations of trying to sew the costumes that they had to wear. Then she asked him about his evening, and he told her of his conversation with George about the rising costs of *lobola*. She sympathised and then asked James how much he planned to pay her father for her. James told her that he was not sure that he would ask her father if he wanted *lobola* for her, and if he did, then even ten ngwee was too much, as she was so much trouble.

What naturally followed, James felt he would remember the rest of his life. The lovemaking in the bath and then again in bed, the nearness of Katrina as he went to sleep, the joy of waking up in the middle of the night to find her next to him. They seemed to fit so well together in the bed, his body moulded against hers. Neither of them wore nightclothes, neither pyjamas nor nighties, so the bodily contact was complete, if a little warm at times. In the morning, when he awoke, he was delighted that she was still there and had not evaporated in the night, so it had not all been a wonderful dream. After an early morning bout of lovemaking, Katrina got up and bathed while James lay contemplating his good fortune and what a wonderful day it was.

When Katrina had dressed and gone into the kitchen, James got up and quickly bathed. As he went into the kitchen, he heard Katrina and Silent engaged in conversation, and then he noticed that there were no settings at the kitchen table. Silent ushered them both into the dining room, where the table had been set, and apparently, all that he was waiting for was for them both to show their faces. Tea or coffee was offered, and then breakfast appeared. James was not sure he could face cereal, a cooked breakfast and then toast, but it had all been prepared, so he dug in and enjoyed the treat.

After breakfast, James asked Katrina if she had any plans for the day. It had started to rain outside, and it looked as if it had set in for the rest of the day. Katrina watched the rain for a while, then suggested to James that, as it looked as though all other options would be rained out, they go to the dam and the boat club and watch the rain in comfort. She rose from the table and went to the bedroom to collect her belongings. James thanked Silent for the breakfast and told him that he would be back later that evening, alone. They left with James driving and made their way, in the rain, through the town towards the dam. Once, James stopped the Land Rover and pulled over to the side of the road as it was raining so hard that he could not actually see beyond the end of the bonnet. They had to wait for about fifteen minutes until the rain subsided enough to proceed. They also discovered that there were leaks in the roof of the Land Rover. The rain caused the culverts to fill rapidly, and in places the road was awash with water as the culverts could not take all the run-off. Overall, the journey to the dam took about twice as long as it would have done on a dry day. At the dam, they sat in the Land Rover and waited for a lull in the rain. The rain was coming down hard enough that they sat for about thirty minutes before there was a lull, and they felt they could make it to the clubhouse without getting soaked.

Inside the clubhouse, they were greeted by the few people already there; most had decided to stay at home because of the bad weather. Katrina saw her parents, and they went over to say hello.

"James *hoe gaan dit?*" asked Koos.

"*Goed, dankie,*" replied James. Yes, he felt good, but here he was exchanging greetings with the man whose daughter he had just spent the night with. It was a little embarrassing. He knew that Koos knew where Katrina had been, and he had to be amazingly naïve to assume they had done anything else but sleep together. However, Koos seemed genuinely pleased to see James and even mentioned to him in an aside that he hoped that they would see him on Christmas Day with a suitable question. James assured him that he would be there and, yes, he probably would be popping the question. James stayed for a while, then excused himself and went home to get some rest.

Monday afternoon, James was back at work with George. He had called Katrina in the morning, but she was out of the office on a job somewhere near Luanshya and not expected back until late. Katrina had been back to practise on Sunday night and had previously told James that they were now in the final stages of rehearsal and would be ready for the performance the following week.

The balance of the week went quickly enough. James got up late each day as Katrina was busy in Luanshya for most of the week, so lunch was out. He went each night to join George in checking on the lashing crews. At the end of the week, he was told that on the following Monday that he was to report back to the Training School for the next two weeks to brush up on the laws regarding explosives so that he could take the test for his blasting licence. He had enjoyed his time with George. George liked to wax philosophical about the *lobola* amounts that were expected at the time. He also had schemes to start a transportation business and would run calculations on the backs of the report forms that they used to show how well he would do when he left the mine.

He had asked James many questions about how to borrow money, how much interest he could expect to pay, and how much he would have to charge for each transportation job in order to make it pay. James had sidestepped most of the questions and had referred George to Suzie Mwamba for professional advice. He had shown George how to set up the interest and loan calculations so that he could work out how big a lorry he could afford. All in all, it had been a fascinating insight into the ambitions and dreams of another, one whom at first sight he had been ready to dismiss as a simple first-line supervisor.

James found himself at a loose end on Sunday. Katrina had taken a low loader to Bancroft on an emergency job and was not expected back until later, and then she had another rehearsal. It was raining early in the morning, and after it stopped, he drove to the Morrison's house to see if Tom and Rita were busy. As he pulled up, he saw them both digging in the garden. They stopped long enough to tell him to get a shovel and help them clean out the drains. The rain had come down hard enough to block the drainage to the back of the house, and their vegetable patches were underwater. James found a shovel among the garden tools strewn nearby and dug as he was directed. With two digging and one directing, they were able to finally open up a diversion and get the water to drain off into the sanitary lane that ran behind the row of houses. When the water had finally drained away, Rita asked James in for coffee.

"No date today?" she asked James. "We hardly seem to see you these days," she continued.
"No, Katrina is in Bancroft today doing something for work," replied James.
"Well, when are you going to pop the question?" Rita asked.
"Maybe sooner than you think," replied James. "But what do I do about an engagement ring?"
"Oh, we have got that far, have we?" asked Rita. "Have you even hinted to Katrina that this might be coming?"
"Not really," said James. "I'm sure she knows, but we haven't actually talked about it yet."
"Okay, so when do you actually plan to ask her?" continued Rita.
"Well, her father suggested lunch on Christmas Day at their house," said James.

"Oh, so you have talked about it with her father," said Rita. "Are you sure that's a good idea, talking to him and not to Katrina?"

"Well, he brought the subject up by asking when I was going to propose," said James.

"Okay. What kind of ring did you have in mind?" asked Rita.

"Right, the ring," replied James. "That's why I'm asking, I don't know what kind of stone she might like and even what size the ring would have to be to fit."

"Do you know what kind of stones she likes?" asked Rita.

"I know that she isn't too fussy, as she doesn't wear too much jewellery," replied James. "But, she did mention once that she likes emeralds."

"Whatever you do, don't buy any diamonds from the Congo guys," interrupted Tom.

"What do you mean?" asked James.

"Well, there are people here who come from the Congo, and they say they have diamonds to sell," answered Tom. "But, I think you would have to be really careful that the diamonds were real and that they weren't with the Zambian Special Branch and just waiting to lock you up."

"Really? I didn't know that sort of thing went on," said James.

"Yes, I learned about it from one of the section bosses I was placed with," said Tom. "They steal the diamonds from the Congolese mines and then sell them across the border here. It's either them or the guys from Tanzania selling the Williamson diamonds."

"Okay, then, where do I get a ring?" asked James.

"There are jewellers in Kitwe," said Rita. "You could try one of them and see what they have to offer."

"What about the size of the ring itself?" asked James.

"Any reputable jeweller would be able to resize it for you," answered Rita.

"Okay, maybe tomorrow after work I will take a look around and see what there is," said James.

"Will you stay for lunch?" asked Rita.

"Thanks, that would be great," replied James.

After lunch, James stayed for a while, and they talked about anything and everything. Rita was having fun working for UTA, Tom, like James, was getting ready to go back to the training school to brush up for the blasting licence test. They were all thinking about Christmas, what to do and who to buy presents for. James had not even thought about Christmas presents, not even for Katrina.

Eventually, he left and went home. He got dinner for himself and sat down to think about presents, what and for whom. Katrina was an obvious, but what about her parents, what about Tom and Rita, and who else? In the end, he decided to leave it all until the next day and take a look around while he was looking for rings. Perhaps for the Morrisons, there could be some booze, and for the Englebrechts, he would have to think a little.

Monday morning, he reported to the Training School with everyone else to go over the requirements for the blasting licence. As well as the trainees who had started together, there were others taking the classes; operators, drillers, and others who would benefit from a blasting licence and who wanted to advance and improve. It was good to see the others who had started out when he had and hear where they had all been. Some he had seen on and off during the past few months, but others he had hardly seen at all and was curious to learn where they had been assigned. The lessons themselves were actually fairly straightforward for James; mostly, they were concerned with what the law said. All pupils were given copies of the regulations, and in some cases, there was considerable time spent explaining in ChiKabanga what the English of the regulations actually said. The regulations were typically written in bureaucratic language, but less so than typical laws. These, at least, were intelligible to the average engineer.

After work, James went into town and looked for jewellers. He selected one and went in to discuss his needs. He told the assistant that he was looking for an emerald. Then he was bombarded with questions as to cut, clarity, carats, and even colour. James learned a whole new terminology, brilliant cut, step cut, rose cut, and marquise. It struck him that for an emerald, the rectangular form with a step cut might be appropriate. He was told that emeralds came mainly from Colombia but that there were emeralds from Rhodesia that were better in quality and colour. He also learned that there were actually emeralds that could be found in Zambia, if one knew where to look.

James was a little overwhelmed by the prices, but eventually he came to an agreement with the jeweller for a simple gold ring with an emerald setting. It seemed to James that emeralds were pricier than diamonds, and he was told that was in fact so, for the stones were of exceptional clarity with very few flaws or inclusions. The rarity of stones without flaws made them expensive. James found one that met his budget and, as far as he could tell, was a reasonable stone. He asked about resizing the ring, if it were to be necessary, and was told that there would be no problem. He was finally asked who the lucky girl was to be, and upon telling them it was Katrina, he received the greatest gift of all, a reduction in the price. The jeweller knew Katrina and her family well and had often wondered who would be the lucky person to marry Katrina.

After making his transaction, he then thought about Christmas presents for others on his list. He decided that booze was a good standby and settled on a couple of bottles of better Scotch that he would wrap later and then deliver. He found some long dangling earrings for Katrina. He had noted before that she did not often wear jewellery, but when she did, she favoured something different. For Sussana and Rita, he was in a quandary, so decided to consult with Katrina later.

Tuesday and Wednesday were the same, with quizzes held to see if they were retaining the information set out in the regulations. James had been in touch with Katrina, but she was getting ready for her theatre show and was very busy. Wednesday night was the premiere performance, and James had purchased tickets for himself and for Tom and Rita. He had actually bought tickets for each performance but decided not to tell anyone about that, as they might see it as a little obsessive.

Wednesday evening, James met up with Tom and Rita, and they drove to the theatre on Kantanta Street. Their tickets gave them seats in the front row and the best view of the performers. All of them were pleasantly surprised at the professionalism of the performance. James was quick to identify Katrina in the dance routine lineups. He pointed her out to Tom and Rita, who asked him how he knew, because the costumes concealed the faces and only gave bodily clues as to the identities. This led to some ribbing from Rita during the intermission as to his familiarity with Katrina and his ability to pick her out. Tom made an aside to him that all the girls in the lineup had figures that wouldn't quit, particularly the one on the end, the left end, as they looked at them. James was not sure who this was, but promised Tom that he would find out and let him know. James saw Koos and Sussana Englebrecht at the bar along with several other people that he knew from either the mine or the boat club. He said his hellos and complimented Koos and Sussana on Katrina's performance. All in all, the show was a great success, and it justified the fact that all the performances had been sold out. James thought that the others in the audience must have had a better appreciation than he did of what to expect, as it seemed to be the norm as far as they were concerned.

After the show, Tom, Rita, and James waited around for the cast to appear and then congratulated Katrina when she came out. She was happy that the first night was over and that there were no major catastrophes. She had remembered all her routines and, as far as she knew, had made no errors or missteps. Then Tom and Rita made their excuses and left, leaving James alone with Katrina. James asked her about the dancer to their extreme left, quickly adding that it was Tom who was asking and not him. Katrina told him that the dancer was Estelle Du Toit. She told him that of all the troupe, Estelle had the best innate sense of rhythm and was easily the best dancer of them all. She also told James that she was envious of Estelle and wished that she had her abilities. James asked her how she was getting home, and she told him that she was riding home with her parents, as she was tired and wanted a good night's sleep before work on Thursday. A little disappointed, James said his goodnights and went home alone.

James saw the Thursday, Friday, and Saturday performances, each following his classes on explosive regulations. He did get a chance on Friday to ask Katrina about gifts for her mother and for Rita. He was directed to a kitchenware store where more unusual kitchen gadgets could be found. Therefore, on Saturday, after class, he acquired an item for each of them, which he took home to wrap. Sunday, there were no classes, but there were two performances for Katrina; one at two in the afternoon and one at seven that night. James was beginning to feel deprived of company and was looking forward to the party that would follow the final performance that night. With the final curtain call, the wait was over, and James hurried backstage to meet Katrina. She had got a ride into town with her father earlier, so would need a ride home after the party. James was introduced to the rest of the cast and met Estelle. It dawned on him that she was a coloured girl, in Brit terms a mulatto. He rather relished the idea of telling Tom about the dancer that he had picked out of the lineup. It would be interesting to see how he reacted to the fact that she was coloured.

The party was fun, Katrina was pleased with the show and her part in it and the fact that it was finally over and there would be no performance on Monday. So, she could now take things a little easier. She also told James that her father would be happier as she could now devote more time to work than she had in the past few weeks. There were things that had been allowed to slide, and she had some catching up to do with paperwork. When, finally, Katrina announced she was ready to leave, she told James that she was going home with him. She would drop him off at the mine in the morning and pick him up at the end of the shift. This sounded fine with James, but his delight was dampened a little when all Katrina wanted to do was bathe and sleep when they did get home. Still, James reasoned, better to have Katrina in bed with him to hold than not to have her at all.

Early Monday morning, James got a few looks when Katrina dropped him off at the mine. When she had dropped him off previously, it had been afternoon shift on a Saturday, and there had been essentially no one there. Now there were the normal crews plus most of the staff and management. For those who did not already know that James was dating Katrina, it was a surprise, and he had his share of comments after she had left. The day was taken up with quizzes to see if there would be any problems with the tests. Some of the candidates had appointments that day, and the rest were on Tuesday. James had an appointment on Tuesday with the Mines Inspectorate. He did not foresee any problems, but he had learned enough in life not to anticipate the result. Later in the day, those who had tests that day began returning to the school. For the most part, the results were positive with only a few exceptions. Those were not unexpected by the staff, and a second test was quickly scheduled, with some extra revision thrown in. As to be expected, each one of them was interrogated as to the actual questions asked by the Mines Inspectors.

After work, Katrina picked him up, but she took him back to her office as she was not finished with work. There was still a mountain of paperwork to catch up on that she had neglected in the past few weeks. As they drove in, Koos was there to greet them.

"James, *howzit* man?"

"Fine, Sir, and how are things with you?" replied James.

"*Goed*, son, and we will see you for Christmas?" asked Koos.

"Yes, Sir, at what time should I be there?" asked James.

"Why don't you come after work on Christmas Eve and join us for a couple of days, or at least until you have to go back to work on Monday?" suggested Koos.

"Are you sure I won't be too much trouble?" asked James. "Does your wife know that I may be coming?"

"*Ag* man, it is the women who want you there," replied Koos. "And, at least there will be another man in the house, too many women sometimes!"

With that, Koos left, and Katrina looked at James.

"You are coming for Christmas, aren't you?" she asked.

"Of course," said James. "I just received the official invitation."

"Oh, good," she said, smiling at him. "Why don't we invite your friends Tom and Rita to come over on Boxing Day and then stay overnight until Saturday?"

"Okay, shall we do that at the party tomorrow night?" asked James.

"Sure, sure," said Katrina. "I presume there will be something to celebrate at this party. You are going to pass this test, aren't you?"

"God, I hope so," replied James. "I cannot imagine the embarrassment or chagrin if I failed. Do you think they would cancel my contract and send me home?"

"No, but your name would be famous on the Copperbelt, and I'm sure they would find all sorts of really bad jobs for you," Katrina replied.

With that, she settled back to her work. It was difficult for James to sit and watch her. She entranced him, and he followed every move she made. Occasionally, Katrina would ask him what he was looking at.

"Don't you have to revise for this test thing tomorrow?" she finally asked him.

"Yes, but I can't do that with you here," replied James.

"Well, you *groot kak*, perhaps you should go home and study and let me finish my work in peace," Katrina suggested.

"No, no, I will be fine," said James.

"Go!" ordered Katrina. "I will see you at the celebration party tomorrow."

"Okay, okay, I'm going," said James.

He gave her a kiss and left the office. He noted that Katrina had her truck parked at the office and would have transportation home.

Tuesday, he reported to the Mines Inspectorate office and waited with the others for his turn in the barrel. Greg came and went with a smile on his face, as did Tom, Felix, Rice, Hippo, and Bill. Then came his turn for the inquisition; he handed in his forms and photographs and awaited the questions. The experience was rather a let down really. After three questions, the inspector commented that he obviously knew the regulations, but what about his experience. James then spent the next fifteen minutes answering questions as to what sections he had been assigned to and what he had learned. Apparently, it was adequate as he was told that he had passed and that the blasting licence was issued.

Upon returning to the mine, the first thing they did was take his blasting licence and put it in his personnel folder. Apparently, they felt it was better to manage things that way, as they then had the original on file should anything untoward occur. James was assured that when he left the mine, he would get it back. The rest of the trainees were assembled and waiting, and he was put through the wringer regarding what questions the inspector had asked. Then they sat around waiting for the last of the group to report back after their tests. Meanwhile, James had noticed a parade of section and shift bosses through the training school offices. He asked what that was all about and was told that they were each reporting in on the performance, attitude, and aptitude of each of the trainees.

Finally, when everyone had returned, the assignments for the New Year were announced. Each trainee had a section allocated to him, either development, production, afternoon shift, tramming and lashing, or night shift. James was delighted to see that he had been assigned a development section. He asked Tom where he was going and learned that he was to start in production. Bill also had a production section, as did Joy; Hippo had a development section, but Greg had been assigned to afternoon shift tramming. Greg was a little pissed off about that and wanted to talk to all and sundry about getting the assignment changed, but fat chance. The assignments were in and, for the next three months at least, there was little hope of a change. James was thrilled with his opportunity and wanted to know who was currently running the section and where they were being moved to. He really wanted some insight into how the section was currently running and whether his assignment was a result of his predecessor's promotion or removal for non-performance. Unfortunately, the office of the training school was singularly uninformative.

James left the school and went to the Englebrecht office. Katrina met him and asked how things had gone. James assured Katrina that everything was in good shape and that he had a section to go to after the immediate Christmas break.
"Okay, Mr. Smart, where do we go tonight for your celebration?" asked Katrina.
"Well, most of the others are going to the Edinburgh," replied James.
"Fine, do I need to change?" continued Katrina.
"What for? You look great as you are," said James.

"Typical," said Katrina. "Only a man would say that. I look terrible, I have been working all day; I need a bath and a change of clothes, but thank you all the same. You really do think I look okay?"

"Yes, I really do," replied James. "Wonderful, in fact!"

"Maybe, but I want to change before we go to this shindig of yours," said Katrina.

"Okay, shall I run you home?" asked James.

"No, why don't you leave your Land Rover here. I will drive tonight. I know what you *ouks* are like when you get together and you won't be in any state to drive later," said Katrina.

The evening went well. Katrina, in James's view, looked stunning, but then it seemed that all the other spouses and girlfriends had gone to some trouble. Now he began to understand why Katrina had insisted on going home to change. She would have been embarrassed to go dressed as she was for the transport office. For some of the English spouses, it was the first time they had socialised with the local Zambians, black or white. For the local whites, it was definitely the first time they had really socialised with the black Zambians. The Training School staff had heard about the plan and had roundly condemned it as foolish, futile, doomed to failure, and never to be repeated.

Before they got too involved in anything, James and Katrina, or more particularly Katrina, asked Tom and Rita if they would join them on Boxing Day and then stay the night. They were delighted, and Tom said that he would get directions from James to get to the farm. Katrina suggested that they come at about ten in the morning. They then spent some time talking to Joy and Suzie Mwamba, and then to Bill Harrison and Mary Chisenga. It looked as if the romance between Bill and Mary was getting serious. They had been together for a couple of months now, and there seemed to be no sign of any dampening of feelings. Greg and Shirley would have nothing to do with the black Zambian trainees or their spouses or girlfriends, and cut Bill and Mary dead. All in all, the group dynamics were fascinating.

The whole group mingled for a while, then split into male and female. James and the other trainees drank too much, told too many would-you-believe-it stories while their respective other halves traded stories about the ills of having a loved one deep underground all day. Katrina learned that the concerns of the black Zambian girls were the same as hers. Where to live, what is my husband/boyfriend going to do with the rest of his life, should we have a family now or later, should I work or stay at home? She knew from the drivers in their employ that family issues were the same, black or white, but now she was hearing it from women of her own age group.

By about ten, the party was winding down, and they all started to make their way home. Most of the men had to be helped home by their spouses or girlfriends. Katrina took James home and put him to bed, then got in beside him. James was asleep in minutes, and Katrina lay for a while thinking about her life and future and when this idiot was going to get around to taking the next step of either asking her to move in with him or asking her to marry him. Well, if he didn't do something soon, she would. With that thought, she drifted off to sleep, comforted by the deep breathing of her soul mate lying next to her.

The next day was Christmas Eve, and James was up early as he had to get Katrina to either drop him at the mine or take him to the office to collect his own transport. They discussed things briefly and decided that Katrina should take him to the office to collect his own vehicle, as he did not know when they would be finished that day. Katrina drove them to her office, where James picked up his own car and went off to work. Katrina told him to go straight out to the farm when he was done with work, as they were taking a half day and would be closed at lunch time. James arrived at the mine in time to get the cage to the training school. Most of his compatriots were suffering from sore heads and cringed every time the cage rattled and banged on its way down the shaft.

The morning was spent on basic instructions for the paperwork that each would have to fill out in their new roles. Each assignment had its particular paperwork, so the instructors went through all the forms as a larger group, then split into three to cover development, production and tramming. Most already knew how to manage the paperwork as they had all taken an interest while they had been on their different assignments. James took the chance in one of the breaks to give Tom directions to the Englebrecht farm and drew a quick sketch map for him.

At about lunch time, a halt was called and they were dismissed for the Christmas break, with reminders to be on time when they reported to their respective shift bosses on the Monday following to begin their new jobs. When James reached the surface, he was told that George Bullock wanted to see him. Wondering what this was about, James went to his office.

"Ah, Martin, come in," said Bullock.

"Yes, sir, you wanted to see me?" asked James.

"Yes, I trust that you are still on for house sitting in January?" asked Bullock.

"Yes, sir, I will be leaving the van de Merwe house on the 3rd of January and will move into yours the same day, if that is still convenient for you?" asked James.

"That's fine, be at the house at nine in the morning, and I will be there with the keys and will introduce you to my people," replied Bullock. "There is one thing, though, that I will insist on," he continued.

"Sir?" asked James.

"I gather that you have had an overnight guest at the van de Merwe house on a couple of occasions," said Bullock. "I'm afraid that we cannot have that at my house. My wife strongly disapproves of such behaviour and will not allow it in our house." He continued almost as though he was trying to shift the onus of the request from himself to his wife.

On that note, James was a little taken aback, but reasoned it was their house that he was staying in for free, and if they wanted to be puritanical, then so be it. He could always find other opportunities to be with Katrina.

"That will not be a problem, sir," he commented. "It is, after all, your house, and you can set whatever conditions you feel are appropriate. I quite understand that your wife may have views on the subject, and I will respect those views."

"Even though you think they are none of our business and clearly a trifle old-fashioned," said Bullock, smiling. "Look, personally, I don't care, but I have to live with my wife, and she will get reports back from the house boy."

"It's quite all right, sir," said James. "I will give you nothing to be concerned about.

"Of course, there is nothing to say you cannot have someone to the house for dinner," said Bullock. "Just not overnight, you understand, I hope."

"Really, sir; it's fine, don't worry," reassured James.

"Okay, good, splendid, we will see you on the 3rd of January then. Have a good Christmas and New Year," said Bullock, indicating that the meeting was at an end. James left and had a laugh to himself. Stupid git, what the hell business of his or his bloody wife what he did. What a bunch of puritanical, holier-than-thou idiots! God only knew what Bullock's home life was like with a wife who could be that narrow-minded.

# Christmas

At home, James sorted out clothes that he thought he might need for the next four or five days and then searched around for the dressing gown he knew he had somewhere but had forgotten where it was put away. He packed everything into a bag, then added the presents he had bought and, most importantly, he made sure he had the ring he planned to give to Katrina. He put everything into his Land Rover, then called Silent and gave him his Christmas, or small cash present, as was the custom; he also gave one, in a lesser amount, to Evansi. He told Silent that he would be gone until Monday, and as Silent and Evansi were also both going to be gone, they locked up everything in the house and then walked around the exterior to check all the windows. When they felt that all was secure, they left, locking the gate behind them.

The dogs were fine; they were being cared for by one of Silent's uncles, who was staying in the *kaia* for a while. He was delighted with the arrangement as he had a quiet place to himself and liked the dogs for company. He was hiding out from his wife and her family. They wanted him to invest in some venture that she had concocted, and he wanted nothing to do with it, so had decamped to Kitwe from Mpika to give them all time to forget the idea. He was determined not to return until the middle of January, considering that by then the venture would have collapsed or have been forgotten about.

James drove to the Morrison's home first, where he dropped off his gifts and said his "Merry Christmas and Happy New Year." Rita had a small package for him and promised that they would see him on Boxing Day. Then James drove out to the Englebrecht farm, not without a little trepidation. He hoped that his proposal would meet with a positive response, but one never knew. The dogs met him at the house but were shooed away by Katrina. She was dressed in a form-fitting Chinese-style dress with a high neck and slits up the sides. The dress was a beautiful dragon print on a deep red background.
"God, you look great," said James.
"Thanks, you don't look so bad yourself. Will you come in?" asked Katrina.

Inside, he was greeted by both Sussana and Koos.

"James, *hoe gaan dit?*" asked Sussana.

"*Goed, dankie,*" he answered.

"Katrina, why don't you show James to your room and help him unpack?" suggested Sussana. That rather took the wind out of James's sails. He had expected to be put in a guest room and then had imagined all the artifices he would need to contrive to spend time with Katrina. Now, here was her mother packing him off to sleep with Katrina. It was a little different attitude from the one that he had encountered earlier with George Bullock. Koos seemed to be fine with this arrangement as well as he ushered them both into the bedroom and asked if James needed anything.

When Koos left, James hugged Katrina and kissed her.

"I didn't expect to be actually sleeping with you this weekend," he told her.

"Why, where else would you sleep? And if we put you in the spare room, where will Tom and Rita sleep tomorrow night?"

"Well, not all parents are comfortable with their daughters sleeping with guys they are not married to," commented James.

"Perhaps, but don't you think they know we have been, if not sleeping together, at least having it off?"

"Yes, but let me tell you about my conversation with Bullock today," said James. With that, he related the conversation he had had earlier that day and speculated on the reasons. Katrina told him that it was just because Mrs. Bullock was far too concerned with the morals of others, a regular "Holy Joe, or Jane in this case!"

James unpacked his stuff, and Katrina showed him where he could store it for the moment. Then they returned to the living room.

"Ah, James, I booked a telephone call for you tomorrow to call your family in England," said Koos. "I thought you might like to talk to them on Christmas Day."

James was surprised, and all he could do was make his thanks inarticulately. He also suspected that Koos was anticipating things a little and was going to provide him with the opportunity to tell his parents about his proposal to Katrina. James had not talked to his parents by telephone since coming to Zambia because very few homes had telephones, and even if they did, overseas calls were not always easily made, hence the need to book a call. Koos told him that at ten the following morning, the operator would call and ask him what number he wished to speak to. Ten in the morning made it eight in the morning in England. His parents had not said anything about being away for Christmas, so James presumed that his call would find them in, if not up.

James asked what their customs were at Christmas regarding presents and such. He learned that they opened presents at midnight. Katrina told him that the house servant and the rest of the staff were now off for Christmas, visiting relatives. Koos had provided each of them with their "Christmas" and they had all been happy with the gift. Koos asked James to join him on the *stoep* for a beer while the women did their thing in the kitchen. James had the good grace to look to Katrina for guidance, and she gave it to him by pushing two glasses of beer into his hands and telling him to go. Koos was in an expansive mood; he talked about the business, politics, and the weather.

The weather finally intervened in the form of a storm that lashed rain down onto the house and even onto the *stoep*. They went inside and joined the ladies. Over dinner, James found himself answering all manner of questions about his upbringing, his family, his aspirations, and his impressions to date of Zambia. It seemed reasonable to him that all Sussana and Koos were trying to do was learn more about him than Katrina had told them. It was difficult to concentrate sometimes because the slits in Katrina's dress showed her legs off to great advantage, and there was a lot on display. James thought once more that Katrina had to be the most alluring girl he had ever known. He felt his love for her welling up and wondered what life would be like living with her.

A little after midnight, they opened their presents. James decided that he wasn't going to wait until morning and slipped the ring box into a little box that he labelled for Katrina, then put it with the rest of the presents. When she got to it, she looked at him in surprise and with questioning eyes.

"*Ini lo?*" she asked.

"It is for you, if you will marry me," said James.

"Marry you!"

"Yes, will you marry me? I know this is not the kneeling type of proposal, but I can't wait any longer. Will you marry me?"

"Yes, oh yes!" said Katrina, who then flung her arms around him and kissed him. "Look, Mom," she said, showing her ring to Sussana.

"This deserves a drink, don't you think?" asked Koos.

"You don't seem surprised, Daddy?" asked Katrina.

"Well, of course I am, are you happy?" responded Koos.

"Yes, I'm happy. When shall we get married?" she asked James.

"We need to talk about that. We need to pick a date that will be best for you, and I'm sure that your parents will also want a say."

"What about your family?" asked Katrina.

"I'm not sure. A lot will depend on when we decide and whether or not they can afford flights out."

"Why don't you two talk about it tomorrow?" suggested Sussana.

Koos handed glasses around and added his voice to the discussion. "*Ja,* tomorrow. Now, if you are ready, Katrina and James, to you and *alles sal regte kom!*"

They talked for a little longer, then Sussana shooed them off to bed. James suspected that she wanted to talk to Koos about his proposal to Katrina and what her marriage would mean for them. Katrina led James to the bedroom and pushed him down onto the bed, then climbed on top of him.

"*Groot kak!* How long have you been planning this?" she asked.

"For a while, but I only got the ring recently," replied James.

"Well, let me show you what it will be like to be married to me," she said.

Christmas morning dawned, and they were finally roused by household noises at about eight. Katrina got up, found her dressing gown, and then told James to get up and go with her to the bathroom. James hunted around trying to remember where he had put his dressing gown, then asked why she wanted him to go with her.

"You are planning to shower, aren't you?" she asked.

"Yes."

"Well, then, let's go. There is room for two, you know!"

With that, James magically found his dressing gown and followed her to the bathroom. In the shower, he started to laugh.

"What's funny?" asked Katrina.

"I know what my parents are going to ask when I tell them that I'm going to get married."

"What?"

"Whether or not you are black."

"Do you really think that's all they will want to know?"

"I really don't know how they will react, but I'll bet that will be uppermost in their minds."

Over breakfast, Sussana asked Katrina if she had had any thoughts about when the wedding could be. They got into a discussion about dates, planning needs and the rest. Koos looked at James, raised his eyebrows and smiled.

"Now look what you have done," he said to James.

"Yes, we've rather lost them, haven't we?" James replied.

"James, all you have to remember is to be there on the right day," said Koos.

At ten, the phone rang, James took the expected call, and the operator asked for the number he was trying to reach. He heard the Zambian operator talking to the British operator, then he heard the phone ringing.

"Hello," said a very tentative, sleepy voice at the other end. It was his sister, Alexandra.

"Hey Alex," said James. "Merry Christmas!"

"James, Happy Christmas! How are you? Where are you?"

"I'm still in Zambia and am actually at my fiancée's house."

"Ah, is this the Katrina you wrote and told me about?"

"Yes, you should come to the wedding and meet her."

"Hold on, James, Dad wants to talk to you," said Alex.

"James! How are you? Where are you? What time is it?" asked his father.

"Hold on, let me call your mother?" continued his father.

"Elizabeth, it's James calling from Zambia," he heard his father call out.

"Well, boy, how are you?" asked his father again.

"Dad, I'm fine. I'm in Zambia and am calling from my fiancée's house," James replied.

"Your what?"

"My fiancée," repeated James. "Her name is Katrina Englebrecht, and I asked her to marry me last night."

"Here is your mother, talk to her!" said his father. "He says he is engaged to be married to some girl called Katrina, God only knows who she is," James overheard his father comment to his mother.

"James, what is this about marriage?" demanded his mother.

"I asked Katrina to marry me last night."

"Who is Katrina?" demanded his mother again.

"Katrina Englebrecht she lives here."

"Englebrecht, what kind of name is that?" she continued her interrogation.

"It is an Afrikaans name."

"Afrikaans, what does that mean? Is she black?" asked his mother in a mild panic now.

"No, Mum and she is lovely."

"She is not English then?" continued his mother, perhaps a little relieved but still suspicious.

"No, Mum, she is Afrikaans," repeated James.

"I am surprised at you, James. You are English, you know, and we had expected you to come back from there and marry a nice English girl. I forbid you to marry this Katronia, or whatever her name is."

"Well, I love Katrina, and we are going to get married."

"Talk to your father," she ordered. "William, tell him that he cannot marry this girl, whoever she is," was her aside to her husband as she handed him the phone.

"You heard what your mother said, boy, you cannot marry this girl," said his father. Duty done, he handed the phone back to his wife. "Here is your mother again."

"James, you need to forget this nonsense about getting married to some girl from the jungle, it's only loneliness after all, and come home to a decent English girl," reiterated his mother.

"Well, I'm sorry you feel that way, Mum, but it won't change my mind."

"Don't expect us to support you in this," said his mother. "I'm sorry you had to wake us up with news like this; it has quite spoiled our Christmas. Goodbye."

James heard the phone click as his mother hung up, then he heard a faint voice on the line say, "What a bitch! It almost makes me embarrassed to admit to being English," and another reply, "Yes, perhaps if she came here to Zambia she would learn that we are quite nice really." He realised that the operators had been listening in on the conversation. Well, they probably didn't really want to be at work on Christmas day, and this would give them something to talk about at the end of their shifts.

James put the phone down and looked at Koos helplessly.

"That didn't go well, did it?" asked Koos.

"No, they seem to think that I have betrayed the family, the empire, and mankind in general by wanting to marry someone who is not 'English'," replied James.

"Well, who are they to comment?" asked Katrina heatedly.

"They are just a little old-fashioned and apparently prejudiced," he said

"So what are you going to do?" continued Katrina.

"Marry you, what else?" asked James in return. "After all, they're not the ones that have to live with you, are they, *suikerbossie?*"

"Do you think they will change their minds?" asked Koos.

"Who knows? I didn't appreciate until now just how narrow-minded they are, or maybe I'm being unjust, and it is just the surprise."

"I am sorry that this had to happen," said Sussana. "I hope it won't spoil your Christmas."

"It's fine, Mrs Englebrecht, I'll write to my sister later today and find out what is happening over there."

"James, why don't you call me either Mom or Sussana?" asked Sussana. "No matter what else, we are happy for you and Katrina. Perhaps when your folks have met Katrina, they will come to like her as much as we love you."

"Thanks, Mom," said James, grinning and feeling a little better.

"We should light the *braai* now," suggested Koos. "Then it will be ready when we want to cook later. *Kom* James, you can help me."

Koos had a fairly sophisticated *braai*; it was a built-in structure with a place for preparation and serving, as well as the fire pit. They cut wood into kindling, lit a fire, and then added large pieces of wood that would eventually burn down to hot embers and be perfect for cooking. Conversation was desultory and focused mainly on the reaction that James's parents had had. Koos thought that he could understand, as he would have had a hard time if Katrina had called out of the blue with similar news. But, he did emphasise that he trusted Katrina's judgement and that his only real concern was would she be happy? James made the comment that he probably could have been a little more forthcoming in his letters to his parents.

The only two people he had really ever told much about Katrina were his sister, Alexandra, and his grandmother. He had mentioned Katrina in passing to his parents, but he had never said very much and had never given any indication as to which way the wind was blowing. Of course, if they had bothered to talk to his grandmother or his sister, they might have learned more. With the fire going nicely, Koos and James went back inside and joined the ladies. Sussana had put together a light lunch, so as not to spoil their appetites for the dinner she had planned. James thought this was quite unlike any Christmas lunch he had had before. Firstly, it was warm outside, no snow or ice anywhere, and secondly, there was no heavy turkey or chicken meal with overcooked vegetables and no Christmas pudding. Altogether, it was very different!

Later, almost as the sun was going down, James asked what they were having for dinner, and Katrina piped up before the others could answer with:

"*Pampoen, rys and vleis!*"

"What's that?" asked James.

"Daddy doesn't think meals are meals unless there is pumpkin, rice, and meat. So for him it is pumpkin, rice, and meat, or meat, rice, and pumpkin, or rice, pumpkin, and meat, you get the picture?" elaborated Katrina.

"So, no sandwiches, Christmas cake, or sugar mice?" asked James.

"I don't know about the sandwiches, but the Christmas cake and sugar mice must be English things because we don't have those here."

"Okay, so what will we have?"

"Daddy plans to *braai* some steaks, chops, and vegetables. Will that suit you?"

"Not quite like the Christmases I grew up with, but yes, that would suit me fine."

"Why don't we take a walk before dinner?" suggested Katrina. "You should have an appetite after a quick walk down by the river."

"I was right, you know," said James when they were out of the house.

"About what?"

"My mother wanted to know if you were black. When I told her that you were Afrikaans, she immediately asked me if you were black."

"You're not serious?"

"Oh, yes. She really asked me that, and then she forbade me from marrying anyone not English."

"Well, when do we get married?"

"Do you have a date in mind?"

"I was thinking of 4th April. Where did you learn *suikerbossie*?"

"That sounds fine to me," agreed James. "I had a little help from your dad on some Afrikaans words."

They walked back to the house and joined Katrina's parents for a sundowner and then dinner. Dinner was cooked on the *braai* by Koos. It seemed to James that cooking on the *braai* was the province of the male of the house. It involved meat, vegetables wrapped in foil, and a lot of beer, much of which was poured or sprayed onto the cooking meat. All in all, it was actually a very good meal, and James was curious to learn what else Koos had put in with the vegetables. After dinner, Katrina announced that they had decided on a date for the wedding. April was fine with her parents, and James added that he would let his family know, and if they wished to come, there would be plenty of time to find flights. Privately, he believed that if anyone came, it would be his sister.

Later that night, in bed, Katrina asked James for a complete playback of the conversation he had had with his family. As far as he could remember, he recited it for her. She was curious why they were so adamant that he marry an English girl. James had to confess to being unsure. He was also surprised at how little he knew about his own parents. He had always thought that they were far more open-minded than they were showing themselves to be. Katrina commiserated and then told him that no matter what, she loved him.

Boxing Day, James was up early and took a walk by the river, accompanied by four of the dogs who had attached themselves to him. It seemed that any time he was outside the house, the same four would always follow him around. James was not sure why these particular four accepted him, but noted that they were also the ones who followed Katrina about the most. He saw crocodiles on the opposite riverbank and some hippo in the river. There was a fish eagle soaring above him that eventually swooped down and perched on a tree heavily marked with droppings, obviously a usual haunt.

There were some people on the opposite bank, and they waved to him. He waved back and then watched them get into dugouts and proceed downstream. He reflected a little on the day before and even laughed at the absurdity of it. He also thought about his lovemaking with Katrina the night before and decided that he had to be one of the luckiest people alive. It was a beautiful morning, he loved and was loved by a truly striking girl, he was fit and healthy, and was about to start a new job that promised to be challenging and fun. What more could anyone want? Feeling in much better spirits, he made his way back to the house and was met on the *stoep* by Katrina.
"Are you okay, sweetie?" she asked him.
"I'm great," replied James. "I feel wonderful this morning. Don't you think it is a beautiful day?"
"Have you been drinking?" asked Katrina, laughing at him.

"Absolutely, drinking in the early morning air and the memories of you!" responded James.

Breakfast was fun with good coffee and animated conversation. James was required to give an explanation as to the origin of Boxing Day. He was not sure that his answers were historically correct, but he told them what he had been told, and that seemed to be satisfactory.

Later that morning, Tom and Rita arrived to be greeted by the pack of Great Danes. Katrina dispersed the pack and escorted their guests into the house. They had not really met her parents before, so introductions were made all around. Katrina then showed them to the guest room, where they dropped off their belongings. Sussana offered them coffee, which they accepted gratefully. While they were drinking their coffee, Rita noticed the glances between James and Katrina and asked; what was the news?

"News, why should there be any news?" asked James.

"Oh, come on," replied Rita. "The way you two are looking at each other, you have either won the Pools or Katrina has something else to tell us."

"Well, actually," said James. "We have some news. Katrina and I are going to get married."

"Well, about time. What took you so long to pop the question?"

"I was waiting for the right moment," said James, a little plaintively.

"If he hadn't asked me this weekend, then I would have asked him!" interjected Katrina. "He is only slow!"

"When is the happy day?" asked Rita.

"We thought of April 4th," replied Katrina.

"I'm sure that you and your mother will be able to handle everything, but if you need anything, I would be happy to help," said Rita.

"One thing you can do," commented Katrina.

"What's that?" asked Rita.

"Make sure that James is at the right place at the right time," joked Katrina.

"I think that will be Tom's job," said James.

"Me? Why me?" asked Tom.

"Well, who else is there?" asked James.

After lunch, the women shooed the men out of the house and got down to serious wedding planning. Koos and the two others sat on the *stoep* considering the greater things of life. There were a number of visitors who stopped by during the afternoon. It seemed that it was the practice on Boxing Day to make the rounds of one's friends and wish everyone well. In between the visitors, Koos got Tom to talk about himself and his aspirations.

James asked Koos if previous Christmases had been this tranquil. Koos told them that it seemed to be the case that he was more often busy over Christmas than not. The mining companies planned major overhaul operations and improvements when there were the fewest number of people actually working underground, so they often needed large items of equipment moving around. That all meant business for Koos and his company, but it also meant that most of their Christmases had been disturbed. He told them that the family had become somewhat accustomed to events and that the previous year, Katrina had managed everything so that he could have the time off. Tom commented to James that he could see them having to take turns and work Christmas and New Year in the future. James had not really thought about that until then, and wondered what other holidays they might get roped into work.

After the sun was down, the women joined them on the *stoep* and announced that they had the plans for the wedding largely mapped out, with just details to fill in. James was instructed to write to his family as soon as possible and find out who, if anyone, might be coming so that accommodation could be arranged. Sussana had decided where the reception should be held, and it was now up to Katrina and James to pick a venue for the wedding itself. Koos joked with them that they should just go to the Boma and skip all the headaches that would come with a larger wedding. Sussana was less than impressed by this idea and told Katrina to think it over carefully. James could see fights happening before the wedding day, so decided that he and Katrina needed to make a decision fairly soon. All in all, it was going a lot faster than James had anticipated, and he was beginning to wonder if he should have chosen a different occasion when there was not so much time to sit around and plan.

Dinner was a *braai* that Koos managed with James and Tom doing the cooking, fetching and carrying. James was still surprised by the amount of food cooked at these *braais* and could not help but think back on his mother's admonitions when he was younger to remember the poor, starving children of Africa. Certainly, there was a huge disparity between the way the Englebrechts lived and ate and the way that most of the people of Zambia lived and ate. Still, he consoled himself with the thought that Rome was not built in a day, and he could not change the system overnight or feed all the starving children of Africa even with the pantry at hand. He did note with some relief, however, that the house servants of the Englebrecht family were well fed and seemed happy enough.

Following dinner, Koos and Sussana told them a little about their wedding and their life in first South Africa, then Northern Rhodesia, and then Zambia, as it became after independence. Tom and Rita then recounted the story of their wedding. Their marital life had not yet been long enough to have much for the telling, so they deferred to Koos and Sussana again. Koos asked them if they had anything planned for the next two days. It seemed that no one had anything particular in mind. James and Tom were both thinking about their new assignments, and Katrina was thinking about how life would change after her marriage.

The following two days were a mix of social calls by neighbours and discussions about the upcoming events. Katrina overheard her parents talking about plans to sell the business and move south. It seemed now that Katrina was to be married, and it looked as if her future was taken care of, that they were thinking about their own futures and how to best manage their retirement. She talked to them about it, and they then discussed the subject at length with Katrina and James. All in all, they had a lot to think about and look forward to.

# Section boss

Monday morning, James reported to the mine office and was told to see Abel Mwewa. Mwewa told him that he would be taking over Isaac Kayumba's section. Apparently, Isaac was due leave and was off to visit his family in the Western Province and do some hunting. As James knew where the section was and who the crews were, all he needed was the latest development plans for the section. He collected his *chola* and went to the cage and found his crews. Once underground and in the section, he quickly made his assignments and set his crews to work. Not that they required much instructing. By and large, they all knew what to do, and the blasting licence holders could start without James inspecting the workplaces.

The first day in his new job went well, and there were no particular problems. At the end of the shift, he lit up the ends and hoped that he had connected everything up correctly so that they would go as required and not misfire. He lingered at the bottom of the ladderway listening to the blasts as they occurred, trying to count the shots as they went off. Whatever happened, the requisite number of ends were fired. Whether or not each hole within the end had gone off, he would only know the next day. Hoping that all had gone well, he walked out to the shaft, joining the general throng of people eager to leave for the day. He met up with Tom, and they talked about their weekend and their respective days. Although neither of them had encountered any problems, James was sure that over the coming months, there would be plenty of opportunities to shine or be an idiot.

Once on the surface, James went to the personnel manager's office at the shaft to talk about housing and the fact that he was going to get married and would be looking for married accommodation. He saw Piet van Rensburg, who leered at him and told him that he had heard that marriage was in the offing. Apparently, Piet was there to check on the progress of the trainees and to see who, if anyone, needed extra time in training. James was redirected to the main personnel office and told to see Henry Mwanza of personnel. James diligently drove to the main offices and found that he was expected and had an appointment.

At first, there was a little discussion because he had signed on as a single employee, but once it was understood that he had no objection to paying the higher rent for the house, his contract would be amended, and a house would be ready for him in early April. In fact, Mr Mwanza suggested that they get him a house at the end of March so that it could be properly cleaned and painted before he moved in. James was told to come back in a week, and they would have a specific address for him. It was likely to be somewhere in the area of Philips or Geddes streets, so would be close to people he knew. James was struck by the difference in attitude towards him and Joy Mwamba. Joy had been married late in the year and had told James a long story about the bureaucratic bull he had had to deal with to get married quarters. What really surprised James was the fact that it was Mr Mwanza who was the stumbling block. He would have thought that Mr Mwanza would have been more favourably disposed towards Joy.

The next stop James made was at the office of the Englebrecht transportation company. He wanted to talk to Katrina about what he had agreed to that day so that she could start planning their move. Katrina was not at the office; apparently, she had taken some paperwork to the government offices. Koos told James that he expected her back in about an hour, so why didn't he take a seat, have some coffee, and wait for her. James told Koos that he had worked out with the personnel people to get a house.

Koos then told James that he and Sussana had been talking about the business and what to do with it. He went on to say that their retirement was essentially tied up in the business assets and that to have anything for their retirement years, they needed to find a buyer for the business. The biggest issue would be to find a buyer who could help them by paying, at least partially if not wholly, outside the country. The exchange control regulations that the government was introducing would limit the amount they could expatriate, and having their assets tied up in Zambia was not a wholly comforting prospect. He had put out some feelers and thought that he might have a buyer in one of the local heavy equipment dealers, but there would be a price for having the receipts paid out of the country. Koos said that he had yet to fully discuss things with Katrina and asked James to keep it to himself for now.

Eventually, Katrina came speeding into the yard and skidded to a halt by the door. She gathered up her papers and belongings and marched into the office.
"What took you so long?" asked James.
"*Verdomde* bloody government officials!" was her reply. "You would think I was trying to export every vehicle we have out of the country, instead of trying to bring one new one in!"
"Ah, but did you have fun? And, by the way, you look wonderful."
"Thank you. As for fun, it depends on what you call fun! I can think of better ways to spend the afternoon. What about you, how did your afternoon go?"
"Better than yours, I think. At first, I thought that the mine was not going to give us a house, but it seems that if I'm prepared to pay the extra rent, then all can be arranged."
"So, where will we live?"
"I won't know until next week, perhaps Philips or Geddes streets."
"Have you talked to any of your family yet about coming to the wedding?"
"No, I thought I would write and see how they respond," replied James. "If I had to guess, I would say that Alex may try and come, but I doubt if anyone else will."
Katrina, all this time, had been shoving papers into folders and then dropping the folders into filing cabinets. She finally turned and studied the office as if looking to see if all was done.

"Are you finished for the day?" asked James.
"Why, have you something in mind that you would like to do?"
James looked sideways at Koos and then back to Katrina and grinned.
"When are you moving out of Vans' house and into the house of that bollock or was it Bullock?" asked Katrina, blushing.
"Soon, I could probably use some help cleaning up and packing."
"Why don't we go and get started?"
"Good plan," agreed James. "*Kom ons ry!*"

"You two should be less obvious," said Koos as they left the office. "Oh, and if you remember, pack something of James's. Will we see you for dinner?"

"*Ja*, we will be there just now," said Katrina, blushing even deeper if that were possible.

Later that night, when James said goodbye to Katrina, she asked him if he fancied going to a New Year's Eve party in Chingola. One of her school friends was having a party and they were invited. James thought that would be a great idea. He told her that he would pick her up at eight in the evening, and then they could drive over. He suggested that she take some extra clothes and that they would return to his place in Kitwe on New Year's Day. He had some cleaning up to do, as they had not actually done much that day.

The following day, James spent his time getting to know his crews a little better. Each of them had good points and also little quirks that he would have to watch, particularly the blasting licence holders who could drill and charge up their own work. James had a total of twenty in his gang, sixteen of whom were assigned in pairs to do the drilling, with the rest detailed off to timber work or extending water and air lines and ventilation ducts. Although he remembered most of their names, he was ashamed to admit that their numbers came more easily to mind when he was filling out his paperwork. He consoled himself with the thought that he was also better known by his number when it came to the mine administration.

Apart from the veteran Kossam, there were three other blasting licence holders, so that meant that James focused most of his attention on the four crews who could not work without him setting up each development end. He was reluctant to change much of the way that Kayumba had set things up too quickly, but there were some things he just felt he had to change. He had observed earlier that the timber crew were actually more capable than a couple of the drilling crews. So, he resolved to switch them around and give the timber crews the job of drilling. He was not sure how well this would be received, but it was worth a try. He spent some time during his quiet period before blasting, laying out who the crews should be and who would take which assignment.

At the end of his shift, James made his way to the surface and was given a message that George Bullock wanted to see him. James cleaned himself up and then presented himself at Bullock's office, who merely wanted to check that everything was still set for the move on January 3rd. They agreed on a time to collect keys on January 2nd and when he would move in on the 3rd. It looked as if his stay in the Bullock household would be his last leave house, because he would be moving into his own house after his marriage on April 4th.

Bullock knew that he had been to see the personnel people and that he was looking for a house that he could have. Bullock made some asinine comments about his wife being pleased that James and his paramour were making it legal. Once again, James had his opinion of Bullock and his wife confirmed; they were a pair of self-righteous prigs. He did have this momentary vision of the two of them up to all kinds of questionable antics behind their closed doors, but he quickly dismissed that as wishful thinking and categorised them as Holy Joes who would probably live out their lives disapproving of almost everyone else. How sad, and what a pitiful way to live life.

New Year's Eve, all of James's crews were eager to get off early, so they came in early and got to work immediately. James assigned work on a *skonkwan* basis or piece work; that is, as soon as a designated amount of work was done, the crews could leave. Unfortunately, because of the blasting schedule, James had to wait long after all his crews had left before he could light up his ends and leave for the shaft himself. James was eager to get home because he was looking forward to his excursion to Chingola with Katrina and wondered if he might meet anyone at the party that he knew, apart from the people from Kitwe whom he had already met.

When James picked Katrina up, it was lightly raining. He ran into the house and greeted Koos and Sussana and then waited for Katrina to appear. When she came out, she had on a red mini-skirt with a black sleeveless top. Her skirt was short but not as short as many James had seen in London in the past few years. He recalled a classic incident in Kensington High Street where he had witnessed several cars crashing into one another as the drivers stared at a girl crossing the road wearing what could be affectionately referred to as a wide belt. Katrina didn't go that far, but her skirt was short enough to draw the eye and make one take a second look. Katrina also had heels on that served to emphasise her height and the shape of her legs.

Katrina said goodbye to her folks and then told James that she was ready to go. She handed him a small overnight bag and an umbrella and waited for him to open the door and escort her to his car. While they were driving to Chingola, James asked Katrina who else was likely to be at the party, and she told him that there would be her school friend Barbara, plus whoever her current beau was. It was also likely that some of the people that James knew from Kitwe, Attie, Darryl, plus their girlfriends, if they were still actually going out and probably some of Barbara's friends from Chingola. Katrina doubted if there would be any other VC-tenners there, but who knew?

Once they got to Chingola, Katrina directed James to Barbara's house in East Chingola. There were already a lot of cars in the yard and on the street, and James had to look around a while for a decent place to park. Fortunately, the rain had stopped, but James still took the umbrella into the house; who knew what would happen later? The party was well underway, and they were ushered in by the house servant who knew Katrina. Once inside, Katrina sought out Barbara and introduced James.

"Oh, so this is the *ouk* you are going to marry," commented Barbara. "James, if you decide you don't fancy a life with a *Boer meisie,* give me a call," she continued.
"*Hande tuis,* he's mine!" said Katrina.
"Have we met somewhere?" asked James. "I'm sure I have seen you somewhere before."
"I doubt it," replied Barbara. "I would have remembered if we had ever met."

"Were you ever in London?" asked James.

"Oh yes, I went to university there, to King's College," she replied.

"Where did you live in London?" James continued.

"In Kensington, just off the High Street," she answered.

"What is this, Twenty Questions?" asked Katrina.

"No, I was just curious," answered James. "Come, let me get you something to drink. Great to meet you, Barbara."

"So what is the story?" asked Katrina when they were out of earshot of Barbara.

"She's the one, the one I saw in Kensington High Street."

"What do you mean?"

James then told her the story of the car accidents and the girl crossing the street dressed in her "wide belt".

"Oh, that would be her," said Katrina, laughing. "She's toned down a little lately, but she always was a little extreme in her fashions."

James got them each a drink and then turned to check out the crowd. He saw Attie and waved to him, and then he saw Lionel and Jane. Several people came up to Katrina and said hello. Katrina, in turn, introduced James to them all. She got quite a few congratulations when she told them that she and James were to be married in April, and not a few veiled hints about invitations to the wedding. A couple of the men seemed less than impressed, or perhaps they were just superbly jealous. James was startled by a tap on his shoulder and turned to face Susan, his old girlfriend, and her husband, Patrick.

"Hello, James," Susan said. "I never expected to meet you here!"

"Oh, hi, Susan," replied James. "Who do you know here?"

"I knew Barbara from college days," she answered. "We shared a flat in Kensington once."

She then looked pointedly at Katrina and raised her eyebrows in interrogation.

"Oh, sorry," said James. "Katrina, meet Susan and Patrick."

"Nice to meet you," said Susan icily. Quite why Susan should have any animosity towards Katrina, James could not fathom, except perhaps Katrina looked stunning and Susan was less than impressive.

"Who do you know here?" asked Susan.

"Katrina was at school with Barbara," said James.

"Oh, are you the one who used to bunk out of school to go to swim in the boys' school pool?" asked Susan.

"I did once in a while, along with about ten others," replied Katrina. "How do you know James?" she continued.

"Once upon a time, before I met Patrick, the love of my life, we were an item," Susan replied.

"When is the baby due?" asked Katrina.

"I'm not pregnant!" retorted Susan crossly.

"I'm so sorry," said Katrina. "Please excuse us, we have to see someone over there."

When they had crossed the room and briefly said hello to Attie, Katrina asked James. "Did you really go out with that?"

"Hey, I was young, I hadn't met you, and at university, there were very few women in the engineering classes," replied James. "Remember it was an engineering school and for some reason, women seem not to go in for engineering subjects."

"Well, to be catty, she's a bit of a bitch. She is trying to stir with snide comments about bunking off school to go to the boys' school."

"Did you? Did you bunk off school, I mean?"

"Of course, we all did. It was disgustingly simple; out of the window, across the roof, and down the trellis."

"Why the boys' school?"

"Simple, they had a pool and we didn't."

"What was that about being pregnant?"

"Silly *teef* deserved it. She's really filled out around the middle, don't you think?"

"You're right," said James, looking back across the room. "What on earth did I ever see in her?"

"We'll never know, will we?" said Katrina.

The next person they ran into was Piet van Rensburg. James was a little surprised to see him, as most of the people at the party were considerably younger than Piet.

"Katrina, *hoe gaan dit?*" asked Piet.

"*Goed dankie oom* Piet," she replied. "Do you know James?"

"*Ja*, I met him when he first came here. *Howzit*, James?" he asked.

"Great, thanks!" answered James.

"What about the other *ouks* you started with?" continued van Rensburg.

"I think they are doing reasonably well," said James. "Now that we all have new assignments, we might see how each of us fares."

"I gather that one of your illustrious number rather thinks that Afrikaners are, what was it, thick as two short planks?"

"Where on earth did you hear that?"

"Young George ought to remember that even if walls don't have ears, waiters do!"

"Hey, I can't control what everyone else thinks," said James, a little alarmed by the fact that their conversation had probably been reported verbatim.

"No, I guess not. Besides, you can't think we're all thick or you wouldn't be getting ready to marry Katrina, would you?"

"You're right."

"Well, *kinders*, I will leave you to your fun," said van Rensburg. "Congratulations on your engagement and best of luck for 1970."

"What was all that?" asked Katrina.

"Well, you've met George," said James. "You have a sense of what he is like."

"Did you ever make any such stupid comments?"

"Probably, but I don't think so since I have been in Zambia."

At midnight, James found a quiet corner to be alone with Katrina, and their whispered conversation quickly turned to the obvious, and they decided to leave and go home. It was raining lightly when they left, and on the drive to Kitwe, the weather worsened and the rain got harder. By the time they turned into the drive of the house, it was really coming down. Just the quick dash between the car and the house was enough to get them both absolutely soaked. Once inside the house, Katrina told James that she needed a hot bath to warm up, and then she would celebrate the New Year with him in an appropriate way.

On New Year's Day, they got up late and Katrina organised breakfast. Silent was off for the day and would return that evening. After breakfast, James thought that they really should organise his stuff and make sure that the cleaning job for Silent was within the bounds of normality. James was not quite sure how far to go with cleaning and tidying and took his guidance from Katrina. They actually didn't have very much to do. Most of their effort was in making sure that they found all the odd items that belonged to James that he had managed to strew all around the house.

"How did your trousers get onto the *stoep*?" asked Katrina.

"Oh, I think I spilt something on them and changed in a hurry."

"Man, how can you have so little stuff and yet occupy so much space?"

"I don't have you to keep me on the straight and narrow."

"Where do you think they will give us a house?"

"I don't know yet. Given a choice, would you rather it were Philips Street or Geddes?"

"Philips, I think," replied Katrina. "Geddes is busy, and there is more traffic."

"What are you going to wear for the wedding?" asked James.

"A dress, probably. But I haven't decided yet exactly what; I need to argue with Mom a bit first!"

"I suppose I need to wear a suit, don't I?" he asked.

"Unless you fancy spending your wedding night in the doghouse, that would be a good idea," she said

"Do you think we've done enough for the day?" he asked.

"*Ja*, let's go to the dam and get a beer," she said.

"Great plan," agreed James. "I can finish up what little is left tomorrow."

Tomorrow came and went. James went back to work on January 2nd and again on the morning of January 3rd, which, being a Saturday, was a short shift as everyone was eager to be away for what was left of the holiday season. As soon as the shift was over on Saturday, he drove to the Van de Merwe house and collected his belongings. He said his goodbyes to Silent and was really quite sorry to be leaving. He had grown attached to Silent and had enjoyed his stay in the house.

Apparently, Silent was also in some measure sorry to see him go and offered his hand to James to shake with the familiar and standard farewell,

"*Hamba gahle Bwana*,"

"*Shala mushle* Silent," responded James. He then got into his Land Rover and drove off to his new quarters at the Bullock house.

The Bullocks were waiting for him. Apparently, they only intended driving as far as Ndola that day, and Mrs. Bullock wanted to see James into the house. It transpired that Mrs. Bullock wanted to do more than just see James into the house. She had a list a mile long of dos and don'ts, most important of which was no overnight guests. James assured her that he understood her concerns and would respect her wishes, even though privately he thought she was more than a little strange. James was introduced to Moses, the house servant and had to endure the indignity of listening to Mrs. Bullock instruct Moses on all the dos and don'ts.

After they had finally gone, James spent a few minutes talking to Moses and learned fairly quickly that Moses was quite happy to have a break from Mrs. Bullock for a while. He as good as told James that whatever James wanted to do was fine with him. Tempting as that was, James knew that someone in the neighbourhood would be bound to report back to Mrs. Bullock, and Moses would be the one who suffered the consequences.

The Englebrecht household seemed refreshingly normal and welcoming after his indoctrination that afternoon. Katrina asked him how things had gone, and James's reply was simply "strange!". Koos laughed at his story but agreed with him that it would not be good to put Moses in a difficult situation. Their conversation then turned to the longer-term planning that Koos and Sussana were doing. They had discussed things with Katrina, and it seemed that they were now seriously engaged in finding a buyer for the business. From what Koos said, it would be about six months before they had a completed sale, and they would be looking to leave for the Cape as soon after that as was practical. They planned to drive down, essentially reversing the route that James had taken on his journey north.

# A new year

With the holidays now truly over, everyone returned to work. James met Tom and the other new section bosses in the changing room, and they all quickly recounted their New Year's Eve stories: parties they had attended, hangovers they had endured, and resolutions they had made and already broken.

James joined his crew at the cage, and they went to work. When he had checked in that morning, he had been given some plans that showed a new raise to be mined between two levels, and he had to find the exact location of the start and finish points and then plan his work. He had been given a hint by one of the other section bosses that this was something of a test, so his performance would be under scrutiny.

Finding the start point was simple enough; he had been given two chains with large washers attached to the ends. Each of the chains was marked with the peg number so that when hung from the roof, they could be used to give a level line and direction in the drive. Indicating the line was done by shining his lamp through the washers and having one of his crew mark where on the drive walls the light beam fell. The tricky part was striking off the right angle to the line in order to get the base of the raise correctly positioned, and then establishing the correct vertical angle to set the centre of the raise that they would follow.

With marks in place, James then set Kossam to work drilling the first overhead blasting round. Unlike a regular end, this was a really messy process. All the water and debris from the drill holes flooded down onto the heads of the drillers. The mine provided waterproof jackets for this job, but for reasons James could never fathom, the drillers rarely used them. Once the round was drilled, charging the holes was awkward, as again, everything was done overhead and was tiring. Getting the explosives to stay in the holes entailed using one of the tricks he had seen before. He used his knife to slice down the length of the explosive sticks so that the wrapping was cut and the stick would deform when tamped into the holes. This was, of course, strictly illegal because using steel tools on the explosives was definitely prohibited.

By the end of the shift, James had twelve blasts to light up, unfortunately spanning the total vertical distance of this section. By the time he was done, he felt that he had climbed up and down enough ladders to almost reach the moon. As James was walking to the shaft, he met up with Hippo, who ran the equivalent development section on the south side of the mine. They traded stories, and James promised to lend Hippo a spare jackhammer he had acquired. At the shaft, they had quite a wait before the cage finally came, and when it did, Greg was among the section bosses who got off.

"James, Hippo," greeted Greg. "I suppose you arseholes are going to gloat over your nice jobs."
"Why would we do that?" asked Hippo.
"Because I have this shitty afternoon shift and you bastards have nice day shift jobs!" Greg replied.
"Yes, but we also have all the shift bosses, mine captains, and underground managers that could appear at any time," countered Hippo. "You will be lucky and see only the shift boss rarely."
"Don't you also have all day to do things and then not finish that late?" asked James.
"Maybe," replied Greg. "But I still think I got the short end of the stick and am being punished for something."
"You must be dreaming," said James. "See you later!"

On that note, James and Hippo joined the others in the cage and rode up to the surface.
"You know that he is right?" suggested Hippo.
"What do you mean?"
"He got bad reports from all the section bosses he was with, and the mine will not give him anything better yet."
"Where did you hear that?"
"I heard," was all Hippo would say.

Once back at his new quarters, James addressed himself to writing a couple of letters to his parents and his sister. Katrina was in Mufulira for the day and not expected back until late, so he was at a loose end.

Moses had prepared dinner, and James ate as he composed. It was difficult to write about Katrina to his parents. Describing the love of his life to people who had never met her was not easy. He had no natural facility with words, and it came to him slowly. He had also been surprised at the antipathy they had felt towards him marrying anyone who was not 'English'.

Just as well, he thought, that Katrina was not also black, as that would have probably driven them to apoplexy. It was probably this as much as anything that made the letter difficult to write. He harboured strong resentments towards them because they were apparently not prepared to just accept his life and decisions for what they were. He had tried to put himself in their shoes and imagine what it was like dealing with the unknown and the fears that went with it, but he had found that difficult.

To Alex, it was a lot easier. He had always been able to talk to her, and he had already told her a fair amount about Katrina. He still had no idea if Alex would come to the wedding. However, he was confident that if she could find a way, she would be there. He was a lot less certain about his parents. This might just turn out to be one of those weddings where the bride lends the groom guests just to balance out the church.

Tuesday morning, James was anxious to see how his first raise blast had gone. The lashing crews had cleared away the broken rock, and he was able to see up into the new hole he had created. So far so good! Before they could drill the next round, they had to create a work platform, so Kossam drilled holes in the wall and they hammered in large steel rods. The next step was to place timbers across these rods and build the platform.

It suddenly dawned on James that they would have to pull all this down at the end of the shift because the blasting would bring it down if they did not. Obviously, this was going to be a slow process that would take some planning for the building and removing of the work platform each day. He also started thinking about how he was going to light up this end when it got a few metres farther up. It was going to mean either a lot of climbing up and down steel rods or a long igniter cord line leading to the fuses. He decided that it would be prudent to ask some of the other section bosses how he might ensure the blast with multiple strands of igniter cord so that the risk of failure was low.

The days turned into a routine of drilling, blasting, and spending evenings with Katrina. On Friday, James went to the personnel department after work to enquire about his new living quarters. Piet van Rensburg had been assigned the task by Mr. Mwanza, and he was waiting for James.

"Well, young James," opened van Rensburg. "It seems we can actually offer you a choice."

"Really?" commented James. "Where?"

"Well, there is one house on Princess Street and another on Philips Street. Which one would you like?"

"Whereabouts on the streets are they? Towards Central Street or the Kafue?"

"The one on Princess is high up close to Central, and the one on Philips is near the top end, not far from the school."

"I think we will take the one on Philips Street."

"I thought you would," commented van Rensburg. "Better to be away from Central and Princess."

"When would we be able to move in?"

"Well, the current residents are returning to the UK on February 20th, then we will take about a week to clean and paint the house, and then it could be yours to move into, on say March 2nd."

"That sounds great!"

"Okay then, why don't you come and see me about the middle of February, and we'll see if there have been any changes."

"Fine, I'll do that."

"*Tot siens* James."

James took the goodbye as a dismissal and left the office. He then drove down Central Street and off to Philips Street to have a look at the house he would be moving into. From what he could see from the road, the current occupants had not done much lately in the garden, and the whole yard had an unkempt look about it. The garden abounded in small walls and posts, all constructed from bricks and painted bright red. Quite what the intention of all that was, he could not fathom; the spaces between the walls abounded in weeds, some small tufts of long grass and a couple of sad-looking bushes.

He drove around the block again and took a look at the neighbours on either side and across the street. The neighbours on both sides appeared to be more enthusiastic about their surroundings, and their gardens were manicured to the point of absurdity. It was quite a contrast, really, within the three adjacent houses. Across the street, it was difficult to see the house because of the huge bougainvillaea hedge that screened it from the road and the solid gates that blocked the driveway. One could only imagine what lay beyond.

The following day, as James studied the results of his raise blast, he suddenly understood what he had been told earlier about the advisability of a pilot hole. It struck him that he was going to have difficulties keeping his lines straight and true without either a guide hole to follow or some clever surveying from the bottom of the raise each day. Kicking himself for not having listened more closely to the advice being given, James sought out the crews that had the diamond drills and talked them into changing their priorities and drilling a pilot hole for him. The drillers had actually been told to put the hole in by the shift boss, but had waited to see if James would ever twig that this was something he should have done and how he would approach them. James went with the diamond drill crew to the site where the raise would top out and found the survey marks that had been painted up and agreed upon a drilling direction and starting time. He would keep a close eye on the progress and only have to pull his own crew out at the last minute before the drillers holed through.

It was probably fortunate that the various levels of hierarchy above him had not paid any visits to discover his omission. He was sure that he would have been reminded again and again of his oversight. Fortunately, the diamond drill crews were not particular talkative and word had not gone around the mine in the way that such similar sins of omission and commission usually did.

For the next week, James kept an anxious eye on the progress of his pilot hole and pulled out his own raise crew in time before the advancing raise met the advancing hole. It was with some considerable trepidation that he climbed up to the top of his new excavation to see where the pilot hole actually came through. Fortune sometimes smiles upon the unwary and unthinking, and he had not strayed too far from the line as to make any material difference. A little sliping here and there, and things would be close to perfect. A useful lesson learned about listening when advice is given.

He had confided in Katrina, and she had listened to his tale of woe but had been unable to help beyond offering a friendly ear. She had her own concerns and worries as the negotiations to sell the transport business had proceeded apace, and it looked as if a deal would be completed within the next day or so. It would take time between the handshake on the deal and the transfer of funds, so that the original timetable of six months had not changed, but the level of certainty had.

Koos had also begun negotiations on the sale of the farm to one of the other businessmen in town who, apparently, had always coveted the location. That transaction might take as long as the sale of the business, but it was at least proceeding. Lastly, there were the wedding plans that Katrina and her mother wrangled about regularly, particularly when it came to the size of the wedding itself, the dress, reception, flowers, just about everything involved. She told James frequently that perhaps it would be better if they just went to the Boma and had a quick and quiet wedding without the fuss and bother.

It was a relief to all when James suggested to Katrina that on the next Saturday afternoon, immediately after work, they take a trip somewhere for the weekend. James had been talking to Hippo and had learned of a tall waterfall out on the road towards Mpika. Hippo had waxed lyrical about the location of the falls and its height and size, and they had worked out that he was talking about the Kundalila falls on the Muchinga escarpment. Katrina had heard of them but had never actually been to them, so James suggested that this would make a nice weekend away. It was not too far that they could not be there before dark on Saturday, if the Great North Road was not too badly washed out and rutted with the heavy traffic.

Friday after work, James went out to the Englebrecht house to prepare for the trip. He had thought that they could get away more quickly on Saturday if they organised themselves beforehand. Katrina had agreed and suggested that she pick him up after work on Saturday, and they would leave straight from the mine. James made arrangements with Tom to be picked up in the morning so that he could leave Katrina his Land Rover with their *katundu* packed.

Saturday, James had some anxious moments as it looked as if everything was going to go wrong and that he would not get away early. However, his crews seemed to have heard from somewhere that he was going away, and all issues were quickly resolved, and they were all able to leave early. When James arrived on the surface, it was deserted. All the *Bwanas* had taken off already, and the only people left were the unfortunate shift bosses saddled with the responsibility of ensuring that nothing untoward occurred. He did see Katrina waiting for him in his Land Rover. She had parked it, rather cheekily, in the covered spot reserved for the Underground Manager. As he had gone, there was probably little risk of her being turfed out. James ran over and told her that he would be back as soon as he had cleaned up a little.

They were on the road south by one thirty with about two hundred and sixty miles to go. Provided that the Great North Road was not too badly washed out, they ought to be able to make that in five to six hours. With sunset at about six-thirty, it would be touch-and-go to make it before dark. As far as Kapiri Mposhi, the road was fine with only a few detours through the bush to avoid large ruts made by the tarmac breaking up under the heavy traffic. The first part of the road from Kapiri towards Serenje was passable, but they quickly ran into problems with deep ruts and no detours. There was standing water on the road in places, and they were forced to wade through several deep puddles. All this served to slow down the trip, and James began to think that they would not make the falls before dark.

Not far past Mkushi River, Katrina told James that the Congolese border was probably less than five miles away to the north. There was a park that took up the very southeastern corner of the Congo; however, roads through the park were uncertain and travel through the Congo was a very hit-and-miss proposition. Once through Serenje, they were actually fairly close to the falls, but their progress was once again slowed by the abysmal road conditions. There were trucks off the road, parked and waiting for help and even a couple stuck in the mud in the middle of the road. Working their way around those was tricky as the bush had not been cleared well back from the road, and there was the danger of hitting a tree stump and taking out the front axle or the engine sump.

It was a relief to turn off onto the side road that led to the falls, as this was a regular dirt road and thus easier to drive on than the patchwork that the main road had become. They reached the top of the escarpment in time to see the sun disappear below the horizon, so decided to leave the falls until the following day. Even in the failing light, it was a spectacular view from the escarpment across the Luangwa Valley. Far below was the Luangwa National Park, and way off to the south, they knew that somewhere was the Zambezi and the border with Mozambique and Rhodesia.

As rain was still a distinct possibility, James rigged a tarpaulin to the back of the Land Rover that would provide ample cover. If it rained too hard, they could always sleep inside the truck. While he was thus occupied, Katrina sorted out dinner. The evening turned cool as the sun went down. He was sure that they had climbed a bit since leaving Kitwe, but it was really hard to tell with all the ups and downs in the road. He asked Katrina if she knew how high they were, and she surprised him by telling him that they were about 4,900 feet above sea level. Curious as to how she knew this, James sneaked up behind her and caught her reading out of an old guide of the area.

"Ha!" accused James. "Caught you, and here I thought it was because you really knew your country!"

"Well, one of us had to be prepared with some information," she replied. "Did you know that we have climbed over 1,000 feet since we left Kitwe?"

"I thought we had probably gone up a little," said James. "But, I was not really sure, the roads do a lot of ups and downs, no wonder it's chilly here."

"Chilly, just wait until June and July, and then you will know what chilly is!" retorted Katrina. "We actually get frost overnight sometimes, did you know that?"

"No, I admit to awful ignorance, but who needs knowledge when you are there to answer for me!"

"*Groot kak*, eat your dinner, and tomorrow we will continue your education!"

Dawn came, and with it the bird chorus. No matter how high they were, it certainly had not diminished the enthusiasm of the birds. James went with Katrina to the edge of the escarpment and looked over. Much of the valley floor was still in deep shadow; James estimated that the valley floor was a good 3,000 feet below them. Katrina told him that they were in the Muchinga mountains and that the escarpment and the valley were remnants of the Great Rift Valley system that dominated much of East Africa. They peered over the edge and spotted the pool at the base of the falls.

There was a rough pathway, so they scrambled down to take a dip. James stripped off his clothes and jumped in, only to come up gasping. The water was cold, and as the falls were in shadow, it was quite an awakening experience. Katrina had seen and heard his gasps, but not quickly enough to forestall her own plunge, so she too was truly jolted into wakefulness. A quick dip was enough for both of them, and they were quite happy to get out, get dressed, and climb back up to their camp. James estimated that the falls must be a good 200 feet tall, so the scramble back up warmed them up nicely.

"I'll bet that is really welcome at the end of a hot day," commented James.

"*Ja*, I believe that people who used to come up from Luangwa made it a stop on the way, just because the water is cool and there is usually plenty of it," said Katrina.

"What else is in this part of the world?" asked James.

"Well, the Livingstone Memorial is not too far away. A little to the north of the main road and past Mpika is Shiwa Ngandu, the English country estate built by Gore-Browne."

"Who?" asked James.

"Gore-Browne, one of you crazy Brits who came here and farmed a big estate in the Northern Province. He was a leading light in the politics of the country through Federation and into Independence," explained Katrina.

"Have you ever been there?"

"No, but pop delivered some stuff there once. He told me that it was an incredible place and that the Gore-Brownes were really nice."

"How come I've never heard of him?"

"After Independence, I think Kaunda and his people in UNIP thought that he was irrelevant and that they no longer needed his advice or counsel, so they dropped him like a hot potato. Shame really, because he put himself at a lot of risk to help these people. He died only a couple of years ago at quite an old age, I think."

As the sun climbed higher in the sky, the valley floor below was finally fully illuminated, and it seemed to James to be just an immense forest riven occasionally with rivers and streams. He added the Luangwa Valley to the list of places that he would one day visit and wondered when he would have the time to do all the things he had on his list. As the day wore on, they could see a rainstorm building and thought it advisable to leave before it rained too hard. As it transpired, it was well that they did, as the drive back to Kapiri took almost five hours, at an average speed of under thirty miles an hour. There were still trucks abandoned in the road, large puddles getting larger by the minute, and a seemingly endless sea of mud. Once back to Kapiri, they were able to pick up speed a little and put the Land Rover back into high range and out of permanent four-wheel drive. It was quite late when they arrived back in Kitwe, and James stayed at the Englebrecht farm rather than make another trip to his new leave house.

For the next few days, James followed the track of his raise and carefully measured the distance by dropping a weighted tape down the diamond drill hole. He got his crew underneath to free the end from the weight and then hold it to the face, allowing him to record the distance left. This allowed him to record on the plans where they were at any time. Finally, they holed through, and the rest of the work to equip the raise could begin. He organised the timber crews who would now install ladders and other services. This would take a while, so he was left with a long walk back and forth to a raise farther away from the working faces.

January 16th was Katrina's birthday. James had found a birthday card and had searched around for a gift. He was really at sea as to what to get her. He decided to seek help and consulted Rita, who was, unfortunately, little help to him because, as she put it,
"You're the one who has to get her something, and you're the one who should know her best by now!"
A fat lot of good that did him. He could hardly buy her a new car or something as large and extravagant as that; she really was not a person who liked jewellery, she liked to buy her own clothes, hated handbags and had her own radio, record player, and camera. So what was he to do? Inspiration finally struck when he remembered that she had waxed lyrical one day about an atlas she had seen in town. It seemed to James an odd sort of present, but at least it was something he knew she had had her eyes on and would probably get for herself one day.

Gift and card in hand, James drove out to the Englebrecht farm to make his delivery. Katrina was delighted with her gift and immediately began picking out those places that she would like to visit in her lifetime. There was a party planned for Saturday evening, staying out late on Friday night was fine except that most of the guests worked Saturday morning, if not all day. James asked about the party and who was coming. The guest list was mostly friends of the family, both old and young, work-related acquaintances, and boating club members. Katrina had decided to hold it at the boat club, rather than at the farm, a lot less work for her and her mother.

The party on Saturday was fun. From somewhere, they had organised a live band, and the party flowed between the inside of the club and the covered veranda, depending on whether the partygoers could tolerate the volume of the music. Rain later in the evening forced most of the outside party to retreat into the main part of the club, but then they hovered close to the doors to save their ears. James thought that it would have been a good idea to bring some earplugs from the mine to save his hearing. He was able to dance with Katrina for quite a bit, but his dancing skills were hardly up to her standard, and he sometimes felt that he was frustrating her.

After a very quiet Sunday at the Englebrecht farm, recovering from the excesses of the party and catching up on sleep, James returned to work on Monday to a completely different set of people and the challenges of the week. Work was progressing steadily on equipping the new raise, and the balance of his development work seemed to be proceeding well. He was surprised one day by a visit from a safety inspector who was, fortunately, a mine employee and not a government inspector. They, according to legend, could be quite difficult and had the power to impose fines, which were payable by the individual and not the company. From the safety inspector, he received five slips on items that needed addressing, from an air line in the magazine to the use of wire to bind hoses to the machines instead of the proper metal banding. He was told to expect a follow-up visit sometime in the next week, when it was expected that all his issues would be addressed and corrected.

James saw Tom quite frequently on his way in and out of the mine. The production section that Tom ran had only been opened up recently, and he was trying to ramp up production as quickly as he could. His section was adjacent to the area in which Hippo was working. As Hippo extended the development tunnels, Tom and his crew would eventually follow up behind them and extract the payable materials. Following James was one of the older section bosses, Elijah Banda. James wondered why there seemed to be a preponderance of Biblical names among many of the Zambians and learned from Hippo that it was the missionary influence in the villages. Elijah met James regularly at the bottom of the ladderways that connected the upper and lower parts of their sections, and they often waited together until all the blasting had been done. As James had to light up his ends by hand, he would climb down to find Elijah waiting at the bottom to connect up his blasting box and set off his charges electrically. James estimated that Elijah was probably in his forties and wondered why he had progressed no farther than section boss, particularly as he was clearly quite competent. One day, while waiting with Elijah for the cage, he asked why he had never been made shift boss. Elijah explained that as an alien from Malawi, he was limited in how far he could progress, as the promotional opportunities were given to the Zambians. He had no animosity towards the Zambians because of this policy; it was just a fact of life and something that they all lived with. One thing that James had also noted was that it seemed that all the Malawians were called Banda; he surmised that it must be a relatively common name in Malawi.

# Greg's tribulations

It was now mid-February, and James was well established in the task of developing his new section in the mine. Living at the Bullock house was not the trial it could have been. James was comfortable enough, and he had grown accustomed to the fact that any and all personal items that belonged to the Bullocks had been stored in a back room that was locked and nailed shut. When they had left, they had mentioned that they were going to 'remove any temptations' from the house. James was not sure if that comment was intended to refer to the house servant or himself, but put it down to the general attitude of the Bullocks. In fact, the house had been so well cleared of any personal items that he might as well have been living in the single quarters, except that the house was bigger and he was catered to by the Bullocks' house servant.

On another front, Koos had finalised his negotiations to sell the business and was set to complete the transaction in mid-March. He had also found a buyer for the farm. That had taken a lot of searching and negotiation because there were very few potential buyers and almost none that were prepared to offer anything outside the country. Getting their money out of Zambia was really the greatest challenge. Koos had arrived at a deal where he essentially converted the cash from the farm sale into more durable items that he was going to take out with him. He was probably stretching the laws about as far as they would go and was a little apprehensive about the treatment that they might receive at the border. He had already decided to emigrate through Botswana, across the Kazungula ferry and then down to Serowe, avoiding Rhodesia and the possible problems there.

Katrina was thinking about where she would work after the business was sold and was talking to several companies in town. She was not sure exactly what she wanted to do, but the buyer of the company had expressed a strong interest in having her stay on as their transportation manager. She had also been approached by a couple of garages in town to manage their parts and service businesses. As her folks were not leaving the country until after the wedding, she had no concerns about where she would live. She had also been acquiring all the things that she felt that she and James would need to set up house together, as James had precious little in the way of household effects.

All in all, life was proceeding about as well as one could expect. There were still rainstorms, but by now the drains had been well and truly cleaned out, and there were few problems with flooding or standing water. Life seemed to have sprung up out of the ground all around, and James was amazed at the things he now saw growing, especially in the bush. There was new growth everywhere, and in places the grass was getting to be so tall it was impossible to see over, and one had to be careful walking through it, never knowing what might lurk. He was now used to the cycle of warm sunshine, then a downpour of rain, and back to sunshine. It seemed to James that the incidence of actual thunderstorms had declined, but he was uncertain if that was in fact true or if he just did not notice them as much.

In letters to his parents, grandmother, and sister, James told more about the forthcoming wedding and had extended the invitation. From Alex, he had heard that she would, in fact, be coming, and she was organising flights to arrive in Ndola about three days before the wedding. His grandmother had written to say that she was delighted with the news, but that she would be unable to attend and asked for pictures of Katrina as soon as possible. From his parents, James had met with stony silence. It was as though he had not informed them, or that they had not received his letters, which he knew they had from information passed on by Alex. He could only conclude that they were not wildly excited about the idea. Ah well, their loss, not his.

He and Katrina had sent invitations to family members and friends, but it looked as if the family members from South Africa would not be attending for a variety of reasons. Other family members of James's from the UK had all declined, and most of his UK friends were now in other countries and scattered across the globe. Local friends of Katrina's family had committed almost to a man that they would be there, and the few invitations that James and Katrina had sent to his friends in Zambia had been accepted. James had watched and listened to arguments and squabbles between Katrina and her mother over the size of the wedding. Katrina favoured something small, but her mother was determined to get her way and have something much grander. On those occasions, James retreated to the *stoep* with Koos and they waited it out. It seemed that even though there were arguments, compromise was always eventually reached.

At the mine, he saw Tom and Joy regularly, and they were both enjoying their assignments and doing well. Greg he saw occasionally, and from what his crews told him, there were problems. He was mulling over what he had heard one day at the shaft station, waiting for a cage, when he heard shouting from the haul road and then a couple of people came running to the station.
"*Chaya na lo surface and kuluma na lo first aid!*" called out one of them.
"*Inindaba?*" James asked.
"*Lo Bwana, fanika lo Bwana ena fili!*" he was told.
"What? What the fuck is going on, Kossam, *bamba lo cage, hamba lapa surface, futi chela lo Bwana lapa, mina azi hamba lapa futi mina azi bamba lo Bwana!*" James quickly gave instructions to Kossam to hold the cage when it came, go to the surface, and tell someone what was happening. He was going to go and find the Bwana, whoever it was, and see what could be done.

Before he went, he grabbed the phone by the shaft and called the surface until he could get someone to answer the phone, then he asked for the first aid station and told them that there was an emergency and to send someone down quickly. With the help of the two people who had first come running into the station, James opened the big, long white cylinder that housed the stretcher and the first aid box and then went to investigate.

On the way, he asked who the Bwana was.
"*Ena lo Bwana Greg*," one of them told him.
"Oh shit," thought James. "Has he had an accident or been clobbered by someone?"
The trammers took him off the main haul road and into a small cross-cut. Greg lay there motionless, his hard hat off in a corner and blood streaming from a large gash in his head. James fought back the gag

reflex that he felt and checked for a pulse. Thank God there was one, albeit weak. Issuing orders like a sergeant major, James organised himself and the others and prepared the stretcher. As far as he could tell from gently probing around the head and neck, the damage was to the head alone. Checking for spinal injuries was going to be difficult with an unconscious patient, and there was a risk in moving him, but he had to be taken to the surface as quickly as possible for real medical attention. Dressings in place to stem the bleeding, James and the others manoeuvred the stretcher and Greg until he was firmly on it and could be strapped down. Then they picked him up and started for the shaft. As a last thought, James picked up Greg's hard hat and put it onto the stretcher.

On the way to the shaft, James looked at the hard hat and decided that the damage was too severe to be caused merely by Greg banging his head on a low part of the roof or an obstruction. It looked as if it had taken a pretty severe blow, so someone had clobbered him after all. Heaven only knew what kind of inquiry and repercussions there would be now, but for the moment, the first priority was treatment. At the shaft station, they only had to wait a few minutes before the cage came and with it the first aid team. They took over immediately and whisked Greg off to the surface.

A mine captain had also come down with the cage, and he detained James. He instructed James to take them to the location where he had found Greg. This mine captain was new to James; he realised that he must be the afternoon shift mine captain, but even so, James was surprised, as he thought that he knew them all. At the crosscut, James pointed out where Greg had been lying, where the hard hat had been, and then detailed what he had done. The mine captain, now introducing himself as David Prescott, wanted to know how James had known of the problem. James then went through the whole story again, starting with the shouts that he heard from the haul road and the subsequent appearance of the two trammers. The two trammers had been tagging along and were hovering in the background, apparently eager to tell their story. James stepped back and let them talk to Prescott while he listened in and tried to make sense of it all.

The story, as the trammers told it, was that they heard some shouts coming from the crosscut, went to investigate, and found Greg lying on the floor. They claimed to have seen no one else and said that they did not hear the shouting well enough to identify who else may have been there. It was all very plausible but at the same time a little rehearsed, so James was left wondering what had actually happened. Apparently, Prescott also had reservations because he sent the two to the surface with instructions to wait for him there. He also asked where the rest of the crew was and learned that they had taken a train to the south side to start pulling ore from the chutes.

"You're Martin, right?" Prescott asked.

"Yes, sir," James replied.

"Well, I've got bad news for you, son," he was told. "Someone has to take charge of this crew and run the tramming shift for a while. You're here, I don't have anyone else handy, so you'll do."

"Could I get something to eat and drink?" James asked.

"Yes, I'll have something sent down for you with the onsetter. Don't expect anything fancy, but it will be enough. Your replacement should be here in about four hours," Prescott said. With that, he went back to the station to go to the surface and told James to be sure and stop by personnel the next morning to give a statement.

James collected himself and started off to find the tramming crews. He had barely walked a few metres when the train came; brilliantly timed to miss all the fuss and ado and the inevitable interviews with the mine hierarchy. He was sure that they were smart enough to realise that there would be an investigation and that they also knew what had occurred and, in all probability, who had done the deed. James decided that discretion was called for, and he simply told them that Greg had been found with an injury, he had been treated and taken to the surface, and that, until a replacement came, he had been put in charge.

He asked the locomotive driver who was the crew boss and learned that it was one of the two sent to the surface. He then asked which stopes they were pulling from and set them onto their appointed tasks. James reflected on the circumstances and the precarious hold they had on the situation. It all hinged on respect, an issue eloquently described in *The Flame Trees of Thika* by Elspeth Huxley. James did not exactly see a risk from armed Africans, but there were risks all the same, particularly if it became clear that you were not the best of *Bwanas*.

For the next three hours or so, James watched the crew and tried to work out who, if any of them, might have been involved. Impossible task! They were the model crew and offered useful suggestions as well as following his instructions. James collected his bread and the salted orange juice normally issued to the ventilation engineers and waited for his replacement. He was relieved when Jimmy van de Merwe appeared and told him that he could go home. Jimmy had also been called in from a day off and was less than delighted with the situation.

"*Howzit,* James?" he asked.

"Pretty bloody shitty," replied James.

"What the hell happened, man?"

"I can't really find out, except that clearly someone clobbered Greg."

"Any ideas who?"

"It could be any one of the tramming crew, or none of them, or just someone on their way out. It all seemed to happen right at about shift change."

"Bloody Greg, he would have to piss off just about everyone he met! What did they use?"

"It looks to me as if it was a large Stilson wrench, but what I can't understand is where it actually happened."

"Why?"

"Well, there isn't enough headroom to swing anything in that crosscut, so I think he was hit in the haul road and then dragged off."

"Well, James, *alles sal reg kom.* You should *hamba lapa kaia* man, you look all in!"

"Thanks, Jimmy. I'll see you probably sooner than we both imagine!"

On that note, James left and went once more to the cage to get a ride to the surface. It was quite late when he finally made it home, but as seemed to be always the case, the news had preceded him, and Moses knew all about the incident and had held dinner until much later. He hovered around, clearly wanting to talk about something.

"Okay, Moses, *ka ini?*" asked James finally.

"*Bwana, lo muntu yena chayili lo Bwana Greg?*"

"*Ja, mina aikôna azi ubani ena chayili yena, kabanga kusasa lo munya muntu yena azi chela tina.*"

"*Kabanga Bwana, munya skati kuluma na lo Phiri,*" offered Moses.

"Sure?" asked James, curious as to how Moses would know this Phiri character was involved.

"Sure, *Bwana!*" Moses assured him.

James wondered which one of the crew was Phiri; he had not really had the opportunity to get to know them all. It also struck him that all the crew were still underground except for the two sent to the surface to give statements. Perhaps one of them was Phiri, and that was how Moses knew something of what had occurred.

Moses brought coffee, and James had just poured himself some when someone pulled into the driveway. Curious as to who this could be, James took his coffee and went to the door. He was delighted to see Katrina.

"James, are you okay?" she asked.

"Of course. Why?"

"We heard about Greg, and then we also heard that you were there. The boys were telling me that you were fine and had only stopped to help, but I wanted to be sure."

"Doesn't it amaze you sometimes how quickly news travels around here and how everyone seems to know what is going on, even before it happens?"

"Not really, that's just the way it is. Now come here and let me check you out and make sure that you are still in one piece!"

"Where did they take Greg?" asked Katrina a little later.

"I think straight to the hospital," replied James.

"Are you going to go and see how he is doing?"

"I hadn't thought about it."

"You should, he has no real friends here from what you've told me, and he and his wife will need some help now."

"Won't the personnel people help?"

"They will do something, of course, but what those two will need now is to know that there is someone else who cares."

"Do you really think so, *suikerbossie*?"

"Sure, James, you must check on him tomorrow, and then we will *maak n' plan*. Do you want to come back to the farm with me tonight?"

"That would be great. Why don't I follow you back? I have to be at the shaft tomorrow and give some kind of statement before I go down."

"Okay, *kom ons ry*!"

The next day, James went to the shaft early and met with his crews before they went down. He shuffled them around a little to assign a blasting licence holder to each work area so that he could afford to be a little late getting down himself. That done, he met with the personnel people and gave his official statement before finally escaping to take the cage down with the shift bosses and mine captains. He had to go through his story again for the benefit of this larger audience and was happy to escape them and go off to his own section. His crews started work, and he only had a few ends to check and mark up himself. Throughout the day, James would catch odd snatches of conversations that clearly were about the incident of the day before, but everyone quickly quietened when he appeared, and he learned nothing.

After work, James drove to the hospital and then sat in the car park for fifteen minutes trying to think what on earth he would say to Greg and Shirley. He went into the hospital and asked at a desk where he might find Greg. He had to answer all kinds of inane questions that would have been obvious to anyone with a modicum of common sense. No, he was not a family member; it was hardly practical to make it from England to Zambia that quickly. No, he was not his supervisor. No, he was not from personnel. Yes, he did know Greg. Yes, he did work with him. Yes, he was the one who had been called and had been credited with finding Greg.

He was finally allowed to proceed, but not before being given a whole set of restrictions, limitations, warnings, and prohibitions. Entering the ward where Greg was recovering, he met Piet van Rensburg, who told him that Greg would have a pretty bad headache, but that his skull was not fractured. He then dropped his bombshell: Shirley had left the country that day. She had just upped and gone, leaving Greg in the hospital. Piet said that they had found out when he had gone to the house to collect her and had been told by the neighbours that Shirley had left early with a lot of luggage. A check with the airline confirmed that she had, in fact, gone.

At the end of the ward, a bed had been screened off, and a Mine Policeman was stationed to prevent casual visitors and onlookers. Piet took James to the screens and then told him to wait until he checked with Greg that he was actually up to visitors. James could hear the tones of the quiet conversation going on behind the screens, but not the words. Piet reappeared and ushered him in.

"Greg, *howzit* man?"

"James, have you come to gloat?"

"Hell no, man, I'm just sorry I was not around a little earlier yesterday so that you might not be here today."

"Well, thanks for your help. God only knows what I'm going to do now. Do you know that Shirley left me?"

"Yes, Piet just gave me the news. I'm sorry, Greg."

"Well, you needn't be," said Greg. "We have been having problems since we got here, and we probably would have split sooner or later anyway."

"Boy, Greg, I don't know what to say. Is there anything I can do?"

"No, hey, I'm sorry I accused you of coming to gloat. I heard from Piet that you were the one who found me and got me out. Thanks again."

"All I did was help," said James. "Some of your crew were the ones who raised the alarm. Do you know what happened or who slugged you?"

"No, I was yelling at some of those wankers to get a bloody move on and the next thing, everything went blank."

"Where were you?" asked James.

"We were in the haul road, which means, from what Piet tells me, that someone dragged me off into the cross-cut where you found me."

During this exchange, James noticed that Piet was listening carefully and comparing what Greg was saying to something he had written. He realised that Piet was checking to see if the story stayed the same or if Greg remembered anything new. James also realised that the ones being yelled at probably knew perfectly well who had done the hitting.

"Can I get you anything, Greg?" asked James.

"No thanks, Piet here seems to be able to either cajole the harridans here into action or conjure up almost anything except a beer."

"What about at your house?"

"We are taking care of that," interposed Piet.

"Should I stop by again tomorrow?" asked James.

"Please do. It's going to be a while before I get out of here, and it would be nice to talk to someone occasionally who doesn't want to stick me with some object."

"Okay, I'll leave you to Piet and see you tomorrow. Bye Greg. *Totsiens, oom* Piet."


James left the hospital in a bit of a daze. He had expected to find Shirley there with Greg, and to learn that she had just up and left without so much as a goodbye was a bit of a facer. He drove to the Englebrecht yard to confide in Katrina. As he entered the office, Katrina looked up from her work and smiled at him, then asked him what was wrong.

"How did you know there was anything wrong?" asked James.

"It's written all over your face," replied Katrina.

"Well, I just went to see Greg in the hospital and apart from being clobbered on the head yesterday, Shirley upped and left today. Poor bastard, I wonder what will happen to him next?"

"Oh, so it was Shirley who left. I heard from some of the drivers that a white woman was raising hell at the airport in Ndola, trying to get on a plane out of the country, but I didn't know it was her. Shame, I wonder why she left and what he will do now?"

"Well, I suppose he must get himself well enough to leave hospital, then I wonder if they will put him back into the same job?" mused James.

"Where did she get the money for the ticket?" wondered Katrina.

"I'll bet she emptied out his bank account. But, you know, that means she must have done that yesterday before the bank closed because today she was already in Ndola before the bank opened."

"She must have heard and reacted awfully quickly to be able to do that, and didn't she go to the hospital yesterday afternoon?"

"I don't know. I just assumed that she would go. You don't suppose that she paid someone to belt him, do you?" asked James.

"Now you're imagining things!" retorted Katrina. "But, you know, it would make a good piece of gossip for the fish wives here."

"Yes, I can just see the headlines in the *Times of Zambia:* "Expat wife in contract hit". Sounds good, don't you think?"

"Well, just make sure you don't have someone *chaya* you!" Katrina said. "Do you fancy a beer?"

"Yes, good idea, shall we go to the dam?" James suggested.

"*Kom ons ry, ou maat!*" answered Katrina, indicating yes and let's go now!

The next day, underground, James asked Kossam if he had heard anything more about the incident with Greg. Kossam talked in a roundabout way for a few minutes, then told James that the mine police were close to arresting someone. James asked Kossam if he knew why Greg had been struck, and Kossam seemed genuinely puzzled. The one whom they all believed had struck him was apparently not part of the tramming crew, but a driller from Hippo's section.

This could mean something or nothing. If he was related to or friends with someone from the tramming crew, it could just be taking care of the problem for them. If he had no relationship with the tramming crew, then the field for speculation was wide open. Apparently, Hippo was of the opinion that Shirley had been seeing the driller after work, and Greg was in the way. That shook James! Miscegenation no less! If that were the case, where did they meet, who went where and oh so many more questions? But, James reasoned, that was all pure speculation, and he still had a job to do and needed to do it in such a way as to avoid getting his head bashed.

At the end of the shift, James met Hippo, who seemed eager to share his opinion and was also full of speculations as to how, when, where, and why. In Hippo's mind, at least the issue was resolved, and it was now just a case of finding a new driller, because the one he could lose was very good at his job. He wondered if he could quietly raid one of the other sections and get a good man transferred to him, but the personnel people might get in the way of that, so he was tending towards making a deal with one of the other section bosses for a trade of people for machines.

He had a couple of spare machines hidden, and they were like gold at the moment, so he could probably make a good deal with them, particularly as he was confident that he could reacquire the machines shortly after he traded them. Such were the everyday machinations of running the underground operations. He even had a scheme worked out to foil the auditor types who came down to take rubbings of the machine serial numbers to verify what units were where. Hippo told James that if he ever needed help in this area or any other area, just to let him know, and it would be taken care of.

At the change house, James ran into Bill.
"Ah, James, just the man I've been looking for."
"Bill, *howzit*?"
"I wanted to know if you and that Katrina of yours would be available to come to my wedding on Saturday after next, the 28th?"
"Ah, set the date, have we?" asked James.
"Yes, it will be in Luanshya at St. George's church at four in the afternoon with a reception to follow at the church hall. I have already asked Hippo, Joy, Tom, and Lionel, so you are last on the list."
"Thanks, I will check with Katrina, but as far as I know, we have nothing on so we will be there. Is there anything particular you need for a wedding present?"
"Nothing really, just a place to live. You wouldn't believe what a bunch of bastards the personnel people are being. They seem to be going out of their way to be unhelpful. How did you get on with them when you asked for married housing?"
"They didn't want to help at first, but I wore them down and agreed to pay the extra in rental without any complaints. But, there is at least one other house available now because they offered me the choice of two."
"You know I'll bet this is their way of disapproving of my marrying Mary, what do you think?"
"Hell, Bill, I don't know. Who knows what they like or don't like, but there is nothing in your contract that says you can't get married. Just go

in there, wave the contract around and sound like a barrack room lawyer and they will probably behave."

"Thanks, James, I might just do that!"

Hippo, who had been listening to this exchange, then added his piece.

"Bill, my friend, let me talk to Henry Mwanza. I am sure he will be happy to cooperate!"

"Really, Hippo, do you think so? It would mean so much to Mary and me if we could sort this out before too long. She is trying to get a job at either the mine hospital or Kitwe Central so that she can work in Kitwe and not have one of us driving the Kitwe-Ndola road every day."

After Hippo had left, James turned to Bill and commented that Hippo seemed to be some sort of fixer, as nothing was impossible for him. Bill agreed and wondered if it was charm, the promise of future favours, money, or physical coercion. Whatever the means, if there were a price to be paid later, he would cross that bridge when it arose. James also asked Bill if he had heard about Greg and learned that Bill shared Hippo's opinion that Greg was in the way of a relationship between Shirley and Phiri. James jolted at that. Wasn't it Phiri that Moses had told him to talk to? He wondered if there could be more than one Phiri involved or if, as was usual, the houseboys knew everything that was happening.

"Do you think Greg knows?" James asked.

"Probably not, poor bastard. Don't they say that the husband is the last to know?"

"But, I've met Shirley and she seemed to me as *verkrampte* as they come. How did they meet? Where? How long has this been going on?"

"I'm sure that in time, old Hippo will give us the lowdown. If Greg doesn't know who's going to tell him?"

"Not me, that's for certain. I think we could all safely leave that to the personnel chaps and let old van Rensburg earn his fifty kwacha."

James asked Katrina later if she would be free to go to Bill and Mary's wedding and learned that she had already been discussing it with Rita. Apparently, they had agreed on travelling together and had already designated Tom as the driver who would drink the least and make sure they all got home safely.

"But how did you know we would be invited?" asked James.

"Oh, simple, one of our drivers knows an uncle of Mary's, and he told me that we were on the list of guests."

"You know, this place amazes me," said James. "Everyone seems to know what is going on, and information travels faster than the speed of sound, if not light. How does word get around so fast?"

"I don't really know, but there are the most incredible stories of people knowing about events that occur far away, almost as soon as they happen. Just remember that when you think you are getting away with something! How much *lobola* did Bill pay for Mary?"

"I don't know. Do you really think he paid *lobola?*" asked James.

"Oh yes, he did. I have it from the drivers, only I don't know how much and whether it was cash or cows."

"Hippo told me that he believes that Greg was part of the eternal triangle. Apparently, according to Hippo, Shirley was having it off with one of Hippo's drillers, a chap called Phiri."

"No man! Genuine?"

"Apparently so. I'm sure that in time all the sordid details will come out. But who'd have thought it?"

"*Ja* man, I'm telling you, the VC tenner wifies, if they don't work, they get bored and then who knows what they will do?"

Thursday of that week, James was sitting on one of his powder boxes, filling out paperwork. He had set the crews to work early and was taking a short respite before starting the charging-up process. He was surprised to see one of the crew from his top level running towards him, clearly very agitated.

"*Bwana, bwana, fanika lo muntu ena fili, buya checha!*"

"*Lo muntu ena fili, Ubani ena fili?*" he asked in a serious panic now. Who on earth was dead and how?

"*Aikôna, lo muntu aikôna fili, buya na mina checha!*" Obviously, it would be a good idea to go with him and quickly find out what had happened.

Not sure just what was going on, but relieved that no one was actually dead, but now he thought about what he had heard and realised that he had been told that a man had almost been killed. He climbed up to the top development level and found Banda very much alive but visibly shaken.

"*Ini lo?*" asked James.

"*Buwawa, mina chaya lapa, futi ena kona lo munya drive lapa side, lo jombolo hamba panzi,*" said Banda.

Making some suppositions and guesses, James concluded that they had hit some kind of open space ahead of where they were drilling, and the drill bit had gone through into empty space. No wonder poor old Banda looked shaken up, the air leg would have pushed the drill right up to the face with no resistance. James walked over to the face and looked. Banda pointed out to him the hole that had gone through and continued with his voluble explanations of what had happened.

"*Okay, Banda, buisa lo gafa stick, meningi,*" James ordered, and Banda and his helper quickly gathered up all the charging sticks they could find. James pushed one into the hole, then added an extension. He kept adding extensions and pushing them into the hole until he had about twenty metres of stick through the hole. This much empty space beyond probably meant that they had hit an old development drive, but James had no information on his drawings that showed him anything.

James thought about it for a while and decided that if it were an old drive, it was slightly closer to the ore body than the drive they were currently extending, and it was one of the side holes in his blast pattern that had holed through. He measured where they were from the survey peg and then sketched up the situation. He told Banda to barricade the drive and move his equipment out, then changed his assignment for the rest of the day to helping him with the charging. He also put a wooden plug in the hole. He could feel air flow through the hole, so there was access to the surface or the ventilation network somewhere.

At the end of the shift, James went to the shift bosses' office and told Abel Mwewa what had happened and asked for guidance. Abel immediately took James off to see Chris Phillips, the mine captain, and James again went through his story.

"Okay, James, now we have to find out what we are dealing with. Abel, take James with you and go to the old planning building and see if you can find any plans or records from the old miners who worked that area. I imagine it would have been about 1946 to 1948 when they worked that section on contract from that old number three inclined shaft. It does surprise me a little that they were that far down at that time. I didn't think they even got down to 2,000 feet, let alone the 2570 level. Well, I suppose you never know, we had better check it out," said Phillips.

Abel told James to follow him, collected his car and drove off towards a group of old buildings. They went into the larger of the buildings and looked around. There were racks of drilling core samples and racks of rolled-up drawings.
"Does anyone ever come here and use this stuff?" asked James.
"Not for many years," replied Abel. "I have no idea where anything that might be useful to us might be hiding; we should just start looking."
"There is no catalogue or index?"
"Hah, these people, I do not think we will find any index. You start over there, and I will start here. We are looking for records or drawings for inclined shaft number three."

James started pulling the rolls of drawings and looking for dates and locations. There actually seemed to be some logic, so he was able to quickly dispose of the shaft number one and two drawings and find the sets that pertained to shaft number three. Now it was a case of looking at each drawing and working out to what particular area it applied and deciding whether or not it was germane. The drawings were old and, in some cases, partially eaten by mice and cockroaches. James was a little concerned with all the evidence of mice and asked Abel what was uppermost in his mind.

"Abel, with all these mice around, do you think there are any snakes in this building?"
"Oh God, I hope not. I hate snakes! Have you found anything yet?"

"Yes, a lot of drawings associated with the number three inclined shaft, but nothing yet that would be low enough to intersect with my upper level."

"I have found a lot of payment records for work done during the period we are looking at, but they all seem to end at levels well above the 2,000-foot line."

"Was there a sub-vertical that we don't know about?" asked James.

"There must have been to go that far down, I wonder where? Is there anything marked?"

"Not yet, I'll keep looking."

After two hours of poring over drawings and records, Abel waved a piece of paper in the air.

"James, this is a payment for a shaft station on the 1950 level that I think is close to your section," crowed Abel.

"Let's see," said James, does it tell us where on strike it was?"

"Yes, 2,500 feet north of the number three shaft."

"Okay, do you have that plan of the current operations, and is the number three incline also marked?"

"Yes, see here is where you are, here is the number three and here is where this new station was going to be," said Abel.

"So, it does look as if they put down a sub-vertical shaft. I wonder how far down it went?" mused James.

"No information," replied Abel. "Keep looking!"

It took another two hours before James found a drawing that had been marked up in pencil with the location of the new sub-vertical shaft and the levels off it. As far as they could make out, it looked as if the level that Banda had hit was the lowest level developed off the shaft. The mark-up did not show the development anywhere near as advanced as it now appeared to be, but Abel assured James that this was not surprising, as the contract miners would only report their progress when they needed the money and tended to "bank" progress to spread their income.

"The next problem is, did they leave any explosives down there, and are there any holes you might hit charged with really old explosives?" commented Abel.

"Oh, shit. Do you really think so?" asked James.

"It's possible. We have found old explosives in the past," said Abel. "They had this habit of just leaving when their contracts ran out, and if the ends were charged, they stayed charged."

"Great, so then what?" asked James.

"We drill your end, leaving out the side holes. Shoot the whole lot and hope that anything old sympathetically detonates with the blast," said Abel. "Then we go in and wash it all down and pump out any holes we see."

"Thanks a lot," said James. "Maybe I'll do that with Kossam and move Banda to another job for a few days. Poor bastard got quite a shock when his drill holed through and the air-leg propelled him towards the face!"

"Okay, so what we need is that drawing and these notes, and I will tell Chris in the morning what we plan to do. You should expect a visit from at least two of us tomorrow to have a look and maybe even the Assistant Underground Manager, so you'd better make sure that the rest of the section is in good order."

"Thanks, Abel. I really need a bunch of *mkulu skopus* coming around. Can't you keep them all away?"

"Sorry, they will be concerned with safety, so also expect people from safety and ventilation to come as well."

"Great!" commented James. "Just what I need. What is all this other stuff?"

"Oh, old exploration records going back to the twenties," Abel replied.

"Really, have you ever looked at any of them?" James asked.

"No, why don't you grab one or two if you are interested and read them at your leisure," suggested Abel. "You never know what you might find."

"Okay," said James, and he picked up a slim folder marked 'BBB', and they left.

Abel was right. The following day, James saw more people in white overalls than he had ever seen in the mine. They all had different opinions about what they were dealing with, and when the planning people showed up, there were some testy words between Phillips and the planners about investigating old workings and providing him with good information. At the end of the day, the plan had not changed, and James was instructed to finish the blast on the next day, but to put up a barricade first that would limit the airflow through to the old workings. James begged for another day so that he could get the timber crew in with a barricade and a door. That was acceptable to everyone, so he put his plan into action.

When James's crew set off the blast that would hole through, he was curious to see what they would find beyond. With Kossam in tow, James picked his way over the blasted material and walked into history. The air was clear enough; obviously, his door worked, but not well enough to totally seal the airway and the leakage had cleared out the blast gases. The old drive was almost the same size as the one he was currently mining, parallel, but slightly closer to the orebody. He could see, looking back, the ends of the holes that had been drilled to extend the drive forward. He checked for misfires and old explosives, but none were evident, so he got Kossam to bring up a water hose, and they washed everything down. Another inspection of the hole ends showed no evidence of explosives, so there either had been no residuals or it had all sympathetically detonated.

James wondered how far down the drive he should go and decided not to go too far today. He told Kossam to wait for him and walked slowly down the drive towards the old shaft. There were remnants of the shaft fittings still in place, but much of the timber looked as if it had rotted. James decided that ever trying to climb out of that shaft would be a very poor idea. Now the planners had to come down and determine how much of the orebody had been mined out and whether or not it was worth proceeding with the current development. Well, that was their problem, not his.

For the week that followed, James went to work and each day heard a little more from Hippo about the Shirley and Phiri saga. The mine police took Phiri away one day and handed him over to the Zambia Police, but there, things stalled because there were no witnesses who could be persuaded to remember anything. Come Saturday, 28ᵗʰ February, James was quite happy to have something else to think about. After work, he went out to the Englebrecht farm to collect Katrina, and she met him at the door dressed in a light tan linen suit and a broad-brimmed hat. James had dug out his one suit, and Moses had done a stellar job in cleaning and pressing it, so he actually looked fairly presentable. They had arranged to meet Tom and Rita at their house, so James drove them into town. It dawned on him while they were driving in that something had been really different at the farm; there had been no dogs.

"What happened to all the dogs?" he asked Katrina.
"Mommy has been working with some auntie in Lusaka who runs a kennel, and they came to an arrangement. They were all collected two days ago."
"You didn't mention it before?" accused James.
"No, I suppose I was a little upset that they were all going, but they could not take them all south, so they are only taking the house dogs," she replied.

Tom and Rita were waiting for them, and they transferred cars and were driven to Luanshya. On the way out, James went through his tale with Tom and Rita. Upon hearing about his grabbing an old exploration folder, Tom asked him if he planned to go into business for himself and become the next Harry Oppenheimer or Ronald Prain. James laughed at that and said no, probably more like Collier or one of the other early prospectors, not the people who made the real money.

The church in Luanshya was busy when they arrived. Most of the guests were congregated on the bride's side of the nave, with only a small group on the groom's side. James led the way towards the front, and they were spotted by Bill. He came back and introduced them to his brother, John, who was there as the best man. They joined the few that were there supporting the groom and took their seats. Joy was already there with his wife, Susie, and so were Lionel and Jane.

The service was familiar to most of them as it was a standard Church of England wedding ceremony. James was a little curious about the priest, a white man with a couple of black deacons. He wondered whether or not the C of E was ordaining black ministers yet. He was sure that they were, but he had yet to see any, not that he had been to any churches, but he was always curious. James was impressed by the singing; the congregation really got into the spirit of the hymns. As the happy couple walked down the aisle, James wondered how the bride's father really felt and how the couple would do, particularly if they went to England at some time in the future.

The reception was held in a hall adjacent to the church and was a buffet rather than a sit-down meal. James and his party joined the throng and were introduced to the bride's parents and other family members. Bill came over briefly and talked to them before his new wife claimed him and took him off to meet some people. John came over to join them and asked them what they thought about Bill and Mary. James and Tom both commented that it was Bill's decision, and they hoped he would be happy. John went on to say that the biggest problem he foresaw was the time when Bill returned to the UK with Mary. He was not sure how the community he came from would accept them both. Rita then asked John if he had given any thought to the fact that it would not be easy for Mary's parents to see her go off into the world with someone else and not know when, or if, they would see her again. John admitted that he had not actually thought about that.

The party looked as if it was getting into full swing and could go all night, and Katrina asked James how long he anticipated staying. Her question was put in such a way that James thought that the proper answer was likely to be not long. Rita then chimed in with the comment that she was tired and would appreciate it if they could start out for Kitwe. On the drive home, Katrina admitted to James that she had felt a little uncomfortable at the wedding reception. It was difficult for her to put into words, but for her whole life until now, her upbringing had been in a society that was segregated, and this was all new to her.

James, Tom, and Rita all commented that their only experiences with other races had been with students at university; they all came from environments that were whiter than white. James thought back and recalled only one black family that lived anywhere near him. They had come from Jamaica in the mid-fifties. Tom and Rita said there were a few more families in Notting Hill, but the groups had never mixed. This was a new experience for them as well.

"It's ironic, isn't it?" said James. "Here, old Bill looks as happy as can be marrying Mary and Greg is struggling to get out of hospital and has to deal with the fact that Shirley ran off."

"Well, that's life," commented Tom. "Maybe if Greg were a little more open, he might find life a little easier."

"You know the people I really feel for are Mary's parent," said Rita. "Their daughter is marrying this white chap and in all probability they will leave Zambia and go to England or somewhere, and who knows when they may see her again?"

"I know," said Katrina. "Daddy is keeping a brave face, but he must also be wondering what will happen to me and where I will go."

"When did he leave South Africa?" asked Tom.

"When I was really small," replied Katrina. "At the time, he came with little or nothing, so was not sure when he would see South Africa again. In fact, I was about eight, I think, when we made the first trip back."

"What is it with Afrikaners?" asked Tom. "They seem to want to get away from everyone."

"True," laughed Katrina. "They used to say that if you could see the smoke from your neighbour's fire, they were too close and it was time to move on!"

# Banns & Birthday

Monday after work, James went to the personnel department and was given the keys to the house he had been assigned. Piet van Rensburg had promised March 2nd, and he was true to his word. James drove to the house and parked in the driveway. The house was a standard mine house for his pay grade, which meant it had a kitchen, dining cum living room, three bedrooms, and a screened-in porch. The floors were like most he had seen, concrete polished with red floor polish. There were bars on the windows, no curtains or shades yet, and a minimum allocation of basic furniture. James wandered through the house and tried to picture what life might be like in his own house instead of leave houses. He cut short his musings to go and meet Katrina at St. Michael's church to register their banns.

The banns would be read out over the successive weeks, and James presumed that no one would find 'just cause or impediment' as to why the marriage should not proceed. The priest was friendly enough and did not seem to mind at all that Katrina was not a regular visitor. James had never actually been into St. Michael's before, so he was totally new. Katrina had been able to talk her mother out of a choir and all the other trappings that can come with a church wedding, so the fees were not all that steep, still more than the seventy-five ngwee it would have cost at the Boma!

James then told Katrina the latest about Greg and Phiri, according to Hippo that was. Greg was out of hospital and had been assigned to the special projects office for a while, known affectionately on the mine as the special rejects office. Phiri was back at work, as there was no real case against him, without any witnesses, but he had been reassigned to one of the other shaft complexes. James was not sure if Greg would return to his previous assignment or whether he was destined to be in the planning office for an extended period of time. The problem for Greg was that the assignment took him right out of the line of any advancement. The mine ran on pretty conventional lines, and the expectation was a stint in each of the various hierarchical levels underground as the path to success and promotion. Any deviation from the norm was difficult for the mine management to deal with, and outliers tended to get pigeon-holed and forgotten.

Katrina asked if anyone had heard anything further from Shirley, but all James knew was that Greg had received some papers that had really upset him, so presumably they were divorce proceedings. He doubted if they would see Shirley ever again. Katrina then went on to voice her hopes and misgivings about their own marriage. She wondered if they were too young; it was such a big step, and undoing it was an even bigger step. James had had similar thoughts, but after a deal of cogitation, had decided that, yes, it was the right thing to do, and he was convinced that it would work. Katrina was happy to hear that and pointed to Tom and Rita for a relationship that obviously worked and seemed destined for longevity. It was probably all about pre-wedding jitters, and it was good to actually air their misgivings and come to an understanding.

With the banns registered and misgivings quelled, at least for the moment, there was still time to check out the new house before dinner. They each drove there, and James showed Katrina around. She took notes of curtain sizes and also had a quick look around the garden to see what else she thought could use improvement. By this time, it was almost dark and time for dinner. James wondered if Moses had cooked anything and was delighted to find that he had prepared a chicken with accompanying vegetables. After dinner, Katrina took off, saying that she had things to organise, leaving James to his own devices.

With time on his hands, James started to read the papers in the file he had picked up. They were prospecting reports for Loangwa Concessions (Northern Rhodesia) Limited, except that Loangwa had been struck out and Nkana written in. The person submitting the reports was a B. B. Brock, and the reports were for 1934. James tried to remember what the history of Loangwa Concessions was and what relationship it had with the company he was currently working for. He felt that it was likely that the Nkana Concessions had some relationship to the Anglo American group of companies, but one could never be sure, as concessions and ownerships changed hands a lot between 1920 and 1940.

Brock was interesting; most of the reports were typewritten, but one, the first of the series, was handwritten. What James was reading were monthly returns of activity and comments on anything interesting found. There was also a basic accounting of time spent and distances travelled, e.g., for one month: "Rivers and Streams Traversed, mileage … 6.8, Straight-line Traversing, mileage … 205.0, Total Miles Traversed … 211.8." In that particular month, Brock spent 24 days traversing, 2 days on test pits on the Kafue River, 1 day on reports and 4 Sundays, which were clearly not work days. He listed any economic minerals that he found and generally described the geology of the area in which he was working. James was intrigued by the attachment to that report on the possibility of gold along the Kafue River and in a later report of gold in the Kasalia Stream. The problem was that he had no real idea where Area X was, and whereabouts along the Kafue Brock was operating. Clearly, he would have to re-read the reports and see if there were clues as to location, or he would have to find a map of the concession area that showed the sub-areas and, in particular, Area X.

The next day, when he saw Abel after work, he asked him if he had any idea where the concession sub-areas were. Unfortunately, Abel had no clue and had no notion of where to find out except in some archive somewhere. James returned to his studies and made copies of the reports that he had so that he could return the folder to Abel, who was now beginning to wonder if it had been the correct thing to take anything from the records. As he read the reports, James was fascinated; he could almost imagine the work of traversing lines across the bush, setting up camp at different locations, and collecting an ever-growing pile of rocks and gravel. He realised that one of the elements missing from the reports was any mention of who else was with him. There had to have been any number of Africans with him, to dig, collect, carry, cook and generally make sure everything could proceed. James also knew that nearly all the major discoveries had, in fact, been known deposits that had been pointed out to the European prospectors by Africans. So who were these unnamed natives with the knowledge?

James asked Katrina if she knew anything about the area he was looking at, and she told him that she would ask the drivers if they knew where the various streams were that he mentioned. She went on to tell him about the copper flower. Apparently, according to legend, where one found a particular type of flower, there was also supposed to be copper. In fact, it was said that it would only grow where there was copper. In her opinion, that plus the workings of the ancients were the major clues that led the European prospectors to potential mine sites. In many cases, they had actually been led to old mine workings that had been hand-dug by people long ago.

"I'm telling you, James," she said. "Those old *madalas* were pretty jacked-up and knew what they were doing."

"Why is there so little said about it?" he asked.

"Well, if you were being paid to find copper, why would you tell the *Bwanas* that you were not needed. All they needed were a couple of *madalas* who knew the area and the history. Much cheaper!"

"It must have been fun, though, don't you think?" asked James. "Exploring the bush with a couple of good guides, game to shoot and eat, camps to make, and other people to carry all the stuff!"

"*Ja*, but what about the rains, man, that had to be no fun," Katrina commented.

"Did anybody ever die on these prospecting trips?" asked James.

"Oh, I'm sure they did, but the only story I ever heard was about some *rooinek* with more guts than gumption who followed a wounded lion into tall grass."

"Were these chaps married?"

"I don't know," replied Katrina. "But, I'll bet many of them landed up like your friend Bill, in spirit if not legally."

"On another subject, how is the sale of the company and the farm going?" asked James.

"Fine, I don't think there are any problems. My folks should be able to leave when they planned and make their way south."

"Where in the Cape are they planning to go?"

"They have a spot picked out near Calitzdorp, a small farm, I think, with some vineyards."

"Where is Calitzdorp?"

"Close to Oudtshoorn"

"I remember a road sign to there, but I didn't really know how to pronounce it. What's in Calitzdorp?"

"Well, for one thing, it's the Hanepoort capital of South Africa."

"What's that?"

"It's a dessert wine, sweet, somewhat like sherry, but better, if you're Afrikaans."

"So, your dad is going to get into this business?"

"Better than ostriches," retorted Katrina. "In fact, I'm rather looking forward to having somewhere nice to go down south that is more in the country, more like here, but drier."

"What kind of place is Calitzdorp?"

"A real Afrikaans *dorpie*, no *Engelsmen* there, the story is they hanged the last one a few years ago!" replied Katrina.

"Well, perhaps one day we can both visit and you can protect me from the local element!"

"Hah, only if you're good!"

"What do you mean, good?"

"Come here and let me show you," said Katrina, ending conversation for a while.

Later, she told him that she had been to the house and had started work on the curtains. She also said that her dad had sent a crew to clean up the garden, mow the grass, and trim the hedges. There was a fence on one side of the house that needed repair, and that would be taken care of the next day. She was not happy with the painting that had been done and had organised for that to be redone as well, and finally, she was not happy with the locks on the doors and had some new ones installed along with better bolts. Katrina suggested to James that he move in over the weekend, after she had had the curtains installed and had stocked the linen closet and the pantry. This was all rather new to James, and he rather liked the idea of someone doing these kinds of things for him. During the balance of the week, he stopped by after work and checked on progress and was delighted with what he found.

Katrina had done a superb job of organisation, and the house now looked almost brand new. James talked to Moses and told him that he would be moving out that weekend, and he also told Piet van Rensburg that he was vacating the Bullocks' house and asked him to keep an eye on things until they returned from their leave.

James asked Katrina one evening what was going to happen to all the staff on the farm and to the houseboys. Apparently, the buyer of the farm wanted the farm crew to all stay on and had met with them. As to the house boys, Seventeen, the *madala*, was retiring and taking the money that Koos had put aside for him and returning to his family's village. Gibson, the younger one, if fortyish, was younger, would be staying, and when Koos and Sussana left, would be coming to work for Katrina and James. If they needed help in the garden, there were always family members of the farm crew who would be happy to earn the extra money.

Friday, after work, James returned the exploration folder to a relieved Abel, who was determined to replace it in the archives, even if the documents were being eaten by termites, mice, ants, and other beasties. James had learned from his own people that the Kasalia stream was in fact fairly close to Kitwe, just a little north and east. As far as he could make out, the Mutundu stream must be to the south of the town. So, when Brock was working in 1934 and filing reports on the Nkana Concession, he must have been working fairly close to where they now were. He found Tom and asked him what he was doing on Sunday. Tom wanted to know what was in the wind, so James told him that he was going to look for the Kasalia stream and asked if he wanted to come along. Tom asked if Katrina was coming, and upon learning that she was, said that he would check with Rita and let him know later that evening.

As it transpired, the drivers at the Englebrecht company had given the same information to Katrina that James had received and had even given some clues as to how to get to the various streams. Katrina and James were discussing their Sunday excursion at the boat club and were joined by Tom and Rita.

"Hello, Katrina," said Rita. "Should we go along on the crazy venture these two are talking about?"

"No, man, it will be fun, I'm telling you," she replied. "Any trip into the bush, even a short one, is fun!"

"So, I'm confused, are we going or not?"

"Yes, didn't I say so? I'm sorry."

"Don't worry, Rita, you'll get used to it!" said James. "It has taken me a while to be sure I always understand."

"Understand what?" asked Katrina. "I don't know what you are talking about."

"*Moenie* worry *nie*," said James. "It's only us who are a little slow."

"So where is this famous stream, and will we find our fortunes in gold?" asked Tom.

"According to both my chaps and Katrina's drivers, it's just north of Kitwe on the other side of the river," replied James. "If we take the Muf road across the river and turn southeast behind the Kafironda factory, we should be able to make our way there."

"Well, how will we know that it is the right one? There must be lots of little streams around," asked Rita.

"We'll ask," said Katrina. "I'm sure that any of the *madalas* we see can tell us which is the right stream."

"What about making our fortunes?" reiterated Tom.

"You'll be lucky," replied James. "Even if we found anything, we have no licence, so we could not legally mine or sell it. This is just for the edification!"

"Maybe, I'd rather sit at the club and drink beer," Tom added.

"Later, after we at least look for the stream," promised James.

Saturday, James gathered up his things from the Bullock house, said goodbye to Moses and drove to his new abode. Katrina was already there, as were her folks and Gibson. Koos and Sussana stayed for a short while, then left for the boat club, asking James and Katrina to join them later. Gibson inspected the house and then gave Katrina a list of things he felt they should have for cleaning, laundry and gardening, and then he checked out the *kaia*. He announced that it would be good to store things in, but that he would prefer to live with his family outside town and ride his bicycle to work. James asked how he would manage if it were raining hard, and Gibson said that, in that case, he would use the *kaia* for an overnight stay. Inspections all done, James locked up the house, and they drove back to the farm to drop off Gibson and then went on to the boat club for a beer and dinner. Katrina went back with James to the new house after dinner and spent the night with him.

Sunday, they were up tolerably early, which was as well, because Tom and Rita showed up at nine to see if the expedition was still on. As it turned out, the expedition was not exactly a wild success. There were a number of smallholdings on the other side of the river, and a whole village had grown up around the Kafironda factory. Navigating their way through towards the streams beyond was a challenge. Then it rained, which made the going difficult, in fact almost impossible, when they got off the principal dirt roads. After a few abortive attempts to progress, they all decided that today was not the day and retired to the boat club bar for a philosophical discussion on the pros and cons of Castle or Lion.

Tuesday was James's birthday, and he received cards from his parents, his sister Alex, and his grandmother. Alex had included details of her flight schedule; she was due to arrive on Good Friday at the Ndola airport on a Zambia Airways flight from Lusaka. She was flying BOAC out from London to Lusaka, via Cairo and Nairobi and then connecting to the local Zambia Airways flight. He had heard that those flights were interesting; the pilots were contracted from Alitalia and were all reputed to be ex-Air Force pilots with a penchant for attacking the runways with gusto. Well, he would ask her about it when she arrived.

He had arranged for her to stay with Tom and Rita. He had not really expected his new house to be ready, so had made alternative arrangements. Rita insisted that Alex stay with them even though James could now accommodate her. James suspected it was to be able to grill Alex on his younger life and get ammunition for after-dinner remarks at the wedding. His grandmother confirmed that she was not coming for the wedding, but from his parents, there was no mention of the wedding or even questions about Katrina. It was almost as though they felt that if they ignored the situation, it would, in fact, go away, and there would be no marriage. His brother was not able to take the time from school, but had included in the card from Alex some suitable or unsuitable comments and remarks about his upcoming honeymoon with Katrina.

Somehow, the crews underground knew it was James's birthday, and he came in for some ribbing. By now, he had learned enough to know to take this in good part; it was better than having them mutter away behind his back. Abel stopped by to see him and wanted to take a look at the old workings they had broken into. They went up to the upper level and into the old workings. Apparently, the ventilation kings had been complaining about leakage through the old workings and were looking for better seals around the door James had installed. That would be an easy fix. They now had some sprayable foam that hardened after a few minutes, and they could seal just about anything with it. James promised to get the timber crew to take care of that.

The planning department had also been busily adjusting the mining plan to take into account the ore that had probably already been extracted and the necessity to leave a crown pillar above the new workings. The upshot of all this was that James was instructed to stop work on his top two levels and concentrate on the lower levels. He would also lose one crew that was to be transferred to another section. The choice of crew was his, so he decided to consult with Kossam and Hippo and see who best to transfer. With the crew, he had to send a drill and all the other *mpasha* that went with it. He was also told to accelerate the development off the new raise he had put in, so that meant some more work for his timber crew before he could really take off.

The end of the shift could not really come fast enough for James. Hippo had offered to do his blasting for him so that he could get out sooner, but James really did not wish to put that onus on Hippo, so he gracefully declined. He had come to rely so much on advice from Hippo on odd things, often not directly related to the job. It seemed that Hippo did have connections everywhere and also had his fingers well and truly on the pulse of the people in the mine.

Hippo was generous and, unlike some of the other Zambian graduates, had no animosity towards the expatriate trainees. The general work force regarded the expatriate trainees as just another set of bosses in the long line that had been there since the mines began, but the new Zambian graduates, at least some of them, felt that they should be getting the opportunities. They felt that the Zambianization program had already been circumvented to a degree by the creation of new posts and the promotion of, perhaps, less than competent persons into those posts. The real problem lay with the mining companies and the past colonial administration, neither of whom had provided the appropriate educational opportunities early enough to have a sufficiently large group of graduate engineers to run the mines at all levels without expatriate assistance.

All that aside, James was far more concerned with the immediate, and the immediate for him was a birthday celebration. He had arranged to meet Katrina at the boat club, and after a quick trip to his new, but mostly empty home, he drove out to the dam. Katrina was there to meet him along with Tom, Rita, Lionel, Jane, Bill and Mary. James was unsure about the reception that Mary was getting. The white club members were looking at her a little askance, and the black staff were acting very aloof. James felt sorry for both Bill and Mary as they obviously were going to have to deal with these attitudes for a long time to come. Still, he was determined to try and accept them both as they were and not judge. He knew that Katrina was having a difficult time coming to terms with the relationship, but he appreciated her making the effort to try and adapt. Somehow, it seemed easier for the English blokes to deal with their Zambian male counterparts than for the women to deal with their spouses. James recalled that in British India, things had muddled along with some level of accommodation until the memsahibs showed up and reinforced prejudice and separation.

Difficulties and discomfort aside, they all had a good time. They made it easier by having their celebration on the veranda, thus avoiding the interplay that occurred when they were indoors. Bill told them that, apparently, Hippo's conversation with Henry Mwanza had been successful, as he was now scheduled to move into his new house that Friday. He had been to look at it, and it needed some clean-up work, but it did mean that Mary could now move to Kitwe and look for a job at one of the hospitals in town, either Kitwe Central, the old Llewellin Hospital, or at one of the mine hospitals. There was competition, of course, but she came well recommended from Luanshya and thought that she stood as good a chance as anyone.

For James, the main event of the evening was opening the presents he received. From Tom and Bill, he got some very welcome Scotch and from Mary, one of the wire cars that he had seen the children playing with in the streets. He had admired them and had mentioned to Bill one day that he would really like to get one. Mary told him that one of her younger brothers had made it, especially for him. Rita gave him a jazz LP, which made him wonder because he had nothing to play it on, until Katrina gave him her gift, a record player. Obviously, the two had been in cahoots.

Katrina followed James to the new house on Philips Street, where they set up his new record player and put on the one LP that he now owned. She told him not to worry about getting tired of the same music all the time, as she would be bringing her collection of records with her shortly. They then went through the latest details of the wedding plans and arrangements, and tried to work out who would be coming to the wedding at the church and then to the reception at the farm afterwards.

The next two weeks went quickly enough. James had plenty to do at work, and after work, there seemed to be a never-ending list of wedding-related issues to be addressed. James did manage to spend a little time in his yard and started laying things out as he and Katrina had decided, and even went as far as finding the Zambia Forestry plantation out towards Chingola and getting some little trees to plant down the back against the sanitary lane. He had also worked things out with Tom and Rita so that Alex would stay with him until the wedding day, and then she would stay with them until she went back to

England. Rita had suggested this with the sly suggestion that he might be less embarrassed by his activities with his new wife if his sister was not on the premises all the time.

Koos had expected the sale of the business to go through in the middle of March, but there had been some minor delays, and the transaction was now set to close on April 7th, a couple of days after the wedding. The delays were mainly associated with ensuring that the monies payable outside Zambia were actually deposited before everything was handed over.

Good Friday was the beginning of a four-day holiday, so there was no problem with James driving to Ndola to meet Alex's plane. Katrina asked if she could go with him, so he collected her first and then went on to Ndola. He watched the BAC-111 as it flew overhead, then back around and down into the airport, then tried to spot his sister as she came down the stairs onto the tarmac. He saw her as soon as she started down the stairs and pointed her out to Katrina. Alex saw James, waved madly and headed his way.

"James! Lovely to see you, you must be Katrina; I've been dying to meet you! Where do I get my bags? How do we get to Kitwe? Do you still have that Land Rover? What day is today?" Alex said as she tried to hug and kiss both of them at the same time.

"Hi Alex, lovely to see you too," replied James. "Yes, this is Katrina. We'll get your bags over there, and then we will drive you to Kitwe."

"Did you have a nice flight?" asked Katrina.

"Yes, most exciting! I saw Cairo at night, the dawn came over the Sudan somewhere, lots of people at Nairobi and then a nice immigration chappie at Lusaka who welcomed me to Zambia. Then some old goat on the plane up here tried to chat me up. That bloke over there." She said, pointing with her chin to an early middle-aged man standing by the luggage.

"Oh, that's Chris Sands from one of the car dealerships here in Ndola," said Katrina. "You're right, he is an old goat, he would chase anything in a skirt and doesn't seem to care if his wife finds out or not."

James recognised Alex's bag and collected it, then escorted the two girls out to his Land Rover.

"How far is it to Kitwe?" asked Alex.

"Oh, not far," replied Katrina. "We should be there in less than an hour."

"Good, I could really do with a bath before I do much more today. Have you anything planned for us this evening, James?"

"Well, yes, if you're not too tired, I thought we could go out and you could meet Katrina's parents."

"That would be lovely, but I need to bathe and change first. What should I wear tonight?"

"Something casual," suggested Katrina.

During the drive to Kitwe, Katrina pointed things out to Alex, who was fascinated by everything and also kept up an almost non-stop barrage of questions for both James and Katrina. James managed to get in a couple of questions about the rest of the family, but Alex brushed those aside and announced that she would fill them both in later. The drive was not too bad, only three diversions off the main road because the tarmac was breaking up. Katrina told them a story about when some of her family had come to visit and they had picked them up in Ndola to drive back to Kitwe. However, instead of taking the main road, her dad had taken the back road that goes closer to the Congo border and the railway line. They had stopped in an African village by a little round hut, and he had started taking the bags out of the car. The family had not known what to do or say, not wishing to really offend but also clearly taken aback by the idea that this was the home that Koos had always boasted of. Her dad had thought it a great joke.

James had organised another bed and Katrina had made it up and set things out in the spare bedroom so that Alex would be comfortable. He and Katrina sat and talked while Alex took her bath and changed. She kept up a long-distance monologue through the bathroom door that was punctuated with splashes and splutters. When she finally appeared, James wondered if she understood what the word casual meant. It seemed to him that she had overdone things a little, but Katrina approved, and Alex felt reassured.

"Aren't you going to change James?" asked Alex.

"No, why?" he asked.

"You really are going like that?" she asked.

"Yes, we are going to a farm, you know, and I may do some barbecuing."

"Oh, I suppose that's fine if Katrina thinks so?"

"He'll be fine, Alex," replied Katrina. "He and my dad seem to have long forgotten what dressing up is all about, but I live with it!"

During the drive out to the farm, it started to rain, not badly enough to force them to stop and wait, but enough that they got the inevitable drip leaks into the Land Rover. James wondered what Alex was doing as she shuffled back and forth on the seat behind him.

"I'm trying to avoid the drips that this stupid car lets in!" commented Alex when James asked her why she was fidgeting.

"Don't worry," said Katrina. "The rain won't last long, by the time we get there, it probably will have stopped."

James craned around and looked behind at Alex's shoes.

"What are you looking at?" she asked.

"Oh, only to see if I may have to carry you into the house so that you don't get your dainty shoes muddy!"

"Oh, buzz off, James, it doesn't matter."

"What do you do, Alex?" asked Katrina

"I'm a solicitor."

"Yes, she stands on street corners and whistles up business, but I'm not sure what kind of business!" commented James.

"*Oppas neerfie ek sal jou klap*," interrupted Katrina.

"What was that?" asked Alex.

"Oh, she was just threatening me with physical violence again," replied James.

"No, he was being rude," said Katrina. "And I told him to watch it!"

"I think we will get on fine, Katrina," said Alex. "I have had to endure this my whole life from this one and the other one!"

"So, and stay quiet, James, what is it that you do?" asked Katrina again.

"Mostly estate law, sorting out how to divvy up the spoils when the old fogies die."

"You don't wear one of those wigs then?"

"No, Katrina, only barristers wear those when they are in court, and I rarely get to see the inside of a courtroom."

"Yes, she pulls her hair back tight, scowls, and frightens the family members into agreeing with her interpretations of the wills," said James.

The rain had stopped by the time they turned onto the farm road, but large puddles still remained. As they pulled up outside the house, it was obvious to Alex that James had been pulling her leg, because the drive by the house was nicely gravelled and there was no mud in sight. Katrina led them into the house and introduced Alex to her parents and to Seventeen and Gibson. Alex enjoyed the evening and was clearly a hit with the family. They made plans for the rest of the Easter weekend, and Koos had some suggestions as to what might be worth seeing and doing for the rest of the week before the wedding.

At about nine, Alex made her apologies to Katrina's parents and asked James if he would take her home as the journey was catching up with her. They left after setting a time and place to meet in the morning.

"Well, what do you think?" James asked Alex.

"She's gorgeous; I can't think what she sees in you!"

"Ha ha! How's your love life?"

"Piss off, James."

"That's very unlawyerly talk."

"Well, you deserve it. Katrina is lovely, and I really like her family. Have you talked about what might happen when you leave here and either return to the UK or go somewhere else?"

"Yes, at length. Her dad left South Africa when Katrina was really small and they had no idea when they might see their family again, but he says that if that's what you have to do, then that's what you must do."

"I think Granny would really like Katrina. I hope they can get to meet someday. Where was it that Koos and Sussana are moving to?"

"Calitzdorp. It's a little town on the edge of the Karoo in the Cape."

"Do you think you will visit?"

"One day, perhaps at the end of this contract, when I either move to something else or get a long leave."

"I wish you weren't so far away. I miss having you around."

"I know what you mean, Alex. Before I met Katrina, there really wasn't anyone that I could confide in."

"Oh, so now you've replaced me in that capacity, huh? Well, I suppose that was inevitable."

"Don't worry, Alex; no one could ever replace you. I will always love you, you're my big sister. Who else could I turn to for advice?" he asked.

Saturday, Alex was up almost as soon as it was light and had found enough things in the pantry to make breakfast. She had taken a wander around the garden and had amused herself picking lemons, guavas, and avocados. She was a little unsure about the guavas, but after trying one decided that they were quite edible. They had arranged to meet Koos and Katrina at the Englebrecht company yard, and Koos was going to take them on a river trip for the day. Koos had suggested that they put the boat into the Kafue at a place called Muchiyas Ferry and then take a trip up and down the river from there and perhaps do a little fishing.

Alex had never been in a jet boat before, and when they started up the river and ran into the first rapids was a little alarmed when Koos headed straight through them. Katrina pointed out to Alex the deeper water channel through the rapids and told her that it was quite safe. On the banks of the river, they saw waterbuck, impala, a couple of old buffalo, and some crocodiles. Koos pointed out the hippo that were in the water at the various pools and told Alex that they were the animals to watch because idiots in propeller-driven boats had ridden over the hippo in the past, and they, consequently, often reacted badly to boats in general and could be very aggressive.

Easter Sunday was a day to relax at the dam, and Alex and Katrina spent much of the day in deep conversation. James wondered a few times just what it was they could possibly find to talk about for so long, but then had to admit that he had had equally long conversations with both Alex and Katrina; they were both easy people to talk to. Monday was also a holiday, something that the mine had kept from Colonial days, and they took a trip out into the bush to look for game. They drove out of Kitwe towards the Kalengwa mine and found a couple of small side tracks that they pulled off onto and then slowly drove along, looking to see what might be around. Alex had her camera along and was snapping away at almost anything that walked, crawled, or flew. She was surprised at the amount of game that they actually saw and, as James had been from the beginning, amazed at the ability Katrina had to spot things in the bush.

That night at home, James and Alex had the chance to talk about things. James went through his experiences to date, from his trip south on the boat, the journey north, early days at the mine, and then the events leading up to the present. Alex told him a little about her life as a lawyer, and then they got on to the subject of family. She told him about the repercussions of his announcement at Christmas and the squabbles that it had caused between their parents and their grandmother. Apparently, his mother had gone off the deep end about the fact that Katrina was not English. Alex was not sure quite what image they had of Katrina, but then she had the advantage over them because James had written to her about Katrina and sent a picture.

"Well, what do you think now?" James asked.
"I really like her, James. She's very exotic; I'll bet she would turn every head in the village."
"I really didn't mean that. I was thinking more along the lines of whether or not the family ructions have settled down."
"Oh, well, I don't think just yet. I think they will have to meet Katrina first, and then they will come around."
"What about you; how's your love life?"
"Oh, it just seems to be an endless string of useless idiots all of whom are after one thing, like a bunch of sixteen-year-olds."
"Well, Alex, there must be some nice blokes in London. There are enough people there."
"Yes, but where do you get to meet them? Most of the lawyers I meet are self-centred pompous asses, the clients I leave well alone, and I can hardly just pick someone up in a bar, who knows what kind of pervert they might be."
"I'm surprised that there isn't someone who takes your fancy."
"Well, there is this one bloke. He lives just down the road, runs his own travel agency, but I don't think he even notices me."

"Did you book your travel here through him?"

"No, I went straight through BOAC."

"Idiot, there was the perfect opportunity to meet him and tickle his fancy by going somewhere off the beaten track."

"Oh God, I never thought of that."

"Well, when you go home, go and see him and book another trip here or to Calitzdorp or Rio or somewhere. You must be able to afford it."

"Maybe, but what if he isn't interested in me?"

"How could he not be? You're good-looking, as sisters go, have a decent job, not over the hill, and generally a good catch. He would be a fool not to jump at the chance of going out with you, not to mention that he might even want to jump you!"

Alex threw a book at him and suggested that he was only thinking about what he and his beloved Katrina got up to all the time. On that note, James retired for the night as he had to work in the morning.

For the remainder of the week, while James was at work, Koos dispatched Alex with either Katrina on some expedition or with one of his drivers. Katrina and Alex found time to spend in town looking at the shops, and Alex was introduced to OK Bazaars and ZCBC. Friday, Alex moved to Tom and Rita's house and made sure that she had plenty of film for her camera. As Saturday neared, the pace of activity increased with more wedding preparations until finally the day arrived. James had worked things out with Hippo so he would cover his blasting so that he could get out of the mine in plenty of time to get cleaned up and be at the church. Tom, Rita, and Alex picked James up from his house, took over custody of the ring and delivered him to the church.

As with Bill's wedding, the customary groom's side of the church was very sparsely filled, and guests that would traditionally be seated on the bride's side were filling up the spare seats. James saw Attie and Darryl with what looked like dates and looked around for Bill and Mary. They had been invited, but James was not sure if they would come or not. Mary had to work in Luanshya, and Bill said that he might have to go over and take care of some business for her family. James was unsure whether this was true or whether he was diplomatically avoiding the situation.

The wedding was generally a blur, but there were a few things that stood out. Koos wore a tie. Katrina was only a few minutes late, and the wedding went off perfectly. No one had just cause or impediment; they did not mumble their lines, and James did not drop the ring. Alex and Sussana both cried, and even Koos could be seen dabbing his eyes with his handkerchief, but of course, that was just the heat in the church with all the people there. The marriage certificate was interesting. It had been printed up as being of Northern Rhodesia, and that had been blacked out and the Republic of Zambia stamped above the black-out. The reception afterwards was in the garden at the farm, and Sussana and Koos prayed that they did not get late-season rain to ruin everything. Seventeen assured them that it would not rain because he had made arrangements with one of the local witch doctors; it had cost him three chickens. Whether or not this made a difference, James would never know, but it did not rain.

A honeymoon as such had been postponed because James had no time off yet, so they promised each other some adventure in the future that would be the honeymoon. Back at work, James had to describe the ceremony, dress, and reception for his crews, who all seemed to take a very proprietary interest in the whole affair. Some of his people wanted to know how much *lobola* he had paid, but they were set straight by others, which then led to long discussions about the peculiar customs of the *wazungu*. James and Katrina met Alex after work for the next couple of days before she was to return, and then dropped her off with Tom and Rita. They seemed to find plenty to talk about and shared dreams, hopes, and aspirations. They also did some last-minute shopping for souvenirs and gifts to take back for various family members. James had picked out a drum for his brother, William, and Alex complained bitterly about having to carry the stupid thing on the plane.

April 7th came, and the sale of the business was closed. Koos and Sussana were now the recipients of the proceeds but no longer the proprietors of the business. Katrina had agreed to stay on and manage the scheduling and operations side of the business, at least for the foreseeable future. That still left her with a lot of flexibility and maintained continuity for the new owner. The next event for them all now would be the actual sale of the farm. Koos and Sussana had decided to have everything they planned to take with them packed and off the property by the date of the sale, so that there was no issue with leaving. It now looked as if the farm sale would be concluded by late May.

Unfortunately, James could not get the time off to take Alex to the airport early enough to catch the plane, so Katrina volunteered to do the honours. James said his goodbyes the night before Alex left and promised to write at least once every six months. Alex promised to send photographs and also promised to make sure that the family got a full report. She also said that she would trail her coat in front of the travel agent and perhaps arrange a trip to Calitzdorp. Koos and Sussana had told her that she really was very welcome there, and Katrina had confirmed that they really meant it and were not just being polite.

That night, Katrina told James that Alex had got off safely, at least to Lusaka. She had seen a couple she knew who were also going to London, and they had promised to look out for Alex. Apparently, it had been a tearful farewell, and Alex had promised that she would write to Katrina.

"So, what do you think of my sister?" James asked.

"She's really beautiful. Are you sure you two are related?" replied Katrina.

"I've often wondered. If you see our parents, I have always wondered how she got to look so good. It must have been a real Adonis of a milkman."

"Excuse me?"

"Oh, sorry; a rather lame joke. I think she takes after my grandmother, who was a real looker when she was young, judging by photographs I've seen."

"Do you think she will go to Calitzdorp?"

"Why not? She likes your folks, and it would be a really different place to go. I suppose there are bigger places around?"

"Well, there is Oudtshoorn, and George, and even Cape Town is not too far away. My dad would love to show her around. Do you know my dad asked her to review his will?"

"No, really! I wonder how different South African law is from English law. I know that English law and Scottish law have differences, and I would have thought that South Africa would be influenced by Dutch law. So, who gets it all?"

"After my mom, I suppose I do, but I don't really know what he said as Alex didn't tell me much."

The rest of the month had a rather dreamlike quality for James. Work was challenging and fun, returning home in the evening now was something to look forward to. He was now eating reasonably well as he and Katrina shared the cooking. They talked about things they might do in their lives, and Katrina presented James with her list of places she would like to see around the world at some time in her life. His love life was wonderful. He was still exploring his relationship with Katrina and was finding her to be a constant source of wonderment, challenge, and satisfaction. Their lovemaking became more creative as they grew more comfortable with each other and experimented with positions, locations, and times of day. Katrina slept in the nude, so James abandoned his pyjamas completely and thoroughly enjoyed the experience of waking up to her lithe body often draped over him. Sundays were definitely the best as he did not have to be up early for work. If they went to the dam or other social outings, he found himself distracted by her presence and her perfume, and often lost track of conversations going on around him. He was very much in love.

# Stoping

With the beginning of May, the rains ended and the nights started to cool down. James was convinced that there was even frost on the windscreen of his Land Rover one morning. There were mornings when it was difficult to get out of bed, mainly because Katrina was nice to cuddle up to, and the house was quite chilly. However, once up, it was good to get underground, where at least it was warm. James had transferred Elijah and Samson out of his section, on the advice of Kossam and Hippo. Elijah was probably the least experienced of his drillers and was the one who required the most direct supervision, even more than Banda.

Monday, waiting at the station for the cage, James met Joy, who was obviously eager to be out and on his way.
"Joy, what's the hurry?" asked James.
"My wife is close to having the baby, and I think it will be tonight or tomorrow, so I want to be out of here."
"Hey, good luck. What do you want, boy or girl?"
"A boy would be good, but a girl would be just as good."
"Will we see you tomorrow?"
"Probably not, I made arrangements to be off tomorrow and wait at the hospital."
"Let me know how it goes, Joy and remember me to Suzie."

The following day, James made enquiries about Joy and Suzie, and no one seemed to know anything. He stopped by the hospital lab on his way home and found Lionel. Lionel took him aside and asked him if he was coming to ask about Joy and Suzie.
"Right, Lionel, what's up?"
"Look, James, you didn't hear this from me, but there was a problem."
"Okay, Lionel, what's up?"
"Their baby died. Joy is pretty broken up about it. I haven't seen or heard much of Suzie, but poor old Joy is in a bad way."
"Really! What the hell happened, man?"
"I'm not sure. I think there was something wrong with the baby; they haven't done the PM yet, so I don't know yet what the problem was."

"Where is Joy now?"

"I think in the ward with his wife. But I wouldn't go in there just now. There are doctors, nurses and priests already there, so the place is pretty crowded."

"Okay, Lionel. I will try and catch up with Joy tomorrow or Thursday."

James drove home, and while he waited for Katrina to come home, he took a beer and sat out on the stoep and thought about Joy. He had learned enough to know that children were regarded as wealth for the future and that any child was valued. To lose their first child must be devastating for Joy and Susie. He hoped that they would recover fast enough to think about having another if they could. When Katrina came home, he told her what he knew. Katrina had known Susie from the bank for a long time from the bank and was upset that she had lost her baby. They had been talking just a few days before, and Susie was really excited about the prospect of the new baby. She had organised for her mother to help with the baby so that she could return to work, but she was talking about the fun she would have with her child. Katrina said that she would stop by the bank in the morning and see if the manager there knew anything more.

Thursday, when he finally caught up with Joy, James was surprised that he seemed reasonably content. He was at the hospital and was getting ready to leave with Susie and a baby. They both waved to James and, with big smiles, got into a car and drove off. James was more than a little confused and went in to find Lionel.

"Lionel, what's the deal? I thought that Joy's baby had died?"

"You never heard that from me, James."

"But what's the deal?"

"Okay, but again, you never heard this from me. A little after Susie lost her baby, we had a girl come in and deliver hers; the baby made it, she didn't, and there was no husband or boyfriend. We talked to Joy and Susie, and they are as happy as larks to have the baby. The baby needed a home, so everyone is happy!"

"Yes, but," James stammered.

"Hey James, no buts, the paperwork at the hospital is sorted out, and the rumour that Joy and Susie lost their baby is just a rumour. Oh, and by the way, the young girl's baby died of a heart disorder and will be buried with her at the city cemetery."

James met Katrina at what used to be the Englebrecht yard and told her the news. It did not surprise her at all. She reminded James that children were looked upon as wealth and that any baby was welcome. This way, the baby had a home, Joy and Susie's parents would not point the finger and speculate as to why the baby died, and everyone was happier. To the outside world, including the bank, everything was normal. As conditioned as he was to rules, bureaucracy, and red tape, James was a little disconcerted by the way this was all managed, but Katrina pointed out to him that away from the towns, this would be regarded as the proper solution to a problem and would not be regarded as in any way out of the ordinary. Bureaucrats and lawyers were the ones who complicated things with the notion that somehow children were property and had to be accounted for instead of cared for.

Ten days went by, and then James was called into the shift bosses' office as he prepared to leave the mine for the day. He was surprised to see not only Abel Mwewa and Chris Phillips but also Jim Brown and Pete Burgess.
"Ah, James," said Phillips. "Good to see you. We have a new mission for you."
"Really, may I ask what?"
"We need you to take over immediately a section for Jim and Pete here," continued Phillips.
"What about the section I'm running now, Kayumba is already in another section?"
"Well, we were thinking of Greg Young. What do you think?" asked Abel.
"He should be all right. I think he would really like something challenging again, not that the Special Projects Office is not challenging."
"Fine, fine, we don't need to dwell on the Projects Office. What we want to know is, is he up to the job or will there be problems?" asked Phillips.

"I really don't know," replied James. "I can't see why not, he's smart enough, and perhaps his recent experience will open his eyes a little."

"Okay, we'll take the risk and give it a try. Now we need you to go and work for Jim here," continued Phillips.

"Thanks, Chris. Okay, James, you spent some time in the section run by Chazeema, right?" asked Brown.

"Yes."

"Fine, well, Chazeema has a problem and is off the job for a while as of today, so we need someone now," continued Brown. "You should report to Pete here in the morning, and he will take you down and show you what needs to be done."

"Be here at six thirty," said Pete Burgess. "I'll take you down and run you through things quickly."

"Okay, I'll be here," said James. "Is there anything else?"

"No, not for you. We're waiting for Young to show up, and then we'll give him his new assignment," put in Abel Mwewa.

James left and went home to give the news to Katrina.

"What do you think happened to Chazeema?" James asked Katrina later.

"Who knows, maybe you'll hear tomorrow."

"How are things going with the sale of the farm?"

"All done today, we should probably go out and visit with my folks and see if there is anything we can do to help."

"Okay, are you ready?"

"Kom ons ry."

When they arrived at the farm, Koos was in the process of explaining to the workers what was going to happen. Now that the transaction had cleared, he planned to vacate the farm and leave for the Cape by that weekend. The new owner was eager to move in and start up a dairy farm. James was not certain how well that would work, but it was hardly his problem. Koos told them that they had disposed of all the items that they did not wish to take and had reduced the rest to more durable goods and to what could be carried in the two vehicles that they had. He had checked with the customs and immigration people and had, in fact, arranged to meet an old friend from the customs department at Kazungula to smooth the way out of the country.

To James, this sounded a lot like bribery and corruption, but probably in the long run, it was the best thing to do and would avoid long delays at the ferry. Botswana would not be particularly concerned about anything, as the goods were merely in transit, and then the next issue would be with the South Africans. Sussana was distressed about leaving but was excited about moving to a new place, particularly as they had already acquired the property in Calitzdorp and she wanted to be in soon and not have it stand empty for too long.

Friends of the Englebrechts had organised a going-away party at the boat club for Friday night, to which James and Katrina had a command invitation. After the party, Koos and Sussana would stay with James and Katrina and then leave on Saturday. James wondered how well they would all fare after the party and how far Koos would plan to drive the first day. He had to go to work and so would miss the final send-off.

James reported to Pete Burgess as instructed, and after a quick review of the logs, they went underground and made their way to the section. James asked what had happened to Chazeema.
"It appears that his wife poisoned him," said Burgess matter-of-factly.
"Wow, why and what with?" asked James.
"As far as I can tell, they were having a few problems at home, and Chazeema did the standard thing, beat her and threatened to send her back to her father and get the lobola back. She objected and poisoned the poor bugger."
"Really? What did she use?"
"I'm not sure. Probably some concoction she made up herself or got from one of the witch doctors," said Burgess.
"How long will he be off?"
"I think quite a while, she did a pretty good job, and he is very sick. It'll take him a while to get over it, maybe three months."
"Could he have died?"

"Oh, quite possibly He was lucky one of his friends stopped by to see him, found him on the floor, and had the good sense to get him to the hospital pretty damned quick."

Once in the section, Burgess was all business. He introduced James to the crews, most of whom he already knew from his time in the section before. The job was straightforward enough; produce appropriate quantities of ore to be hoisted to the surface to feed the concentrator. To do this, he needed to keep his crews drilling and follow up with the blasting. They were a little behind schedule, and Burgess wanted them to catch up so that the tonnage hoisted met targets. After the final pep talk, Burgess left.

James spent the rest of the day with each of the drilling crews in turn, trying to work out what he could do to pick up production and meet the demands of his bosses. It would not be easy unless he could acquire some more equipment from somewhere. He needed to talk to the crews and find out who was above and below them and how alert they were. He doubted if the powers that be would let him have any more equipment through the proper channels, so it was time to improvise. A chat with Hippo might also be useful, at least to find out who had what and who would be willing to let a machine go or if more illicit means might be called for. As he sat at the station at the end of the shift, James mused on the turn of events and wondered if any of the new crop of students going through their degree courses had any idea that some of the most useful attributes in the world of daily production would be dishonesty, stealth, and the ability to dissemble.

Once on the surface, James asked Burgess about getting another drill and was surprised when he was told that one would be forthcoming. In fact, if he could get organised, he could have the new machine in the morning. Wonders would never cease! All that he had to do now was organise how to get the equipment down and to the section, which would be the challenge for tomorrow.

Friday, Koos and Sussana showed up at James's house at around four with their two vanettes. They looked as if they were loaded to the roof, and there was barely room for a driver in each. Koos had arranged for some of the drivers from his old company to come to the house for the evening and night to guard his vehicles. Packed as they were, they were probably tempting targets for anyone with a light-fingered frame of mind. James was not sure quite what the durable goods were, but he reasoned it probably had to be emeralds or something similar. James was sure that was one of the reasons Koos had arranged for his friend from customs to see them through the procedures at Kazungula.

The party at the boat club was large, really large. James had not appreciated just how many people Koos knew and had done business with over the years. Most of the people who had been at the wedding were in attendance, plus others, some of whom James recognised and some of whom he was sure he had never seen before. Listening to the conversations, it was clear that there were people there from the other Copperbelt towns and a few from Broken Hill. Katrina identified most of the people for James, but there were even a few whom she did not know. James watched the action and concluded that it was going to be a hell of a job getting Koos out of there and ready for the road the following day. He decided he would take the easy way out and leave that mission to Katrina and her mother.

In the end, James left and went home to get some sleep, and one of the drivers took his Land Rover back to wait for the rest of the family. When James awoke to go to work, Katrina was there next to him, but at what time she had returned, James had no idea. He hesitated about waking her to say goodbye, decided to risk it and was rewarded with a smile and a kiss. In the kitchen, he found Koos and Sussana, already up and drinking coffee.

"More Meneer, Mevrou," he managed.

"Morning, James, lovely day for a drive, don't you think?" replied Koos.

"What time did you *ouks* get in?"

"About two hours ago," said Sussana. "We probably won't go far today, maybe to Broken Hill, and then we'll take a break."

"How do you manage it?" asked James.

"Experience, James, experience," replied Koos.

"Well, I have to go to work. Good luck on your trip, and Katrina and I will be sure to visit as soon as we can."

"*Ag* James, *moenie worry nie*. Visit when you can, man, you have to worry about you and Katrina now and not what the old folks are doing!" said Koos.

"Okay, well, I really must be going. Drive safely," James said, edging towards the door. Before he could leave, Sussana got up and hugged and kissed him and then Koos gave him a hug. Raised as he was in a conservative, repressed British household, hugging and kissing all and sundry was a new experience for James and one that he was still getting used to.

That afternoon, James got the rundown on the departure from Katrina. Apparently, Koos and Sussana had left around noon after a tearful farewell. Katrina was trying to deal with the situation as best she could, but in the past, it had always been she who left and went away, particularly when she had been going away to boarding school. Koos had given her the 'now that you are married, your place is with your husband' talk, but that did not help with the feelings of loneliness and deprivation. It was one thing to do the leaving, knowing that you were coming back, but quite another to be left. Obviously, it was going to take a little time to get used to the situation.

# Midwinter

Throughout June, life settled into another pattern. James was getting the hang of the stoping business and had more than caught up with the delays in production. In fact, they were now making noises about taking some of his resources away from him. Katrina enjoyed her job but found it was not quite the same working for a company rather than for your own enterprise. Greg seemed to have found his niche and, although the departure of Shirley still rankled, had actually been seen out with one of the famous sunshine girls from the hospital. Joy was delighted with his new child; he had talked about the situation with James one day as they sat waiting for the cage to come and had come to terms with their loss and gain. Tom and Rita were frequent guests at the Martin household, and Katrina was even teaching Rita a few Afrikaans words. Bill was happy, and Mary was expecting a baby. Koos and Sussana had made it across the border with no problems and were now in the process of establishing themselves in Calitzdorp. All in all, everything was fine.

The last Sunday of the month, James was awakened by a car hooting at the gate. It was Tom, and he was clearly eager to talk about something. James let him in, put on some coffee, and asked him what was so all important to drag him out at that hour of the day.

"I've just been asked to identify a body," announced Tom.

"Who and why you?" asked James.

"It was Lionel! I think they called me because he had my name and address in his wallet, so it was a place to start."

"What happened? Did he come off that bike of his?"

"I think so," said Tom. "As I understand things, he was coming back from Chingola and ran into a train."

"How the hell did he do that? Was he drunk or what?"

"I don't know. You know that there are a few unmarked crossings on the road. Possibly, maybe when Jane wakes up, she can tell us."

"You don't mean to tell me that he had a pillion passenger?"

"Yes, she is a little banged up; nothing obviously appears to be broken, but she is in a coma."

"What's this about Jane?" asked Katrina, who had just come into the kitchen.

"She was on the back of Lionel's bike, they ran into a train on the Chingola road, and Jane is in a coma, and Lionel didn't make it," summarised James.

"I'd better go and see her," said Katrina. "Do you know if anyone has told her folks?"

"Don't know," said Tom. "I think that the government hospital people had called the Lamprechts, and they were trying to work out what number to call in England to tell Lionel's folks."

"Some phone call that will be," commented James. "Hello, Mr and Mrs Fairfax, we are just calling to tell you that your son has been killed in a traffic accident. What do you think they will do, bury him here or ship him back to the UK?"

"No idea, James," replied Tom. "Perhaps we'll learn something this week."

Katrina went back to the bedroom, dressed, and then came back to ask James if he was going with her to the hospital. Tom took his leave, and they left for the hospital. Once there, Katrina quickly found out where Jane was and led the way. They found Jane's parents, who were waiting anxiously to hear what the extent of the injuries were. The doctor reached them at about the same time that Katrina did, so she heard the prognosis; she was in a coma, and they could not really tell how much damage had been done, except there were no breaks to her arm or leg bones.

With the family around, Katrina decided that there was not a lot she could do at the moment, so promised to look in on Jane the following day and also told the Lamprechts that she would be around to see them. On that note, Katrina indicated to James that they should leave and return home. On the drive home, they talked about what had happened and speculated on how. Katrina related to James an incident that had occurred to her a couple of years earlier when she had been convinced that there was a train on the crossing, whereas in fact there had been no train. To her, it had been as real as daylight, but it had been only an apparition or mirage. Katrina was not sure what, but to her it had been very real at the time. So who knew what Lionel had seen or not seen?

The next day, underground, the crews seemed to know all about the accident, even which crossing it had occurred on and at what time. James was again struck by the speed at which information travelled and the peculiar mechanism by which it seemed to pass; his people even knew who the engine driver was! They then proceeded to give him all the folklore tales about train collisions, particularly with magazine lorries from the mine, which occurrences usually ended with a big bang and not much left to show for the truck or the train engine.

James finally had to pull them all back to the present and the task at hand: that of charging up a large stope blast and properly wiring it up for blasting. At the end of the day, he finally remembered that he had forgotten to bring his blasting box down with him. He asked Ben, his crew boss, who might have one in any of the sections around them. Ben considered this for a short while and then announced that George below them might have one, but that there was another solution which would involve a lot less time and effort. Now, James was curious and asked what and how. Ben said he would show him when they got to the haulage level at the end of the shift, but that for now they should just proceed as normal and connect everything up for a regular blast.

Agog with curiosity, James went to the haulage level when they had wired everything up and settled in to wait until their appointed time. He asked Ben how he planned to initiate the blast without a blasting box. Normally, they would connect up the wires to the box, wind the handle until the light came on and then press the button to discharge the capacitors. Ben grinned and pointed to the overhead power line for the trains and to the tracks.

"*Ena lo, Bwana*," said Ben. "*Tina azi faka lo one waiya lapa, na lo munya lapa, munya skati yena azi hamba.*"

James considered this for a minute. Ben was proposing putting one wire onto the overhead line and the other on one of the rails. This would complete a circuit and provide power to the blasting circuit.

*"Okay Ben, kanjani tina azi faka lo one waiya pezulu?"* James was curious as to how the wire would be touched to the line above.

*"Sure Bwana, tina azi faka lo one waiya panzi na lo mahefu na lo munya pezulu tina azi faka na lo stick pezulu na lo waiya."* With that pronouncement, Ben rifled around in the rocks by the side of the tracks and produced a stick that had been split at one end. In the end, he fitted one of their cable ends and cleaned off about a three-inch length of insulation. The other wire he placed onto the railway track and held it down with a large rock. Now all was ready, all they had to do was touch the first wire to the overhead line and the job was done!

It occurred to James that this was obviously not the first time this technique had been used, as all the tools of the trade, so to speak, were ready to hand. James went along with the suggestion, and when they got the word from the section above that all was clear and had heard back from George below that he was ready for them to blast, he tentatively raised the stick and touched the cable against the overhead line. There were a few small sparks, but nothing of consequence, and then he heard the very satisfying blasts going off above them. Ben quickly dismantled their makeshift blasting circuit and hid everything away.

*"Bwana, wena aikôna kuluma na lo,"* said Ben.

*"Sure, Ben, mina aikôna azi kuluma na lo,"* reassured James. He was not about to test the legalities or niceties of this method of blasting, so would keep his own counsel. James had been envious of those who had large sections with built-in blasting circuits and semi-permanent blasting boxes mounted on the haulage level. For them, no lugging of a heavy blasting box every day, only some lengths of cable to connect their circuit to the permanent lines.

At home, James asked Katrina how Jane was and was told that she was not out of the coma yet. Katrina was very concerned and upset and was going through the 'what ifs' in her mind. After she had calmed down a little, she asked James about his day. James told her the basics of the day and then confided in her that he seemed to be learning something new every day from the very people he was supposed to be supervising. Katrina told him that one of the problems of the country was that so many people considered the Zambians stupid and gave them no credit for any intelligence. She went on to remark that there were instances where their lack of experience and exposure sometimes limited what they could do, but that that did not make them any less intelligent. James thought about this a little and came up with many instances underground where initiative and creativity were obvious.

Katrina told him that one of the problems they often had was that because the Zambians did not want to appear uneducated or sophisticated and would say that they understood when they truly did not, and therefore, it was difficult to know when they were merely being polite and when they truly grasped things. It was usually wise to find a polite way to get them to relay back what the instruction or information was and help them with their explanation. That way, they could avoid having to admit that they did not understand. James commented that that problem was by no means unique to Zambia as it occurred only too often in England. People were people, and insecurities were the same everywhere!

Later that evening, James realised that it had been a year already since his final year at college had finished. Time was certainly racing by! He had a lot to reflect on for a year: a new car, a boat trip, the drive north, a new job, and best of all, a new wife!

For the rest of the following week, Katrina visited the hospital, and there was no change in Jane's condition. The Lamprechts were getting worn out just sitting by the bedside and waiting, so Katrina had sent them both home for a while and had stayed, promising to call if anything changed. It was hard for her to watch her friend lie helpless and unresponsive, and she tried not to think about the worst possible outcome.

Meanwhile, James was busier than ever and was trying hard to balance work and his need to support Katrina while she watched over Jane. Things were further complicated one day while he was making up his paperwork; he was surprised to see Pete Burgess walking along the drive towards him.

"Pete, *howzit?*" asked James.

"Fine, James, fine, but we have a problem. It seems the concentrator is not happy with the junk you keep sending them. Junk is their term, not mine."

"Why, what's wrong with it?" asked James.

"It seems there is a lot of waste, some timbers, some steel, and other additions," replied Pete.

"Okay, but do you want tonnage or good stuff? They only get what they ask for, you know."

"I know James. Some bright spark in the planning office says we should get x tonnes a month from this section at an average grade of y, so that should suit the mill."

"What do they want exactly then?" asked James.

"Well, it seems that they have finally decided that perfectly uniform flow is nice, but may not be as productive as a varying flow with more uniform grade. That way, they say they could get better recovery and more usable concentrates," opined Pete.

James tried to think back and remember what he had been taught about flotation cells and the influences on them. He decided that that was a problem he was not going to solve.

"So, what does that mean, for us exactly?" asked James again.

"A change in targets to tonnes of contained copper, so we had better work out how to get geologists and assayers down here more frequently," replied Pete. "Do you know any of the geologists?"

"No, I've never had the occasion to get to know any of them, and none of them shows their faces here. I think they spend all their time on really new development areas."

"Well, you're right there. We may have to rely more on the assayers with an occasional blessing from a geologist."

"Is it the same everywhere?" asked James.

"Yes, I'm making my rounds of all the sections to break the news. We should have new targets in a few days. Expect there to be competition for the services of the assayers!"

"I'm about ready to blast, are you staying or going?" asked James.

"I'll stay and then walk out with you," replied Pete. "It's been a long day, and the next two weeks promise to be chaos."

On the surface, James went with Pete to the geologists' office and found that they were already swamped with visitors. Pete told James not to wait but that he would arrange for one of his old school friends to visit him the next day and work out a plan. James had had only passing dealings with any of the geologists at the mine. He knew that there were some who dealt only with the true exploration aspects and went out actively looking for new deposits, and others who were engaged in the production of the current known deposits. His own focus in geology was on how it related to economics. One of the greatest debates always seemed to be the statement of reserves and the classification of reserves as proven, probable and possible. Depending on the sale price of copper and the extraction costs, large blocks of the ore deposit could move between these categories. This was geology much removed from most classic images of geologists as people who identified rocks and interpreted their probable origins and changes through the ages. Even then, there was debate; the geologists James knew from college could sit around a table, look at a rock and argue all night about what it actually was.

When Katrina came home that evening, she was obviously upset. James asked what was wrong, and Katrina sat down and told him that Jane had died that afternoon.

"What happened, sweetie? I thought she was doing okay, or was at least stable," said James.

"I'm not sure; it seems that she had injuries that they didn't find."

"How are her folks doing?"

"Not too well. They are in shock. It was always possible, but still unexpected."

"What about you, sweetie? How are you doing?"

"I'm not sure, it's all so odd. One minute she seemed to be doing fine, and the next minute she's dead," said Katrina, finally breaking down and crying. James knelt down next to her and wrapped his arms around her, and just held her until the sobs slowed and finally stopped.

"Will there be a funeral?" asked James.

"I presume so," Katrina answered. "I'm sure we will hear this week."

"Is there anything I can do for them, for you?" asked James. He was really lost. Katrina was really having a hard time and was obviously

317

deeply upset, and James felt a little useless. He was not sure what to do or say. James had never before in his life been faced with a situation that he could not correct or fix in some way.

"No, it's okay, I'll be fine. I've known Jane all of my life, and it's hard to think of her not being there any more. Just promise me one thing!"

"What?" asked James.

"Don't ever get a motorbike!" Katrina said. "It seems that even with helmets, you can come to grief easily, especially if you argue with a train."

"Okay, I won't get a bike," promised James.

The next day, as James reported in for his shift, he saw a note in the logbook that he would be visited that day by Sandy Bennet, one of the geologists. There was not much else to the note except that Pete Burgess added that he would be with Sandy. James had never met Bennet and asked the other section bosses if they knew him. A couple of them said they did, and they described him as 'a short one' with '*lo maglas*'. So he was a short man who wore glasses, which did not tell him too much.

Once underground in his section, James quickly went through all the working areas to be sure that there was nothing that Burgess could complain about, or that would embarrass Burgess in front of Bennet. When they finally did show up, James was surprised to see that Bennet was not short and did not wear glasses. Clearly, this was not the person the other section bosses had been thinking of. Pete Burgess made the introductions. Sandy was a contemporary of his, and they had in fact gone to college together, travelled together and started on the mine at the same time. He had been spending most of his time in the new fold section that had been opened up. That section, with its folded orebody, presented challenges to the miners and opportunities for speculation to the geologists.

James explained what he was doing and then took Burgess and Bennet on a tour of the section. They peered into the open stopes where they could get access and then went down to the haulage level to get some samples from each of the stopes that were being pulled at the moment. Bennet surprised James by climbing up onto the chutes and grabbing the samples himself. James had, perhaps unjustly, assumed that he would get one of the haulage crew to do the hard work. Perhaps Bennet was okay! Burgess took his leave of them as he had other issues to attend to, and James asked Bennet what he planned to do next. Bennet said that he had no other particular plans for that day, only to get his samples to the lab that afternoon. James saw the haulage crew and asked them to take Bennet and his samples to the station on their next trip; that would save him the trouble of having to carry all the bags to the shaft. Bennet said he should have the results in a day or so and would be back with his recommendations.

Once on the surface, James learned from Pete Burgess that there was to be a funeral for Lionel at St. Michael's church in Kitwe and that Lionel's parents were due that day. James asked if anyone had gone to meet them, and Pete told him that Piet van Rensburg was taking care of everything, from meeting them off the plane to arranging accommodation and even meals. The funeral was planned for that weekend on Saturday afternoon, so James immediately talked to the other section bosses and made sure that he had coverage for his blasting time. That way, he could leave early and get to the church in time. At home, he told Katrina what was going on, and she suggested that she call Piet in the morning and see if Lionel's parents wanted to do or see anything while they were there, or eat somewhere other than the mine club. She told him that there would also be a funeral on Sunday for Jane, with a wake to follow at the boat club.

The funeral was a sombre affair. There were not a lot of people there, mostly co-workers from the mine who knew Lionel and some of Jane's family and friends. James really felt for Lionel's parents. They had flown to a country where they knew no one to bury their son and would fly back again with a gaping hole in their lives.

After the funeral, James introduced himself to Lionel's parents and tried to tell them how sorry he was for their loss. They truly looked bemused and mumbled their thanks and moved on. He did note that the Lamprechts had taken Lionel's parents in tow and were now looking to their welfare. As James thought about it, it would have been so easy for the Lamprechts to blame Lionel for their daughter's death and thereby blame his parents. However, they seemed to have rather taken the approach that the two families had experienced severe loss, and the best thing to do was to comfort each other.

Jane's funeral was similar, but with a much larger turnout. Obviously, there were many more people in Zambia who knew Jane and who would mourn her loss. James noted that Lionel's parents were also there and that they sat with the Lamprechts. After the funeral, everyone retired to the boat club for the wake. Katrina had only a couple of drinks and then asked James to take her home. For her, there were too many people and memories for the moment, and she wanted some peace to remember Jane.

At work, on Monday, James was introduced by Pete Burgess to one of the assayers, Sisha, who would be spending time with him. Sisha went with James and was shown the section and the working stopes. He collected samples from each of them and also had with him the results from the samples that Sandy Bennet had taken the week before. Based on that information, James went down to talk to the tramming crew and tell them which stope to pull from. He then asked Sisha about himself and got a life story. Sisha had various business enterprises, quite apart from the mine job, including part ownership of a house of ill repute in Lumbumbashi. It seemed that Sisha had family in Zaire and spoke French fluently and visited Lumbumbashi regularly to collect his share of the earnings. James asked him how he crossed the border with money on him and learned that Sisha did not use one of the regular controlled border crossings, but some bush paths.

There was an element of risk associated with that, but he had contacts on both sides of the border and had a system worked out. In the event that the system broke down and he was ever approached by the Zairean border guards, he reasoned that a few Zaire here or there would facilitate passage, provided they had not been drinking too much and were not trigger-happy. James asked him how he knew where the border actual was, as it looked to a casual observer to be difficult to discern. Sisha told him that the border was marked by a series of cairns and markers that were actually defined and that his father and grandfather had shown him when he was younger. James then wondered how the border came to be where it was and who actually laid it out. Sisha had the story for that, too and told James about the Rhodesia/Congo border commission that negotiated and marked out an arbitrary line through the bush. It was not as if there was a nice, convenient landmark like the Limpopo or the Zambezi, as on the borders to the south. Even there, the system came unstuck at the western edge of Rhodesia, where Zambia, Rhodesia, Botswana, and the Caprivi Strip came together. Such was the legacy of colonial rule. As for the western boundary of Zambia with Angola, a nice straight line drawn on a map hardly matched up with reality.

When James arrived home, he was surprised to see some cars in the driveway. Katrina had apparently invited the Lamprechts and the Fairfaxes to dinner. When James joined them, they were telling stories about Jane and her exploits and telling Mr and Mrs Fairfax a little about the life that Lionel had led before his death. James was content to sit back and watch Katrina delicately weave the conversation back and forth, and also get the Fairfaxes to open up a little and tell them all more about Lionel before he came to Zambia. Once again, James was amazed by his new wife and the seeming never-ending depths of her talents and compassion. He knew that what she was doing now, he could not do it anywhere near as well or as diplomatically.

Dinner, considering the circumstances, was a success. Gibson had done them proud and produced a banquet fit for any occasion. He offered his condolences to the Lamprechts, whom he had known for many years, and asked them to pass on to Lionel's parents his wishes that they go well and in peace. At the end of the evening, Mr. Fairfax surprised James by inviting the Lamprechts to stay with them in England, when and if they should come, and was gratified when his invitation was accepted. The Lamprechts had a business trip that had been planned for some time the coming September and had decided that they needed to go away for a while. England was just far enough away and was also somewhere that Jane had never been, so it would not stir memories. All that was left for them to do was arrange the details of when they would be going and how to get to the Fairfax house.

After they had all gone, James asked Katrina if she had had any inkling that something like that would happen. She admitted that she had known that the Lamprechts were probably going to go to England and had thought that it might work if the two families got together. As she remarked to him, all she needed was to *maak 'n plan, jong*!

Stoping continued apace, and James spent an appreciable amount of time with the assayers and the tramming crews pulling differing quantities of broken ore from each draw point. The tramming crews complained a little about the extra work they felt they were being put to because of the variations, but for the most part, it was good-natured. James saw Greg fairly often now that he was on a regular day shift schedule. Greg confided in him that Shirley had filed for a divorce in England, citing abandonment! James thought that it was the other way around, but was sure that there was some lawyer out there who would take the case and make it sound good. Greg told him that he had been careful with his dating because he was unsure who might still be in contact with Shirley and who would see fit to tell her what Greg was doing. Giving her grounds for divorce through infidelity would be the ultimate irony, particularly as the case was being heard in England and he would not be there to gainsay anything. He was completely disillusioned with marriage at the moment and was still trying to come to terms with his situation and Shirley's betrayal.

Friday, James decided that Katrina needed a break from Kitwe and the past week, so he suggested that on Saturday afternoon and Sunday, they take a drive into the bush, south and west of Luanshya. Katrina was happy to go and set about organising their *katundu* for the weekend. She also suggested that they borrow a boat from Koot Strydom and take a trip down the Kafue to the Luswishi. She would take care of getting the boat and petrol for it. They did not really need much, just food and something to sleep on, as there was no chance of rain. James had been captivated by the weather service announcement that he had heard on the wireless. There will be no more weather until October: Goodbye. It just seemed so appropriate for a climate where, for about six months of the year, it was the same every day. Cool in the mornings, clear blue skies and 75° by about ten, cooling down again overnight. He knew that by the time October rolled around again, it would get hot and sticky, but for now, it was perfect and to be enjoyed.

On Saturday, when James went in to work, there was a message for him to see Koot Strydom before he went down. James went to the office, and Koot immediately took him out, showed him the boat, and suggested that if he left his car keys with Koot, he would get the trailer hooked up for him while he was underground, he would also drop off the Land Rover and boat at James's house so that Katrina could load it up. That way, she could collect him straight from work, and they could leave without delay.

When James came to the surface on Saturday, he saw Katrina waiting for him, parked under the shade normally reserved for one of the Assistant Underground Managers. She grinned and waved. The others who were with James were curious as to who this was. Most of the long-time residents knew Katrina, but many of the newer batches of expatriates had never met her. A couple of them even remarked that they did not know that the manager had such good taste. James disabused them of the notion that Katrina had anything to do with that august personage. He told them that she was his *ou vrou,* which amused the long-time residents and confused the newcomers.

Away from the mine, Katrina asked James what he had been talking about with the other section bosses, and he related the tale. She leaned over and punched him on the arm for the *ou vrou* remark and then went on to say that all she knew about the Assistant Underground Manager was that he was an idiot that had been promoted well beyond his intelligence, that he regularly got drunk and beat his wife, and it was rumoured that he had a compound girl on the side. He had been around forever, and that was probably his only claim to fame.

After they reached Luanshya, James asked Katrina for directions. "Take the road out of town that goes towards Mpongwe."

"Fine, which one is that?" asked James.

"Left here, then right, then after about a mile left past the tailings dam."

"What's the road like to where we're going? James asked.

"No, man, it's not bad, dirt, usually a bit corrugated with some soft patches."

"How far are we going?"

"About eighty-five miles to the Kafue. We'll put the boat in there at Muchiya's Ferry and then go downstream," replied Katrina.

Katrina was right about the road. It was generally corrugated, which meant a shaky ride unless they went really fast or really slowly. Fast seemed like a better plan. While they were driving along, James had a feeling that he had been there before and thought that he recognised some things. When they reached the river, there was a ferry, a simple, large pontoon with ramps on each end that looked as if it were pulled across the river with basic manpower. Next to the ferry docking bank was a boat ramp. James recognised the place at last. Koos had brought them out here when Alex was visiting. James turned the Land Rover around and, after untying the boat and helping Katrina up into it, backed the trailer into the river until the boat floated off. Katrina started the engine and backed out into the river. She spun the boat around a few times while James was parking away from the boat ramp. He locked up and went down to the riverbank to be picked up.

Katrina spun the boat around, expertly navigated the few rapids that they encountered and then they tore off downstream. Eventually, they came to the confluence of the Kafue and the Luswishi and saw a herd of hippo in the tributary. James was by now wondering where they would camp for the night, and he asked Katrina if they should stop as the light was failing and it would be dark very soon.

"*Ja*, now now. We'll be pulling into the bank just over there and will camp under those tall trees," she said.

"Won't there be a problem with the hippo as they come out of the river to feed at night?" asked James.

"No, man, it'll be fine. They like to go to the west, where there is good grazing, there just isn't much to eat for them under the trees."

"Okay, where do we pull in?"

"Just here, when I pull in, just jump out with the bow rope and tie us off," instructed Katrina.

She spun the boat around and pulled over slowly to the east bank. James dutifully leapt off with a rope and pulled the boat into the bank and tied it securely. He then helped Katrina unload their stuff and carried it to a clearing under the trees. It looked as if the trees actually suppressed any new growth, so there were no bushes or long grass to trample down to form a campsite. James noticed the remnants of previous fires and collected together the rocks used to create the fireplace.

After the drive down the river, it was quiet on the bank. The only sounds were those of the bush, the honking of the hippo in the river and the calling of fish eagles. A scops owl started up and was answered by another, and James heard some rustling sounds. He looked around in alarm and was relieved to see that it was only a group of francolins roosting for the night in one of the trees. He asked Katrina if they were safe.

"*Ag* man, *moenie* worry *nie*. We'll light a fire and keep it going for a while, remember most things in the bush are more afraid of you and will stay away," she replied.

"If you say so," he said, a little disbelieving.

"No, man, I do have a gun with me, so if we are really in trouble, I will use it," she added.

"Really, I didn't see it when I unloaded the boat unless it was in that long roll over there!" he said.

"Just come over here and help me get something to eat, and then we can think of something else to do under the stars," she said.

Katrina had brought plenty of food, and James quickly lit a fire and set up a grill to cook over. After dinner, Katrina sent James to the river to get water and more water, which she then heated over the fire in a large kettle. She then asked James to build up the fire for the night, unroll the sleeping bags and make sure that they were clear of debris, insects and animals. She finally unrolled a rubber mat, stood on it, stripped off and then told James to get busy.

"What do you mean?" he asked.

"Wash me, what do you think I heated the water for?" she asked.

"Oh, okay, I can do that," he said.

James took the sponge Katrina was holding and mixed hot and cooler water until it felt fine to him, and then began washing her down. With the only light being from the campfire, it was an amazingly erotic experience as the firelight played over her skin, which shone differently where it was wet or dry. As he worked his way down her body, he gently shifted her legs apart and washed between them, then knelt down and kissed her and worked his tongue up and down her. She pulled him into her and opened her legs wider to give him better access. When she came, it was with big gasps and shudders, and she just held James to her until the spasms subsided.

Katrina then told James to strip off, and she would wash him down. James discovered that although the experience was truly wonderful, he would have liked some heat from a fire on both sides. The side of the fire was nicely heated, but the other side would cool off quickly, particularly when wet. Now he understood why Katrina kept rotating when he was washing her. He wondered if she would return the attention, but apart from washing his fully erect penis, she seemed more intent on getting him into bed and inside her.

With both of them now clean, they quickly moved to the sleeping bags that Katrina had laid out earlier. Their lovemaking was passionate as they had both been strongly aroused by the mutual cleansing and James's oral attentions. Afterwards, they both lay back and looked up towards the sky, where they could see stars through the branches of the trees.

"Do you know what is wrong with these sleeping bags?" asked Katrina.

"Yes, no room to move around!" laughed James.

"Yes, unzip them and let's do that again with a bit more freedom for me to get on top of you!"

"Okay, you don't think you'll get cold?"

"Were you cold just now?"

"No, I was sweating," admitted James.

"Well, then?"

Without the constriction of the sleeping bags, Katrina was able to straddle James and ride him until he came again. When they were both finally sated, they relaxed with Katrina nestled in James's arms.

"You know, this is what I had thought we would do that weekend we went to the Mita Hills dam," commented Katrina.

"Wow," replied James. "I thought I might have been lucky but would never have expected anything as great."

"Why not?" she asked. "Do you think it only happens to people in X-rated films?"

"No, but I suppose it's just something that the staid and sober English never discuss or advertise except in x-rated films."

"Really?"

"Shh!" said James. "Did you hear that?"

"Oh, the rooting in the leaves, pass me the torch and I'll show you what it is," Katrina promised.

She shone the torch around until she found the culprit. It was a porcupine, busily searching for food and rooting around in the leaves and debris at the edge of the clearing formed by the trees.

"Oh, I wondered if it were something more dangerous," commented James.

"No man, just a porcupine. Don't go and try to play with it though, I don't want to spend the rest of the night pulling out quills!"

"How did you know it was a porcupine?" asked James.

"Man, didn't you see the spoor when we landed and the pellets and the odd quill?"

"No, I was more worried about securing the boat and about the hippo across the way," replied James.

In the morning, the early bird chorus got them up. There were the francolins from the night before, guinea fowl, eagles, and seemingly innumerable other smaller song birds, all bound and determined to make their presence known. James collected more water from the river and relit the fire. He was struck again by how quickly the sun came up. From pitch black to brilliant daylight had to be less than thirty minutes, not at all like the long, dragged out dawns of the northern latitudes. With the water heating nicely, James wondered if there would be a repeat of the previous night, but his hopes were dashed when he heard a boat approaching and a hail.

"James, fancy seeing you here!" said a voice.

James looked and tried to make out who it was. By now, Katrina had joined him, and she laughed.

"It's Barbara. You remember, from the New Year's Eve party?"

"Oh yes, who is with her?"

"I can't see yet," replied Katrina. Then she called out to the boat, asking them if they wanted coffee and breakfast.

"Thanks, we'll pull in behind your boat, whose boat is it by the way?" asked Barbara.

"It belongs to *Oom* Koot, so don't scratch it," cautioned Katrina.

As James helped them in, he realised who else was in the boat, Susan and Patrick and, of all people, George, whom he had not really seen since the first aid classes. Now he thought he understood all the trips to Chingola. Well, he thought, why not? Barbara was pretty hot stuff, and if he had not met Katrina, he might have taken an interest himself.

"James, do you know everyone?" asked Barbara.

"Yes, come on up, and I will get coffee going."

"So it was your fire we saw last night," commented Barbara. "What were you doing all night?"

"Not much," replied Katrina. "What about you?"

"Oh, we got some binoculars and enjoyed the show," said Barbara with a sly grin.

"Oh, stargazing were you?" asked James.

"You might say that," said Susan. "Except our stars kept moving around and were being obscured by the trees and bushes!"

"I thought that the hippo were doing a lot of grunting last night," continued Barbara. "But then I remembered they were all off eating, so someone else must have been doing the grunting."

"Coffee anyone?" interrupted Katrina.

"Hey, thanks," said Patrick. "You know you girls are so full of shit."

"Why so, Patrick?" asked Katrina.

"Well, we saw a fire all right, but we were camped about a mile or so up the Luswishi, and even the firelight was only partially visible."

"Well, thanks a lot, Patrick," said Barbara. "I was well on the way to convincing Katrina that we had witnessed all so that she would confess!"

"So, what were you doing last night?" asked Patrick.

"Star gazing and chasing after a porcupine," laughed James.

With coffees in hand, Barbara and her group took a little tour of the area, which gave James a chance to confer quickly with Katrina.

"Do you think they were watching last night?" he asked.

"It wouldn't surprise me," she replied. "But who cares? I don't see any cameras, do you?"

"No, but where do you think they were last night. I didn't hear a boat, and there were no other cars by the ferry."

"If they crossed the Kafue on the pontoon, the next river they would hit would be the Luswishi, so I'll bet they put the boat in upstream and motored down," Katrina suggested. "They probably stopped well short of here, which is why we didn't hear them last night."

"Makes sense to me," James agreed.

Patrick and George came back to join them. Apparently, the two girls had gone off to use the facilities. George told them that he had seen their Land Rover by the pontoon and that it had been an interesting ride over. He guessed that they had camped about two miles upriver from the Kafue, but had been concerned by the number of hippo in the river and their aggressive behaviour. When Barbara and Susan came back, Katrina offered them breakfast, an offer that they all accepted with alacrity. Somehow, James had the feeling that they had not eaten particularly well the night before, the way they shovelled down the food. He was right. Patrick started to tell them about their adventure and the loss of their food box in the river. They had dropped it while unloading the boat, so they had spent a fairly hungry night. Fortunately, the beer had not also gone, so they consumed all that instead of solid food. That probably also accounted for the blurry looks and red eyes.

After breakfast, Patrick and George helped James wash up and stow his gear while the girls talked. James was curious to know how George had met Barbara. It seemed that he knew Patrick somehow, and the introduction had been through Susan. James wanted to ask what happened to the antipathy towards 'local yokels', but decided to leave it alone. Barbara and Susan came over and asked if George and Patrick were ready, as they were going to try their hand at fishing. James said his goodbyes and helped them get their boat away from the bank.

With their visitors gone, at least for the moment, James and Katrina turned their attentions to loading the boat. They were also going to try fishing. James asked Katrina what they might catch, and she thought possibly bream or pike.
"We must go down to Kariba one weekend and do some fishing there," she suggested.
"Why?" asked James.
"We could go after tiger fish and perhaps vundu," she answered.
"What are they?" he asked.
"The tiger fish is a smallish fish with lots of fight and teeth; the vundu is a kind of big catfish," she elaborated. "My dad used to catch vundu with blue soap!"
"Blue soap?" James wondered.
"Don't ask me why they like blue soap; they just seem to. You catch them at night, and they can only get big!" Katrina commented.

They took the journey back up the river towards the ferry in leisurely stages. The fishing was actually pretty good. By lunch time, they had caught far more than they would use in the next week or two, so Katrina hailed a group of fishermen and unloaded most of their catch onto them. There were rapids to negotiate in the river, but the jet boat was built for such waters, and Katrina was able to easily find her way through the rocks and stay in the best water. At the ferry, they put into the shore, and James collected his Land Rover and backed the trailer into the river. While they were loading the boat, they saw the others arrive on the opposite bank and watched them drive onto the pontoon. They waited for them to cross and asked about the fishing.

"Fishing, what bloody fishing?" asked Patrick. "All we saw were hippo and more hippo. That river must be crawling with them."

"Any problems?" asked Katrina.

"Only one," said Barbara. "One cantankerous old bull decided to charge us, but we got away in time."

"James, I'm telling you, that bastard came out of the bottom of the river so fast, it looked like a bloody express train!" said George.

"That's what happens when stupid idiots ride over them with outboards and piss them off!" said Barbara. "They all develop this hatred for boats and attack."

"So, race you back to Kitwe?" suggested George.

"No, it's okay, George," replied James. "You go on; you have farther to go to Chingola."

"Okay, see you around!"

James recalled that Koos had said exactly the same thing about the boats and the hippo on his previous trip to this part of the river. Well, he surmised, there were probably idiots in all walks of life and in every country.

# New regime

When James reported for work on Monday morning, he was surprised to see Pete Burgess in earlier than usual. He asked if there was anything special going on and was told that they were getting a new Mine Captain that day. Apparently, there had been some emergency elsewhere in the group, and they had taken Jim Brown to solve the problems. They were going to get Harry Penrose. James had seen him once or twice around the mine. His impressions were of a late middle-aged man, rather dour, overweight, and prone to shouting. Burgess told him that Penrose had come to Zambia right before the War and had struggled to get anywhere until Independence and the onset of Zambianization. That had finally given him the promotion to Mine Captain. So he was a rather embittered man who probably hovered on the brink of being deported for his treatment of the black Zambian workers, both orally and physically. It seemed the greatest crime one could commit was to call the Zambian workers 'stupid' and Penrose usually used that, plus any number of expletives, to better emphasise how stupid. Fortunately for Penrose, he also called all the expatriate shift bosses and section bosses stupid, so was quite fair and even-handed in his abuse. This had probably saved him a time or two, as he could hardly be accused of discrimination.

Burgess also gave him his other news. That year's crop of students had arrived for their summer vacation work experience, and he was to get them for the next two weeks. That meant that Burgess was going to have a group of seven students trailing around after him while he was trying to adjust to a new boss. James gave him his deepest sympathy but wondered what that had to do with him. Then Burgess let it drop that they would be spending a fair amount of time in his section because it was a good example of the type of mining they were engaged in and was reasonably well run. He also said that after the two or three days of general introduction to each section, James was going to get one of the students for a month.

James took the cage underground and joined his crews. He told them about the change in hierarchy and about the students. He then began to get the tales about Penrose and the opinions as to why he had taken so long to climb the promotional ladder. It seemed that wherever Penrose went in the early days of his career, death followed. It was never possible to actually pin any of the accidents directly on him, but the general opinion was that he was a *mube bwana* and that working for him usually led to bad things. Well, with two layers between the operators and Penrose, James felt that he and Burgess should be able to insulate the operators from any really bad decisions. However, they did have a problem in that Penrose looked upon 'college boys' as some form of inferior being and delighted in creating difficulties for them.

Later that morning, Penrose came through the section briefly with the Underground Manager, so their tour was brief and limited to introducing Penrose to his new sections. After they had gone, Burgess came by with his herd. James found it hard to imagine that a mere two years before, he could have been one of them. They were a mixed bag from the mining schools in England and from Delft and Leoben. As Pete Burgess did the introductions and explaining, James watched the reactions. There were the few really keen types, the ones who probably were first in line for everything and sat at the front of the bus, the mediocre, and the more relaxed ones who were more likely rebellious and questioning. He wondered which one of them he was likely to get and if he would have any say, or just get saddled with whoever they gave him.

Burgess and his tribe stayed long enough to watch the wiring up of the blast for the day, then they all trooped down to the haulage level for the blasting. Fortunately, James had brought his blasting box with him in anticipation of this happening, so was not faced with the problem of his illicit firing line. The resulting thumps from the concussion waves of his blast impressed even the most blasé among them. He was asked on the way out to the shaft if he enjoyed his job and how he had decided to come here rather than one of the other options open to a graduate: the National Coal Board, Ghana, Australia, Canada, or South Africa. James told them that the Coal Board had just not looked very interesting, and he had never been that keen about coal mines. The offers from the rest of the companies had all been much of a muchness, and in the end, it had been the interviewer who had swayed him.

James then asked his own questions and learned that there were twelve students in all, living in two houses on Fifth Avenue. Seven he had met, and the other five were assigned to the concentrator and the smelter. One of the mining students was a local chap who was going to university on a company bursary; he told them that there was another scholar with the smelter group. Burgess told James that there was to be a party for the students at the boat club on Saturday night and invited him and Katrina. One of the students asked him if he had been married before he came out, and James told them no, he had met and married his wife in Zambia. When the cage finally came, Burgess and James got on the lower deck but sent the others to the upper deck as the cage was now pretty full. The cry was soon taken up by many in the cage, *chaya four one, chaya four one*. The onsetter took a look around and decided that they were full enough, if not a little over the posted limit for persons per deck, so he rang four one to take them direct to the surface. As they passed other stations on the way up, they were hailed by those waiting, and the response was calls of derision from those in the cage lucky to be riding directly to the top.

On the surface, James asked the students if they had any transport, and as they had none, he offered to drop them off at their houses. What they also wanted was to replenish their beer stocks, so he threw in a trip to the bottle store. He told them the tale of one group of students the previous year who had been loaned a car, and it had caught fire on the road to Kariba. The students were rescued by a passing fisherman, but the one who had been loaned the car then had the problem of getting it back to the Copperbelt. Life was certainly never dull!

At home, James relayed all his news to Katrina, who told him all the folklore about Penrose. Apart from all the other sins with which he was credited, it was generally held that he beat his wife, usually when drunk. He seemed like a really nice chap all round. Katrina was interested in the students and asked James if he had been on such trips when he was at university. James told her that he had been to Ireland and to Canada because there was a requirement for graduation to have worked so many shifts in a mine. Hence, the summer vacation jobs. His summer jobs typically started with the wonderfully fulfilling task of cleaning drains underground; back-breaking work with few rewards. He had progressed to cleaning out working areas with mechanical devices, known as slushers, and had even become a roof bolter. The Irish had even foolishly entrusted him with explosives! All in all, the Zambian opportunity looked like one of the better deals. You got flown out to Zambia, shown around the mine, you were not allowed to actually do much work, then you could either fly home or make your way to Cape Town and take the boat back.

For the rest of the week, James saw Pete Burgess and his tribe frequently, once accompanied by Penrose, who apparently was taking delight in pointing out all the sins of omission and commission that the section bosses had or were committing. In his section, Penrose found little to gripe about but still managed to get in some harsh words about James's magazine. Apparently, the air supply to the magazine did not go far enough into the controlled space, so James was told to fix it. Oh well, if that was all, James could live with it. In some of the working areas, James had erected supports and had sized them to take up most of the drive so that a large person could not pass by. Penrose could not enter but could not complain because the safety inspector and a Government Mine Inspector had just been in and pronounced the area safe. They then asked Penrose to accompany them to another area where they had found issues. Burgess was happy to see him go and even happier that it was not in one of his sections. Some other poor bastard was going to get the heat later.

Saturday, James and Katrina drove out to the dam and joined the party. The mine had provided a bus and a driver for the students, so they were taking full advantage of accepting any beer that was offered. There was a pretty good turnout. James saw most of the expatriate section and shift bosses, the new local Zambia section bosses who had started with James and Tom, and even some of the mine captains and the Underground Manager. There were also others there that James assumed must be from the concentrator and the smelter, and perhaps even the different engineering services. Katrina saw Rita and Tom and directed James to join them. They were talking with two of the students whom James had seen underground.

"Oh, James, let me introduce you to Bill and Ben," said Tom, indicating them in turn.

"Okay, so where is the Little Weed?" asked James.

"Who?" asked Katrina.

"Sorry, bad attempt at a joke," apologised James. "Hello, this is my wife, Katrina. I saw you two underground, didn't I?"

"Yes," replied Bill. "We were with Pete Burgess when we stayed and watched your blast."

"Not much to see, I'm afraid. Just a lot of noise until the next day when all sins are revealed!" commented James.

"James told us that you two met here, Katrina," said Ben. "How long have you lived here?"

"Most of my life," she replied. "My dad came north when I was really little and, apart from boarding school, I have lived here all my life."


"Bill was telling me that he goes to Nottingham and Ben to Newcastle," said Rita. "I haven't found out yet if they might want to come back here."

"That rather depends on whether they will actually offer us jobs and what any other offers may be," commented Bill.

"Well, I for one don't regret my decision to come at all," said James. "I think for Henry Zimba and Joy Mwamba over there, it was a pretty easy decision. They could come home and get a good job."

"I'm glad I came," agreed Tom. "It has been great so far. We had a nice boat trip out, and the drive up was fun. Rita got a job as well, so we can remit more money back home, so we are doing okay."

"Do you see yourselves in competition with the local Zambian section bosses?" asked Bill.

"Not really," replied Tom. "I will do my contract, then if all is going well, I will consider another, but doubt if I would go beyond that. Those chaps are here for the long term, so will probably stay at the mine indefinitely."

"Do you get on well with them and the other Zambians?" asked Ben.

"Yes," replied James. "I don't know that I would go as far as to say we socialise, but at work we are fine. I like them, particularly Joy and some of the non-graduate section bosses, and have had good dealings with my operators."

"We heard that there have been problems with some of the white bosses and the workers," said Bill in a conspiratorial undertone.

"Oh, occasionally something happens that often gets defined as white on black or black on white, but the same issues could come up in an all white or all black group," commented Tom.

They were joined by the Underground Manager, Colin Winter, who was making the rounds and introducing himself to the students. He was probably on a recruiting drive, as other mines in the group seemed to be getting more attention than his. James and Tom had never actually met him, so for them it was a first. After a few moments talking to him, James wondered what Winter had done to be saddled with people like Penrose, Ross, and Hagley. Winter seemed actually like a reasonable bloke that you could talk to. As far as James could tell, Winter seemed well educated; he certainly had no chips on his shoulder about college graduates, and in fact, he told them stories about his university days and his career to date with the mine. Winter then excused himself and went over to talk to Kayumba and Zimba.

"Seems like a nice bloke," commented Bill.

"That's just the public appearance," said Ben. "In real life, he's probably like all the rest, mean and nasty."

"Perhaps one day you'll find out if you come back here to work," laughed Tom.

"Are there any dances or anything in this town?" asked Bill.

"Sure, the right person to ask is Piet van Rensburg from Personnel, he knows everything that goes on in this town," replied Tom. "There he is, you must have met him when you arrived."

"Yes, he's the one who collected us from Ndola. Come on, Ben, let's go and see what we can do for entertainment," said Bill.

"Well, how are you two?" asked Katrina. "It seems ages since I spoke to you last."

"We are just fine," replied Rita. "How are your parents doing down south?"

"The last I heard, they were settling in. Things are a little different down there, so they have some adjusting to do," Katrina replied.

"Tom, be a dear, you and James go get us a beer while I have a chat with Katrina," suggested Rita.

"Okay, come along, James, let's go talk shop while the girls talk about whatever," Tom said. On that note, Tom and James exchanged news about their respective assignments and the changes in management that had just occurred. James also told Tom about his weekend trip, well, the expurgated version of the trip, and his encounter with George. Tom was as surprised as James was that George had apparently softened his antipathy towards the 'local yokels', love conquers all, so there was hope for him yet. At the bar, they met Greg, who was there on his own and who was now looking in pretty good shape. James asked him if there were any residual headaches or other pains. Greg said that he was fine now, and apart from the powder headaches he had when he started back, he was now in great shape.

Delivery of the beer to the girls took a little longer than expected, but apparently, they had anticipated that and got some from a waiter who was hovering around. The waiter knew Katrina and was happy to help, as his brother had worked for Koos and now had a job with the new owner and was doing well. That made Katrina a good one, madam, in his book, so anything he could do to make life easier for her, he would. Katrina had found a table, and she and Rita had been deep in conversation when James and Tom returned. Joy came over to the table to say hello, and James asked how the new baby was. It was doing well, and Joy was happy to be a family man. Joy told them that his wife and child were taking a few days to visit her parents, so he was on his own for a while. Then Joy was gone, snared in conversation with two more of the students who were there, one of whom Joy had briefly met while at university. The rest of the evening went quickly enough, and James and Katrina were happy to leave and go home to more pleasurable and personal activities.

Monday, it was back to the regular routine, except that James did see Burgess still shepherding his little flock around and did wonder which one he would get. The week passed quickly enough until Thursday, when James was ready to blast and called to George below to see if he was ready. There was no answer, so James waited about fifteen minutes and called again. Once again no answer, and he was now getting agitated because he wanted to leave for the day. He called again, and still no answer, so he asked Ben what he thought. Ben suggested that they just blast and go, because, in his opinion, George must have already left. James thought about that for a while and then agreed. They set off their blast and left for the surface. James did not see George in the cage nor at the surface in the change house. So he waited until the next cage came out to see if George would be in it. No George.

Now, James started to imagine all kinds of scenarios. His blasting gases had overcome George, and he was lying somewhere in the mine, unconscious. The more he thought about it, the more disturbed he became and the more bleak the scenario. As each cage came up, he went to the doorway and checked who got out, but still no George. James was beginning to think he should go to the shift boss's office and confess all, but caution or shame got the better of him, and he waited.

Finally, after about forty-five minutes, George appeared, smiling and happy. James asked him how things were, and George said he was sorry that he had not been at the raise at the appointed time, but that he had been delayed with his own problems. He had realised that James might blast on time, so had taken himself off to a safe refuge and waited for the explosions, then had given himself another thirty minutes for the smoke and gases to clear. James wanted to hit him for making him worry so much, then had the good grace to realise that he was the one at fault, so he apologised to George for not waiting. All he wanted to do then was get out of there and go home.

At home, Katrina asked him why he was so late, and he related the story, telling her that for at least half an hour he had been convinced that he had killed George and that he had been working up the courage to tell someone of his fears. He told her that he now realised what a stupid thing it had been to do and vowed not to do that again. He was certainly not going to tell Burgess or Penrose. It would be the kind of thing that he thought Penrose would love, a college graduate making a huge blunder.

James was assigned his student in the last week of July, David Thomas, a coal miner from the Midlands who had apparently seen the light and left the coal mines of Nottinghamshire for hard rock mining. His father, uncles, and grandfather were all coal miners. He was full of new expressions, out-bye, in-bye, and the one James really liked, panzer. Up until then, he had always thought that a panzer was a type of German tank, but found it was also a coal mining machine. Out-bye and in-bye meant away from or towards the working face.

He had one vice that James came to hate: he was forever smoking. Obviously, in a coal mine, that would have been a major problem, but in the copper mine, it was often only an inconvenience for those immediately around him. One day, James was surprised to see him even start to light a cigarette as they were charging up holes. Ben reached over and crushed the lit cigarette in his hand, and made it clear that any further attempt to blow them up would be met with real violence. He seemed unabashed and quickly settled into his diatribe about the evils of copper mining and the niceties of coal mining. James came to thoroughly dislike Thomas as he rattled on for hours about his bloody coal mines and about how mismanaged the copper mines were.

James had toyed with the idea of introducing his student to Katrina and of entertaining him while he was assigned to him. However, it only took the first day for him to decide that the idea of spending more time than necessary with this bloke was more than he could bear. Sometimes Ben would look at James and shake his head and then rattle off in ChiKabanga so fast that there was no way that Thomas, even if he had learned a word or two, could follow. Ben was definitely unimpressed and really did not like the fact that Thomas never shared his cigarettes with the members of the gang. He told James that Thomas talked worse than three women together, which made James laugh and then put him in the spot of inventing a translation for Thomas. It was obviously going to be a long and trying two weeks.

At the end of the first week with Thomas, James noticed that someone had been helping themselves to his lunch and his coffee. He suspected Thomas because this was new, but was unable to catch him. There were times when James went alone to do certain jobs, and then he left Thomas at the place where they had their powder boxes and the boxes for their equipment. He asked Ben what he thought and learned that some of the others felt that their meagre lunches had been examined, if not sampled.

After work on Saturday, James stopped by the hospital lab to see Catherine. Fortunately, he found her at work and put his problem to her, asking if there was not something he could dose his coffee with to metaphorically smoke the bastard out. Catherine thought for a short while and then grinned and disappeared, only to reappear with a small vial of liquid.

"Phenolphthalein," she announced. "Just the ticket. Make your coffee good and strong to mask the taste, and the bugger will be shitting through the eye of a needle."

"Really? Is this enough?" asked James.

"Oh, trust me," said Catherine with a big grin. "With that dose, anyone who pinches your coffee won't be worth much for the rest of the day. Just one thing, though."

"What?" asked James.

"I didn't give this to you, and don't drink any of this yourself," she whispered.

"Hey, thanks, Catherine, I'll let you know if I'm right or if it is some other bastard."

James told Katrina of his woes and his plan, and she immediately set about getting him another matching coffee flask so that he could take his regular flask in on Monday but have another that he could conceal and use for himself. She was highly offended by the idea that someone was helping themselves to the lunches that she made for James and was delighted that Catherine had a potential solution. James then switched the conversation to her job and how things were going. Apparently well enough, but as she had noted before, it was different being an employee rather than being one of the owners, albeit a very small and junior owner. The new owners of the business were very nice, but it was still not the same, and she did not have the same commitment that she did before.

In the mail was a letter from Katrina's mother telling them about the progress in Calitzdorp. Apparently, they now had a place to live and were working on sorting out the vineyards that they had. Koos had decided to keep the grape vines that he now had and send the production to one of the wineries. He also had some sheep that he was raising in the Little Karoo that he planned to do something with one day. Their appearance in South Africa had also prompted some of their relatives to contact them and visit, something rarely or never done while they lived in Zambia.

Monday morning, James was eager to try out his doctored coffee, so he made sure that it was strong and sweet to disguise the taste of the phenolphthalein. Once underground, he drew Ben aside and told him what he had done.

"*Mushle wena aikôna puza lo coffee ka mina,*" he told Ben. "*Mina azi fakili lo muti, futi lo muntu ka puza lo, yena azi hamba lapa chimbusu zonke skati!*"

Ben grinned an evil grin and looked sideways at Thomas, and replied. "*Tina azi buka ubani yena bamba lo coffee, kabanga yena lo bwana lo.*" He was saying that they would see who was taking the coffee and that perhaps it was Thomas. James tried hard to maintain his normal routine so as not to give the game away. He did make sure that his undoctored coffee was stashed somewhere else and then waited for results.

By very early afternoon, it looked as if they had struck gold. Thomas came to James and Ben and asked where the toilet was. He said he must have eaten something the night before that disagreed with him, and he needed to go. James directed him to the toilets on the haulage level, then went to check on his coffee. There was about one-third of it gone, but it was still too early to pin it on Thomas. There was still a possibility that it was one of the regular gang members. By the time they were done with the shift, the evidence was pretty damning. They had hardly seen Thomas for the rest of the shift. He had spent all his time at, or near, the toilets and no one else in their gang or the one above had shown any signs of discomfort.

At the station, while they were waiting for the cage, James asked Thomas directly if he had helped himself to his coffee.
"Hey, Thomas, did you try any of my coffee?"
"You bastard, what did you put in it?" spluttered Thomas.
"Ah, so it was you," said James. "Just something to smoke out the prick who has been pinching my coffee. You'd better be careful if you do that again, others may not be as charitable as me and may be more inclined to just mete out immediate retribution."
"But I saw you drink out of the same flask. Why aren't you running to the loo every few minutes?"
"Because you miserable turd, I have another flask that looks just the same."
"So what did you put in it, and how long can I expect to feel like this?"
"Phenolphthalein. I suggest that you drink plenty of water tonight, and tomorrow you can go to another section. You're not coming back to mine," replied James. Once on the surface, James saw Pete Burgess and told him the story and told him that he did not want Thomas back in his section. Burgess agreed and took Thomas into his office for a bollocking, which was interrupted three times by the need for toilet breaks.

On his way home, James stopped by the hospital and told Catherine the results of their doctoring. She asked who the miscreant was, and upon learning that it was Thomas, told James what else she had heard from a couple of the other students that she had met at a party on Sunday. Apparently, there had been fisticuffs at one of the student houses when Thomas had been caught pinching beers from the other student house. The other students had taken a dim view of this, and one of them had gone a little beyond yelling and had thumped him. The fracas had been broken up by the Dutch chap, who was concerned lest they all be shipped back with bad reports. James's guess was that there was one student who would not get a job offer, but who knew, the ways of the world are sometimes strange and irrational, and someone could actually take leave of their senses.

Katrina was also interested to learn the results of the doctoring and who the villain was. She took the contaminated flask and washed it out thoroughly, but set it aside so as not to use it for a while, until she was satisfied that there was no risk of James being caught in his own trap. She had no doubt that the story would now follow Thomas, no matter where he went in the mine or within the group. The Africans, with their uncanny system of communication, would ensure that everyone knew what the problem was and also what the response had been. In her mind, it also did not hurt James's image as he was now held, in a very minor way, in the same esteem as the witch doctors. It was doubtful that anyone ever again would touch his food or his coffee, unless it was a *muzungu* unversed in the ways of the world.

When James reported for work the next day, there was a note to see Burgess. He wondered briefly if there had been any repercussions from his run-in with Thomas, but no, Burgess had two very different things to discuss. The first was that on Wednesday, a week away, he had to report to the Pneumoconiosis Bureau for his annual check. The appointment was at eight, so he could go straight there and report to work later. The next item was that James was due some local leave, and if he planned to take a week in early September, he needed to let them know so that they could arrange for a substitute while he was gone. James told Burgess that he would let him know the next day. Their conversation had just ended when Tom arrived and told them that he was to appear for his annual physical the following Wednesday. He then added that he had some leave coming. James asked what he and Rita might do, and Tom was unsure. James suggested that he get Katrina to talk to Rita, as it might be fun to go off for a week and do something together.

Later that day, as he was waiting to blast, James saw Joy in the haulroad and asked how things were going. Joy had been for his annual check-up and was also taking about a week off, the last full week of August. He told James that he was going to visit relatives in the Western Province, near the Angolan border. James asked him how close to the border, as he had heard stories of minor incidents along it. Joy assured him that they would not be that close. He was going to Kalobo, just across the Zambezi from Mongu. It would be a long drive as they would go south first to Lusaka, then essentially straight west to Mongu. At least this time of year, the roads would be passable; in the rains, it was always a chancy business. The flood plain around the Zambezi near Mongu should also be reasonably dry. He planned to do some hunting and fishing with his uncles.

At home, James told Katrina that he had been asked about local leave and that the second week of September had been suggested. He also told her that Tom and Rita would be off that week. Katrina then suggested that they go and see Rita and Tom and see if there was somewhere they would like to go for that week. Later, after beer, a *braai*, and some discussion, they settled on the Kariba Heights hotel in Kariba, just over the dam wall into Rhodesia.

That plan would have been fine except for events that took place the following week. James was in his section when one of the crew from Tom's section arrived out of breath and sweating profusely. This was unusual, to say the least, as their section was some way off.
"*Bwana, bwana, buya checha, lo bwana yena ifwa!*" he finally managed to get out after he had recovered his breath. It looked as if he had run and climbed all the way.
"*Ini wena kuluma, lo bwana yena ifwa?*" asked James. Was he telling him that Tom was dead?
"*Sure, bwana lo bwana* Tom, *yena ifwa, buya checha.*"
James told Ben to take over and then headed off to Tom's section, all the while thinking that it had to be a mistake.

Ten minutes of hard and fast going later, James climbed his last ladder and ran down the drive that the crew pointed to. Things were a mess. Tom was on the ground, breathing but obviously in a bad way. There were two others also down, one obviously dead and the other still breathing but also not very well. James asked the others if they had

345

notified the surface and gone to get the first aid box and stretcher. They had the stretcher and box arrived as they were speaking. While he mechanically tore open Tom's overalls and started to apply dressings and pressure to stop the bleeding, James looked around and tried to work out what had happened. They were next to what looked like the remains of a bar machine drill. There were bits of steel embedded in the walls and the roof, and upon closer examination in Tom and the others. The dead helper had no hands, and the operator was severely cut about the chest and face.

James and some of the others loaded Tom and the other live operator, called Banda, onto the stretcher, and they started towards the raise to get them to the surface. The dead operator they would collect as soon as they acquired another stretcher. As they were manoeuvring the stretcher down the raise, they were hailed by some of the first aid station team. They took over and ran the two stretchers to the station. James was hard-pressed to keep up as they were setting such a pace. Some of the team had stayed behind to collect the third casualty, but they would take more time and get the next cage up. The cage was waiting for them, and they rushed on board, taking up the cry of '*Chaya four one, chaya four one*'. As with any mine accident, the onsetter did not need telling, and he rang them straight to the surface.

At the top, an ambulance was waiting, and it whisked Tom and Banda away. Then James walked around the back of the shaft and threw up. Everything that he had eaten or drunk that day came up until he was dry-heaving. He finally sat down with his head in his hands and cried. Pete Burgess found him sitting in the corner and sat next to him and asked how he was.
"What the fuck do you think?" asked James. "My best friend here looks like he met a meat grinder. What the hell happened?"
"We don't know yet, but I'm sure that in time we'll find out," replied Pete. "We're sending an investigation team down now to see what they can learn. Why don't we go to the hospital and see how things are?"
"Has anyone told Rita yet?" asked James.
"Yes, I just called her and she will meet us at the hospital," said Pete. "Are you OK to go?"

"Yes, I'll see you there," said James.

"No, I'll drive and drop you at home if I have to. You are in no state to drive," said Pete with some finality.

At the hospital, they found Rita, who immediately broke down and, between sobs, wanted to know what had happened. James had to tell her that they did not know yet and that he had done what he could for Tom while he was underground. Katrina arrived almost immediately and sat with her arms around Rita while they both cried. The waiting was bad; there seemed to be no one with any information, and all they were told was that the surgeons were working on both the victims and they would tell them of any progress. James caught sight of himself in a mirror, and he looked a mess. He still had his overalls on that were spattered with blood, dirt, and whatever else. His face was filthy, and his hair was plastered down to his head because of the sweat and the effects of the hard hat.

When a doctor finally appeared at the door, James's heart dropped as he guessed the news. The doctor came over and asked who Mrs Morrison was, then he took her hand and told her in a quiet way that they had been unable to save Tom. He let her hand go, and Katrina immediately took over. James looked at Pete Burgess, and all he could think to say was "Why?" Pete looked back helplessly and then turned to the door as some others arrived, Penrose and Tom's shift boss, Jones. They had been on the golf course and had been told of the accident. Burgess gave them the news and then intercepted them as they made to go to Rita. He suggested that now was definitely not the time and to let Katrina handle things. As he said that, Colin Winter arrived, and he quickly sized up the situation and motioned for Penrose and Jones to go with him.

James took Katrina and Rita home, and they made up the spare room for Rita. It seemed best to do this and not let her sleep at her own house, alone. Katrina had called her company and told them the situation and had taken the next few days off. She reasoned that Rita would need help in all kinds of ways. James took a shower and threw away his overalls, and then went and sat under the mango tree and cried for his friend. Katrina came to join him and told him that she had given

Rita a sleeping tablet so that she could get some rest before trying to face the situation.

Later that evening, Piet van Rensburg and Henry Mwanza came to the house, and Katrina told them that Rita was resting and that they should return in the morning. Mwanza had checked in Tom's file and had found an address in the UK for his parents, and had sent a telegram and provided a telephone number at which he could be reached. James asked about Banda and was told that he, too, had died. Mwanza and van Rensburg were now on their way to see Banda's family and Mwewa's, the third casualty. They told James that the investigating team was still down and not expected up before late that night because there were fatalities, the Government Mines Inspectorate had been informed, and they, no doubt, would conduct their own investigation.

Sleep was difficult for James; he kept seeing Tom and the others lying in pools of blood with bits of steel sticking out of them. Eventually, he just gave up and made himself some tea and sat on the *stoep* thinking about his good fortune and the bad fortune that had befallen Lionel and now Tom. When at last dawn came, Katrina got up and came to find him. She told him that she would take care of Rita and that he should go to work and try and find out what happened.

At the shaft, James was surprised to find Winter already there. Underground managers normally did not start with the common folk. He saw James and told him that he wanted him to take him to the site and explain what he had seen and done. James was about to say that he had his own section to run when Pete Burgess spoke up and told him to go and that he, Pete, would run the section for the day. James rode down with Winter, and they walked to the section that Tom had been running. It was hard to visit the actual scene again, and James had to quickly excuse himself and throw up his breakfast into the drain. Then he felt better and began to relate what had happened the day before, beginning with the summons from the operator. Winter was curious as to why they had fetched James, and James suggested that their operators all knew that he and Tom were close friends.

As they looked around the workplace, Winter told James what the investigating team had found, and it all began to fit with what James had seen. Apparently, the area they were in had rock that kept shifting. That meant that between the time that they drilled holes and charged them with explosives, the holes often closed, and they could not load them and had to re-drill them. That was putting them behind schedule, so Penrose and Jones had come up with a scheme to immediately charge the holes after drilling and then put in the detonators at the last minute. The problem was that the charged holes were then really close to the drilling, and the new holes did not exactly go in straight. In fact, the holes wandered all over the place. So what had happened was they had drilled through a charged hole. The water tube in the drill string had filled with explosives, and when they had been pulling out the drill string, the action of striking the connectors to break the thread contact had caused the explosive to detonate. That explained why the helper, Mwewa, had no hands. They had been blown off. It also explained the bits of steel everywhere, including those buried in Tom and Banda, and the wrecked bar machine that James had seen. It was by mere chance that Tom had been there while they were pulling the drill string and had been caught in the blast.

Winter said that the notion of pre-charging had been under review and they had been close to coming up with a method of operation, but that Penrose and Jones had jumped the gun and started on their own. The method that was to be proposed left at least two lines of empty holes between the charged holes and the new ones being drilled. They felt that that would accommodate the natural deviations in drilling direction.

Winter finally told James that he was free to go back to his own section, and there he found Pete Burgess. Pete told him that Penrose and Jones had been suspended and that, in all probability, they would both 'retire' early and leave the mine. He commented that it was a sad commentary that it was only because an expatriate had been killed that such drastic action was likely. If it had been just Banda and Mwewa, the probability was that Penrose and Jones would have both been fined fifty to one hundred kwacha, and the matter would have ended there. The official investigation by the Mines Inspectorate was due to start in two days' time, and it was entirely possible that Penrose and Jones would have left the country by then.

After making sure that James was up to the day, Burgess left to check on his other section bosses. James asked Ben where they had finished up the previous day, and Ben told him that George had come up, checked the wiring for the blast, and they had set it off. James now felt that he was again in George's debt and would talk to him later in the day. He then unburdened himself to Ben, telling him what he had found when he arrived in Tom's section and also what the preliminary conclusions were for the cause of the accident.

At home that night, James found Rita alone; Katrina had gone into town to run some errands. James was not really sure what to say except that he was sorry and promise to do what he could for her. Rita opened up a little and told him about her day. She had been visited by Henry Mwanza and Piet van Rensburg, and they had started on the process of repatriation. The mine was going to pay the way for Tom's parents to come out for the funeral, and then they would pay Rita's fare home plus shipping expenses for her household goods, such as she wished to take. The debts that Tom owed the mine for the outbound travel and the settling-in bonus, etc., all died with him. It was still hard for her to accept that Tom was not going to walk in the door any minute ever again.

James had learned of one of the more macabre items obtainable from the mine stores, a pine coffin with brass handles. One had been requisitioned for Tom and charged to the section budget as an operating expense. Two others, plywood with rope handles, had been requisitioned for Mwewa and Banda and also charged to the section budget. The funeral for Tom was set for Saturday afternoon at St. Michael's church. Tom's parents were due to arrive on Thursday, and van Rensburg would meet them at the airport in Ndola. They would stay with Rita until she was ready to leave and return to the UK. There would be a lot to do in the week following the funeral to clear up all their affairs before she could leave the country. James felt a certain sympathy for Piet van Rensburg. It could not be at all easy having to meet people who had lost their sons; this was the second time in a short while, and James hoped that the old adage of bad things happen in threes was not true.

When Katrina came home, she hugged James as if it were a miracle that he was home at all. James appreciated the sentiment as he had had occasional misgivings about going back underground again. He had conquered his fears, and now that he had some idea of what had happened to Tom, he knew that, whatever might happen to him, he would not die that way. Katrina and Rita then discussed what she would do when Tom's parents arrived, and it seemed that her parents were coming as well to lend their support. Rita would stay with Katrina and James until the others arrived; that way, she would not be in the house alone.

The following morning, James was able to sleep in as his appointment with the Pneumoconiosis Bureau was not until eight. The process was fairly simple; get an X-ray, then get weighed and measured and then wait for one of the doctors for a review. The doctor that James saw was, to him at least, an elderly woman who sat smoking a cigarette, coughing away while she lectured James on the problems of lung diseases. She commented on the fact that he was now 5lbs lighter than when he had had his medical before signing on. James listened to all this with a good degree of scepticism, as she hardly seemed the best one to talk about lung disease. He noted that all around the room, there were jars of pickled lungs, all with various stages of disease. Some of them were so far gone that it looked as if they were full of sand. She did make one interesting comment, examining the baseline X-rays, those of Europeans were always more shadowed than those of the Africans. In fact, an African with lungs as clouded as James's would never he taken on as a miner.

Thursday afternoon, James arrived home to find Piet van Rensburg there with Tom's parents and Rita's parents. Gibson had kept himself busy providing tea to all and sundry and was even thinking about dinner for the whole party. Katrina suggested that they stay for dinner and come for lunch and dinner at least for the next few days. That arrangement suited Rita, who really did not fancy having to cater to four others. She, by now, appreciated that it was not a particularly great burden for Katrina, as Gibson actually did most of the work.

The funeral on Saturday was attended by all the class that started with Tom and James, and many of the other section and shift bosses, but without Penrose and Jones. Pete Burgess saw James at the funeral and, in an aside, told him that the two had in fact left the day before. They must have worked amazingly fast to have everything sorted out that quickly! It was almost as if they had received one of the infamous forty-eight-hour deportation notices!

Following the funeral, James asked van Rensburg what had been done for Mwewa and Bamba and learned that their families had taken charge of the bodies and had already had their services. The Banda family were headed back to Malawi, and the Mwewa family were going back to Abercorn.

At the wake held at the boat club, people queued up to offer their condolences to Tom's parents and to Rita. It was obviously a trial for Rita, who was having a very difficult time keeping herself together. Katrina kept a close eye on her, and a couple of times when she felt that Rita was getting too overwrought, she took her aside and gave her the chance to compose herself. The family party left early and returned to James's house for dinner. For the rest of the mining types, it was a chance to reflect on the fragility of life and the risks that they all took every day. There were undoubtedly going to be a few sore heads in the morning.

The following week, James met Pete Burgess and learned there had been a general shake-up and that appointments to new assignments had been made. Burgess had moved up to Mine Captain, and now there was a vacant slot for shift boss. Winter and Tom Slater, the daytime Assistant Underground Manager, wanted to see James after his regular shift that day, so speculation was now rife about whether or not he would get the vacant slot. When James reported to Winter's office, he saw Slater, Ross, and another man there. The other, he did not know until he was introduced to George McIntosh, the Superintendent of Mining. McIntosh opened the proceedings by telling James that, as he was sure he knew, there were now two slots open for shift boss. One created by the exit of Penrose and the promotion of Burgess to replace him, and the other created by the exit of Jones. McIntosh went on to say that his dilemma was that whereas Tom Slater and James Ross argued for promotion by seniority, Colin Winter argued for promotion by capability and demonstrated adaptability. Where, asked McIntosh, did James see himself in this picture?

James was pretty sure the decision was already made, as he could not see anyone taking Slater's or Ross's opinion over that of Winter. However, the job was still his to lose by making a hash of things at this review. He talked about his experiences to date and the views that he had of managing the different sections. He was peppered with questions by all four but felt that he held his own. He was then excused for a few minutes. When he was called back in McIntosh had left, and only Winter, Slater, and Ross were there. They congratulated him on his promotion and told him that he would be taking over the sections vacated by Jones immediately. James would have loved to have been a fly on the wall at their private discussion, but doubted whether he would ever hear what truly went on.

As he left the offices, James saw Pete Burgess and went to talk to him about his new assignment. Burgess said that he would go with him in the morning to the sections, and they would talk about how to get things going again after the accident. James asked who he would get as a section boss for that area, and Burgess told him that it would be Isaac Kayumba. James also asked about the reasons for the meeting with Winter, Slater, Ross, and McIntosh, and Burgess told him that Slater had essentially been overruled by McIntosh and Winter, who had delivered bollockings all round and asked why they were clinging to unqualified, incapable people just because they had been there forever. It almost looked as if Slater's star was waning and that he was on probation, as it were. Burgess also promised one more thing: to stay as a buffer between James and Slater, who was generally reputed to be vindictive and who would not take kindly to being overruled by Winter and McIntosh.

Katrina was delighted to hear the news of James's promotion, but thought it a shame that it had to come partially as a result of Tom's death. James had thought of that and had also promised himself that he would sort out the issues and make sure that Tom's legacy was one of safety and success, not death and failure.

James toured his new sections with Pete Burgess the next day and met Isaac and his three other section bosses. They worked on a plan for what they would do to recover the area affected by the accident and how to safely begin to recover the lost schedules. It was going to be a challenge. James asked Pete about his local leave and was told to take it anyway. As he would be gone for only just over a week, they could cover for him and with a plan of action in place, there would be no reason to delay. Pete told him that in his view, everyone needed time away so as not to become stale and complacent.

Saturday, Rita and her family were ready to leave. Rita had disposed of their cars and most of the things that belonged to Tom. All she was taking home were memories and her personal effects. It was horrifying to think that less than a year earlier, they had been on the boat together, coming to a new life, full of promise and expectations. Now it had all changed in an instant, and she was going back alone to try and start a new life. Katrina and James took them to the airport and said their tearful farewells. Rita promised to write, as did Katrina, and James wondered if they actually would or if Rita would try and excise this whole experience from her mind and build another life. On the drive home, James told Katrina that it was, in fact, one year to the day since they had sailed from Southampton. Such a lot had happened in one year!

James now had two weeks to organise his operations before he took his local leave. That was actually less complex than it might have appeared. His section bosses were all experienced, and he had no intention of putting them in the situation that Jones put Tom in, one of extreme peril. He visited each in turn and went through a detailed plan for the next month to be sure they knew exactly what they would be doing. Then he went through ideas of what they might do if everything did not go as planned. Between them, they re-equipped Isaac's section and found replacement operators. They set them to work, and the only issue was the discovery one day of one of Mwewa's fingers that had not been recovered by the investigation team. To be presented with a finger in a brown paper bag with the announcement that, *ena kona lo into ka lo muntu*, was a new experience for James. He was a little surprised that the crew did not seem unduly bothered by the discovery.

On the home front, Katrina suggested that, as Tom and Rita were no longer going to be with them on their local leave, perhaps they change their plans and go camping at Siavonga instead of crossing the dam into Rhodesia. That suited James. Siavonga was a beautiful place on the banks of Lake Kariba, and they could fish, enjoy each other, and forget about the rest of the world for a week at least.

For the next two weeks, James put in long hours until he was satisfied that each section was in good order and that he could afford to leave them in the hands of someone else for a week. Burgess was going to pull in one of the night shift bosses for the week to ensure that things ran smoothly. It was unfortunate that the events of the past month had precipitated promotional moves early. Normally, such moves would be made after local leave was taken, but events had rather overtaken everyone. Katrina made arrangements with Koot to borrow his boat again, and then she and Gibson worked out what they would need for the week. She instructed Gibson to take the time off and visit his family. If she had not done so, he would have assumed that he was going with them to cater to their needs at Siavonga.

# Siavonga

Early Sunday morning at about four thirty, James and Katrina locked up the house and set off on the drive south. Katrina liked to set off early so that they could get established in their campsite while there was yet light. They were well past Kapiri Mposhi by the time it was light, and by the time they reached Kabwe, James was ready for a coffee break. It was still early in the town, and there was little activity, so Katrina directed James to the old Boma site, where there was a big tree and space to park. Kabwe was like Kitwe; its reason for existence was the mine, but in the case of Kabwe, it was a lead and zinc mine. There was a great quote about the railway ending in a burnt-out vlei at Broken Hill, now Kabwe, but James could not remember where he had heard it.

Once on the road again, they passed through Lusaka and on across the Kafue Bridge, with its ever-present and vigilant, sometimes guards. James wondered why they bothered, but supposed it was like putting guards at the post office; it made somebody happy and kept the army busy. With the antiquated arms the Zambian army carried, anyone with some determination and firepower would make short work of the poor soldiers detailed to guard these assets.

After the junction with the road to Livingstone and Vic Falls, the road to Chirundu and Kariba started down the escarpment. James remembered driving up on his way to Kitwe when he first arrived. There were lorries off the road that had crashed into the bush, and in places, they could still see remnants of the first road that had been replaced with one of a new line that meant less severe gradients and curves. It was the kind of drive down where it paid to know who was behind you and if they had any brakes! Once, James pulled off the road for a break and to let a small convoy of heavy transport trucks go by. If any of them had problems, he wanted to be uphill of them. In the valley bottom, it got hotter and more humid. They went through the tsetse fly barrier and were sprayed by one of the 'fly men'.

Before they reached Chirundu, the road to Kariba and Siavonga turned and ran almost straight south towards the lake. The map showed a nice straight road, but in fact it curved around hills and swooped in and out of stream valleys all the way down. They had left the tar behind, and the surface was now a fairly well-maintained gravel road. Twice, they were stopped by groups of elephants crossing the road, and once, James managed to hit a large pile of elephant dung. He did not see it until it was too late to take evasive action, and the smell lingered with them for a while. At last, they could see the lake and then the dam, and across the river, the power lines coming from the generating station and heading off north and south. Katrina told James where the Siavonga turn-off was, and he worked his way around to Siavonga east, away from the motel and the harbour. They found a cove and a suitable spot close to the water and set about making camp. Launching the boat was fairly straightforward. The beach was gravel, and James made sure that there were suitable trees ahead of him, in case he mired in the gravel and had to winch himself out.

From their cove, it was not possible to see the dam or the facilities at Siavonga. Clearly, the cove had been visited before and used as a campsite, but not that often, judging by the number and age of old fire pits and flattened areas of grass. Katrina did wonder briefly if she had done the right thing by sending Gibson off to see his family. Had they had Gibson there, he would probably already have had tea made and would have been working on getting hot water and a shower rigged up. She reasoned, however, that she and James could surely manage those tasks themselves for once!

There was still some of the late afternoon left after they set up camp and organised a shower. James rigged a bucket in a tree and put a curtain around it, then made a grating of sticks and placed that above a short trench that he dug to drain the water away. That way, whoever used the shower would not be standing in mud. Katrina had brought a second bucket that already had holes punched in the bottom. So all they had to do was hoist up the full bucket of hot water, upend it into the second bucket and enjoy the shower; at least that was the theory. They had yet to try it out.

Katrina got each of them a beer, and they sat looking over the shore and watched the sun go down. James asked if there was a danger from crocodiles if they got close to the shore, and Katrina told him that in any water in Zambia, there was a danger. They saw a couple of boats running in from higher up the lake into the marinas on the Rhodesian side. James asked if the lake was patrolled by either side. Katrina said that she thought it was, but both sides left people alone who were obviously just out fishing.

James commented as the sun dropped from view that he was always surprised at how quickly it went down. He told Katrina that sunsets now made him think of Tom. There was no gradual ageing as there would be in the higher latitudes, just here one minute gone the next; a quick snuffing out of a life that held so much promise. He wondered what Rita would do now and how she would pick up the pieces of her life. The mine could do very little except help her return to the UK and offer condolences. She was now truly on her own again. He felt truly lucky that he had met Katrina and had someone to share his life with. Katrina told him that her biggest concern was that she one day would get the telephone call or the message to say that he had not come back up. She tried to rationalise it all and tell herself that the statistics were in her favour, but that never totally conquered the fears.

With the light gone, they could see how many other people were camped relatively close by. There were over a dozen campfires dotted around, none too close, but it was not as deserted as the Kafue had been. There was a glow in the sky from the lights at the dam and in the town of Kariba on the Rhodesian side. James lit an oil lamp and then started to fix some dinner. For their first day, Katrina had pre-prepared some items so all he really had to do was heat them. That made life easy for the day.

After dinner, he heated water so that she could take a shower and then set up their tent and mosquito net. James was not sure that they really needed it for the mosquitoes, as for all the other flying insects that were around. The shower device worked, mostly. It tended to deliver a little fast, so they had to be ready to soap and rinse fairly quickly, but it did work. He heated water for himself and washed off the grime from the trip and the fire building. Ensuring everything was properly stowed, he then joined Katrina, who had already made up their bed.

For the next three days, they did the same thing; got up early, had coffee and something light, loaded food and drink into the boat, and then headed on to explore the lake. Most of the islands on the eastern end of the lake seemed to be more on the Rhodesian side, and James was a little reluctant to spend too much time over there. However, one day they decided to take a trip across the eleven miles or so of lake to Fothergill Island just to take a look. Katrina told James the story about Rupert Fothergill and his Operation Noah, which was put together to rescue animals caught by the rising water behind the dam wall. She told him that an appeal had gone out for nylon stockings to make nets and ropes to catch animals and then transport them to the shore. Apparently, the nylon was less abrasive than other ropes and did not inflict the rope burns that would otherwise have occurred. She told him tales of catching snakes, about recalcitrant rhinos, and about a leopard that did not eat the buck on the same island it was on but seemed to prefer to fish. Katrina also told him about the Batonka people who had been displaced by the dam and the lake, and about whom neither government had seemed to care too much.

There were several other boats over by the island, some from each shore, but the emphasis was definitely on fishing, not espionage. The only espionage that was going on was to see what bait or lures others might be using to get the best catch. It was on the way back from the island that James caught his first tiger fish. Katrina was right, they did seem to be all teeth and put up a real fight. She caught several for James's two, so maintained her supremacy in the area of fishing. James was not overly concerned by this; he just enjoyed being with her and watching her, whatever she was doing. He was just glad to be alive after the events of the past couple of months and to have someone in his life.

On Thursday, they decided to take a ride up the lake and find a nice secluded spot for lunch. After they had gone about forty miles or so, James noticed that the lake narrowed considerably. Katrina told him that beyond this point, it did open out again to a long stretch of the lake that led up to the end of the gorge that came down from Victoria Falls. They turned back and headed more inshore, looking for a likely spot to pull in and have lunch. There were small islands now on the Zambia side, and one of them looked promising. James went completely around the island while Katrina looked at the bottom for snags and at the beaches for good places to pull into. She also looked to see what kind of animal life was on the island, as she had no desire to meet up with anything unpleasant. After the first complete tour, she directed him back for a second look and was now peering into the water quite intently. James asked what she was looking for, and she told him snails. Then she elaborated and told him that before she got into the water, she was looking for the snails that are part of the cycle to transmit bilharzia. Apparently, the water conditions were not suited to reeds or water grasses on this island; therefore were not suited to the snails, as she saw none at all in their trip around. Finally, she picked a spot that she liked and directed James towards it.

They nosed the boat ashore, and Katrina jumped onto the beach and made the boat fast to a tree. James followed, and they looked around and took stock of their lunch site. The island was about one and a half miles from the Zambia shore; it was perhaps half a mile long and about half of that again wide. Looking at the beach, it was clear that even if there were no animals on it now, it was visited from time to time by animals swimming out from the main shore. However, there were birds, rodents, mongoose, and a small herd of buck. There appeared to be no people at that time, but again, judging by the evidence, it had been used by fishermen a number of times. There were old campfires and fish bones scattered around. There were no slides evident that would indicate crocodiles, and the grasses were probably unattractive to hippo, so they would probably all be on one of the main shores.

James and Katrina found a clean spot under a tree on a rise overlooking the shallow bay that they had pulled into and set out their lunch. James swept the ground clear of small rocks and sticks and unrolled the blankets he had brought with him. Katrina looked at that and asked if there was a special reason for the blankets, and James suggested that perhaps lunch could wait for a while. When Katrina shed her clothes, James could see the effect of the past three days on her tan. The tide lines where her bra and pants would be were now very much evident as she had darkened up very quickly. For himself, he had to be much more careful and had been exposing himself to the sun in small doses. The tree would provide shade for the day, so James was happy to also shed his clothes. After three days of fishing, getting back late and falling straight to sleep, they were both ready for each other, and their first bout of lovemaking was passionate and quick.

Afterwards, James understood why Katrina had been so concerned with snails, as she suggested a dip in the lake to cool off and clean off. She raced James to the water and dived in. It was refreshing and cool; however, whatever ideas may have been forming in James's mind about making love to Katrina in the water were quickly dispelled when they heard a boat approaching from the other side of the island. They raced back up the shore and put some clothes on, which was as well because a Zambian patrol boat pulled around the island and they were hailed. The guys on the boat had to have known what they had been doing, but asked anyway. James told them that they had been fishing and had stopped for lunch. Asked what they had caught, he went to the boat and pulled out some fish they had caught earlier in the day while they made their way up the lake. James offered some to the border guards, and they thanked him and took all that he offered. While he was handing over the fish, one of the guards leered at James and asked him, "*Wena enzili lo jig a jig na lo mfazi?*" to which James replied. "*Sure, futi mina azi enza lo futi skati zonke wena hamba!*" basically telling them that he would do it again after they had all gone. The boat crew let out a great shout of laughter and pulled away, all making the gesture for intercourse.

Katrina guessed what had been said out of her earshot and blushed at the gestures. She suggested to James that they have lunch now before doing anything else in case the boat crew decided to take a quick trip back to try and catch them at it. A wise move, as it transpired, for twenty minutes later, James saw the boat creeping around the headland. He waved, and they waved back and were obviously joking with each other about the situation, then James saw money change hands and realised that they had been betting on whether or not they would catch James and Katrina in the act. James wondered how long this cat and mouse might go on, but then he heard their radio and they turned and sped off down the lake with a final wave goodbye.

With that distraction out of the way, Katrina and James went back to the water and cooled off again. Then they made their way back to the blankets and the expectant audience of Zambezi lovebirds, who were sitting in the tree, chattering.

"What do you think they are saying?" Katrina asked James.

"I don't know," he replied. "Probably having a discussion about whether or not we are going to perform for them."

"Well, do you think we should?" she asked.

"*Suikerbossie*, I'm always ready for you, any time, any place," said James rashly.

"Really, any time, any place?" she asked.

"Sure, but here and now would be good, what do you think?" he asked.

"Lie down and let's find out how ready you are," instructed Katrina. Then she straddled him, guided him inside her, and started to move up and down. She rode him until they both could no longer contain themselves and came together in his last thrusts upwards.

"Did you like that?" she asked.

"Oh yes, you can do that anytime you like," he replied. "But what about you?"

"All I can say is don't ever die on me because I don't know how I could replace you!" she said.

"I won't, believe me. I can't imagine life without you," commented James.

"Lovey, as much as I would like to stay here and do that again, we might want to think about heading back before it gets dark," she said.

"Okay," James replied. "You steer and I'll watch!"

"Shall we come back here tomorrow?" asked Katrina.

"Great plan," agreed James. "We'd better make sure we catch some fish on the way in, case those nosey guards come around again."

On Friday, they spent more time talking about possible plans and dreams than lovemaking, but did manage a couple of times, much to the annoyance of the Zambezi lovebirds, who seemed to object to their presence. James asked Katrina what she thought about leaving Zambia, as he was a contract employee, and even if he renewed his contract, it was unlikely to be a long-term career. Katrina admitted that she would be apprehensive and would obviously miss Zambia a lot, but if he had to go, then she would be with him, no matter what.

Saturday, it was time to think about going home. They could have stayed another day and driven back on Sunday, but neither of them relished the idea of coming back from a break and having to go straight back to work. James told Katrina that it was one year to the day since he signed on at the mine, and what a year. During the drive north, they each went through the year and highlighted the events and what it meant to them. Obviously, the good things included finding each other and getting married. The not-so-good parts included the deaths of Lionel and Jane and of Tom. They also included the departure of Koos and Sussana and the sale of the business, and the farm. That Katrina confided had made her feel very much alone for a while. Fortunately for her, she had James to rely on and be a friend as well as a lover and a husband.

James then speculated about what the next year would bring. He had a new job and, in the normal scheme of things, could expect to be there for the next year at least before any other moves would be considered. It seemed that the move up to Mine Captain usually happened at the end of the first contract, or after three years. Anyway, they would see.

For now, James would be going back underground and found himself looking forward to it. He liked the job and the people, and thought that for him, the one thing he would remember most was being in a crowded cage with all the operators yelling 'Chaya four one, chaya four one!'

363

# Glossary

**Note:** ChiKabanga was the adapted language used on the mines in Zambia. It is a very contextual language: words will have varying meanings depending on the context in which they are used. ChiKabanga was derived from Fanagalo, the language developed in the South African mines. Many words in ChiKabanga remain the same as those in Fanagalo. Other words used are from various origins, including Afrikaans, Zulu and Bemba. Many of the words listed below are slang derogatory terms and would be better not used. However, in the period of this work, they were commonly used.

| | | |
|---|---|---|
| Afs Slang | abbreviated form of "Africans" | |
| Aikôna | Afrikaans | no |
| Azi | ChiKabanga | will, know |
| Aziko | ChiKabanga | no, no problem |
| Bakkie | Afrikaans | light delivery vehicle, bowl |
| Bala | ChiKabanga | count, write (Zulu: bala) |
| Bamba | Zulu | take, fetch, bring |
| Bichana | ChiKabanga | little |
| Bioscope | English | South African term for cinema |
| Bliksem | Afrikaans | scoundrel |
| Boerwors | Afrikaans | boer-sausage, homemade sausage |
| Boetie | Afrikaans | diminutive form of boet (brother) |
| Braai | Afrikaans | grill, barbecue |
| Bundu | ChiKabanga | bush |
| Bwana | Swahili | boss |
| Chaya | ChiKabanga | hit, strike (Zulu: shaya) |
| Checha | ChiKabanga | quickly (Zulu: shesha) |
| Cheesa | ChiKabanga | to burn, to blast |
| Chimbusu | ChiKabanga | toilet (Zulu: chambusu) |
| Chitenge | Bemba | thatched umbrella-like structure |
| Chola | ChiKabanga | bag |
| Crosscut | English | tunnel running 90° to main tunnels |
| Dankie | Afrikaans | thank you |

364

| | | |
|---|---|---|
| Drift | English | tunnel |
| Doppie | Afrikaans | detonator |
| Faka | Zulu | put in |
| Fili | ChiKabanga | dead |
| Fosholo | ChiKabanga | shovel (Zulu: ifosholo) |
| Futi | ChiKabanga | again (Zulu: fhuti) |
| Grizzly | English | a large sizing device for rocks |
| Goed | Afrikaans | good |
| Hamba | Zulu | go |
| Haulroad | English | tunnel equipped for transportation |
| Houtkop | Afrikaans | slang term for black African |
| Howzit | South African | greeting: contraction of "How is it?" |
| Ifwa | Bemba | dead |
| Indaba | Zulu | matter, affair |
| Inindaba | ChiKabanga | why |
| Inzwa | ChiKabanga | listen |
| Isabi | Bemba | fish |
| Isolo | ChiKabanga | yesterday |
| Jombolo | ChiKabanga | drill steel (Zulu: ijombolo) |
| Juba | ChiKabanga | cut |
| Kaia | ChiKabanga | house (Shangaan: kaya) |
| Kaffir | Arabic | unbeliever |
| Kaffir | South African | derogatory term for African Bantu |
| Kaffir boetie | Afrikaans | little brother to kaffirs |
| Kanjani | Zulu | how, how are you |
| Katundu | Bemba | luggage, equipment |
| Kêrel | Afrikaans | chap, fellow |
| Kuluma | ChiKabanga | talk (Zulu: khuluma) |
| Kona | ChiKabanga | there, have (Zulu: khona) |
| Kudala | Zulu | long time |
| Kupela | ChiKabanga | only, merely |
| Kusasa | Zulu | tomorrow |
| Lash | English | shovel out |
| Lekker | Afrikaans | sweet |
| Lightie | English | diminutive term for child |
| Lobola | Bemba | bride price |
| Maak | Afrikaans | make |

| | | |
|---|---|---|
| Mabuna | ChiKabanga | Boer, derogatory term |
| Madala | ChiKabanga | old man |
| Malabishi | Bemba | rubbish |
| Mali | ChiKabanga | money |
| Mangaki | ChiKabanga | how many |
| Maningi | ChiKabanga | much, many |
| Manje | Zulu | now |
| Manzi | Zulu | water |
| Mboo | Bemba | buffalo |
| Mealie | English | Maize |
| Meneer | Afrikaans | Mr. |
| Mevrou | Afrikaans | Mrs. |
| Mgwala | ChiKabanga | crowbar, pinch bar |
| Mkubwa | Swahili | big, important |
| Mkulu | ChiKabanga | big, important |
| Moenie | Afrikaans | do not |
| Môre | Afrikaans | morning, good morning |
| Moontlik | Afrikaans | maybe, perhaps |
| Mulilo | Bemba | fire, safety match brand |
| Munt | Zulu | derogatory: African (Zulu: umuntu) |
| Munya | ChiKabanga | other |
| Mushle | ChiKabanga | good, well |
| Muti | ChiKabanga | medicine (Bemba: úmúti, tree) |
| Muzungu | Swahili | white man |
| Namusha | ChiKabanga | today (Zulu: namuhla) |
| Neefie | Afrikaans | diminutive form of nephew |
| Nuwe | Afrikaans | new |
| Oom | Afrikaans | uncle |
| Oppas | Afrikaans | careful |
| Ou | Afrikaans | chap, fellow |
| Oukie | Afrikaans | diminutive form of ou |
| Panzi | ChiKabanga | down, low (Zulu: phansi) |
| Pezulu | ChiKabanga | up, high (Zulu: phezulu) |
| Picinin | ChiKabanga | small (Portuguese: pequenino – tiny) |
| Powder | English | explosives |
| Raise | English | vertical or near vertical small shaft |
| Rooinek | Afrikaans | derogatory term for Englishmen |

| | | |
|---|---|---|
| Ry | Afrikaans | ride, go |
| Sandu | ChiKabanga | hammer (Zulu: isando) |
| Scrubber | English | slang term for loose woman |
| Sebenza | Zulu | work |
| Session | English | dance |
| Shateen | ChiKabanga | bush (possibly Bemba: shetani –hell) |
| Shebeen | Gaelic | illicit bar |
| Skat | Afrikaans | sweetheart |
| Skati | ChiKabanga | time, occasion |
| Skopu | ChiKabanga | head |
| Slim | Afrikaans | crafty, sly, cunning |
| Soek | Afrikaans | look for |
| South West | English | outdated term for Namibia |
| Soutie | Afrikaans | derogatory term for Englishmen |
| Sterek | ChiKabanga | very (also heard as stelek) |
| Stoep | Afrikaans | porch |
| Suikerbossie | Afrikaans | diminutive of suikerbos, sugarbush |
| Sumali | ChiKabanga | nail |
| Tailings | English | concentrator waste discharge |
| Tekkies | Afrikaans | Anglicised to takkies, tennis shoes |
| The moer in | Afrikaans | angry (mixed language slang) |
| Tina | ChiKabanga | we |
| Tot siens | Afrikaans | goodbye |
| Tumbu | ChiKabanga | hose (Zulu: ithumbu) |
| Umfazi | Zulu | wife, woman |
| Vala | Zulu | close |
| Verdomde | Afrikaans | damned |
| Verkrampte | Afrikaans | unenlightened |
| Vula | Zulu | open |
| Waiya waiya | ChiKabanga | waste time |
| Wena | Zulu | you |
| Yona | Zulu | they |
| Zams | English | slang, abbreviated form of Zambians |
| Zonke | Zulu | all, all of them |

References:

Nuwe Praktiese Woordeboek: H. J. Terblanche, Afrikaanse Pers-Boekhandel, Johannesburg, 1966.

Bemba Pocket Dictionary: Rev. E. Hoch W.F., The Society of the Missionary for Africa (White Fathers), Ndola, 1960.

Fanagalo: J. D. Bold, J. L. van Schaik, Pretoria, 1995.

Scholars Zulu Dictionary: G. R. Dent & C. L. S. Nyembezi, Shuter & Shooter, Pietermaritzburg, 1993.

# Select bibliography of Zambia

1. Bancroft, J. A., 1961, *Mining in Northern Rhodesia*, The British South Africa Company
2. Burawoy, Michael, 1972, *Colour of Class: From African Advancement to Zambianization*, Manchester University Press for the Institute of Social Studies, University of Zambia
3. Carr, Norman, 1963, *Return to the Wild*, Collins
4. Carr, Norman, *Kakuli*, CBC Publishing
5. Clements, Frank, 1960, *Kariba: The Struggle with the River God*, G.P. Putnam's Sons
6. Coleman, Francis L., 1971, *The Northern Rhodesian Copperbelt 1899-1962*, Manchester University Press
7. Crawford, Dan, *Back to the Long Grass: My link with Livingstone*, George H. Doran Company
8. Ferguson, James, 1999, *Expectations of Modernity: Myths and Meaning of Urban Life on the Zambian Copperbelt*, University of California Press
9. Gann L. H., 1964, *A History of Northern Rhodesia*, Chatto and Windus
10. Hall, Richard, 1963, *Zambia*, Pall Mall Press
11. Hansen, Karen Tranborg, 1989, *Distant Companions: Servants and Employers in Zambia, 1900-1985*, Cornell University Press
12. Kaunda, Dr. Kenneth D., 1969, *Zambia shall be free: An autobiography*, Heinemann
13. Lamb, Christina, 1999, *The Africa House*, Viking
14. Letcher, Owen, 1987, *Big Game Hunting in North Eastern Rhodesia*, St. Martin's Press (originally published in 1911)
15. Owens, Delia and Mark, 1992, *The Eye of the Elephant*, Houghton Mifflin
16. Pauling, George, 1926, *The Chronicles of a Contractor*, Constable & Collins
17. Powdermaker, Hortense, 1962, *Copper Town: Changing Africa, the Human Situation on the Rhodesian Copperbelt*, Harper Colophon Books
18. Richards, Audrey, 1956, Chisungu: *A girl's initiation ceremony among the Bemba of Northern Rhodesia*, Faber & Faber

19. Roan Consolidated Mines, 1978, *Zambia's Mining Industry: The first 50 years*
20. Rotberg, Robert, 1977, Black Heart: *Gore-Browne and the Politics of Multiracial Africa*, University of California Press
21. Tabor, George, 2003, *The Cape to Cairo Railway and River Routes*, Genta Publications